TICKET TO BERLIN
A Novel

For Esther and George,
With much love,
Irene

TICKET TO BERLIN

A NOVEL

Irene Magers Gingold

VANTAGE PRESS
New York

Published by Vantage Press, Inc.
516 West 34th Street, New York, New York 10001

Manufactured in the United States of America
ISBN: 0-533-12478-6

Library of Congress Catalog Card No.: 97-90766

0 9 8 7 6 5 4 3 2 1

To the memory of my father

ACKNOWLEDGMENTS

I thank the many people who encouraged me in the writing of this book: Marianne Farrin, who wore out her eyes reading the raw copy and, finding sufficient merit, challenged me to rewrite it. Gratitude also goes to Cynthia Wang-Toxby, whose keen sense of mystery pointed out important areas to be developed. I thank Joan Rothman for her willingness to discuss the story and listen to my woes over the course of several years. A resounding appreciation goes to the dedicated librarians of Westchester who found and dusted off old books and maps for my research. I am indebted to Michael Balfour's exacting book *The Kaiser and His Times*, and to Martin Kitchen's *Germany*.

Last, but not least, I owe a great deal of gratitude to my husband, Julian, and to my sons, Tom and Laurence, for their enduring patience while I worked.

TICKET TO BERLIN

A Novel

ONE

Dorrit was crouched at the side of the bed. But she was by no means immobile. Her hands—a child's hands typically refusing to be still—were kneading a corner of the bedclothes. Her lips, too, moved, twitching in prayer for the man who lay prostrate on the cot in the alcove next to a tidy living room two floors above a greengrocer.

"Please, God, ...," Dorrit murmured in a voice tight with unshed tears, "please don't let Papa die...."

Somewhere in the small apartment, a clock chimed the hour of eight, the jingle quickly followed by other clocks pealing the hour. For whatever the flat lacked in fine appointments, it had a number of rare old timepieces. But the cheerful bell-like concert sounded incongruous this terrible night. The girl shivered, her teeth made odd noises in her mouth. She clamped her lips shut, which made praying difficult. But maybe it didn't matter. God was probably tired of listening. It might be more expedient to concentrate on Dr. Kozlowski. In Dorrit's anguished state of mind, the two were synonymous anyway. "Please hurry!" she now begged the doctor, temporarily letting God off the hook.

Outside, a storm raged. Sleet scraped against the slanted roof, where a skylight rattled on its rusty hinges with each blast of the icy wind. Dorrit was about to get up and stuff a towel around it, when her heart lurched in panic as she heard her father struggle for air before another violent spasm consumed his chest. Forgetting all about the noisy window, she remained by the bed, too frightened to move.

"Papa!" she cried after his seizure passed and he was no longer coughing. "Papa!"

He didn't answer.

She dabbed at the beads of moisture on his furrowed brow with her sleeve. His eyes closed, his thin lips quivered, and his gray-streaked beard moved with his labored breathing. Still, he didn't speak.

1

"Papa...?" Dorrit tried again, whispering. She knew better than to press him. He had suffered these disabling spells before. Winters were hard on Herman Zache's lungs, and this winter of 1895 was more so than others. January had dumped two feet of snow across Poland, and now February brought ice storms. Dorrit didn't know which was worse, but she realized the weather was the reason the doctor was late. The streets of Bialystok were paralyzed, choked under what some said was a glacier forming right under their noses. People, wrapped to their cheekbones in woolens, purchased footing on slippery sidewalks at great expense to knees and elbows. Old friends eyed one another with suspicion, wondering who had left the door to Siberia open.

Resting her head on the edge of the stiff horsehair mattress, dank with the body's attempt to rid itself of sickness, Dorrit again implored Dr. Kozlowski to hurry; it was difficult to be understanding of bad road conditions when her father was so desperately ill.

Herman Zache was a physician as well, but he didn't practice. His daughter didn't know why not. He never talked about it. The times she'd asked, he had become tight-lipped and melancholy. And because she couldn't bear to see him unhappy, she had decided long ago not to pry. Which was also why she'd never asked for an explanation the day she came across some hidden papers and discovered that he had changed their last name from Tzacheroff to Zache. Furthermore, one document stated that she was born in Saint Petersburg, not Minsk, as she'd always been told. She wondered about the discrepancy but assumed there was a perfectly good answer.

A loud rap on the front door tore Dorrit from her musings.

The doctor!

She straightened, let go of the corner of the sheet she'd wadded into a clammy mess, and struggled to her feet, brushing lint from her blue plaid frock. Her legs were stiff, her knees numb from the hard floor.

"The doctor is here, papa!" she announced with overwhelming relief and gently touched his shoulder. Their downstairs neighbor, Frau Weiss, had obviously been as good as her word when she promised to send her husband out in the storm to summon Dr. Kozlowski. And as Dorrit now ran toward the door, wrapping a knitted shawl around her slim shoulders, she decid-

2

ed to thank Frau Weiss tomorrow by bringing her the begonia plant from the window sill in the kitchen. Despite the weak winter light, a large pink flower was just about to unfurl; surely a pretty blooming plant would please the landlady.

Dorrit threw back the latch and flung the door open to the hall.

"Good evening, my dear," Dr. Kozlowski wheezed, short of breath, and stepped clumsily into the small foyer. His beard was peppered with melting ice particles dripping down on his lapels, awakening a musty tobacco redolence. He reached out his hand to pat Dorrit's head. She shrank back, not because his gloves carried the rank smell of wet leather, but because of habit. People invariably tried to stroke her hair; something she minded only because it made her father very uncomfortable. In fact, if anyone fussed over her appearance, her coloring for instance, he grew even more so. Once, when a neighbor had suggested it was odd that father and daughter did not resemble each other in the least, Herman Zache became visibly agitated. The very next day he made plans to move.

"Good evening," Dorrit curtsied and quickly closed the door against the draft from the stairwell before she turned to help the doctor remove his coat and hat, items she placed over a chair because there was no clothes rack. Dr. Kozlowski kept his scarf around his neck against the chill in the flat, for there was also no coal for heating. The wood Dorrit gathered daily in the small park around the corner was used for cooking, and before her father fell ill, they kept warm nights, sitting by the potbellied stove in the kitchen. Tonight, she had compensated for the lack of heat in the apartment by piling every blanket they owned on her father's bed, insuring his comfort. She herself ignored the cold.

"Now, what seems to be the trouble?" Dr. Kozlowski bent down to retrieve the black bag he'd deposited on the floor. He had been here once before. About a month ago.

"Papa has trouble breathing." The words tumbled out with the impatience of the girl's extreme youth. "I . . . I think he's running a fever. He's been coughing something awful. He can't speak. Do you . . . do you have the medicine? The syrup? It helped him the last time." Without waiting for an answer, Dorrit suddenly turned and dashed into the living room to a clock perched on a shelf that also held books. Standing on tipped toes, she

3

opened the front of the ancient timepiece and reached into the pendulum well, losing her grip on her shawl in the process. She removed her hand from the clock and was holding two crumpled bills. "I hope this is enough . . ." she said and held out the money to Dr. Kozlowski before she bent down to retrieve her wrap from the floor, "enough for the medicine and your visit?"

"It'll do." The doctor tucked the bills into his waistcoat pocket and produced a bottle of thick dark liquid from his black bag. "Use it sparingly," he cautioned as he handed the bottle over.

"One teaspoon every half hour," Dorrit said, repeating the instructions from his previous visit to prove that she remembered. And, clutching the precious medicine to her chest, she also remembered her manners. "Thank you," she said and, too distraught to smile, frowned with gratitude.

A frown clouded Dr. Kozlowski's face as well, but it was of a different origin. He was dismayed that a child of twelve should fret so. He had four children of his own, and among the lot of them, he'd never seen such anxiety. Not even last summer when his youngest fell out of an apple tree and the others had run to the hospital to report that their brother's arm hung at an odd angle.

"Your father has suffered bouts of congestion before," he said, compelled to calm the girl's fear. "All things considered, he's a sturdy individual. Worrying yourself sick serves no purpose." His eyes swept over Dorrit's thick red curls, so shiny they glimmered like fire in the dim lamplight with the slightest move of her head. "Besides," he reached out and patted her cheek before she could step away and avoid him, "if you persist on frowning, you'll get ugly lines between those astonishing eyes of yours." *Unusually fetching,* he thought to himself, *a color peculiar to the Romanovs.* Out loud he said, "Tell me, who did you inherit those vivid green eyes from? Your mother?"

Dorrit raised her thin shoulders and let them fall, indicating she didn't know. Her mother had been dead for years. She had no memories of her and no photographs. In fact, she knew absolutely nothing about her—something she'd never admit to a virtual stranger—because in the same manner that Herman Zache refused to explain why he had quit the medical profession, he never mentioned his wife. This left Dorrit free to tinker and fabricate, which she didn't mind. Making up an imaginary per-

4

son was really quite exciting, and of course, she nurtured the idea that her mother was as beautiful as an empress and as kind as God.

Dr. Kozlowski looked queerly at the girl. Although she was much too skinny, she was remarkably pretty. He glanced toward the alcove. The man in the bed was quite the opposite. Homely described him. Ordinary, at best. But only if one wished to be kind.

Smoothing his long beard, now hanging with something which resembled dew, Dr. Kozlowski crossed the sparsely furnished living room. Dorrit followed on his heels, praying that her father hadn't overheard the comment about her eyes, because it was precisely that kind of talk which upset him. And sick or not, he'd no doubt make plans to move. Dorrit didn't want to move again. Certainly not in the dead of winter. They had a wonderful apartment. Two whole rooms; this living room plus an extra room next to the kitchen that her father insisted be her very own, staunchly declaring he much preferred to sleep in the alcove. "I like being near my books," he said the day they settled in. And, of course, Dorrit was happy with the arrangement. This was the first time she'd ever had a room all to herself. She would hate to leave it. Moreover, this house was close to the synagogue. Her father could walk to *shul* on Saturdays, and he could also walk to the university where he filled in for professors who were on sabbatical or were otherwise indisposed.

While Dr. Kozlowski fumbled with his pince-nez and bent over the bed to examine the patient, Dorrit fell to her knees on the other side. She groped under the blankets for her father's hand.

"The doctor is here, papa," she whispered. "You'll be fine now. And look! Look...here's your medicine!" She held out the bottle so that he might see it. She plucked at his sleeve to rouse him.

Dr. Kozlowski positioned his stethoscope on the man's chest and prepared to listen. His grave mien didn't escape Dorrit's eye. She bit her lips to keep from crying. *Please, papa,* she begged silently, *please get well. Don't die. You're all I have in the world. You can't die. I...I love you so....*

Despite her misery, she remembered to pray in German. Her father would like that. He had taught her several languages, but

5

exhibited a preference for German; this, while he was peculiarly eager to have her forget what little Russian she still knew. She suspected that he was hoping to live in Berlin one day. He often spoke of a great university there, and each of the many moves he'd undertaken all had one thing in common. They invariably pointed west.

TWO

"Whoa!" Johann pulled rein so sharply, the stallion flared its nostrils, whinnied, and stumbled backwards, its hind legs digging into the soggy forest floor while its front hooves boxed the air.

The sudden groan of splintering wood shattering the rainy silence had alerted horse and rider to danger only a split second before a massive tree trunk toppled to the ground in front of them, bringing down lesser growth in its crushing plunge. A jumble of roots tore from the wet soil and, flailing in an unaccustomed environment, spit sod and last summer's rotting leaves in all directions.

Clamping his thighs into the sides of the rearing animal, Johann dared the beast to unseat him. It didn't. It wheeled in a tight circle, tossing its black mane, before yielding to a will stronger than its fear. The minute all four hooves found solid footing, Johann eased up on the reins.

"That's a good fellow," he said and reached down to pat its shiny neck before brushing at the splashes of mud on his suede jacket, something he shouldn't have bothered with, because he only managed to spread the muck around. Cursing under his breath, he turned up his collar for what little comfort it afforded against the steady April rain plastering his dark brown hair to his head and seeping down his back. His square jaw clenched, his gray eyes glinted with irritation. How could he have been so dumb and forget to grab a hat before going out in this stinking weather? Johann von Renz was never at the mercy of the elements. This was a first, a very unpleasant anomaly, and decidedly uncomfortable. While mentally flogging himself for stupidity, he led his horse around the fallen corpse of the ancient oak.

Sometimes it didn't pay to get out of bed.

Actually, the morning had started out well enough. It was not until his mother succumbed to hysteria when her husband didn't return from his ride at the precise time he was expected that things began to fall apart. By midday, having worked herself into a frenzy, Annedora von Renz had ordered every ambulatory servant out in the rain to search and, in a burst of democratic impartiality, dispatched her son as well.

Caught up in the charged atmosphere that ensued whenever the baroness raised her voice to the employees, Johann left the house without dressing properly. But at least he'd had the presence of mind to bring a pistol. And now, fingering the cold metal securely tucked into his belt, all the while listening for the menacing snorts of wild boar known to roam these woods, he urged his recalcitrant horse on, grateful that at least the gun remained dry.

When would this damned deluge stop? April showers, hah! This was rain of prophetic proportions. The entire county lay under water. When had they last seen a sunny day? And why the hell had his father gone out alone?

Actually, Johann knew the answer to that. Their land manager, along with a number of grooms, had fallen victim to a virulent fever sweeping the countryside, giving new meaning to biblical plagues and leaving Baron von Renz with no escort. Finally, after weeks of being housebound, he refused to truckle to inclement conditions any longer, brushed aside all caution, and rode alone.

Johann huddled his broad shoulders inside his jacket, but experienced no relief from a sudden chill. He shivered involuntarily, the gloomy weather underscored his mood. He felt a strange premonition of doom. But why? He was twenty-one years old, healthy, strong, and sole heir to a noble title and a large parcel of Prussia, which had supported his family in splendor for generations. Particularly ever since his great-great grandfather, an illustrious *Generalfeldmarschall*, served Emperor Frederick Wilhelm III in the battle of Leipzig with such distinction, it cost him his life, but added ten thousand acres to his estate.

Now emerging from a narrow bridle path leading out of the woods, where fragile new leaves hung limp and dispirited on drooping branches, Johann came to a road that traced its origins in Poland and meandered lazily through Bernau—the village of his birth—where it straightened and paid rapt attention on its last leg to Berlin some twenty miles directly west. His brow crimped, he stopped and glanced at the flooded ruts in the old

8

road. He had no clue where to go next. However, since others involved in the search had probably gravitated toward the Black Wolf on the green in Bernau, there to swap stories and inquire about the whereabouts of the baron in total comfort, he decided on the opposite course. He turned his horse east toward Ladeburg and a tavern of equally seedy reputation, where he too could get in out of the rain for a spell. The month-long monsoons that had postponed spring planting throughout the region had caused boredom to reach epidemic proportions—a bonanza for any establishment of ill repute—and there could be no doubt that Karl-Heinz Konauer, friend since the cradle, was addressing his malaise at the Ladeburg tavern. On the strength of their long association, Johann figured that he could be persuaded to brave the elements, relinquish a warm chair for a wet saddle, and join him in the search. All at once anxious for company, he forced his horse into a fast lope; no small feat on the muddied road.

Ten minutes later, he rode up to the Ladeburg Inn, tossing the reins to a lackey who stepped out from under a roof overhang where he'd taken shelter. The man touched his grimy cap respectfully, for although this rider was soaked to the skin like any other mortal in this ungodly weather, his garb was of a finer quality and his saddle was studded with silver.

"Ye fixen' to stay?" the old man wanted to know, gumming the words for there was not a tooth in his mouth, something his grizzled beard concealed nicely.

"No," Johann said as he swung down from the saddle. "I'll only be a minute."

"I shan't bother smithy then."

"On the contrary. I suspect that my friend is inside. He'll need his horse."

The lackey knew all the inn's regular customers by name, and it didn't require much guesswork to identify this well-heeled individual's friend.

"Herr Konauer...he be inside," he reported with a mischievous and knowing grin. "I'll fetch his horse." He secured Johann's black brute to a post, received a perfect set of teeth marks on his wrist for his trouble, and now prudently giving the animal's hindquarters a wide berth, sloshed across the courtyard to the blacksmith, his rubber knee boots making squishy sounds in the mud as he went.

9

Johann took the steps to the tavern in one easy leap and, hand poised on the doorknob, shook himself like a shaggy dog before he went inside, where he immediately spotted Karl-Heinz at a corner table with a gypsy girl, some twenty pounds on the wrong side of svelte, on his lap. Her waist-long, blue-black hair glistened in the meager light, as did the golden hoops in her ears when she threw her head back in a guttural roar at something Karl-Heinz was whispering.

Raking long, slender fingers through his wet hair, Johann strolled across the uneven plank floor, nodding to the proprietor behind the bar counter and several idle farm workers sitting astride three-legged stools near the source of their newfound contentment. The smoky heat in the place felt good. Johann figured his clothes would dry in a jiffy.

Karl-Heinz looked up the minute his friend's shadow fell across the table. He put his wine goblet down and discharged the wench with a slap on her ample posterior. As she slipped away, she gave the tall, lean, and exceptionally handsome newcomer a sultry look. It was rare to see a clean-shaven man among this inn's clientele.

Plunking himself down, Johann reached over and took a gulp from Karl-Heinz's glass.

"Hey, get your own!" the latter protested and motioned toward the bar for a refill. "And how about some grub?" Sniffing appreciatively, Karl-Heinz eyed the huge stone fireplace near the door to the kitchen, where a side of pig was rotating on a spit; a large, bubbling kettle hung over the hearth at the other end of the room, and the entire place smelled of burnt pork rind and cellar cabbage boiling in sugar and vinegar. He rubbed his hands together and licked his lips. He was coping with the long, wet spring in the way he knew best, eating and drinking. "It ought to be ready any minute now."

"I don't have time to eat." Johann wiped his mouth on the back of his hand and set the wine down. "I'm out looking for my father. Have you seen him?"

"Mm... sure. But not in this place. Last I know of, he and my old man were wading knee-deep in muck and lamenting the loss of their fields."

"Where were they?"

"Where?" Karl-Heinz pursed his lips and contemplated the

10

coarse ceiling beams, slung so low his mind didn't need to stretch itself. "At the old crossroads, I believe. Near the kaiser's game preserve." A pitcher of hot spiced wine arrived at the table. Karl-Heinz checked it for any floating flies before pouring. "Want any?" he asked as he filled his glass.

"No." Johann put up his hands. "About when was this?"

Karl-Heinz worked a fine resonant belch to the surface and looked pleased with himself.

"Huh? What did you say?"

"When did you see them?"

Blowing across the top of the glass to cool it, Karl-Heinz sipped gingerly.

"Late afternoon, I believe," he mumbled. He put his drink down; it wasn't worth ruining a set of perfectly good tonsils. "So . . . , actually, I guess it must have been—" he suddenly nodded vigorously. "Yeah, it was yesterday."

"*What!*" Johann sputtered.

"Yesterday. Late in the afternoon."

"I heard you." Swallowing his impatience with great difficulty, Johann persevered. Karl-Heinz could be a trial when binging, and he was no sage. But he had something else going for him. He was loyal to the bone. "How about today?" he asked one last time. "Have you seen my father at any time today?"

"No. Mostly 'cause I've been right here. Had a game of cards earlier with that new Polish fella . . . what's his name? The new manager at Hotzendorf's place." Johann shrugged, he didn't keep track of the local work force. "Anyway, I took five marks off him," Karl-Heinz announced proudly. "Money I was about to spend on that piece of work over there." He nodded toward the gypsy girl at the bar and looked momentarily disgruntled, because he would probably have to start wooing her all over again. "I'd almost talked her into going upstairs when you showed up."

"Sorry," Johann murmured.

"Yeah, sure. Anyway, since when does the baron frequent a place like this?" Karl-Heinz threw his arm around a room in great need of some human kindness. "This establishment is strictly for the likes of you and me. What's up? Is he really missing?"

"According to my mother, yes. She feels he has stayed out too long, considering the lousy weather. She's sent everyone but

11

the dogs out to chase him down. I just spent an hour combing his favorite haunts. Damned near got killed doing it."

"I can tell." Karl-Heinz perused his friend's unusually shabby appearance; hatless and soaked, there were splotches of mud on his clothes. "You look like the devil. Got thrown, huh?"

"No." Johann decided not to elaborate on his close call with a ton of timber. It was more expedient to rouse Karl-Heinz to the rescue, and if he wasn't quite sober, so be it; the rain would work like a cold slap in the face. "Look, . . . " he said, coming straight to the point, "if my father is stranded in the back acres with a lame horse, which I'm beginning to think is a likely scenario, two good Samaritans are better than one. How about it? Are you coming?"

"Uh, well, I . . . I suppose so." Karl-Heinz's stomach was growling so ferociously, it interfered with a prompt response. He threw a regretful glance toward the sizzling meat and the girl busying herself at the bar counter. *Chrisakes, she's already dallying with another customer!* He sighed, dejected, and it was with precious little enthusiasm that he rose and reached for his coat slung over an empty chair. "All right, I guess we might as well be off," he said and dropped some money on the table before following his friend outside to where the lackey was tending two horses. When Karl-Heinz saw his gelding, saddled and ready, he scowled. "You took a lot for granted," he griped to no one in particular.

The two riders were soon plodding across fields stripped of topsoil, and while Karl-Heinz carried on, *ad infinitum,* about the high price of wheat come September, Johann dismissed any concern. Farming was a tiresome occupation, one he was glad to leave to others. Physical science intrigued him, and if not for his parents, who made no demands on their son except that he present himself at the dinner table regularly, he'd be attending the university in Berlin right now, studying biology and related sciences. Anything but agronomics.

The search had used up a perfectly good hour, when Karl-Heinz, who had the liveliest respect for his own welfare, concluded he was near death from starvation and halted his horse at the crest of a hill a mile from the Konauer spread, second in size only to the von Renz property. In front of him, low plumes of wet clouds drifted across a meadow—now a fine lake—where a few stalwart trees stood up to their armpits in water. Beyond, obscured by the mist, the gorged and swollen Havel River dragged its heavy load to the sea. The noise of rushing water carried the distance. It was about all one heard. There was no pleasant twittering of birds. Clever critters, they had clearly extended their hiatus down south until the weather improved.

"You know what?" Karl-Heinz pretended to study the dismal view while trying to extricate himself from this wild goose chase. "I'll bet your old man's got enough sense to get in out of this rain. He's probably dropped in on mine. Feet to the fire and a good bottle of port between them, I'll wager they've lost track of time and simply forgot to send word. My father waded through enough mud yesterday to last him a lifetime."

"You could be right." Against his better judgment, Johann let his horse nibble on last summer's leftovers, slimy tufts of yellow grass poking through the mud.

"Of course I'm right!" Karl-Heinz typically displayed a mulish streak. He removed his wide-brimmed hat and, tousling his matted blond hair with unnecessary roughness, beat it against his knee to shake off some water. "For all we know, they're as sodden as the soil. No one's at home to keep them sober. Mother went to Oranienburg this morning." Karl-Heinz made a fist and reshaped the top of his hat before replacing it on his head.

"Oranienburg? Why?"

"Cousin Hilda is failing."

"Hildegard Gersdorf?" Johann knew the frail widow and was not surprised at news of her decline, nor was he particularly interested in this Konauer relative.

"Yeah, Gerlinde sent word at the crack of dawn. She was frantic."

"I can imagine," Johann agreed, bored. Hildegard Gersdorf's daughter, a nervous girl of bland appearance, was easily frightened. He knew her to be seventeen but she could pass for twelve. "What's the complaint this time?" he asked without the slightest interest in the woman or her plain daughter.

"That nasty fever making the rounds has all but done her in."

"She's dying?" Johann straightened in the saddle, his indifference vanished somewhat.

13

"I'm afraid so. Mother is leading the death knell." Karl-Heinz looked dour. "She'll probably bring Gerlinde back home with her."

"Well, cheer up. She won't eat much." The quip slipped out before Johann could consider if it was appropriate and he immediately attempted to cover the callous remark. "If I recall correctly, she is quiet as a stone," he said. This was a veritable compliment, in that he didn't particularly like chatty females. "You'll never notice her except as a shadow on the wall."

"Actually, it's not Gerlinde who concerns me," Karl-Heinz shrugged. "I'm more bothered by the fact that no one's at home to keep my father out of trouble. And given the bad influence of yours, one can expect the worse. Wanna come? If he's there, it'd save you some trouble." Johann shook his head. "Well, suit yourself." Home and hearth lay a short distance away; the road was easily accessible from here, and Karl-Heinz's stomach insisted that he take it. He shifted in the saddle and held his chin at a stubborn pitch. "This is where we part ways," he said, figuring he'd given more than enough of his time in the name of friendship.

"You break my heart," Johann laughed, flashing a row of glamorous white teeth. He fished a handkerchief from an inside pocket to wipe at the rivulets of water seeping under his collar. "I'll continue a little while longer. As far as to the river."

"Are you crazy?" Karl-Heinz pointed to the swampy landscape between them and the Havel. "You'll sink into oblivion long before you get there. You and your horse. And that, my friend, would be one helluva waste of an expensive animal." Karl-Heinz eyed Johann's horse with a touch of envy, every black ounce of it thoroughbred. It had small white markings around the neck, which he had learned to think of as a fallen halo. Johann had once gotten mad as hell when someone likened it to a necklace.

"To ease your mind," Johann allowed with a grin at his friend's play on priorities. "I'll loop around to the left. Close enough to my house so someone will hear me holler if I begin to sink."

"Why go at all?"

"Because I'm curious to see if any sand has survived the high water. My father pays a fortune to have the stuff hauled in. Since I'm this close, I'm sure he'd appreciate a report. He might be

14

there himself. He takes great pride in maintaining a beach a hundred miles from the real thing."

"Oh, yeah, I forgot. Eccentricity runs in your family," Karl-Heinz sniped, forgetting the many summers he had enjoyed the swimming hole, with its white banks imported from the Baltic. But hunger made him testy. He clucked to his horse and prepared to turn right. "I still say he's at my place," he hollered over his shoulder as he fought gravity negotiating the slippery downhill path.

"If he is, kick him out and send him home."

"Count on it." Without turning, Karl-Heinz raised a fist, thumb pointing up.

THREE

Baron Edmund Bernhard von Renz was not at the Konauers'. Johann found him some twenty minutes later lying face down on a wooded path near the river. A magnificent roan stallion, pitifully crippled, was sprawled nearby, thrashing and foaming at the mouth in pain. One glance told Johann there was no hope for the animal, and loathing what had to be done, he slipped the pistol from his belt before he could get into any maudlin arguments with himself. Aiming carefully, he pulled the trigger. The bullet entered the skull and the huge beast shuddered with one final spastic jerk, then lay perfectly still. Now bracing himself for the worst, Johann jumped to the ground, tethering his horse to a dwarfed spruce in one fluid motion before kneeling down and turning his father over.

The breath caught in his throat at the sight of an ugly deep abdominal gash, a laceration that along with a subsequent loss of blood had rendered the baron unconscious. Reaching for the pistol for the second time in as many minutes, Johann glanced around for whatever vile creature had ambushed his father and might still be laying in wait.

His eyes flicked over the immediate area, a site of a furious struggle, evidenced by trampled patches of muddied grass. Following a thin trail of blood diluted by rain, he spotted the boar; dead, thank God! Even so, its eight-inch tusks jutted menacingly from under the shrubs where it had crawled with a hunting knife—one Johann recognized as his father's—plunged into its gray belly, mottled and swarming with bloated ticks. Johann's skin crawled. He quickly put the gun away and turned all his attention back to his father, speaking to him, trying to rally him; alas, to no avail.

Digging into his pockets, he found a clean handkerchief, which he pressed against the wound. The white linen absorbed the blood like a sponge. Leaving it in place, Johann ripped off his suede jacket, turning it inside out to expose the warm dry

16

lining before placing it under the battered head. Shivering as his shirt was pelted by rain, he now pushed up his sleeves and got to work stemming the flow of blood as best he could, using another handkerchief he found on his father's person. The elder von Renz moaned and finally opened his eyes. The minute he recognized his son, a shadow of a smile passed over his sallow face.

"What happened?" Johann asked in a raw, emotion-charged voice; not that it wasn't obvious his father had been thrown and gored, but he wanted to test his faculties.

The reply was a rasping whisper.

"A...a boar...mad as anything...came out of nowhere. Hamlet spooked...fell. I think he broke a leg. Maybe two.... He must be in...agony. Put him down."

"I already did." How typical of his father to concern himself with the stallion before anything else, Johann thought and shot a glance toward the horse, his attention more keenly focused on the huge boar lying belly-up in the bushes, however. He hoped to God it wasn't rabid. "Does it hurt when you breathe?" he probed his father, this while trying to dispel a mounting alarm; in the last couple of weeks there had been several cases of rabies reported.

"Terribly."

"You might have broken some ribs. You can't ride, or I'd put you on my horse." Johann realized a stretcher was needed. His father was a big man; it would require several people to carry him back to the house. "I'll have to go for help," he said. "I won't be long. Try not to move while I'm gone."

"Don't worry...I...I won't budge. For the simple reason that I can't." Baron von Renz grasped his son's warm hands and held on tightly for a moment as if attempting to draw strength from them.

Johann smiled reassuringly even as his silvery-gray eyes dulled and the muscles in his square jaw tightened involuntarily with the seriousness of the situation. Despite the cold, he realized that he was perspiring; something other than rain was running down his back and gathering above his upper lip. He ran his sleeve across his face, and after checking the makeshift bandage, swung up on his horse and, with no concern for his own safety, galloped off, taking dangerous shortcuts across slippery

17

fields and driving a priceless stallion into death-defying jumps over hedges and ditches.

It was an hour before the baron was brought home. A doctor was summoned. When he finally left, he was grim-faced.

Word spread. Villagers began to assemble outside the tall iron gates that marked the entrance to the barony, an enormous red brick residence enclosed in a graveled courtyard dominated by a marble nymph fountain rising above a reflecting pool where schools of goldfish swam in blissful circles under showy lily pads. Ancient ivy clung to the north face of the house, while climbing roses had the run of the walls along the eastern exposure.

Johann and his mother spent the night keeping a vigil by the bedside. Eventually Johann dozed off only to be awakened some time after midnight by Annedora's heart-wrenching sobs.

His father was dead.

It was barely a month after the baron's funeral when Annedora von Renz became ill with the same fever that had cut a wide and merciless swath through the countryside earlier in the spring, leaving the strong weak and the weak dead.

The baroness was soon laid to rest next to her husband.

FOUR

"Christ! What's the matter with you?" Karl-Heinz barged into Johann's library, unannounced, and in such a state of anger, he neglected to notice that large chunks of dirt were flaking off his boots, leaving brown spots in the pastel Aubusson. His rudeness this morning in June included slamming the door behind him, sending the papers on Johann's desk flying. "Where the devil were you?"

"What?" Exasperated, Johann looked up and spread his fingers over his paperwork to keep it in place against Karl-Heinz's temper. "Where the hell was I supposed to be?" He narrowed his eyes and glared at his friend, not at all happy with this intrusion. He had to wade through his father's investment portfolio before the solicitors arrived. Due at noon, they took pride in being punctual and would probably be early. Attorneys and accountants were doing their damnedest to assure he had no peace. Now it would appear that Karl-Heinz was joining the conspiracy.

Admittedly, Johann had neglected their friendship. During the past month, along with mourning his parents, he'd had to come to terms with his new and vast responsibilities. Everything on the estate needed his attention, and every employee expected him to have quick answers, when in fact, he hadn't the foggiest idea what made the place run, nor did he care; something he'd rather die than make public, of course. The Berlin house needed his attention as well. But for now he simply sent bank drafts in hope that the caretakers, a husband and wife team by the last name of Schmidt, would be motivated to keep the roof tight and the basement dry. Something they could probably be trusted to do, since they lived on the premises and no doubt enjoyed that comfort enough to want to maintain it.

"Last night . . . ," Karl-Heinz persisted, his voice rising, "you, of all people, were conspicuously absent!"

"Absent from what?"

19

"From what?" Karl-Heinz rolled his eyes, wondering if Johann had been simple-minded all these years without anybody catching on. Now leaning across the desk, he planted his palms on a pile of documents, while his angry blue eyes bore into a person he'd known since creation. "The Konauers throw a bash to proclaim the end of my bachelor days, and guess who doesn't bother to show up?"

"Wait a second!" Johann's eyebrows snapped together; Karl-Heinz had finally secured his attention. "Did I just hear correctly? You're getting . . . married?"

"That's right." Karl-Heinz began to rummage through the sea of papers on the desk, invading private territory bold as you please. *It's got to be here somewhere*, he thought to himself and wondered how a person, who was so meticulous about his own appearance that shaving was a daily obsession, could tolerate such a mess. "Ah-hah!" Karl-Heinz shouted triumphantly a moment later when he found what he was looking for. "Here it is! Unopened!" He held up a gold-edged envelope, which Johann immediately snatched out of his hand.

Foregoing the letter opener, he tore roughly at the seal. His eyes skimmed the contents written in Ursula Konauer's neat hand.

"Damn!" he swore under his breath; to have ignored this invitation was unforgivable. He would have to apologize to Karl-Heinz's mother forewith. "I am sorry about this," he said and looked squarely at his friend. "I've had a hell of a time lately, as you know. If it'll make amends, I'll sack Rolf for failing to bring this card to my attention."

"Nah, keep the ol' boy on. Senile or not, butlers are hard to come by." Some of Karl-Heinz's petulance had left him the minute he spotted the unopened letter. It was clear that negligence, not intent, accounted for any insult.

"But . . . ah, so tell me, who are you marrying?" Johann wondered how an experienced rogue like Karl-Heinz had been fool enough to get himself trapped. A pregnant bride was obviously the explanation for this sudden engagement.

"Gerlinde."

"Who?" Stealing a sideways glance at a porcelain clock on the black marble mantelpiece, Johann realized that precious time was passing. "Who . . . who did you say?"

"Gerlinde Gersdorf." Johann still looked confused. "Come on!" Karl-Heinz began to scowl; it was unlike Johann to be so thickheaded. "Dammit, you know Gerlinde! Surely, you remember Hildegard? She died in April. Gerlinde is her daughter."

"Oh...? Oh, yes, of course..."

"Congratulations, pal! There ought to be a prize for such swift comprehension," Karl-Heinz mumbled under his breath.

"But wait! Back up a minute." Johann still cherished the hope he might have heard wrong. "Are you telling me that you're marrying that Gerlinde? Gerlinde Gersdorf?"

"None other."

"But why?"

"Why?" Annoyed with his friend's reaction, Karl-Heinz was, furthermore, irritated that he had to explain himself. "Because..." he began slowly as if addressing an underachiever, "because Hildegard, in her dying breath, made my mother promise that we'd look after Gerlinde. You know, sort of make sure that she didn't fall into the clutches of some ne'er-do-well looking to improve his prospects. And what, I ask you, what better way to foil a greedy suitor than to have Gerlinde marry... yours truly? *Moi?*"

Johann could think of a dozen, but said nothing. He got up from his desk and went to stand by the double bay windows facing out over acres of sloping virid lawns. He pushed at the green satin drapery and pretended something outside had caught his interest, while his mind slowly absorbed what he'd just heard. If he remembered correctly, Karl-Heinz had never even liked the girl.

"You actually consented to this?" he finally asked, turning around. The question escaped like a hiss, but he didn't care if his voice betrayed him. Gerlinde Gersdorf was so pathetic... so colorless... so small. Thin as a needle. The proverbial runt. The one that's drowned at birth. A door knob had more personality.

"Consented?" Karl-Heinz scoffed and fell into a comfortable arm chair. "My friend, you are looking at a happy man!"

"I see." Johann didn't believe that for a minute but kept his peace. And rounding the massive oak desk, he walked over to one of the bookcases lining the walls of the spacious library. He opened a false front, revealing a mirrored liquor cabinet. "Felicitations are obviously in order," he said. "It's uncivilized to drink before noon, but I think we can make an exception today. What'll it be?" Silently, he acknowledged that he needed a drink to help this disaster sink in. He was very familiar with Karl-Heinz's taste in women, and had Gerlinde been a boy, she could not have been further from the mark.

"I'll take some brandy. A splash of that rare Napoleon you're hoarding." Karl-Heinz shrugged out of his jacket, threw it across a sofa, and prepared to enjoy himself. "And for once, try not be miserly with it."

Johann poured liberal amounts into two snifters. He handed one to Karl-Heinz.

"To your bride!" he said and sat down on the corner of his desk. "And to your happiness!" The first did not impact the latter, but he lifted his glass and tried to be cheerful. "When's the wedding?"

"Early September. In Oranienburg. You'll get the details in a letter." Karl-Heinz propped his dirty boots up on a pristine white damask ottoman and leaned back in the soft chair. "So, for chrissake, open your mail once in a while!" He accepted the cheroot Johann was offering him.

As Johann struck a match and held it out, he eyed his friend for signs of a twisted arm. Gerlinde Gersdorf was so unappealing, it offended the senses. But if Karl-Heinz was being railroaded, he sure didn't show it.

FIVE

Of Lilliputian physique and as if to compensate for this paucity of stature, Viktor Gersdorf amassed an enormous fortune investing in gold mines in South Africa, where he had spent his youth and most of his middle years, too preoccupied with making money to be practical in the ways of the flesh. Marriage did not occur to him until he suffered a serious illness that brought any dreams of immortality into the harsh morning light. He immediately retired to Germany and acquired a house so large, it cried out for a mistress. A trusted friend introduced him to Hildegard Kollmer, a woman of such cardinal virtues that she'd been overlooked by less discriminating gentlemen.

Happily settled down in domestic bliss, Viktor Gersdorf, sadly, did not have long to enjoy it, nor did he live to see his only child born. But his daughter would not lack for attention. Viktor Gersdorf's two maiden sisters arrived for his funeral, carrying large suitcases; woe be it for them to turn their backs on a bereaved sister-in-law in her hour of need.

In due time, the three women set about to raise the fatherless infant; a responsibility they took to heart and carried out admirably, drawing on their combined inexperience.

Gerlinde was fifteen when *Tante* Angelika died; *Tante* Amelia passed away a year later, and when Gerlinde's mother followed the aunts into the grave this past April, Gerlinde was so desolate, she agreed without deliberation when Ursula and Karl Konauer suggested that she marry their son. She was not the slightest bit fond of Karl-Heinz, but was even less thrilled at the thought of living alone.

The wedding took place on a brisk September day bursting with the first rich colors of an early autumn. Standing next to her robust groom in a three-centuries-old church, the diminutive ashen-faced bride was completely overshadowed by the splendor of her surroundings and would have blended into the background altogether if not for the fifty yards of beaded ruffles in her wedding dress that screamed for attention.

At the gala that followed in the Gersdorf's large, primly decorated formal parlor of sensible, brown upholstered furniture—protected by embroidered lace doilies on every armrest and vulnerable wood surface—Johann claimed the perfunctory dance reserved for the best man and drew Gerlinde into the adjoining salon where only slow waltzes were played in respect for the bride's recent loss.

"I hope you'll like living in Bernau," he said when it became clear that Gerlinde wasn't going to inaugurate the light conversation the dance required. She demonstrated a rate gift for silence; a trait he grudgingly admired. "I suppose it'll be quite a change for you. Our sleepy little village can hardly be compared with the bustling metropolis of Oranienburg."

Gerlinde stiffened, unwilling to admit that she knew little about her place of birth because she'd never been allowed into town except to attend church with her mother and her aunts. Teachers had come to the house to instruct her in reading and needlepoint and whatever dance steps were required of a girl of good breeding.

"I expect Bernau will suit me," she said tonelessly and lowered her light-blue eyes, lacking in both sparkle and wit. Karl and Ursula brushed by. Gerlinde saw them out of the corner of her shuttered eye and heard her father-in-law humming along with the music. She wished she were dancing with him. Or better still, ensconced in a corner of the salon, sipping tea with Ursula. Older people tended not to unnerve her. "Ursula will be a wonderful companion," she said, and meant it.

Johann raised his eyebrows. *Ursula?* This girl had married Karl-Heinz, *not* his mother. But he said nothing. It was none of his business if she preferred an old woman to a young husband. Inwardly he chuckled. Karl-Heinz had his work cut out for him. No wonder he was taking his bride to Italy for their honeymoon; her maidenly screams damned well wouldn't carry the distance.

"I . . . I hope you'll consent to being our very first guest once we return from Venice," Gerlinde said in the very next breath, a quivering breath she drew with some effort, as if she'd read Johann's mind about the wedding bower.

"Nothing would please me more."

"Good. Then I shall expect you to come without ceremony."

She raised her small pale face to his and, emboldened by what she took to be sincerity in his expression, stretched her lips into a semblance of a smile. "It'll be ever so nice to have family nearby," she added staunchly, glad when the waltz began to wind down.

"Family?" Johann's gray eyes narrowed as he looked down at her. He didn't realize Gerlinde had any to speak of. Why else had the Konauers made the supreme sacrifice of tying this pitiful piece of baggage to Karl-Heinz? They didn't need her dowry and could certainly have pawned her off on some more deserving soul without breaking any deathbed promises.

"Oh, f . . . forgive me!" Gerlinde blushed a deep crimson that went clear to the roots of her beige hair. "I . . . I'm being presumptuous of course. But, uh, Ursula told me that she thinks of you as family. She said that you and Karl-Heinz are like brothers. And, . . . well, I just . . . ah, thought . . . That is . . ." The rush of blood to her face accompanied by a sudden roar in her ears, interfered with her ability to continue.

"Well, by all means then," bored and amused at the same time, Johann inclined his head in a slight nod, "consider me *brother* Johann." Suddenly his face broke into a grin. "That sounds a bit pious though. And I'm afraid that I'm not blessed with any corroborating qualities."

A giggle like a polite hiccup escaped Gerlinde's throat. But she dared not comment further. Intuition told her that he spoke the truth. Johann von Renz was no saint, and, worse, he was *proud* of it. She lowered her head to stave off further conversation while her original embarrassment subsided.

Before the dance ended, and although it was rather awkward to lead a girl around on the floor when she was determined to study her shoes, Johann found himself warming toward this nondescript person drowning in shyness and yards of white silk. Her flaming cheeks pulled at a man's heartstrings, if not his passion. He conceded that Karl-Heinz, the quintessential scoundrel, might possibly get a rise out of such a timid creature.

Traveling back to Bernau the following day, nursing a world-class hangover, it occurred to Johann that in the span of one short summer, he'd been stripped of all companionships, those that mattered anyway. His parents were in their graves, and although Karl-Heinz was still his neighbor, he suspected their

25

friendship would never be the same again. Karl-Heinz was now a married man; his priorities and obligations would change. He might even be a father before a year passed.

Johann arrived home feeling uncharacteristically depressed, something he attributed to the lingering headache.

Frau Erdmann, cook and housekeeper on the von Renz estate, had prepared a sumptuous dinner for his homecoming, but although he hadn't eaten since breakfast, Johann had no appetite and stabbed abstractedly at his plate, soon pushing it away.

The large dining room felt oppressive; the tapestries on the walls seemed to close in on him, and though the double French doors were thrown open to the terrace and a cool September breeze was flapping the curtains, giving proof of circulation, Johann experienced a crushing lack of air. He suddenly rose from the table as if he'd broken bread with the devil, rose with such clumsy movements that the tapers in the silver candelabrums flickered and spilled splotches of hot paraffin on the exquisite rosewood.

Frau Erdmann whisked her rotund bulk through the swinging doors from the pantry with uncanny grace and, using the blunt edge of a knife, began to scrape the wax from the table top at the same time she vigorously applied polish; her synchronized grunts reminding the maids—whose dewy eyes were following the handsome young baron—of their immediate duties.

With the strong smell of lemon oil in his nostrils, Johann left the room, crossed the hall in a few long strides, and settled down in the library with the evening papers. However, his bleak mood, as acute as it was bizarre, stayed with him. He found that he couldn't concentrate. Eventually he threw the papers aside in disgust with himself.

Aimlessly, he glanced around. This room had been his father's domain, but since his mother had been partial to pastels, the sofas and chairs were upholstered in white satin and damask, strewn with plump pink pillows. The draperies, framing the large bay windows, were the color of sea mist and hues of this same green were worked into a leaf pattern in the border of the pink Aubusson on the floor. Only the dark wood-paneled walls with built-in matching bookcases filled with brown, leather-bound editions, insured that despite Annedora's best efforts, the room was respectably masculine.

Loosening his collar while toying absentmindedly with the gold chain on his waistcoat watch, Johann felt at odds with his world, a trespasser in a familiar milieu. His headache had dulled, still he experienced an unremitting sense of restlessness. He couldn't read, and, dammit, he couldn't even get comfortable. Unbuttoning his vest, he moved forward, balanced himself on the edge of the chair and reached behind him for a superfluous pillow, which he flung on the floor. Now leaning back, he pushed his legs out in front of him, crossed them at the ankles, and tried to confront the baffling mood that had nagged him ever since this morning and that could no longer be ascribed to a hangover.

Moments later, galling as the thought was, he realized that in some inexorable way, he was utterly bored. And as he puzzled with this new revelation, repeatedly opening his watch and clicking it shut, he came up with no answer that satisfied him. Only one thing was certain; life on the estate presented no immediate challenge. The dormant season was about to quiet the landscape, and Klausen—the new manager he'd hired when the former man failed to regain his health—had proven himself capable of running things. The workers respected him; one stern word, and the laziest among them were galvanized into activity.

The spring floods, the funerals, the change of command had been unsettling for all concerned. But normalcy had returned, and everyone had again fallen into a routine, a long-established routine that Johann suddenly didn't fit into. Of course, he had long known that in regard to agronomics, he was not cast from the same mold as his land baron ancestors. When all was said and done, he could expect to maintain the status quo and grow old knowing that he had held the estate together for his heirs with embarrassingly little effort.

Heirs?

Johann glanced around the room where pictures of his ancestors were prominently displayed, as if reminding him of his duty. And whereas he'd never wished for any siblings, he all at once did and shrugged wearily. He supposed that marriage was inevitable, although he had yet to meet a female sufficiently fascinating not to irritate him any sooner than absolutely necessary. Even the ones who were good sports and enjoyed a roll between the sheets quickly lost their allure.

That said, he got up, stretched, and sauntered over to the fireplace. He took a slim cheroot from a gold case on the mantelpiece, lit it, and narrowing his eyes against the tobacco smoke, leaned a shoulder against the black marble. Studying the countless rows of books along the walls, he recalled that three years ago, when he'd outgrown the various tutors and insipid ladies who came to teach him French and English, he had fully expected to attend the university. However, his parents had looked positively stricken with the idea of losing him to Berlin. As stricken as when he'd marched into breakfast one morning at the age of fifteen and announced that he wanted to marry Ingrid, a new parlor maid who'd slipped into his bed the night before where she'd convinced him that she was an angel. She received her walking papers, and he got a stern lecture about squandering his name, his title, and property on a female with no ancestry.

Grinning with the memory and clamping the cheroot between his teeth, Johann bent down, lifted a log from the brass bin next to the hearth, and tossed it into the fire. A shower of sparks rose in a frenzied dance, while the flames retreated under the heavy bulk for a moment before regrouping to lick the new morsel.

Johann straightened, wiped wood chips from his hands, and made a snap decision. At first light tomorrow, he would move to the house in Berlin and enroll at the university. And if he was older than other newcomers to the hallowed Humboldt Halls, so be it. He'd simply take competency exams and catch up with his peers.

Let it be said here that Johann von Renz was not the least bit vain except in matters of intellect. There he considered himself above the fray.

28

SIX

Berlin five years later—1900

"Dear me, I do believe the temperature is dropping." Frau Schmidt walked briskly into the library, pushed at the heavy red velvet drapery, and squinted through thick eyeglasses at the thermometer attached to the outside of the window to confirm what her middle-aged bones were already telling her. "Only November, but I dare say a fur-lined coat will be necessary for anyone venturing out tonight." She fingered some strands of black hair—carefully dyed to conceal any gray—and stayed put, peering out toward the dark street, checking it for the elegant carriages that regularly negotiated Lindenstrasse. There were precious few this evening, something she carefully pointed out to her employer before turning away from the window to stoke the fire and rearrange the pillows in the supple red leather sofas. That done, she attended to any other housekeeping detail that might justify her presence.

From his place at his desk, Johann made an unintelligible sound. Frau Schmidt regularly busied herself within his earshot to inform and opine. But during the handful of years he'd now lived in Grunewald—a fashionable residential section west of the general hub of Berlin—he had perfected a deaf ear to the traffic of the city as well as that generated by his housekeeper's vocal chords. Despite these irritations, he'd never once regretted that decisive September day when he arrived, catching the resident caretakers unaware. A substantial raise helped them recover. Schmidt starched his collars and acquired new black butler attire along with a snappy livery uniform for when he drove the coach. Frau Schmidt hired additional maids, delighted in lording it over these inferiors and occasionally forgot her own station when she waltzed into the sanctuary of the baron's library without summons. Such as tonight.

"Might you have plans for this evening, *mein Herr*?" she finally asked, now that her circuitous comments about the weather had failed to elicit a response and nothing else in the library required her attention. She looked down her sharp nose at a yellow chrysanthemum plant on a coffee table; the least it could do was appear a tad less cheerful to justify a bit of pinching.

"No."

"No? You won't be needing my husband then?"

"That's right." Johann worked his jaw and looked up from his reading with an expression that dared the woman to ask him to explain himself.

She didn't of course. Instead she hurried from the room, tugging at her apron. She had her answer. Her husband, thank heavens, could stay in on this bitter night. He suffered from arthritis, aggravated by cold weather. She'd fix him some chamomile tea, then they'd retire to their quarters and enjoy a game of cards.

Johann went back to his work, as relieved as the meddlesome housekeeper to be spending a rare evening at home. The "season" was in full swing, with the usual abundance of soirees and balls. He glanced across the desk at a pile of invitations, put his book down after inserting a marker so he wouldn't lose his place, and reached for a letter Schmidt had placed on a separate tray. Turning the envelope over, Johann recognized the seal of Kaiser Wilhelm II. The invitation was not unexpected. Since moving to Berlin and because of his family's past associations with the Crown, he'd been to any number of receptions at the Imperial Palace on Unter den Linden.

Putting the gilt-edged card aside, Johann flicked through the other invitations; he would send his regrets to most of them. He was growing tired of dancing attendance to Berlin's debutantes, whose zealous mothers—determined to have marriageable daughters off their hands—were prone to unattractive sycophant behavior. That Baron Johann Maximilian von Renz was twenty-seven and still remained a bachelor, chafed the grande dames of society.

Silently praising Schmidt's brave attempt to make order out of the chaos on the desk, Johann picked up a letter in a tray that, like the invitation from the palace, stood apart from the clutter. It was from Gerlinde—postmarked two days ago—which meant it had only just been delivered. Good. He couldn't be accused of neglect. And since his reading on infectious tropical diseases was now interrupted, he might as well attend to the mail tonight rather than save it for the early morning hours, as was his habit.

He opened Gerlinde's letter. After reminding him that he was expected for Christmas, she'd devoted the rest of the page to her son's latest mischief. Johann leaned back in his chair as he read, a smile tugging at his finely-formed wide mouth. He was immensely fond of the lad, his godchild, a charming boy with straw-colored hair and fat sturdy legs. Born a year to the day of Gerlinde and Karl-Heinz's marriage, Hans's birth had brought great joy to the Konauer household, though his entrance into the world was almost poor Gerlinde's exit. She had hovered between life and death for months, and her son turned four before she reclaimed her premarital state of delicate frailty.

With the passing of time, Johann came to love the unassuming Gerlinde. Small of body, he soon discovered that she owned an uncommonly large heart, one that loved all God's creatures with democratic zeal. He who would have moved heaven and earth to have talked Karl-Heinz out of the marriage, now occasionally found himself envying his friend such a philanthropic wife.

*   *   *

Dorrit walked across the floors in the apartment for one final check to make certain nothing was forgotten. She felt a touch of sadness at leaving. She and her father had lived in Warsaw for five wonderful years, the longest they had ever remained in any one place since abruptly moving from Bialystok in the spring of 1895. A move, Dorrit suspected at the time, that had a lot to do with Dr. Kozlowski who'd treated her father the preceding winter when a lung infection had almost been the end of him.

Come spring, and with Herman Zache's restored health, the doctor, nonetheless, continued to stop by. Dorrit thought he was being awfully nice, because he never charged a fee for these visits. Her father, on the other hand, wondered about a hidden motive and grew increasingly leery. His suspicions bore fruit the day Dr. Kozlowski brought along his eldest son. The young man had a terrible complexion and stared rudely at Dorrit. But worse, he asked personal questions, far more than the visit warranted. Knowing how much her father hated any kind of probing into their private affairs, Dorrit was not surprised when he politely cut the *tête-à-tête* short.

When a matchmaker came to the door days later, Herman Zache was no longer polite.

Trying to listen to an exchange that she was not allowed to participate in, Dorrit pressed her ear against the closed door to her room.

"Ivar Kozlowski is prepared to wait and marry your daughter only when she becomes of age . . . ," she heard the *shadchen* explain. Dorrit's heart dropped. She strained to listen to her father's response. He was speaking rapidly, but she garnered enough to realize he would have none of it. She sank against the door, relieved. In the next instant she heard the woman warn that he might never receive a better offer. "You ought to be grateful that a family of property, such as the Kozlowskis, are willing to accept a bride without a dowry," she admonished him, at which point Herman Zache's pride came into play, and he all but tossed the woman out the door.

The minute she was gone, Dorrit tore from her room.

"Papa, . . . oh, I'm so glad you didn't consent!" She threw her arms around him.

He held her tight and stroked her beautiful red hair.

"Then I was right to assume that you didn't care for the young man?" Herman Zache allowed himself a small grin of satisfaction.

Dorrit nodded.

"Even if the angry red spots on his face diminish and his property doubles, I would never marry him. Besides, I . . . I couldn't leave you . . . ever!" she protested. "You are the dearest papa in the world." A dark cloud suddenly settled across Herman Zache's face. His smile vanished, he let go of his daughter and turned away. His posture seemed to crumple; it became apparent that he wished to say no more. Dorrit, recognizing the signs, gave his arm a quick playful pinch and went into the kitchen. "I'll make some tea," she said over her shoulder. "And we'll have biscuits with marmalade." This bit of extravagance was added as a diversionary tactic to his mutable mood.

Indeed the exchange with the matchmaker had taken a toll on Dr. Zache's nerves. Before going to sleep that night, Dorrit heard him pace the apartment like a caged animal.

The next morning, he severed his professional ties in Bialystok.

"It has become necessary to move," he said to Dorrit, without elaborating.

She was not surprised. This sort of thing had happened before. Without demur, she packed her things and helped her father box his clocks and books for shipment. He squared his bill with Frau Weiss, gave her the two extra months on the lease, but no forwarding address.

Heading west, Dr. Zache found a temporary teaching post at Warsaw University. The following year, it became permanent, and three years later, he took over as head of the department of medical history when the present man died of advanced age and the professor next in line succumbed to a liver complaint. It was a meteoric rise that Herman Zache had never dreamed possible. Dorrit supposed they were not quite so poor anymore.

Warsaw suited her father, proof being that although the weather was as harsh as in Bialystok, he was ill less often. Once, when Dorrit commented on this wonderful development, he revealed that the distance he had finally put between himself and Mother Russia was the reason for any improved vigor. However, when she asked him to be more specific, he immediately clammed up and disappeared behind that rueful expression she had come to recognize, never understood, and was never able to penetrate.

But now they were leaving Warsaw as well. Dorrit should have known it wouldn't last. Still, this move was different from all the rest. There was no sudden sense of urgency. Her father wasn't fleeing. He had carefully planned this change over several months.

Opening and closing the last drawers in a bureau, Dorrit confirmed that the apartment was empty except for the furniture which belonged to the landlord, who'd come over this morning to determine that no piece had suffered damage beyond normal wear and tear.

Handing Herr Kmetz the keys, Dorrit walked over to a window to have a quick glance at the street below. Her father was standing on the curb with the suitcases. He had gone down ahead of her to hail a public coach. So far without success. He looked up, saw her, and smiled ruefully. She waved, indicating that she'd be right down.

"Hm, I'm afraid they're scarce this morning," she mumbled as she buttoned her coat.

"What? Coaches?"

Dorrit nodded.

"Yes, it's a real shame about the rail strike." Herr Kmetz looked appropriately concerned, but in the next instant, he was smiling at the seventeen-year-old girl as she stopped in the middle of the living room, pivoting gracefully for one last nostalgic look around. Her coat was a dull brown, but one scarcely noticed when the morning light, filtering through the windows, put such a fiery glow in her abundant auburn hair and left a lovely pink blush on her finely chiseled cheekbones. The girl was exquisite. The landlord wished himself thirty years younger and, mesmerized, followed her as she turned her back on the room, walked into the hall, and headed for the stairs. Closing the door behind him, Herr Kmetz was tempted to apologize for the plain flat she and her father had occupied.

"Yes, it's a real shame," he repeated when they reached the ground floor, where he held open the door to the street. "The strike, I mean. A great bother for all concerned. Still, I trust you and the professor will have a good journey. At least you'll see more of the countryside from a coach." He extended his hand. "Best of luck in Berlin."

"Thank you." Dorrit turned dazzling green eyes on Herr Kmetz and shook his hand before she pulled a hood securely over her head and stepped out of the doorway. She hurried across the sidewalk to the curb, where she linked arms with her father anxiously eyeing the street for some form of transportation that could take them to the depot and the noon coach bound for Poznan. From there, it was a day's ride to Wielkopolski and the German border.

Dorrit glanced up at the sky. Clouds were blowing in from the west, dulling the sunlight and further chilling the air. Except for a constant worry about her father's weak lungs, she was excited about this trip, albeit inconvenienced by the railroad strike. Trains across Poland sat idle, and if the job action spread into Germany, they'd be obliged to ride a horse-drawn rig the entire way.

"Let's hope the coaches aren't drafty," she said, airing her concern and huddling close to her father to keep warm.

"I'm afraid December is not a choice month for traveling," Herman Zache conceded and patted her hand on his arm. "But if I had requested a postponement until warmer weather, they'd have discovered that I am a decrepit old man and then they would probably have invited someone else. It was something I couldn't chance. The position at Berlin University is too important."

Indeed, Herman Zache had campaigned hard and long for the post; a crusade that included sending copies of books he'd co-authored, never profited from, but which had now tipped the scales in his favor.

Dorrit was not surprised at her father's show of resolve or at his defiance of the season. Of course, some might question his sanity. After all, he was giving up a distinguished and tenured position in Warsaw for a part time spot in Berlin; surely, a step down on the professional ladder. But Dorrit knew it was a dream come true for her father. He finally had his ticket to Berlin.

*　　*　　*

After picking up debris the wind had scattered about during the night, Schmidt swept the front walk and brought the baron's coach out to the curb where he harnessed it with horses from the public stables across the street in Grunewald Park, a forest which ran the length of Lindenstrasse and lent the neighborhood its name. Working swiftly under a gray overcast sky, Schmidt put hot bricks under the floor boards and had the travel conveyance ready to depart well ahead of schedule and hopefully before the storm broke loose. The clouds were thick as thieves and as menacing. Why anyone would want to set out for the country with a blinding blizzard just waiting to test one's holiday spirit was beyond him. But it was not his place to counsel Herr Baron.

As it were, the storm held off long enough for Johann to arrive in Bernau and for Schmidt to make the return trip to Berlin before it unleashed its fury, dumping a foot of snow overnight.

Come morning, the sky was making no frivolous promises. But it was the day before Christmas, Johann was expected at the Konauers', and he was not about to beg off because of weather. After fortifying himself with a hearty breakfast, such as Frau Erdmann took pride in serving, he grabbed his things and headed for the stables, deciding he would ride. His coach would have a difficult time on roads not yet cleared.

Otto, a head groom of long employ, removed his cap respectfully the minute his employer walked into the compound. When he realized the baron was dead-serious about having Asmodeus saddled, a stallion not known for caution, he replaced his tufted knitted cap and stoutly volunteered to ride along.

"Supposin' he was to hit some ice and come up lame," he said as he bent down to pick up a net of hay he'd been preparing. "You'd be out alone in this crotchety weather where a body could freeze in minutes and not be found till spring." Otto hung the hay over a stall where a horse was making loud noises, signaling hunger. And motioning to a stable boy, he hollered: "Hey, let's look alert in here! Let's get goin' with the feed bags. We've got forty hungry animals wantin' breakfast." Turning back to Johann, he said: "I best tag along with you."

Glancing at the aging groom, Johann concluded he would be of little help in an emergency.

"Thanks, but no, Otto," he said. "You stay put. I'll take an extra horse though. One to carry my gear."

Muttering under his breath about some folks' lack of proper regard for ice and snow, Otto knew better than to press his point with the baron. He called for a groom to saddle Asmodeus, while he went to the stalls himself to carefully choose the spare. The hazardous conditions required a slow, sure-footed animal to help restrain the stallion.

Minutes later, Johann put a booted foot in the stirrup, swung up in the saddle, and with the extra horse in tow, rode off, wryly noting the latter had legs like an elephant. What on earth had possessed Otto to trouble a poor plow horse in this weather?

Deferring from well-known shortcuts, Johann stayed on the mile-long private drive that led to the main road. The drive was obliterated by snowdrifts, but a row of poplars on each side, brandishing naked limbs like lashing tongues excoriating the lead-colored sky, served as markers.

Once out on the village road, Johann bore left, heading straight into a nor'easter with a bully attitude. It was a grueling four miles before he caught sight of the Konauers' approach, which was similar to his, a long avenue flagged by trees that offered guidance but no protection from the wind stabbing at his face, using darts of swirling ice and snow. A layer of feathery crystals covered his coat like goose down, and a white mantle lay across his shoulders like an extra cape; neither warmed him of course.

He pulled his hat down as far as it would go and dug in the spurs. The stallion responded and generally set a good example, but it required repeated black threats and violent tugs on the reins to convince the lagging beast of burden that it was in its best interests to try to keep up.

At long last, the Konauer residence came into view, looming like a huge apparition in the distance, gray and blurred by the hostile elements.

Moments later, squinting through frozen eyelids, Johann caught sight of welcoming lights burning in all the windows. Instantly the surrealistic scene took on an inviting aura.

SEVEN

The horses were taken to the stables, and Johann was ushered into the great hall, where a roaring fire was burning in the large stone hearth.

"Welcome, Herr Baron!" The butler relieved the guest of his coat and gear, stiff and crystallized with ice. "I trust the weather was not too punishing."

Flexing his fingers in front of the fire, Johann glanced at the frozen articles the butler passed to a valet, they spoke for themselves.

"I've been out in worse, Gunther," he sufficed as he pushed a hand through his dark hair.

Accepting a folded cloth from the man, he ran it across his wet collar before brushing the remaining ice particles from his well-fitting tan riding breeches. He rearranged his neck cloth, completely unaware of the devastating effect his masculine primping had on a couple of maids watching from across the foyer.

Hearing a commotion in the hall, Karl-Heinz thundered down the stairs. The two old friends embraced enthusiastically.

"Country life sits well on an old rogue. Even in winter." Johann laughed and slapped Karl-Heinz none too gently on the shoulder, noting his friend was in as fine a fettle as when he'd last seen him in July.

"I recommend it." Karl-Heinz landed a couple of reciprocal blows. "Why don't you give it a try instead of wasting away your best years in Berlin. What's it been now? Five? Six?" Karl-Heinz had felt personally defrauded the time he returned from Italy to learn of Johann's defection, and to this day never missed an opportunity to air his grievance. True to form, he managed a few snide remarks as he led the way to the library, where another roaring fire banished the last chills from Johann's limbs.

Karl-Heinz pushed a couple of winged chairs so close to the grate, they were in danger of being scorched. He motioned for

38

Johann to sit down and be roasted alive.

"By the way, Lillian is back," he said and plunked himself down ahead of his guest. "She'll grace our holidays with her presence."

"I see." Johann vaguely remembered that Karl-Heinz's cousin had been away at school. "How nice."

"'How nice...'? That's it? That's all you can say?" Karl-Heinz grimaced. "You could do worse, old boy. Lillian's a peach."

"Yes, I suppose so." Johann dawdled, wondering if he was missing the point of some brilliant observation. He sat down and reached for a bowl of nuts on the coffee table. Now that he was no longer cold, he realized he was hungry from his trek. "Do you have a nutcracker anywhere around here?"

"Huh? Oh, yeah." Karl-Heinz got up and went to fetch one from the Louis Quatorze desk in the corner of the mahogany-paneled room, where both the ceiling and floor borders were embellished with intricately carved moldings. "Catch!" He threw what looked like a pair of silver pliers at Johann. "Now, as I was saying—"

"I know what you were saying. You want me to seduce Lillian." Chuckling, Johann cracked a plump hazelnut and popped it into his mouth.

"Hell, no! That's not what I was saying." Karl-Heinz pretended to be offended. After all, Lillian was family and should be treated accordingly—with respect. "I merely meant to suggest that you might...well, you know, look her over. Being that she has just returned from that female academy in Switzerland, I figured that you two educated types might hit it off."

"Actually, I was tempted years ago when she was still a tomboy."

"You pervert!"

Johann laughed.

"Well, at least she displayed some spunk back then. Remember the summer she came visiting from Berlin just when we had stretched a poor rabbit's entrails across your courtyard?"

"We?" Karl-Heinz snorted and reached for the bowl Johann was balancing on his knees. He grabbed a fistful of walnuts and proceeded to crack them with his hands. "As I recall, you were the weird one, trying to measure the stinking mess." He separated out the nutmeats and tossed the shells into the fire.

"Who was doing what is not the point. Lillian didn't throw a fit or faint. That's the point. It impressed me."

"So you're telling me that you like girls with strong stomachs?"

"No. But I prefer a little more than a pretty face. The last time I saw Lillian, she'd become decorative without any . . . what can I say? esprit de corps. Believe me, Berlin has plenty of pretty ornaments. Like the glass globes we hang on the Christmas tree. Bright and shiny on the outside, but tap them, and you get a hollow echo. Forgive me for being so blunt."

"Never!" Karl-Heinz promised, chewed vigorously, sucked his teeth, and reached for some more nuts, wondering if he ought to feel insulted on Lillian's behalf. "Ornaments . . ." he mimicked. "Well, remain a bachelor then. Let that be your punishment. I still say Lillian might be your last chance at happiness. She likes Bernau. If you and she clicked, we could become one big happy family out here."

"Do you really think a nonpareil city girl like Lillian would be content in the country?"

"Unless she'd prefer a broken neck."

"Don't trouble yourself," Johann laughed. "Besides, Berlin . . . not Bernau, is in my blood. And you're on my back. Shall we drop the subject of my heart?"

"Only while I tell you some great news."

"Such as?" Johann put the bowl of nuts aside, brushed shell remnants from his lap, and became attentive.

Slouching back in his chair, Karl-Heinz stretched his legs out in front of him.

"Gerlinde is expecting," he said. "The baby is due in June."

"Good God!" Johann leaned forward and turned to stare at his friend. "That is good news? If I remember correctly, having Hans nearly killed her."

"Sure, but that was ages ago! Dr. Speckmaier says she's stronger now. And apparently it's easier the second time around."

Johann looked toward the ceiling as if begging God to forgive this mortal blunderer sitting next to him.

"Christ Almighty, Karl-Heinz! You know better than that, even if Dr. Speckmaier and a dozen midwives don't. Gerlinde is no stronger today than she was five years ago. Another baby might—"

"I know." Karl-Heinz held up his hands to stop the tirade; he had expected a pat on the back, not a lecture. "But what do you want from me? Gerlinde has had her heart set on another child for a long time. It's all she ever talks about. She goes all mushy whenever she sees someone else's baby. Hell, she'd like to have a baker's dozen! And I can tell you there's no one around here who's more excited about this than the little mother herself," he added in an attempt to exonerate himself.

"I don't doubt that," Johann said grimly. "And, of course, it's too late for a second opinion. Just promise me one thing."

"Sure. What?"

"Bring her to Berlin when her time draws near. Admit her to Wirchow."

"A hospital! What on earth for? She's not sick. She's just having a baby."

"Yes, but for whatever it's worth, I'll be on hand. I start my residency at Wirchow first thing in the New Year." Even as he said this, Johann knew that God alone would have to intervene on behalf of one of His most deserving creatures if He meant her to survive.

"Hm, they're sure cranking out doctors fast nowadays." Karl-Heinz was glad to change the subject.

"Not really. I've been doubling up on lab work. It has allowed me to move along a bit quicker than most."

"What happened to your internship?"

"Over and done with. By special imprimatur at Charite."

Impressed, Karl-Heinz whistled.

Just then Hans darted into the library. He treated Johann to a sticky hug and, keeping his arms around his neck, plied him with a string of questions about what he'd brought him for Christmas.

Tousling Hans's blond hair affectionately, Johann managed a fair amount of evasiveness in order to keep the boy in happy suspense.

Gerlinde followed in Hans's wake. Johann put the youngster down, rose to greet her, and was almost knocked off his feet as she drew closer and the light in the room fell across her bird-like form. Her pregnancy didn't show yet except in her face, which was like a death mask. Chalk-white cheek bones protruded unnaturally, while her blue eyes were sunk into deep purple circles. Her pale hair was pulled into a severe bun, which didn't improve the overall picture. As he embraced her, Johann managed not to communicate his shock.

"Johann! How wonderful to see you!" she cried. "I am sorry I wasn't on hand when you arrived. Ursula insists I take a nap before lunch. Most of the time I just lie in bed, watching the clock. Today I actually slept." She tilted her small plain face up to look at him. "How were the roads? You must have had quite a time getting here. I'm so glad you made it."

"Nothing could keep me from spending Christmas with my favorite girl," he grinned and released her. But he kept her cold hands in his for a moment longer while surreptitiously attempting to read her pulse. "Moreover, I've just heard such happy news," he said, somewhat mollified because Gerlinde's pulse seemed normal.

"You mean about the baby?"

"Yes. Congratulations!"

"Thank you. We're all so excited about it. But I'm afraid it's turned the house upside down. Karl and Ursula tiptoe around as if a loud noise will knock me over."

Johann laughed, then remembered that Karl-Heinz had not given his word to bring her to Berlin. He sobered and decided he'd have to insist when the time came.

Ursula and Karl joined the group in the library moments later; Ursula bubbling with excuses as to their tardiness.

"I simply had to finish rearranging the upstairs bedrooms to accommodate everybody tonight," she explained as she greeted Johann. "I couldn't relax and come down before the job was done. But enough of that now. We've kept you waiting long enough. Let's have lunch!" She waved her hand gracefully around the room to gather the flock before she took Johann's arm and led the way to the dining room. "You must be starved, my dear boy," she chatted gaily and looked up at him. "How were the roads?"

Lunch was an unequaled treat for the palate, insofar as the Konauer cook had formerly been in the kaiser's employ; something Ursula never tired of reminding one and all. And of course no one was ever sufficiently tactless to question why he no longer held the royal post.

Today the chef's delicately seasoned pheasant in a rich wine sauce did not agree with everybody however. Just as the meal concluded and everyone prepared to leave the table for the solarium, where coffee and dessert would be served, Gerlinde rushed from the room, hands clapped over her mouth. Ursula, quick on her feet for a woman of fifty-five, gave chase. She knew where several chamber pots were hidden from view and where the poor girl could retch.

With this abrupt departure of the women, Hans followed the men into the solarium, crawled up on Johann's lap, and was soon bending his ear with talk about plans to stage a raid on the kitchen to supplement the bread he'd squirreled away in his pockets during lunch.

"I'm gonna steal some raisins and bacon and stuff," he was saying. "Then I'm gonna hang everything in the pine tree outside the dining room window. You know, the one that's as tall as the house." He raised his hands above his head for emphasis. "It's got a lotta birds living in it. Do you wanna come and watch 'em eat?"

"Sure." Johann smiled, not surprised at Hans's concern for the sparrows that wintered in Bernau. The boy was soft-hearted like Gerlinde, and had been known to beg that a window be opened to free a fly beating its brains out against the glass.

"You, too, *opa?*" Hans looked toward his grandfather, who was bent over a humidor, sniffing the tobacco appreciatively while making a selection.

"Absolutely, my boy! I wouldn't want to miss it." Karl Konauer picked out a cigar, clipped and lit it, then went on to tell everyone how his grandson had come across a dead bird in the courtyard a few days ago. "Hans became convinced it'd perished from hunger," he chuckled. "Now he's committed himself to feeding its surviving relatives."

"Yeah," Hans chimed in. "But ol' Nanny Kruse thinks the bread and stuff will only attract ru...ah, ro.... What do you call 'em, Uncle Johann?"

"Rodents?"

"Yeah, that's them! Rodents and rats." Suddenly, Hans jumped down from Johann's lap and ran off, sliding like a skater across the hall toward the kitchen. Fraulein Kruse materialized from the dining room, where she'd been helping to clear the dishes. She was immediately in hot pursuit.

"Thievery will require a bit more stealth!" Johann laughed and held his cup out for a refill when the maid came around; he declined a second helping of a delicious fruit torte, however.

"What do you say we go exercise some fat, good-for-nothing horses?" Karl-Heinz yawned, put his coffee down, and got up. Stretching unselfconsciously, he walked over to look past the pots of red geraniums hanging by the large mullioned windows, where they bloomed in spite of the season. "The weather looks pretty good."

"Good?" Johann grimaced. "You obviously haven't been outside today." But that said, he finished his coffee and got up. He was game. He was in need of fresh air. Karl Konauer's cigar was making the air in the solarium unpleasant.

EIGHT

"Ladeburg?" Karl-Heinz asked when they were saddled.

"As good a destination as any, I suppose." Johann studied the sky; the clouds were the color of pewter and seemed as heavy. "As long as the weather holds."

Karl-Heinz glared at the gray mass pressing down on the landscape, daring it to spoil his plans.

"It won't snow for hours," he said stoutly.

"I wouldn't bet on it."

"I would!" Karl-Heinz happily placed wagers on the most trivial matter. "Snow by . . . say, four o'clock, and I'll pick up the bar tab. No snow, it's yours. Deal?"

"All right."

Once out on the main road, the horses found some fresh carriage tracks, set a steady pace, and aside from the large puffs of white mist their breaths sent billowing into the wintry air, neither animal gave proof of exertion in the bone-jarring cold.

"Has the old place changed much?" Johann asked after a while of riding along in silence; the air was too sharp for much conversation.

"Nope. Same crummy decor. Same brew. Same greasy grub."

"And the girls?"

"The girls?" Karl-Heinz shrugged negligently. "They come and go like the seasons. Restless fickle creatures. I guess it's the gypsy blood in their veins."

"Any particular one these days?"

"Hell, no!" Karl-Heinz turned in the saddle to look at Johann. "What do you take me for? With Gerlinde knocking herself out bringing heirs into the world, you've got some nerve accusing me of taking my marriage vows so lightly." He pulled up his collar and looked for all the world as if he had been vilely insulted.

"You're a good man," Johann chuckled, not at all sure his friend was being candid.

There was no lackey at the inn today; to stand about in this cold guaranteed frostbite and no tips, because with the holiest night of the year fast approaching, business invariably dropped off. The riders took their horses directly to the blacksmith, who counted on trade from the public coaches that stopped here on their regular runs between Warsaw and Berlin, whatever the season.

Once the horses were sheltered, the two friends crossed the yard and climbed the steps to the inn, making use of the sturdy doorposts to knock the ice and snow from their varnished boots before entering.

It was hot as August inside. The stone fireplaces at each end of the tap room were hissing with melted fat dropping from slabs of meat hung inches above the flames. A skinny kitchen boy ran back and forth cranking the spits to insure an even roasting. He licked his lips. He'd get plenty to eat tonight because, except for the help, the place was nearly empty. From behind the bar counter and the minute he spotted paying customers, the proprietor motioned a serving girl to look alert.

The newcomers made their way to a spot by a window, peeled off their gloves, removed their heavy coats and hats, threw them over a couple of chairs, and sat down opposite each other. Karl-Heinz swept some dead flies off the lopsided table with the back of his hand and broke a chunk of wax from a thick candle burning on a tin plate. He threw it across to Johann.

"Right the deck, will you," he said and pointed to a wobbly leg on the far side that didn't make contact with the worn floor planks.

Johann bent down to stuff the wax under the leg.

"This is precisely what I find so irresistible," he mumbled, tested the table, then wiped his hands on his chamois vest and unbuttoned it against the heat in the room.

"What?" Karl-Heinz said absently; his attention was on the girl approaching their table. "What did you say?"

"I said, I like the general state of disrepair around here. The coarse flavor is strangely appealing. The old century is alive and well between these peg walls. Somehow, that's very comforting."

"And don't worry. The place will collapse from wood worm or other natural causes long before it occurs to anyone to renovate." Karl-Heinz eyed the girl as she put down two mugs. "What have you got in there?" he asked, pointing to the pitcher she was resting on her generous hip.

"Mulled wine. House specialty. Want some?"

"Is it nice and hot?"

"Sure."

"Good." Karl-Heinz signaled for her to go ahead and pour. "We'll both have some," he said before Johann could get it into his head to order a more genteel drink.

As she filled the cups, her heavy black mane fell across her shoulders, obscuring half her face.

"Want something to eat?" she asked, gathering her hair and twisting it into a rope that immediately came undone the minute she let go.

Both men shook their heads.

Her warm eyes settled on Johann. She set the pitcher down and reached, unabashed, for his hand, turning it palm up.

"Maybe you want your fortune told?" she purred in a husky voice while tracing her thumb over the lines in his hand. She appeared to be concentrating on his long slender fingers. "You don't work the land," she said.

"That's right," Johann admitted.

"Um, I see beautiful woman . . . and—"

"And that's all very fine and dandy." It was Karl-Heinz who spoke up. He was a regular here, didn't take well to being overlooked, and couldn't resist pinching this wench's derriere for her neglect. "We just want the drinks. Okay? Anyway, my friend here is committed to a life of celibacy. No women. So, be off with you! But leave the pitcher."

"Maybe you change your mind later?" Ignoring Karl-Heinz, she smiled at Johann then walked away with an exaggerated wiggle on her hips.

"Maybe," he grinned, turning his attention to the brew in front of him.

After testing the temperature with his finger, Karl-Heinz lifted the mug to his lips. *"Prosit,"* he said, before quaffing his wine.

"Prosit!" Johann took a swig, wiped his mouth on his sleeve, and looked around. Few tables were occupied. Nonetheless, the old gypsy fiddler moved among them, playing his viola and stomping his feet with the same enthusiasm he'd bestow on a

full house. When he hit upon a familiar tune, some of the customers belted out the words at varying decibels and levels of musical achievement.

The two friends emptied their glasses and poured another round.

It was getting on toward four o'clock and already growing dark outside. The fiddler was taking a rest, as was the serving girl who'd found the lap and the palm of a customer; her loud giggles promising him the moon.

Johann cleared a circle on the misty and dirty window with the cuff of his sleeve. Peering out into the semidarkness, he spotted carriage lights. A coach was approaching on the road from the east. A mail coach he judged from its size. It was probably carrying passengers as well. With no end in sight to the crippling rail strike, people were hopping aboard any vehicle that moved.

"Hmm, it seems that I've lost the bet," he said after confirming that no snow was blowing across the beams of the flickering carriage lights. "The weather appears to be holding. What do you say we get going?"

"As soon as you pay up, old man." Karl-Heinz sloshed the last of his wine around in the glass to incorporate any spicy sediment before swigging it down and reaching for his coat.

Johann dropped a larger than normal sum on the table before walking up to the bar to stuff several folded bills into the fiddler's jar, and one into the kitchen boy's apron as well. The lad beamed. After wishing the proprietor a Merry Christmas, the two friends left.

The coach Johann had seen through the window had come to a stop in front of the inn. Setting the brakes securely, the driver spit a stream of tobacco juice into a snowbank, where it quickly melted into a small discolored crevasse. Now jumping down with a thud, he opened the carriage door and spoke to those inside the compartment.

"This'll be our last stop before Berlin," he announced. "The horses will need a good rest before we can continue." He reached under one of the seats, pulled out a mail sack and threw it onto the landing where Johann and Karl-Heinz had stopped to button their coats.

"How long will we be here?" a passenger inquired. He spoke German with a Russian accent and experienced some difficulty

48

climbing out of the coach. No sooner did he have both feet on the ground when he bent over, consumed by a terrible cough.

"An hour...give or take," the driver said as he turned and busied himself with his team of bays. "It'll be nice and warm inside. This place is famous for a hot spicy brew. It might soothe your chest."

"I suppose I could do with a hot drink." The traveler had recovered enough to speak as well as to help another passenger from the coach. They appeared to be the only two people on board, and as the latter stepped out, her feet disappeared in the slush of the road which immediately swallowed the hem of her coat as well. She could do nothing to save her shoes, but she quickly hitched up her skirts, and in so doing, displayed a pair of shapely ankles as she took the man's arm and walked toward shelter.

Johann started down the steps ahead of Karl-Heinz, then suddenly stopped, his hand stilled on the last button of his coat as his eyes skidded over the travelers. One was a mere slip of a girl, but so exceptional that he couldn't draw his gaze away. Everything about her held his attention.

When the man halted in midstep, succumbing to yet another hacking fit, Johann saw the girl's delicate brow crease in a deep and worried frown; something that did nothing to diminish the enchanting picture she presented.

"Papa," he heard her say as she let go of her hems to help pull a scarf up around the lower part of the man's face, "it's been a long day. There's really no reason for us to push on. Why don't we stay here tonight and continue on another coach tomorrow?" Her speech, unlike her father's, carried no noticeable accent; every nuance and intonation was unusually cultured for one so young. She appeared to be no older than sixteen or seventeen.

Johann stood rooted to the spot, growing more fascinated by the minute.

"Berlin can wait a day," she went on. "Remember, papa, you're not supposed to exhaust yourself." She wagged a finger playfully at him, then turned to inspect the inn and showed no sign of disappointment at its shabby exterior. Friendly lights were burning in all the windows, she noted, happily, and smoke was curling out of two chimneys. There'd be a choice of fireplaces by which to thaw her feet, stiff and numb inside her

49

shoes from their long imprisonment and, now, wet as well. "This looks like a wonderful and comfortable place." She started to walk again, drawn by the wish of a warm fire. "A far better spot to spend the night than a drafty coach. We need only ask the driver to bring in our bags. And . . . oh, listen, papa! Do you hear the viola?"

The man made a comment, but it was lost behind the woolen folds covering his mouth and nose. His cloak appeared travel-worn. These people had come some distance, Johann surmised as he continued to study the girl in particular. She was wearing a brown coat of coarse cloth and common cut. But for all its un-flattering lines and best of intentions, it did not conceal her lovely slender figure. And as she walked with her father, both of them carefully avoiding the deepest ruts in the road—he with a downcast face and a clumsy limp—she alone moved with the natural grace of the aristocracy, although she carried none of the trimmings.

They were mounting the steps, when the girl raised her head to the cheerful light pouring from the windows.

At that moment, Johann saw her face clearly. It was a masterpiece of astounding perfection. Large, wide-set eyes, a straight nose, an elegant chin, and full, softly curved lips were balanced in a flawless translucent oval. No artist could have created a more perfect harmony of features. Johann felt a strange light-headedness and cursed the proprietor's hot brew, because women, let alone a young girl, had never before wrought such an effect on him.

A gust of wind swept off the roof and pushed at the girl's hood, freeing some glossy curls, the color of paprika. She let go of her father's arm and reached up to gather her headgear together without missing a step. Behind him, Johann heard Karl-Heinz whistle under his breath. His friend, a practiced roué, was not blind of course.

Upon reaching the landing, the girl looked squarely at the two individuals blocking the way, obviously wondering if they were planning to step aside. Karl-Heinz, the consummate gentleman despite his many rough edges, retreated immediately. Johann was slow to do so. The bright green of her extraordinary eyes, the charming sight of her windblown red hair, caused him to forget manners fastidiously handed down over six generations. He compensated for any lapse with a broad smile.

"Forgive me," he said, finally stepping back, addressing both travelers while keeping his eyes on the girl, "but I couldn't help overhearing your concerns about traveling to Berlin tonight."

"Oh." The girl looked eagerly at the tall, dark-haired stranger; perhaps he'd help persuade her father to postpone the last leg of a long journey. Herman Zache was a stubborn man and adhered to his schedule whatever the costs. "Are the roads bad west of here?"

"Yes. They're practically impassable. My friend and I traveled the main link about an hour ago. Not a stretch was cleared. An unwieldy coach, such as the one you're traveling in, might find it rough going."

This pleased her enormously.

"Did you hear that, papa?" she said, turning to her father and squeezing his arm in her excitement. "We could become stranded along the road. Let's stay put. It's already dark. Why take chances."

"If our driver is willing to go on," the traveler rasped behind his scarf, "I see no reason why we should stay behind. It's only another couple of hours to Berlin."

"Under normal circumstances," Johann pointed out. "But after last night's storm, all bets are off. West of here took the brunt of it. And it looks like we are in for more of the same tonight."

As he spoke, he wondered why he was anxious for these people to remain in Ladeburg. For all the girl's allure, he couldn't be here with her. So why on earth was he making a case for this dilapidated inn? He and Karl-Heinz had quite a distance to go themselves. And standing about inhaling this bitterly cold air was sure to invite a host of assorted ailments; something the traveler substantiated with another coughing spell.

Once he could speak, and as if he, too, was loath to court pneumonia, the man mumbled from behind the wool across his face.

"We'd better get inside," he said and took a firm hold on his daughter's arm. "I guess we'll heed your warning and spend the night here." He bid Johann good-bye, thanked him for his concern, and nodded to the shadow of Karl-Heinz as he passed him on the landing.

51

A smile, more radiant than a July morning, broke out on the girl's face.

"You've been very kind to trouble yourself," she said, and just before she was ushered inside, she looked back at Johann with the sweetest expression this side of heaven.

His gaze followed her until the door closed on her wet hems. And had she turned around, she would have seen streaks of silver flashing in his gray eyes. Unmindful of the frigid air, he took a deep breath to steady a strange pounding in his chest.

He felt as if he had just seen his future. And it was a spectacular sight.

NINE

By five o'clock, when the riders returned from Ladeburg, the Konauer household was under siege by arriving relatives and friends, all bemoaning difficult journeys on snow-covered roads, as if the discomfort suffered en route was fair exchange for the lavish hospitality they were about to enjoy. While Ursula and Karl greeted guests in the hall with pomp and ceremony, Karl-Heinz and Johann avoided the crush altogether by using a back entrance.

"I don't wish to run into our insufferable free-loaders any sooner than necessary," Karl-Heinz groused as he and Johann climbed the servants' stairs to their respective rooms. He stopped on the landing to the guest wing. "See you back downstairs around seven. And do try to be charming tonight. I fixed it so Lillian will be your dinner partner."

"Terrific!" Johann grinned apocryphally and slipped into his room.

Sitting on the edge of the four-poster bed, he was pulling off his boots, when a maid, carrying prewarmed towels, knocked to ask if he wanted a bath run. Johann nodded and let her in. While she busied herself with the valves on pipes feeding a free-standing tub behind a tapestry screen, he stepped into an adjoining dressing room to peel off his riding clothes. He emerged wrapped in a terry-cloth robe. The girl indicated his bath was ready and that he need only ring if he required more hot water. She pulled the drapes across the windows, took his coat and hat from the bed and put them into a tall armoire, and polished the two oval mirrors on its doors with a few efficient strokes of a cloth she produced from her pockets. Then she curtsied and left.

Johann sank into the warm water; it relaxed his body, but his mind remained in turmoil, wondering about the girl he had seen at the Ladeburg Inn. And before he got to work with sponge and soap, he realized that any interest in Lillian tonight would stand a better chance if only he could shake the vision of those

53

beguiling green eyes in that exquisite face.

Who was she? Where was she from? He knew she was going to Berlin, but precisely where? and for how long? And, *dammit,* why hadn't he gotten her name? He had wasted precious moments talking about the weather when he should have asked questions instead. Of course, any personal overture was taboo during short and incidental meetings between total strangers. Still, he'd never been a stickler about protocol and should at least have managed an introduction.

Irritated with this lapse, Johann scrubbed himself till his skin smarted. Soon he stepped out of the tub and reached for a towel, shivering for an instant before he began to rub himself dry. He dressed quickly in the formal attire the evening required and was running a comb through his hair with distracted detachment, when a valet entered carrying his black evening jacket, freshly pressed.

"Good evening, Herr Baron," the man said as he crossed the floor, brushing nonexistent specks of lint from the smooth material before he hung it on an ornate brass wall hook and turned to help the guest fasten a striped, silk neck cloth with a diamond and ruby pin. Next the valet helped thread matching cufflinks through the crisp white fabric of Johann's shirt sleeves, edged with a hint of a ruffle. That the Baron von Renz depended on the best tailors in Berlin was obvious to the trained eye of the attendant when he stepped back to assess the completed *tailleur.*

A giant grandfather's clock in the hall below struck the hour of seven as Johann walked down the stairs. Most of the guests were already in the drawing room, grouped into conversation clusters around an enormous Christmas tree. Johann remained in the doorway a moment, content to let his eyes roam the festive gathering before deciding which group to approach first. His eyes fell on the slim form of Gerlinde. He smiled inwardly. She was wearing a showy cherry-red gown—totally out of character—and deliberately worn, he suspected, to defy her weak constitution.

Hans, dressed in a blue velvet sailor's suit, was standing at her side, clutching her full skirts in awe at being the youngest among so many. His blond hair was slicked back with water, the track of the comb was still visible, and while several older children hovered around the Christmas tree, touching the decora-

54

tions within reach and pointing to the more delicate ones that weren't, Hans was examining a tray of canapés a maid was passing around. Wrinkling his nose at the sharp smell of Camembert and smoked salmon with dollops of caviar, he was wondering what adults found so appetizing in those revolting little morsels, when he looked away, found a crack in the wall of people and spotted Johann in the doorway. A smile broke out on his face as he barreled through the maze of gowns and tuxedos.

"The birds ate all the stuff I hung out!" he said breathlessly and grabbed at the knife pleats in Johann's impeccable trouser legs. "There must have been thousands. You should have seen 'em."

"Yes, and I'm sorry I didn't. But it was late by the time your father and I got home. How about tomorrow? I'm sure the birds will be hungry again and be back."

Hans cocked his head and jutted out his lower lip.

"Promise you'll come? Promise?" he wheedled.

"You have my word." Johann picked up the boy and gave him a flying tumble in the air. Hans squealed with delight and, all charged up, now ran off toward his contemporaries still eyeing the tree. He knew which paper baskets held chocolates, something the group would probably appreciate knowing.

Johann followed Hans into the drawing room and began the required rounds, involving himself in pleasant conversation as he worked his way around the room to where Lillian stood in a swirl of turquoise satin among a host of admirers.

Considering the lateness of the hour when the festivities finally ground to a halt, Johann woke extremely early the next morning.

He raised himself clumsily onto one elbow, reached for his watch on the bedside table, then groaned. Seven-thirty! It would be hours before anyone stirred. Only servants and thieves were about at this hour of a holiday morning.

He tried to go back to sleep but found that it was impossible.

Eventually, he threw off the covers, got up, and staggered over to the windows. He pulled back the drapes. Instantly the room was flooded in bright light, forcing him to retreat and clap a hand over his bloodshot eyes. Seconds later, now squinting carefully, he again braved the glorious dawn.

The heavy sky of yesterday had been replaced by a brilliant blue dome blemished only by the fading moon, a small wispy sphere that would soon go down before the rising sun tinting the white landscape in hues of pink, across which tall, naked trees cast long amethyst shadows. It was a sight that beckoned this recalcitrant soul. He made a rash decision, found his riding clothes, and made quick work of getting dressed. His boots had spent the night by the fire and were toasty warm. Grabbing his heavy coat and hat, he left the sleeping house, tugging his hat down hard against the cold morning.

The glistening snow squeaked pleasantly under his feet as he crossed the courtyard with a briskness of purpose; the thought of his destination infused him with energy. He took a deep breath of the crisp air, spiced with the pungent smell of burnt wood rising from the chimneys. The servants, bless them, did an excellent job keeping the fireplaces alive throughout the night.

Johann walked into the stables, surprising the lone groom on duty. His horse was saddled. Minutes later, he was on the road toward Ladeburg, formulating a plan as he went.

He assumed the dazzling redhead was in the tavern having breakfast. Yesterday, her father had been in a great hurry to get to Berlin. They were obviously heading for a family holiday and so would want an early start today. Johann would simply walk over to their table—casual like—and inquire about the comfort of their stay. Introductions would be accomplished, and after sharing a few words about the vastly improved weather conditions, he would probably be invited to sit down.

If, on the other hand, father and daughter were still in their rooms, something the innkeeper could be trusted to divulge, Johann would make himself comfortable, order breakfast, wait until they appeared, and then commence with the business of getting acquainted.

Digging in the spurs, he forced his horse into a trot. But even though the animal was fresh and eager, he was circumspect and balked in spots where the ground was unsure. An instinctive and admirable prudence, but one that today grated miserably on the rider's impatient nature.

Nearing the inn, Johann saw a mail coach pull away. The

driver laid the crop across the horses' backs, they responded with appropriate alacrity, and by the time they approached Johann, they were going at a remarkable clip, considering the slippery terrain.

Just before he was forced off the road and almost off his horse when—startled by the flying coach—it reared up, Johann caught a fleeting glimpse of the two passengers through the small carriage window.

Uttering a string of obscenities in tribute to his poor timing, he was sorely tempted to charge after the speeding conveyance.

However, as quickly as that foolish notion entered his head, he rejected it. He'd look like an idiot. Worse, he'd run the risk of being mistaken for a robber and shot. Mail was more sacred than human life.

TEN

Dorrit Zache flew down three flight of stairs as if her life depended on how fast she could propel herself. It didn't of course. She was not chased by a villain and she was young and healthy. Her father, however, was not and it was the sound of his labored breathing, reverberating in her ears as she ran that lent her wings.

She reached the bottom steps, flung open the door to the street, and dashed out in such a hurry that she forgot to shut it behind her. She was two blocks away before she realized her neglect. The spinster, Fraulein Strutzenberger, who lived on the ground floor would complain bitterly to the landlord about lost heat, but Dorrit couldn't go back now. She had no time to waste and would face the music later.

A newcomer to Berlin, Dorrit knew few of her neighbors except for Fraulein Strutzenberger who had taken an immediate dislike to the tenants from Warsaw but still considered it her civic duty to be acquainted with everyone in the building in order to report on crimes and misdemeanors. Dorrit managed to avoid her as much as possible and took comfort in the fact that at least she was on good terms with the neighborhood grocer, Herr Ziegler, a kind man who never sold her yesterday's milk and always inquired about her father. Best of all, he had a telephone that he let his regular customers use.

Racing down the street, oblivious to a cold March wind, Dorrit's red hair flew about her face like a beautiful fire storm, while her green eyes were black and dilated with fear for her father. And though her cheeks were flushed crimson with the exertion of her desperate sprint, her lips were white as parchment as she burst into Herr Ziegler's small shop.

"Why, *guten tag*, Dorrit!" The portly man behind the counter, cluttered with candy jars and packaged edibles, looked surprised, because this was her second trip to his store today. His young and very pretty customer was usually organized far be-

58

yond her years and always shopped with a carefully compiled list. "Did you forget something this morning?" he asked. "Perhaps the Ceylon tea that your papa is so fond of?"

"No, Herr Ziegler. No, thank you. I need . . . that is to say, I'd like to borrow your telephone." She stopped to catch her breath and quiet her heart. "My father is ill. He's coughing something awful suddenly. I have to call a doctor." She pushed the hair off her face and only now realized that she was wearing a tacky housedress and worn slippers. In her rush, she had completely forgotten to throw on a coat which would have helped her overall appearance considerably. But if Herr Ziegler wondered at her slipshod state of dress, he made no mention of it.

"Professor Zache has had spells before," he said. "What makes you think he needs a doctor today? Some lozenges might do the trick, my dear. Here, look. . . . " He pointed to a bin under the counter, "I have some nice honey and licorice-flavored drops."

Dorrit shook her head. She knew from past experience that her father needed something stronger, something only a doctor could dispense.

"He needs r . . . real medicine," she stammered.

"Surely he can't be that ill." Herr Ziegler arched his white bushy eyebrows and looked over the wire rim of his spectacles at Dorrit. "Why, I saw him only yesterday. He looked quite fit when he walked past my store on his way home from the university. He seemed in wonderful form and was enjoying the jaunt, I dare say."

"Yes, he likes walking. But he wasn't supposed to walk yesterday." Dorrit cried. "The weather was much too raw." She ran the back of her hand across her eyes, fighting back tears of frustration. Her father had decided to walk rather than hail a cab, insisting he needed the exercise. "He got himself chilled to the bone. He didn't sleep well last night, and now he's having trouble breathing. I must call a doctor. Please, . . . may I use your telephone?"

"Yes, of course. But calm yourself, girl." The grocer opened a flap in the counter top and let her through. "There now, . . . take it easy." He patted her on the shoulder as he pointed to the apparatus hanging on the wall next to a picture of Kaiser Wilhelm that appeared to have been removed from a book and framed. "Go ahead. Help yourself."

"Thank you." Dorrit tore the receiver off the hook and absently studied the kaiser's blond hair, large mustache and fine regalia while she waited for an operator to come on the line. Wilhelm II is a splendid looking emperor, she decided, the same time she prayed for a quick telephone connection.

"Yes, hello! Please, can you connect me with a doctor?" she all but shouted when she finally heard the nasal hello of the operator.

"*Jawohl.* Who?"

"Who . . . ?"

"Yes, Fraulein. I need a name or a number."

"I don't have one. But anyone will do. Please, anyone!"

"Sorry, I cannot connect you with . . . ah, *anyone.*"

"Oh, I see. Just a moment." Dorrit held her hand over the mouthpiece and looked toward the grocer who was scooping ground coffee into a bag for a woman who'd come into the store. Sniffing the wonderful aroma, the woman indicated she wanted a full pound. This just when Dorrit was in a terrible hurry. "The operator needs a number or a name," she whispered, although she knew it was very impolite to interrupt Herr Ziegler when he was with a customer.

"Well, of course. Don't you have one?" he said over his shoulder as he weighed the coffee and sealed the bag.

"No."

"All right then, hang up and let me think a minute."

Dorrit thanked the operator for her trouble and replaced the receiver.

Herr Ziegler put the coffee and the woman's other purchases into a net she held open. After he had counted out her change and seen her to the door, he turned and gave his full attention to Dorrit.

"I gather it's Hannah's day off, or you wouldn't be in such a pickle?" he said, crossing the floor and again taking his position behind the counter.

"Yes. She doesn't come on Wednesdays or Saturdays."

"Well, then, the best thing to do . . . as I see it . . . is for you to run over to Wirchow."

"The hospital?"

"Sure. Why not? It's only a few blocks from here. It will be quicker to fetch a doctor there rather than call one and then wait around until he shows up."

That made sense to Dorrit.

"Do you know where Wirchow is?"

"I . . . I think so." She sounded unsure.

"Look . . ." Herr Ziegler motioned her through the opening in the counter and walked with her to the storefront window where he pointed. "Follow Niederlag Gasse in that direction," he said. "Make a left at the second intersection, and then go three blocks. Wirchow will be on the south side. You can't miss it. The building is huge. It's red brick. It's got hospital written all over it."

"I think I've seen it." Dorrit nodded.

"Good. But don't go to the main entrance. Go to the emergency ward around the corner. It's clearly marked, and there's always a doctor on duty. Detail your father's symptoms. Someone on the staff is sure to go back to the apartment with you. And if they don't believe the case is serious enough, at least they'll send a nurse."

"Uh . . ." Dorrit lowered her eyes, suddenly embarrassed.

"What? What is it?"

"Do . . . do the doctors at Wirchow ch . . . charge an awful lot?" Dorrit knew it to be a big and important hospital. Fraulein Strutzenberger had mentioned it once.

"No. Not if you go to the emergency ward, where most of them are residents and still learning the ropes, so to speak. Any charge will be minimal."

Dorrit opened the door in a flash.

"Thank you, Herr Ziegler. Thank you so much!"

"*Gott im Himmel,* girl! Wait a minute. It's cold outside. You'll need a coat." The grocer clucked his tongue as his gaze swept her inadequate housedress, which made her look awfully thin and vulnerable. He looked down at her bare feet in the slippers. "And you must wear some proper shoes. Why, you—you look like a waif."

"There's no time to go back home," Dorrit cried, anxious to be on her way.

"Well then, at least take this." Herr Ziegler handed her a large woolen scarf a customer had left behind months ago. It had hung on a hook near the door since November and was so ugly that no one admitted to owning it.

Dorrit accepted the shawl and wrapped it tightly around her head and shoulders.

"I'll return it tomorrow," she promised.

"Keep it. You'll be doing me a favor." Herr Ziegler turned to search for something else she could have. "Hm,...now let me see..."

When he suddenly heard the door slam, he realized that he was talking to himself.

"Hey, wake up!" Dr. Kurt Eckhart came into the emergency ward and found his colleague slumped in a chair at the reception station. He scanned the scheduling sheet and noted that Johann had been on duty for eighteen hours. "For crying out loud,..." Kurt poked his friend's elbow, "wake up and go home! You're doing overtime on your overtime."

Johann straightened in the chair with a glazed look in his eyes. He rotated his shoulders, checking for signs of life.

"Did you hear me?" Kurt prodded.

"Loud and clear."

"What did I say?"

"You told me to get lost."

"That's right. You're in no condition to treat a nosebleed if one came in now. I'm on my lunch break. I only came down to see if you were hungry."

"Hungry...?"

"Forget it! I'll eat alone. Under the circumstances you wouldn't be much company. Go home. I'll cover for you till your replacement arrives."

"Thanks." Johann glanced around the empty room. He had treated two gunshot wounds and a stabbing during the night, plus a woman suffering false labor pains and three drunks who'd gotten into a fight. One had fallen on his bottle and been impaled when it broke. Early this morning, there'd been a couple of youngsters with earaches and high fevers and an elderly lady with a sprained ankle. But the cases had eventually tapered off. At the moment, the emergency room was empty, even of staff. The nurses had apparently slipped down the hall for coffee. He seemed to remember one of them asking him if he wanted some.

"Speaking of the devil, here he is." Kurt Eckart nodded toward another resident doctor coming down the hall. "Well, what do you know?" he said a moment later. "It's Philip. He must have been kicked out of the labs and ordered to come here and do some real work."

Kurt, Johann, and Philip had gone through medical school together and had remained fast friends, although their interests were now taking different turns. While Johann preferred the challenge of the emergency ward, Philip von Brandt liked the slow and methodical work associated with research. He hailed from an aristocratic military family; his mother was a Hindenburg, and his father, General Ludwig von Brandt, had attained great fame in the Franco-Prussian War of 1870. When Philip declined to follow his two brothers in their distinguished military careers, he somehow landed in medical school, where he soon discovered that he was repulsed by blood and gore and eventually drifted toward research. Chemical compounds, lab animals, tests and experiments with either, fascinated him.

Kurt Eckart came from a long line of physicians. His father had recently retired as chief of surgery at Wirchow, and Kurt was expected to follow in his footsteps. However, he was given some flexibility last year when his sister married a physician, more ambitious than he; for if the truth be known, Kurt's heart was not in medicine. It was in politics. But being a pragmatic man, he applied himself to the healing profession until such a time when he would come into his inheritance, old money on his mother's side, which would make him independently wealthy and enable him to set his sight on a career in public service. To keep abreast, he regularly attended debates at the Reichstag.

Johann struggled from the chair, stretched, and shrugged out of his white hospital coat. Concluding it was too bloodied to wear again, he tossed it into the laundry bin before he reached for his overcoat in a metal locker.

"Where are the nurses?" Philip had walked in and was looking around, uncomfortable with the thought that he might be stuck here alone; it'd be just his luck to have a patient with a severed leg dragged in.

"Relax," Johann grinned, reading his mind. "They'll be back. If not, kick the panic button. Anyway, Kurt here will keep you company for a while. Right?"

"Wrong. I'm out of here." Kurt checked his watch. "As it is, there's only twenty minutes left on my break. Pray for fast service in the lunchroom." He turned and quickly headed up the hall toward the elevator, before Philip could beg for mercy..

Johann bent over the roster taped to the reception station and signed himself out, then handed the pen to Philip so he could sign in.

"Where did you say the nurses' call button is?" Philip ran his hands over the desk like a blind man.

"Right there on the wall behind the chair." Johann grinned at his friend's lack of fortitude. "Good luck. I'll see you tomorrow." He stuffed his arms into the sleeves of his coat and, with a quick wave over his shoulder, walked through the swinging doors and into the crowded sidewalk. It was midday; workers from factories in the area were out and about on their lunch hour.

Fumbling in his pockets for his gloves, Johann bowed his head against the chilly March wind. He prayed Schmidt had brought the coach around, something he generally did by early afternoon whenever Johann pulled the graveyard shift. Schmidt figured, and rightly so, that after an all-nighter, his employer was not in the mood to look for public transportation.

Johann was rounding the corner and happily spotted his sleek black carriage parked a few yards away when someone brushed past him at bullet speed, knocking him off balance. Cursing he turned to glare at the back of the rude fellow who hadn't stopped or uttered a word of apology.

Huh . . . ? A girl? Yes, and obviously a street urchin. She was wearing no overcoat and had a hideous rag tied around her head and neck. He saw her dash into the emergency ward. But judging from her speed and agility, she certainly didn't appear to be in need of medical attention. He shrugged. She was probably just lost.

Johann climbed into his comfortable coach, sank into the soft leather squabs, and, dead tired, closed his eyes.

Schmidt pulled away from the curb.

ELEVEN

Minutes before the gold-tasseled lamé curtain rose on the last opera of the season, Johann entered his private balcony box with one of Berlin's well-bred beauties, Louisa von Tirpitz, raven-haired daughter of Admiral von Tirpitz, on his arm. The box had the enviable distinction of being adjacent to the Royal Parterre, regularly occupied by Germany's monarch and his empress. Tonight proved to be no exception. Before the lights dimmed in preparation of the overture, Wilhelm and Augusta Victoria swept in. An immediate rustling of satin gowns ensued as everyone on the floor below turned to watch the kaiser and kaiserin exchange greetings with the titled occupants in adjoining enclosures. And after acknowledging the Baron von Renz with a cordial nod, Kaiser Wilhelm paid special attention to Fraulein von Tirpitz. Her father was his aide and personal confidant.

"My dear Louisa, . . ." Using her Christian name fondly, he reached past the partition for her hand, "the hall is enhanced by your lovely presence this evening." He put her hand to his lips with great ceremony.

"Your Majesty, . . ." Louisa executed a flawless curtsy all the while fluttering her fan to demand the attention of everyone in the opera house, "you are much too kind," she protested demurely, although the kaiser spoke the truth. After all, she was wearing a particularly fetching rose gown that complimented her creamy skin and black hair. Both her mother's diamonds as well as her own were fastened around her slender throat and, together, fell like a glittering waterfall to the very edge of the swell of her revealing décolleté.

During the intermission, while strolling the grand mezzanine on the arm of her suave escort and sipping champagne and exchanging pleasantries with friends, Louisa again attracted attention from the incurably curious. She relished it and suspected one and all were trying to recall if she'd been seen with the Baron von Renz often enough for them to assume that an announcement was forthcoming. Naturally she did her best to give that impression. She clung possessively to his arm, dimpled prettily at his every word, and appeared for all the world as if there was a secret "understanding" between them. She aspired to becoming the Baroness von Renz and had, in fact, carefully prepared herself for his proposal this past New Year's Eve at the Count and Countess von Beckstein's dazzling ball. However, after employing the full force of her feminine charms, much to her chagrin, the evening passed without a declaration from him.

Days later, after having swallowed her frustration with commendable grace, she gave her disappointment some serious thought and realized that after returning from his Christmas holiday in Bernau, there had been something vaguely different about Johann. She couldn't put her finger on it, but he'd seemed distracted, particularly during the Beckstein ball, where, and although he was her escort, he had danced with far too many other women. Furthermore, he'd gone to the smoking lounge to play cards with a group of men shortly before midnight, leaving her to dance with a number of unattractive partners and watch the fireworks without him. She was furious but was careful not to show it, suppressing her anger beneath smiles that were all the more charming because an inner umbrage ignited her eyes.

And as if that snub wasn't bad enough, after midnight, when the last dance was announced, she was obliged to suffer it with *Graf* Zollern when Johann invited Lillian Schindel to the floor. They appeared rather cozy throughout the waltz, causing Louisa to wonder if anything had passed between them during their Christmas holiday with the Konauers in Bernau, where she knew they had spent at least two nights under the same roof. Of course, she didn't really believe that a silly goose like Lillian could hold Johann's interest for very long. It was hard work keeping him charmed. Louisa had invested an entire year in the arduous endeavor. Therefore, it naturally never occurred to her that a nameless girl of no account might have managed it in a matter of minutes and with no effort at all.

Three months had passed since that brief meeting on the steps of the Ladeburg Inn, yet a strange girl's enchanting face and smile teased Johann to this day, and his bedevilment often interfered with a good night's sleep. There was no scarcity of beautiful girls in Berlin, but he only wanted the one he couldn't find. It was nothing short of ludicrous, and the possibility that she and her father had come to the city for a visit and had long since returned to God knows where did nothing to dampen his desire or ameliorate his strange bondage to a memory.

A practical man, Johann often told himself, would put the trifling encounter to rest. And yet, he—practical to the bone—mentally competent and emotionally stable, thank you, had not been able to do so. Moreover, he had gone so far as to send a private investigator to Ladeburg to interview the proprietor and have a look at the guest registry. Unfortunately, like everything else about the inn, the ledger was sloppy. The proprietor had not seen fit to record one night drop-ins. He recalled the lovely fraulein and her less than robust father, but as much as he was threatened and bribed, he could not—to save his life or reap a fortune—remember the name the traveler had given. Nor could he recall any other pertinent information that might be traced.

*   *   *

Karl-Heinz shifted restlessly in his seat as the carriage rattled through Schwanebeck on its way to Berlin. He glanced out of the windows at the beloved landscape, which was rapidly changing—green fields giving way to clusters of ugly houses sidling up to breweries and other tall buildings associated with various industries thriving on the outskirts of any large city. With each passing mile and smokestack, he prayed that Gerlinde would experience a change of heart so he could order his driver to turn around. Surely it was not too late to scrap this harebrained junket and go back home.

"For pity's sake . . . ," he muttered for the hundredth time and shook his head, "how can you prefer a cold, austere hospital and a bunch of strangers to the comfort of your own home and family? It's nothing short of bizarre."

Gerlinde sighed and looked at her husband with a small, controlled smile. He enjoyed nothing better than bellyaching, and she was not about to deny him some pleasure on a trip he'd been staunchly opposed to.

"Johann is no stranger," she reminded him softly. "And he has promised to be on hand."

"Yes, and isn't that just peachy? I suppose it doesn't bother you one iota to have him . . . uh, well, you know . . ." Karl-Heinz suddenly looked ill at ease. "Anyway, . . . I think you know what I'm trying to say," he finished lamely.

Gerlinde reddened. She knew. And, sure, it bothered her. She was inherently shy. But she was more afraid of her coming ordeal than modest. She needed a medical miracle this time around and only hoped Wirchow was up to the task. And if it meant that Johann would see her in a state of total undress, well, so be it. She'd stand naked on a street corner to bring her babies into the world. Of course, this she didn't admit to Karl-Heinz. He'd be shocked.

As it were, he was still venting his spleen as they skirted the picturesque Wannsee Lake and soon entered the forested suburb of Grunewald. Once the carriage turned into Lindenstrasse, he felt hopelessly trapped. What on earth had possessed his sweet and pliable wife to become stubborn and side with Johann and his outlandish schemes?

"I suppose you think it's odd that our kaiserin gives birth at home?" Karl-Heinz asked in a last ditch effort to make Gerlinde see reason. Having come this far, he was willing to spend a pleasant evening with Johann and then go back home tomorrow.

Gerlinde mumbled something he couldn't hear while she studied a small imperfection in one of her lace gloves.

"Did you ever stop to wonder why," he pressed her, "why all the kaiser's children are born at home?" She shook her head. "Well, let me tell you. It's the correct thing to do. Simple as that. It's proper and it's traditional. Hospitals are for the sick." Karl-Heinz shuddered visibly. "God only knows what diseases one might contract there."

"But with twins to consider, Johann says—"

"Yeah." Karl-Heinz rolled his eyes. "He says something, and we all jump. Huh? Is that it? Well, I say, not that anyone listens of course, but I say that he has no business meddling in the private affairs of others. Living in Berlin has done strange things to him. City noises have rattled his brain. Now he's on some cockeyed mission to upset the established order of things. What's good enough for the royal house is suddenly not good enough for the Konauers. Furthermore, he's forcing me to abandon my lands during the prime growing season."

"You don't need to remain in Berlin."

"Oh, I don't? And how would it look if I didn't?"

"Anyone rude enough to wonder could simply be told that you have to stay with Hans."

"That'd be insulting to my parents as well as to the employment of Fraulein Kruse."

"Um, I suppose so," Gerlinde acquiesced softly. "But you don't need to stay in Berlin the entire time. My due date is not for another four weeks. You could travel back and forth."

"Are you suggesting," Karl-Heinz demanded hotly, "that I leave you alone for an entire month in the house with a debauched bachelor?" "Debauched" came out sounding an awful lot like a compliment.

"In my condition, do you really think anyone would talk? Besides, Lillian could come and stay with me."

"Lillian? Oh, great!" Karl-Heinz snorted. "That would only make matters worse. Johann has escorted her around town on occasion. How would it look if they were suddenly cohabitating? It'd be delicious fodder for the rumor mills, that's what! Berliners have an insatiable appetite for gossip. They feed on it like vampires on blood. It makes them all pink and happy. Lillian's reputation would be in shreds within a day. And woe be it for us to blacken her fine family name. It's my mother's, too, don't forget."

Gerlinde smiled secretly. Ursula was not worried about gossip, except that generated by her son if he abandoned his pregnant wife for even one day.

Frau Schmidt and Nurse Gneist were stationed on the top step near the front door of number 77 Lindenstrasse as a coach slowed down along the street. Nurse Gneist, in particular, had spent the past hour eyeing the traffic, greatly worried that the ride from Bernau might have started her patient's labor, in which case there'd be nothing for her to do except bring the mother-to-be to Wirchow and then go home and wallow in disappointment. Nurses actively vied for plum private assignments, and Nurse Gneist was pleased to have landed this one. The accommodations were exceedingly grand, and with so many maids under foot, no one would ask her to lift a domestic finger. She smoothed the pleats in her pristine white uniform and adjusted her dark blue cape.

The coach came to a complete stop; there was a familiar

rasping sound of brakes being set.

"They're here!" Nurse Gneist exclaimed, pushing Frau Schmidt aside before rushing down the marble steps. The housekeeper had been pleasant company during the wait but was not needed now.

Nurse Gneist shuffled swiftly along the walkway and out through the tall wrought-iron gates. Stopping at the curb, she tucked some strands of gray hair under her white cap and folded her arms across her ample chest while she watched Herr Konauer climb from the coach. She eyed him with a severe expression. She had seen enough women die in childbirth to have developed a healthy dislike of men. To her credit, she'd managed never to marry one and now made short work of the required formalities with this male person, shaking his hand as if he were a leper, and quickly turning a cold shoulder on him as she edged him out of the way to personally assist Frau Konauer from the coach. *Let him make himself useful with the luggage,* she thought.

"There now, easy does it." Nurse Gneist changed to a much kinder tone as she helped her patient to the sidewalk suddenly dabbled with the first soft splashes of rain. "I'm Nurse Gneist. Welcome to Berlin!"

"Thank you," Gerlinde smiled, and once her feet were securely planted and her awkward weight balanced, she offered her hand. "I'm so glad to finally be here."

"Well, I should say so. And don't you worry about a thing now. Leave everything to me. I'm here to take charge of you. Since Herr Doctor's hours at Wirchow are long and unpredictable, he wanted a professional person available to you at all times. But, dear me, let's not stand about and chitchat in a drizzle. We're in for a bit of rain, I'm afraid. Not that we need it in May." Nurse Gneist frowned at the gathering clouds. "Now, . . . into the house with you. We'll have a spot of tea, and then you must take a long nap. I'll have to insist."

Gerlinde smiled inwardly. She liked this domineering woman and wondered how Johann had guessed that this was precisely the kind of person she'd be most comfortable with. Indeed, Nurse Gneist was an uncanny mixture of two maiden aunts Gerlinde had once loved so dearly.

Walking up the path toward the house, she eyed the lovely

large flowerpots that bordered the walkway and were overflowing with pink petunias. A row of elegant birch stood guard in front of the ground floor windows, their pale green leaves fluttering as large drops of warm rain bounced off them. She inhaled the air appreciatively. It was pleasantly scented with the fragrance of lilacs growing along the south side of the house.

Reaching the bottom step, Nurse Gneist glanced up and gave Frau Schmidt a look such as the clouds had gotten a moment ago. *Why is that busybody still standing there...gawking,* she thought, uncharitably. *One would think a housekeeper had things to do.* But no, and instead of disappearing into the house, Frau Schmidt stepped boldly forward, wiping her hands on her apron as she did so.

"Welcome!" she said with a wide smile for the guests. "We've been awaiting your arrival."

"Thank you." Winded from the short climb up the marble steps, Gerlinde stopped to catch her breath and extended her hand. "I hope we're not putting you out?"

"No. Not at all." Frau Schmidt declared quite truthfully, because this house guest and her husband had been here before and she recalled that this petite woman was easy to deal with and not a bit demanding. "We're delighted to have you."

Brushing the housekeeper aside, somewhat rudely, Nurse Gneist led her patient into the rotunda-like hall just as Schmidt materialized from the direction of the basement steps. *No doubt the man's been sampling spirits in the wine cellar,* she decided, but at least he had the good grace not to show it. He stopped briefly to greet Frau Konauer and then, remarkably steady on his feet, bounded out of the house to help Herr Konauer and the driver carry the valises inside.

"Have everything brought to the downstairs guest rooms," Nurse Gneist hollered after him, and still holding Gerlinde's arm as they crossed the hall, she said: "I insisted that you be settled on the ground floor. We can't have you climbing stairs."

Gerlinde eyed the long curving staircase to the upper floors, grateful for the nurse's wisdom.

TWELVE

Gerlinde's water broke at a most inopportune moment one evening, just as she pushed herself away from the dinner table. Doubling over, she clutched her stomach and turned deathly pale as a puddle of water spread in a dark circle under her skirts.

"Oh, dear God!" she moaned, mortification buckling her knees, while a wave of nausea further threatened her dignity. She wished herself dead as she eyed the mess on the priceless blue Persian carpet. "Johann, I . . . I am s . . . sorry—"

"Nonsense," he protested and was at her side in a flash, his arms around her, for she appeared on the verge of fainting.

"I say! What's going on here?" Karl-Heinz bellowed. Stymied in Berlin, he felt entitled to some excesses and regularly drank an entire bottle of Beaujolais with dinner. Therefore, he was slow to grasp the situation. However, as he watched Johann take Gerlinde into his arms and lift her clear off the floor, he rose to the occasion. "Hey! Unhand my wife!" He threw down his napkin and clumsily followed the duo into the hall, where Johann had brought Gerlinde and was now giving orders. Schmidt ran to bring the carriage around, and Frau Schmidt went to summon Nurse Gneist. The commotion flushed several maids from their rooms on the third floor, and leaning over the banister to witness the whirlwind of activity, they were glad Frau Konauer's time had come, glad for her because her ordeal would now soon be over. For the past week the poor thing had barely been able to walk.

Karl-Heinz collapsed on a hall bench next to an upholstered chair where Johann had gently deposited Gerlinde while he went to grab their coats from the closet.

Once he'd helped Gerlinde into her wrap, Johann bent down to speak to Karl-Heinz, who was in no condition to leave the house.

"I'm taking Gerlinde to the hospital," he said as he threw on a coat. "But it'll probably be hours yet before you have anything to celebrate. As soon as Schmidt has dropped us off, he'll come back. The coach will be at your disposal. You can follow at your own leisure. I'll try to telephone you from Wirchow. Don't set out until you hear from me."

"All right." Karl-Heinz had no problem with that. He didn't like hospitals, was in no particular hurry to see the inside of one, and this sordid business of Gerlinde giving birth in an institution for the ill had certainly not been his idea.

Carrying Frau Konauer's valise, packed days ago, Nurse Gneist walked briskly into the hall and took her patient in tow with unflinching professionalism, while the dire look she directed at the latter's husband folded over on the bench spelled "useless man" so clearly that she might as well have shouted.

Gerlinde had been in labor a number of hours when Johann concluded that a caesarean section was her only hope. However, he had no seniority and came up against a stone wall when he tried to convince the attending physician to consider it. One baby was in the breech position, yet Dr. Ercklentz—a man with thirty years experience—insisted it could be turned, although its twin left no room and Gerlinde's small frame was stretched like a jib in a squall.

Cursing a system where vintage doctors were allowed to play God, Johann ground his teeth and continued to carefully monitor the patient. The babies' heartbeats were strong, but Gerlinde's was growing weaker. Agonizing minutes dragged by where he realized that, as it were, she would have been no worse off at home with a country midwife. Why the hell had he upset the Konauer household and brought her to Berlin? If she died, Karl-Heinz would flog him, Ursula would never forgive him, and Hans? Dear God, how could Johann ever look that wonderful boy in the eye if his mother died while in his care?

In the next instant, Johann gave himself a quick mental shake, forced all morbid speculation from his mind and went back to concentrating on the patient's vital signs; this was not the time for negative thinking.

But when Gerlinde's blood pressure began dropping the same time her heartbeat rose dramatically, he recognized all the signals of acute distress and realized she couldn't go on like this. Regardless of Dr. Ercklentz's opinion to the contrary, Johann

73

knew for sure she would never deliver these babies, and that every second was now critical. And insofar as he had already reasoned with the senior man to no avail, he suddenly and brazenly seized command. Come hell or high water, it was time to broker a miracle.

"Let's get this patient into an operating room!" he barked and motioned the attending nurse to send out the alert. "Now!"

"I beg your pardon?" Dr. Ercklentz's face appeared almost comical as his head popped up from between Gerlinde's thighs. With a wave of his hand, he indicated the nurse was to remain at her station. "The patient is fully dilated. She is making good progress," he said, as he got up off the stool to stretch. "In a moment I'll be able to get the forceps around the first baby's head."

"I respectfully disagree," Johann bit off.

"Oh," Dr. Ercklentz looked annoyed but kept his professional composure and, above all, remembered to keep his voice low so that the one being discussed wouldn't hear him. Women in the throes of giving birth might be blinded by pain, but in his experience they never suffered any hearing loss. "Her condition is much too fragile for a C-section," he said under his breath. "She might not come out of the anesthesia. The procedure is too risky. She's too weak."

"Which is precisely why she can't go on like this," Johann hissed between clenched teeth and was about to remind the doctor who'd gone over to the water basin to dab cold water on his face that he had suggested a C-section hours ago, when the procedure was still very feasible. But he held his tongue. He figured Dr. Ercklentz was only a year away from retirement and probably more interested in covering his ass than anything else.

Or...? It suddenly occurred to Johann that perhaps the man had never performed a caesarean. Of course he couldn't hold that against him, for neither had he. But he had observed several, one as late as last week and every step was fresh in his mind. He flexed his fingers. He could do it blindfolded. He was almost sure of it. And the sight of poor Gerlinde, mortally white on the bed, unconscious from her struggle, cleared away any doubt. He'd have to force the issue, though, and it would probably mean dismissal, which was okay with him as long as he was fired after the operation.

Without another word, he kicked the locked wheels of the gurney free.

Sensing unusual activity, Gerlinde surfaced to a feeble plateau of awareness. Her small fingers fumbled with the tangled sheets and grasped for the arm guiding the metal rails on the bed. What was happening? Why was the gurney moving? Spent and exhausted, her hollow eyes searched her surroundings. It seemed an eternity since she'd entered a world of pain with only fleeting moments of blurred relief.

Johann leaned over her, took her hand and squeezed it.

"We'll have to operate," he whispered hoarsely.

"N...no..." Gerlinde rolled her head from side to side, clutching his hand in both of hers, but with as much pressure as that of a bird's wing.

"It's the only way."

"I...I'm afraid...I..., I don't want...ether."

Johann realized Gerlinde had overheard Dr. Ercklentz's remark about not coming out of anesthesia.

"Darling, don't be afraid. I'll see you through it. Every step of the way." He winked and tried to look more confident than he felt. "You've done enough work. Now it's my turn. Trust me in this. Please."

A ghost of a smile parted Gerlinde's white lips before a hollow moan escaped her chest as another violent contraction tore through her body.

Johann pushed the gurney forward.

Dr. Ercklentz was at the door, blocking the way.

"Dr. von Renz!" he fairly shouted. "May I remind you of your position at this hospital. As a resident doctor you have no authority—"

"Oh?" Johann cut him off, sorely tempted to ram the gurney right through the man's middle.

"That's right. I repeat. No authority!"

Glaring, Johann stood his ground.

"I will accept full responsibility. This patient is a close friend of mine."

"Which might be clouding your judgment," Dr. Ercklentz said tersely.

"I have her husband's full sanction in the matter," Johann lied without qualm. But surely Karl-Heinz would approve of whatever lifesaving measures he chose.

Dr. Ercklentz bent down over the shadow that was Gerlinde and placed his stethoscope on her swollen belly. He was tired and suddenly unsure of his own diagnosis. Forceps were of little help in a situation such as this. And, he concluded, she would probably die either way. Here or on the operating table. What did it matter? Her bone structure, her small brittle body, was not made for childbearing. And twins? Well, that was just her bad luck. Twins doubled the chance of disaster even for a much more robust woman. He straightened himself and looked squarely at Johann.

"You will perform the surgery?" he asked, all at once glad to wash his hands of this patient.

"Of course."

"All right." Dr. Ercklentz motioned for the nurse to follow the younger doctor's orders.

As Gerlinde was wheeled down the corridor, Johann shouted directions right and left, gathering an anesthesiologist and a team of surgery nurses about him.

Four weeks later, on the last day of June, an auspiciously warm and sunny day, Gerlinde was discharged from Wirchow along with her two beautiful baby girls.

On the heels of the Konauers' departure from Berlin, Johann removed himself as well to spend the rest of the summer on his estate in Bernau. At the time when he was offered the residency at Wirchow, he had made it clear that he would not be on duty during the months of July and August, something of a brass announcement, and one that had initially given the administration pause. But had they objected more vigorously, he would simply have accepted a position at Charite or at another more "understanding" competitor. For although the practice of medicine occasionally humbled Johann, it never caused him to lose the arrogance of his breed.

On a day in August, a day of a torrential downpour, Karl-Heinz nonetheless rode the distance and strolled into Johann's library, trailing buckets of water and tossing his cloak negligently at Rolf. The butler immediately removed the dripping garment, carrying it well away from his pristine person as if it presented an offensive odor.

"Being a mother of three has gone to my wife's head," Karl-Heinz scoffed and proceeded to unravel several large blueprints he pulled from the inside of his shirt, where they had survived the rain nicely. "Not only does she think that she's entitled to her own house, it has to rival the marble Palace of Potsdam!"

"And why not?"

"Yeah, why not?" Karl-Heinz concurred with a sly grin. "Which is why I spent a fortune on that thieving architect you recommended."

"There's none better in all of Berlin."

"There's none richer now that he's picked my pockets!"

"Does Gerlinde like the plans?"

"Like them? She loves them."

"Then your money was well spent."

"Let's withhold judgment until we see the finished product." He'd mellowed with age, but Karl-Heinz displayed a stubborn streak now and again for old times' sake. Now using a heavy inkwell and a crystal cheroot tray as weights, he anchored the blueprints down on Johann's desk. "Alrighty. Take a look here," he said and pointed to several highlighted areas, explaining each at great length and in great detail. "The playroom for the kids will be on the ground floor of course," he finally finished. "Not awkwardly tucked away near the attic as it is now. Which, come to think of it, is a damn danger in case of fire."

"Something the architect no doubt pointed out."

"Huh?"

"I thought so," Johann laughed. "By the way, have your parents reconciled themselves to separate households? Or haven't you told them yet?"

"Being that I'm no coward, of course I've told them." Karl-Heinz cleared his throat noisily, rolled up the blueprints and slipped a rubber band around them. "Actually Gerlinde broke the news. They were distressed at first but felt better when they learned that we were planning to build right down the hill from the old manse. Hell, any time they want to hear the kids holler, all they have to do is open a window."

THIRTEEN

Over the course of the summer, after giving his professional future a great deal of thought, Johann decided to specialize. Few doctors did, but he felt it was the way of the future and inasmuch as he didn't need to make a living, he could afford to be selective. Reconstructive surgery intrigued him. Risky procedures engaged his imagination, and the bloodier the better, he discovered with some astonishment after Gerlinde's caesarean. He had certainly not embarked on this occupation to administer routine medicine.

In September, when he returned to Berlin, and as much as time allowed, he began visiting his alma mater to hone his skills on cadavers and to observe experiments performed by such world famous surgeons as Theodore Kocher and Hugo Knonecker.

It was on one such occasion, while watching from a front seat in the gallery, that Johann heard talk about an open forum dealing with the history of radical surgery. The lecturer, a professor from Warsaw University, had written books on the subject which further aroused Johann's curiosity. He decided to attend and rearranged his Friday schedule in order to do so.

As the professor pottered into the lecture hall, Johann craned his neck to see past the rows in front of him. There was something vaguely familiar about this individual. Johann was ready to swear he'd seen him before; even his voice had a certain ring to it.

But any prior association became unimportant once the lecture began. The man was a well of knowledge, produced illustrations to prove his theories, and claimed brain as well as blood vessel surgery would one day become reality. Before he began to feverishly take notes, Johann concluded that the professor simply reminded him of other instructors he'd known. Members of the intellectual community shared undeniable similarities: beards in need of a trimming, small wire-rimmed glasses, precariously balanced on the very frontier of the nose, and baggy attire. This pedagogue fit the ranks right down to his rumbled tweed coat, frayed bow tie, and sensible black gabardine vest.

Johann attended each of Dr. Zache's seminars throughout the fall, frequently remaining behind to challenge the professor with provocative questions after everyone else had left. It was during one such private discussion in December that Dr. Zache offered Johann the loan of several books that he had co-authored while at Warsaw University.

"They are no longer in print," he cautioned as he handed them over. "If lost, they would be irreplaceable."

Fingering the important volumes, Johann promised to return them in good order at next week's seminar.

"That is, unless you'd like them back sooner?"

"No. Next week will be fine. In fact," the professor chortled, "I'm sure I'd be insulted if you were finished with them any sooner than that."

A cold pea-soup fog had hung stubbornly over Berlin for days, and on the afternoon when Johann brought the books back to the university, he found a group of his colleagues milling about outside the lecture hall, reading a note pinned to the door that explained that Dr. Zache was ill and would not be available until after the Christmas recess.

As the crowd scattered, Johann lingered. He felt uneasy about keeping the treasured publications over the long holiday period and to simply deposit them in the professor's cubicle here by the door seemed unwise. They might be stolen. Of course, with the lecture canceled, he had an hour to kill before reporting to Wirchow. He could use the time to deliver the books.

A department official down the hall provided the address, and with the scrap of paper in his pocket and the books under his arm, Johann left the university compound, walked through the Humboldt Gates and out to the tree-lined avenue, Unter den Linden.

A stiff wind from the Baltic had blown in, dispersing the fog, instantly turning it into sleet. Flying slivers of ice obliterated the gothic-columned State Opera House across the street, where the huge *platz*, separating it from the library and the National Archives building, was now deserted of both pedestrians and pigeons.

Johann shivered, turned up his collar, and glanced up and down the wide boulevard, where a sudden coating of ice had slowed traffic to a crawl. Spotting his coach parked half a block away, he hurried along the slippery sidewalk, dodging in between other hardy souls in various stages of skidding.

"A slight detour," he said to Schmidt and fished the slip of paper from his pocket. "I want to make a stop at this residence before you drop me at Wirchow. I believe it's near the hospital."

"Very well." Schmidt studied the address, nodded, climbed into the driver's box and clucked to the horses. He turned off Unter den Linden at the very next corner and continued east for a couple of blocks. Progressing along Niederlagstrasse, he shortly pulled into Niederlag Gasse, an alley bearing the same name as the thoroughfare.

As the coach rumbled over the uneven cobblestones, Johann glanced out of the window, surprised to see the street rapidly deteriorating and, moreover, to learn that the professor lived in such a community. But he supposed it went hand in hand with the neglected attire; those devoted to academia wasted little time on luxuries. And although the teaching profession was highly respected, it was not especially lucrative for a nontenured part-timer, such as Dr. Zache.

Again checking the paper for the address, Schmidt found the number and came to a halt in front of a square, three-story, brick structure so ordinary it defied description. As he jumped down and opened the carriage door, pulling out the steps in one fluid motion, he contrasted these surroundings to the magnificent neighborhoods where he normally dropped off his employer. He hoped the baron's business here would be quick; the overall squalor of the area was not comforting, and darkness came abruptly in December.

"I'll only be a minute," Johann said as if he'd guessed Schmidt's concern. He crossed the sidewalk in two long strides and, once inside the building, stopped at the base of the stairs to read the names on the mail boxes to determine which apartment Dr. Zache occupied. A door on his right squeaked and opened a crack. Without turning, he knew he was being spied upon.

"Who are you looking for?" a voice, as rusty as the door hinge, wanted to know.

Johann spun around and caught a glimpse of a shock of gray hair before the door slammed shut, followed by the frantic rattling of keys as the tenant made herself secure.

"I am looking for Dr. Zache," he said, addressing the locked door. "Perhaps you can tell me which apartment he's in?"

"Top floor. Last door on the left."

"Thank you." Johann turned toward the stairs.

"Make sure the front door is closed tight before you go up!" the woman hollered from inside her apartment. "And it wouldn't hurt to remind the professor's daughter to do the same. Constantly running in and out, she is. Costing us a lot of heat. And God knows what rabble is invited in when the street door is left wide open. This used to be such a proper building . . ."

Ignoring the tirade with a shrug, Johann made his way up the dimly lit stairwell against the unpleasant odors of fried liver and onions coupled with the noise of quarreling children behind closed doors. Of course, if what he smelled was their supper, it was no wonder they were brawling.

He began to regret his decision to come here, and when he tripped over a bicycle some thoughtless yokel had left on the second landing, he realized he should have sent Schmidt. He reached the uppermost floor and rapped on the professor's door, wishing himself elsewhere.

A chubby girl with a thick blond braid wrapped around the crown of her head, answered his knock.

"Fraulein Zache?" Johann believed her to be the irresponsible daughter the woman on the ground floor had complained about. "My name is Dr. von Renz. I'd like to see your father for a moment."

The girl clapped a hand over her mouth to stifle a giggle.

"Oh . . . ? I'm not . . . what I mean to say, sir, is . . . I'm the maid. Name's Hannah."

"I see. Well, Hannah, I have some books for Dr. Zache."

"Here . . . give 'em to me." The girl held out a hand while carefully guarding the door with the other. "I'll see that he gets 'em."

Although she was probably just following instructions not to let in strangers, her suspicious manner irritated Johann, and he was certainly not about to requite her lack of trust by handing over the books. The silly wench might put them down in the

81

kitchen and forget to inform her employer of their safe return. Perhaps it'd been wrong to come here, but there was no reason to compound one mistake with another.

"Thank you, but I wish to deliver these personally," he said, emphasizing the last word.

"Well, the professor...uh, he's kinda ill today. Lemme go see if he can have visitors. Wait here."

She was about to shut the door and no doubt secure it, such as the woman on the ground floor had done, when Johann put his hand out against the insult; it was not his style to talk through locked doors. But he only managed to keep the door slightly ajar, because Hannah had planted her foot solidly on the floor inside like a stopper. Having challenged him, however, she was suddenly unsure about what to do next. Only one thing was certain, she could not leave the door unguarded. Two weeks ago, the family one floor below had been robbed by an intruder who'd been all gussied up like a gentleman. As far as she knew, he'd never been caught. This might be the same con artist.

"Hannah?" Someone inside the apartment was coming toward the door. "Is anyone there?"

"Yes," Johann spoke up before the maid could clear her throat, "I would like to see Professor Zache. I'm returning some—" speech died on Johann's lips. Even in the dim light, he recognized her. "Good God!" he sputtered.

The girl walked up to the door, smiling tentatively, obviously bemused at the expletive.

Silent and benumbed, Johann stared at the face that had haunted him during an entire year. He now suddenly realized, why Dr. Zache had seemed familiar at the initial seminar months ago; he was none other than the weary traveler at the Ladeburg Inn whose face and voice had been obscured by a woolen scarf. Astonished at his dumb luck of landing on these very people's doorstep, Johann failed to conceal his surprise as his eyes raked over the girl. She had grown. She seemed taller, and standing here in this dingy hallway, lush copper curls cascading freely over her shoulders, she radiated such glamour that her plain frock and dismal surroundings appeared even more so in contrast.

"Are those my father's books?" the girl asked the tongue-tied caller, her eyes traveling to the bundle under his arm. When he still didn't respond, she repeated herself. "Are those my father's books?"

"Uh," Johann absorbed the shock he'd sustained with a couple of shallow breaths, finally allowing him to speak. "Yes, they are," he said, breaking his silence.

"Well, please, . . . please come in." The girl, more trusting than the maid, opened the door fully. "My name is Dorrit Zache," she said and extended her hand.

"How do you do? I'm Dr. von Renz." Johann reached greedily for her hand and wondered if she recognized him. It appeared that she didn't, for there was not the slightest trace of recollection in her lovely, black-fringed, green eyes.

"My father is ill," she said as she stepped back to allow him inside the small entry. "But he's not so ill that he won't be cheered by company. Are you a colleague of his?"

"No. Time permitting, I attend his seminar." Shifting the books from one hand to the other, Johann shed his coat and gave it to the maid; she hung it in a hall closet before she disappeared into the kitchen. "Your father was good enough to lend me these books last week. When his lecture was canceled today, I decided to stop by and return them. I didn't want Dr. Zache to worry about their whereabouts over the holidays."

"That's very considerate of you." Dorrit led the guest along the apartment's narrow corridor. "I hope it wasn't too far out of your way?"

"Far? No, not at all. I'm on duty at Wirchow tonight. It's practically around the corner. Coming here was no trouble at all." Johann consulted his watch; he still had the better part of an hour before reporting.

"Wirchow? You're a medical doctor?"

"Yes."

"My father was a practicing physician at one time before he turned to teaching."

"So I understand."

"He was a very skilled surgeon," she added, with pride ringing in her voice. "But that was long ago, when his hands were steady and his health was sound. His lungs are weak. Raw weather doesn't agree with him. It would have been a disaster to let him go to the university today. I'm the one who insisted that he cancel his lecture. And now that it's sleeting, I'm glad I did." She turned to Johann with a small apologetic smile. "I hope it wasn't terribly inconvenient for everyone."

Johann assured her that it wasn't.

A damned miracle, he thought, because how else would he ever have discovered that Dr. Zache was the father of this enchanting girl? For with all due respect, and looking at the professor in the best of light, one would never guess he could have sired such a lovely offspring. The girl was perfection. The man was a gnome.

Dorrit had led Johann into the living room, a small rectangular parlor with a lone window that looked out onto the tiled roof of the neighboring building where a sagging rain gutter hung on by prayer alone. The professor was sitting in a sofa, his feet resting on an ottoman, a tartan blanket spread over his knees and several pillows propped up behind his back. The small table next to him was set with two cups and a large teapot under an embroidered tea cozy. An open newspaper, strewn on a wing chair, suggested Dorrit might have been reading aloud to him when interrupted.

Despite its lack of fine decor, Johann decided the room was wonderful. Shelves all around the walls buckled under the weight of hundreds of books haphazardly stashed amid a collection of old clocks, cranky with age, for not a single one was keeping the correct time.

Among the clutter, he spotted some exquisitely framed portraits of a child in various stages of development, plus what appeared to be a recent photograph of father and daughter together. There was no woman in any of the pictures, he noted. Evidence of Dorrit's mother was conspicuously missing.

Johann found it odd.

FOURTEEN

After twelve hours of duty in the emergency ward, where he had free reign with any radical procedure required when a hapless victim of a grisly crime or accident came in, Johann returned home early Saturday, suspecting that unless infection set in, he had probably saved one or two pitiful souls. A nap and a change of clothes, and he was ready to catch up with the mail and the newspapers. Frau Schmidt brought a breakfast tray into the library, her employer rarely used the dining room when he was alone, and placing the food on a table by the sofa, she opened the red velvet drapes to the street, wiped the window sills with the corner of her apron, and put another log in the fire before she took her leave.

The large windows on both sides of the fireplace were fashioned in hundreds of small leaded-glass panes that gave a kaleidoscopic view of the tall birch trees just outside and the patch of grass that lay like a carpet between the house and the wrought-iron fence that ran the length of the sidewalk. Its rigid palings were softened by climbing wisteria vines, heavy with pendent clusters of blue-violet flowers during the summer months. On the far side of the street, groves of elm and chestnut marked the eastern perimeter of Grunewald Park. The trees were now brown and bare, but come spring they came to life in a variety of lush greens.

On Saturdays, in addition to the regular Berlin papers, Johann had the *London Herald* and a Paris weekly delivered; he read while he ate. He enjoyed keeping his French and English alive; there was much to wade through, and it was generally a labor of fascination. However, today his interest seemed to be lacking. Each time he came to the end of an article, he realized he hadn't the foggiest idea what he'd just read. Moreover, for some reason, the food was tasteless on his palate.

Irritated with himself, he tossed the papers into a heap on the floor and got up. He felt restless and needed to move about.

Of course, he didn't have to exercise his legs to determine that it was Dorrit Zache who interfered with his peace. Underlying his lack of attention this morning was a prickly feeling that something had not gone well yesterday. For although Dorrit had welcomed him warmly, a short while later she appeared to be peculiarly anxious to be rid of him. He had barely sat down and accepted a cup of tea when she began to glance at the various clocks in the room, indicating his speedy departure would be desirable.

What had he done to warrant her change in attitude?

Perhaps he shouldn't have accepted the tea, which, in truth, he had only taken to prolong the visit; in retrospect probably a mistake. But even if he had wanted to leave, how could he possibly have done so without insulting the professor's splendid colloquy? A born rodomont, the man had talked nonstop from the minute Johann arrived, boasting shamelessly—particularly about Dorrit—and only drawing breath when he coughed, not a sterling time for a visitor—a physician, yet—to head for the door.

"My daughter has had more education than most males her age," Dr. Zache had vaunted, looking over the rim of his cup to discern the impact his words were having on his guest. And the minute he noted Johann's interest, there was no stopping him. "I had little in the way of material goods to give her," he continued self-effacingly. "But I made sure that she was schooled. Dorrit," the professor held out his cup for a refill, "display your proficiency with the French language."

"*Papa*, . . . really!" She turned crimson.

"Well, never mind, then." Dr. Zache shrugged and looked slyly at Johann. "You'll just have to take my word for it. And, of course, long before we came to Germany, I made sure that my daughter's speech was as polished as that of a born Berliner. Certainly, you agree, Dr. von Renz, that she's far too pretty to have any harsh sounds on her tongue."

Johann agreed.

Dorrit rolled her eyes in the direction of a rather large wall clock.

It suddenly now occurred to Johann that she'd probably hated her father's swaggering, and getting rid of the guest was the only sure-fire way to stop him. Also, conversation obviously taxed his lungs; he'd wheezed and coughed a great deal. Indeed, she had every reason to worry. Herman Zache was not a well man. Johann guessed pulmonary disease was slowly ravaging his lungs. There was no treatment except rest and warmth, and his daughter clearly made it her business to make sure he got plenty of both.

That was why she'd been watching the clock!

Coming to that conclusion, Johann felt better at once. He stopped pacing and sat down to finish his breakfast. The eggs were cold. He shoved them aside and scooped jam on a *semmel* roll, chewing it absently between sips of coffee he poured from a silver pot, all the while making plans for Dorrit.

He would enjoy nothing better than to take her to a night-club, such as Ciro's, loosen her up with champagne, and commence with his courtship, which he intended to make as short as decently possible. However, he suspected that, initially, at least the professor would have to be accommodated, if only because Dorrit probably wouldn't accept an invitation which didn't include him. That ruled out Ciro's but left other options open, such as a night at the opera followed by supper at the Adlon. The old elegant hotel on Pariser Platz had an exceptional dining room, a favorite with the after-the-concert crowd. He assumed Dr. Zache was a music enthusiast; intellectuals usually were.

Johann got up. Left the supple red-leather chair for the hard-backed Bierdermeier at his desk. He sat down and scanned his calendar. He had signed up for an inordinate amount of night duty at Wirchow during the coming week in order to have the holidays off. Next Thursday was his first free moment, but it was also the day he was supposed to travel to Bernau. Well, he'd have to forget that. He'd dispense with tradition, cancel Christmas with the Konauers, and corral the Zaches instead. He would ring Karl-Heinz at once and explain. But first a note to Professor Zache and Dorrit. He couldn't call them. Yesterday he'd learned that they didn't have a telephone.

Johann rummaged impatiently through the drawers in his desk for something other than gold-initialed vellum, which might strike the spartan educator as garish. One had to be careful when dealing with avant-garde intellectuals, and finally coming across some simple parchment, Johann formulated an invitation for Thursday night.

Using the blotter, he proofread the note before summoning Schmidt.

"Deliver this to Professor Zache on Niederlag Gasse," he said, handing the envelope to the butler. "And I'd like you to return with a response."

"*Jawohl*, Herr Baron."

"Oh, and Schmidt, omit that kind of formality around the professor and his daughter. I want them to be comfortable."

"Very well, Herr . . . uh, *Doctor?*"

"Fine," Johann smiled.

Schmidt's eyes skimmed the back of the envelope where his employer had simply scrawled, "Johann von Renz. 77 Lindenstrasse. Grunewald." Well, it can't get any less formal than that, he mused as he walked out of the library to do the baron's bidding.

Feeling nothing but confident anticipation, Johann went back to the comfortable chair near the fire and picked up the newspapers.

FIFTEEN

Johann's good spirits were short-lived. Schmidt returned within the hour bearing disappointing news. Fraulein Zache had declined the invitation.

"Why?" Johann asked, flabbergasted.

"She gave no reasons, sir."

Johann dismissed the butler with the flick of his wrist. Once he was alone, he got up, grabbed the poker and used unnecessary roughness on the logs in the fireplace. Showers of sparks flew out onto the marble fire guard, coming dangerously close to singeing a rug, a destructive blaze that would not be altogether unpleasant; such was Johann's ire.

What on earth was wrong with the girl? he fumed. Had he dispatched a similar note to anyone else in Berlin, it would have been accepted at once. People rearranged their calendars to accommodate him—dammit!—and a hand-delivered invitation was nothing less than a social triumph! And if she and the professor had a previous engagement, why didn't she just say so? A clarification avoided bruised feelings and left the door open. A plain no made it damned awkward to suggest an alternative date. Hands on hips, Johann stepped back from the fire and the thought came to him that she might already have a suitor. Beauty such as hers attracted notice. Plenty of it.

Johann replaced the poker and stood for a moment staring at the roaring bonfire he'd created, jealousy slowly seeping into the deep dark recesses of his soul. Areas never before tapped rumbled to life with ugly feelings as he visualized Dorrit in the company of another male, someone who couldn't possibly be worthy of such a treasure.

Scowling, Johann turned his back on the fire and turned his attention toward the windows. He glanced idly out toward the street and beyond to the park. The trees swayed their skeletal limbs in a benign breeze. After days of dense fog followed by yesterday's icy drizzle, the sky finally showed patches of blue. He ought to go riding, a reliable tension reliever, and the public stable in Grunewald offered surprisingly good stock. He had plenty of time. He was free until tonight when he was committed to escorting Louisa to a richly attended, but conversationally destitute, soiree.

He grimaced at the prospect of the evening ahead. Louisa von Tirpitz was beginning to bore him. Lately, she'd started to play coy, something he distinctly disliked. Expecting to wring a proposal from him, and believing it'd hasten his declaration, she flirted mercilessly and teased him with provocative gowns, then immediately became a pillar of virtue the minute he tested the sincerity of her dalliance.

He massaged the tight muscles at the back of his neck; God knows he could use some pleasant diversion. Of course, the gathering tonight would be sprinkled with a predictable number of women who were bored with their marriages or angry at their husbands. Among them, one could usually be counted on to risk scandal. The evening need not be a total loss. And tomorrow . . . ? Tomorrow he would make a new plan for Dorrit Zache.

That decided, he settled down and resumed his reading.

Frau Schmidt came in to remove the breakfast tray.

Dorrit arrived in front of the house where she remained on the sidewalk for endless moments peering at the huge magnificent villa. She was convinced that she had made a mistake. A physician, even the most gifted, didn't live in a house such as this. Digging into her coat pocket, she took out the crumbled envelope to check the address again.

Seventy-seven Lindenstrasse!

The number corresponded to the one on the gate. There was no mistaking it, just like there was no mistaking the fact that she hadn't wanted to come but had gone to considerable trouble to get here. After taking a westbound trolley to the end of Kurfurstendamm, she transferred to a tram going south on Koenigs Allee. She sat right behind the driver so he could alert her to the appropriate stop in Grunewald. And when she hopped off, he kindly pointed her in the right direction. It took some walking, but eventually she found Lindenstrasse. After that, it was only a matter of persevering until she reached the correct number. But now that she'd found it, her resolve evaporated. Surely no ordinary mortal dared pass uninvited through these elegant gates. She, the most ordinary of mortals, definitely had no stomach for it and couldn't for the life of her understand why her father had sent her on this mission. She also couldn't understand why a man who shunned all social interaction had suddenly become unreasonable about an invitation.

"Mein Gott!" he'd exclaimed when he returned from synagogue and immediately saw the note from Dr. von Renz. "The opera? Dinner at Hotel Adlon? A pricey place, indeed," he mumbled, standing in the hall while examining the invitation. "What did you tell the person who delivered this?"

"Nothing, papa."

"Nothing?"

"Well, naturally, I said we couldn't accept."

"That's all you said?"

"Yes. I didn't think it was necessary to explain that you don't socialize. You've always told me not to . . . you know, not to tell people anything personal." Dorrit still remembered her father's life-long wish to keep his affairs private. "Of course I told him to thank Dr. von Renz," she smiled confidently. At least she hadn't forgotten her manners.

The professor raised his eyes devoutly toward heaven. Was this his amercement? Had God finally seen fit to punish an old sinner by dulling a child's mind? He cleared his throat.

"Let's hope no harm has been done," he said and put the invitation down on a shelf in the foyer while he hung up his coat.

"Harm?" Dorrit seized on the word, puzzled at her father's strong reaction. "What do you mean . . . 'harm'?"

"Maybe there's still time to set things straight," Herman Zache continued as if he hadn't heard her. He went into the living room where, instead of sitting down, he began to pace back and forth in front of the window. His right hand, balled into a fist, was pounding the palm of his left until he apparently hit upon something.

"I've got it," he said and turned to Dorrit, who was watching him anxiously. "You must go at once and see the good doctor. Heaven forbid he mistakes you for a social ignoramus and thinks even less of me for not teaching you better. There might still be time to salvage the situation. But it requires a personal visit if it's to have any impact. You must go and explain yourself. Tell him you made a mistake. After consulting with me, you discovered we'd be delighted to accept his invitation."

"We would? You'd actually venture out at night? Is that wise, papa? In December? And suppose in the course of the evening, he begins to pry about stuff that's none of his business?" Dorrit was thinking of past occasions when nosy individuals had literally chased them out of town.

"We're in Berlin," Herman Zache said simply. "Things are different here. We can talk freely. Now go wash your face and comb your hair. Pull it back neatly. You're a lady of good breeding."

"A what?"

"You heard me. And wear your new blue suit with some proper shoes."

"The blue suit? Why?"

"Don't argue!" Uncharacteristically, Herman Zache raised his voice. "Just do as I say! And see that you hurry!"

Dorrit had rarely seen her father so emotionally engaged, and unless she was missing something, she saw no reason for all this fuss. But she didn't question him further; it would never do when he was so agitated. He might work himself into a bronchial attack. Yesterday's rest had only partially restored his precarious health.

When she had changed her clothes and polished her appearance to his satisfaction, her father thrust trolley fare into her hands, helped her into her coat, and all but shoved her out the door.

"Take a westbound train!" he instructed, giving her the envelope with Dr. von Renz's address. "Grunewald is west of town. Ask the conductor for directions."

Not until she was seated on the trolley, did Dorrit realize why her father had acted so bizarrely. His odd behavior was obviously due to the new medicine he'd taken this morning. It was supposed to clear his chest but had apparently muddled his mind instead.

Now standing here on the pristine sidewalk of Lindenstrasse, she sighed in abject desperation. To turn around and go home, claiming no one had answered the door, was an attractive option. But could she fib convincingly?

Again her eyes fell on the forbiddingly large and elegant

house of gray marble and stone majestically set behind a row of white birch. The garden was meticulously groomed. A neat flagstone walk cut a path to the front steps and a huge oak door with polished brass hardware. The roof was entirely of slate, something she had once heard the landlord on Niederlag Gasse bemoan as outrageously expensive when a roofer had suggested it for his building. She sighed. The tall windows on the ground floor facing the street reflected the bleak winter sky, as dismal as her mood. They seemed to be staring at her; blank, unblinking, warning her not to come any closer.

Dorrit's spine went soft, sagging under the weight of acute inadequacy. Weak-kneed and miserable, she reached out to the wrought-iron fence for support. Her fingers grasped the cold metal and the gnarled dormant wisteria vines clinging to it. She felt breathless, similar to the way she'd felt in Warsaw once when she'd come within a hair of being run down by a speeding coach. Another pedestrian had pushed her to safety a split second before disaster, and after the danger had passed, she leaned against a lamppost, trembling and feeling light-headed, precisely like now. Of course, that episode was a foolish comparison, she told herself severely, for in spite of her fear, neither life nor limbs were in danger here.

SIXTEEN

"Ahem..." Schmidt cleared his throat as he walked into the library. "Herr...*Doctor!*"

Johann looked up from his reading. Was there to be no peace? Was a conspiracy at work within his own four walls to test his patience?

"A young lady," Schmidt announced, economizing on words, something the baron was sure to appreciate, "the one I delivered a note to earlier is at the door."

"Huh?"

"A young lady, the one—"

"I heard you," Johann snapped.

"Very well, sir. Shall I take her coat and show her in?"

"Yes." Johann said, contriving to manifest unconcern.

Schmidt disappeared.

Resisting the urge to rub his hands together, Johann put down the newspapers, got up, and walked over to the fireplace. Dorrit Zache...here? How extraordinarily convenient. She might not be so troublesome after all. He braced one hand against the mantelpiece while the other engaged the iron poker. Thus, stabbing at the logs, he kept his back turned on the French doors, pivoting around only when he heard hesitant footsteps.

"Ah, Fraulein Zache..." Johann arched a dark eyebrow, and although he could control his voice to a smooth faultlessness, flecks of silver flashed in chaotic abandon in his eyes as they narrowed and swept over the girl standing in the doorway. "What a pleasant surprise!" This was as truthful a statement as any he'd ever made.

"Good afternoon," she said in a tight voice, unnerved by the opulence all around her and suddenly immensely glad that her father had insisted on the blue suit. "Forgive me for intruding—"

"You are not intruding." Johann approached her, wryly noting that she took a step backwards and glanced over her shoul-

94

der—for Schmidt no doubt. "Please, come in and sit down." Johann took her arm and ushered her to the chair he had just occupied near the fireplace, and although she dragged her feet the entire way, it was pleasant to escort someone not a whole head shorter than himself. He was six feet four inches tall, and most women barely reached to his shoulder. But Fraulein Zache was taller than most.

Dorrit lowered herself stiffly to the edge of the seat, silently declaring she wouldn't be troubling him long. The glow from the burning logs enveloped her like a down comforter, only now did she realize how cold she'd been, standing on the street outside. And while Dr. von Renz discarded some newspapers in a bin by the fire and turned a matching red leather chair around to face the one she occupied, her eyes flitted over the beautiful library.

Wonderful mahogany bookcases, some with glass-fronted shelves housing collections of leather-bound editions, dominated the high-ceilinged room. Behind a long red leather sofa, a sliding ladder allowed access to books on the uppermost shelves. A sand-colored Afghan was draped over the sofa's back, and tables at either end held decorative reading lamps. Dorrit could well imagine curling up under the Afghan with a book. It'd be heaven! Her eyes fell on a card table in the corner of the room that held an exquisite chess set, its game pieces crafted in alabaster and jade.

In fact, everywhere Dorrit looked, she saw objets d'art that appeared to be priceless. The ornate inkwell on a large oak desk was probably solid gold, and she knew enough about antiques to realize the escritoire under one of the windows facing the street was worth its weight in the same precious metal. As her eyes kept traveling, she recognized several paintings by French Impressionists, such as Monet and Pissarro. Above the fireplace hung an almost life-sized portrait of a young girl sitting in a beautiful rose garden. But although Dorrit could spot and identify a great number of artists, she did not recognize that particular work. And this was not the proper time to ask, because, having seated himself, Dr. von Renz's eyebrows were lifted into a questioning arch. He was obviously waiting for her to explain this impromptu visit.

"I . . . that is to say . . . my father . . . ," Dorrit began clumsily, and found she had to clear her throat several times. Though she was warm, she was far less comfortable in this magnificent library than she'd been outside on the windswept sidewalk, an antithesis she blamed on Dr. von Renz, who was staring at her in an odd way. Yesterday, he had appeared quite the gentleman, but today, he seemed the wily sort her father often warned her about. Why papa wished to socialize with this individual was beyond her.

"You were saying?" he prompted, when she stalled repeatedly.

Dorrit pushed at a strand of hair that had come loose from the ribbon holding her riotous curls in place at the nape. "I . . . uh, I was about to explain that my father was not at home earlier today when your note was delivered. He was quite upset to learn that I had declined without consulting him. So he sent me here to tell you that if the invitation is still open, we'd be able to accept after all."

"It's still open." The phrase was deliberately businesslike, conveying no emotion one way or another. For some irrational reason, it gave Johann sadistic satisfaction to see her squirm.

Dorrit swallowed hard, his clipped tone did not escape her and seemed to insist on more by way of an explanation. All right. Papa had said it was safe to talk freely. And so she would. But not to satisfy this man. Only to follow papa's instructions.

"My father rarely ventures out at night," she began, anxious to get it over with. "And never during the winter months, when he tries to avoid large crowds, such as one would find at the opera . . . much as he enjoys music. His lungs are weak, and just as he had to cancel his lecture yesterday, there's always the possibility that he'd have to cancel a social event at the last minute. Which would be a terrible shame if you'd already bought opera tickets and reserved dinner at the Adlon. That's why I declined. Plus there's the problem of our religion. We don't observe Christmas. Next Thursday is Christmas Eve, I believe. We are Jewish. So I'm sure you realize that we'd not be able to celebrate in the same manner with your other guests."

"Other guests?"

"Well, I just assumed—"

"You assumed too much, Fraulein Zache. I was planning on no one else. Nor was I necessarily planning a holiday supper."

Johann was relieved to learn that apparently Dorrit had no other suitor. His only "competition" was her religion, and that he could handle. Live and let live, he's always maintained. He was not an obeisant Christian himself and only attended church sporadically, usually at the Deutsche Dom on the Gendarmenmarkt, and then mainly to hear the famous choir. Dorrit Zache could hardly object to him on religious grounds. And he had no quarrel with hers.

"I have an idea," he now said. "Suppose we skip the opera and the Adlon, avoid crowds altogether, and suffice by having dinner here at the house, where I can ensure your father's comfort."

"Dinner here? In your home?" Dorrit was troubled with such intimacy on a short acquaintance.

"Why not? In the event you find you must cancel, only my housekeeper will be inconvenienced."

Studying her hands tightly clasped in her lap, Dorrit remained silent while she wondered what her father would think about this.

Johann took the opportunity to press his point. "Next Thursday happens to be my first free evening," he said. "That's why I chose it. Not because it is Christmas Eve. And in view of your religion, something I wasn't aware of until now, I could lean on Frau Schmidt to cook . . . what's the word . . . kosher?"

"Yes, but you needn't trouble your housekeeper on that score," Dorrit said. "We don't keep a kosher home. My father follows the laws of the Torah but eats what he likes. His poor health often requires a glass of hot milk with his supper and he figures that if God wants to keep him alive, He'll forgive any dietary indiscretions."

Johann took that as an affirmative. He smiled.

"Then it's settled."

"Settled? Well . . . ah, all right. And . . . and thank you," Dorrit added perfunctorily and placed her feet squarely on the floor; mission completed, she was anxious to be off.

However, instead of rising and escorting her to the door as she so clearly wished, Johann stretched his legs out in front of him, indicating the interview was not over. With the skill of a pantomimist, he signaled Schmidt hovering in the hall just outside the double doors.

A tray of refreshments materialized almost instantly.

Plates of smoked salmon, aromatic cold cuts, and goose liver pâté stared Dorrit in the face, as did a nearsighted maid who eyed her bluntly as she put down a basket of sliced bread. The butler brought in wine and crystal goblets. His wife poured coffee. Everything came about so efficiently except the moment of Dorrit's departure, because she didn't think she could insult the staff by running off before she had sampled their efforts. However, she promised herself that as soon as she returned home, papa would suffer a piece of her mind for putting her in this spot.

"Guten appetit!" Frau Schmidt was the last to leave the room.

"Thank you," Dorrit croaked and once she was again alone with her host, she wondered if she'd be able to choke down a single bite. It had been a long time since breakfast, but she experienced not the slightest hunger, and although her plate contained all her favorite foods, she eyed it with a touch of nausea.

"My housekeeper likes to see people eat," Johann grinned at the wide array of edibles—the woman was a marvel. "Hungry?" he asked.

"Um . . ." Dorrit mumbled noncommittally, and pretending some interest, took a fork and lifted a slice of salmon off her plate. She bit into it before realizing that she should have cut it first. Her teeth were not able to halve it, but rather than spit it out, she pushed the whole piece in. The fatty salmon immediately stuck like glue to the roof of her mouth. She gagged. Her tongue worked the logjam furiously, but once the salmon was free, she didn't dare swallow it whole for fear of choking. And to chew it properly meant displaying big lumps in both cheeks. Of course, spitting it out was even more unattractive.

While caught in this dilemma, the room grew oppressively quiet. Dorrit was convinced the entire household could hear her struggle. It'd never occurred to her that so much noise and effort was involved with the simple task of eating. And when the salmon finally slipped down, the ensuing gulp echoed off the walls loud as a cannon. She cleared her throat but only managed to wake a dry tickle, which shook her shoulders in a most unladylike fashion.

Out of the corner of her eye, she saw Dr. von Renz smile.

He's laughing at me, she cried inwardly and her mouth went bone dry. In desperation she reached for the wine. It was velvety smooth and lubricated her throat nicely. She felt better and took another sip, for although her father had repeatedly cautioned her about spirits, she didn't believe something the color of rubies could be harmful.

It became easier to eat. She ate a piece of pumpernickel with pâté and truffles without incident and could even glance at her host without embarrassing side effects. And—*Gott im himmel*—for all the devilish arrogance in his silvery eyes, he cut a grand figure. Yesterday, she had determined that she'd never come across a more handsome or a more well-groomed individual. Even here at home and at leisure, his gray slacks were pressed with knife-pleats and his shoes were shiny as a new coin. His shirt was crisp and spotless, and although he had rolled up the sleeves, wore no tie, and his dark hair was a bit ruffled, he looked positively elegant. Of course he also looked old. Thirty if he was a day. Still, there could be no question but that he was enormously attractive.

Vexed at the silence between them, Johann ate what was on his plate, soon depositing it on the coffee table, but leaving his napkin across one knee so Fraulein Zache wouldn't get the idea that he was finished and thus be encouraged to take off. Her discomfort, her springboard position on the chair, was a clear message.

"Tell me about your family," he finally said, a stab in the dark to raise some sort of conversation.

"My family?" Dorrit looked up from her food as if she'd been ambushed. "I have no family," she said. "Only my father. And him you know."

"You must have had a mother at one time." Johann was remembering the photographs in the apartment, conspicuously missing a woman. "I assume your father is a widower."

"Yes. My mother is dead, but I can't tell you much more than that, because I have no memories of her. I was very young when she died."

"Your father doesn't talk about her?"

"No." Dorrit took another sip of wine; it was amazing how much better it made her feel. "He thinks about her a great deal though. Sometimes I wish he wouldn't. It makes him terribly melancholy."

"How long has he been a widower?"

"Sixteen years."

"Hm, that's a long time to mourn," Johann conceded. "What did your mother die of?"

"Consumption, . . . I think. She died while we lived in Saint Petersburg."

"Saint Petersburg? You're not from Warsaw then?"

"Well, yes and no. We lived in Warsaw for about five years before coming to Berlin. Prior to that, we lived in a number of different places."

"Such as?"

"Well, besides Saint Petersburg, where I was born, we lived in Minsk, Kiev, and Bialystok. In that order. There were other places in between, but they're not important enough to mention, because we didn't stay long. In fact, we moved so often, I think my father became confused."

"Confused? It's hard to visualize the erudite professor as confused." Johann grinned.

"Yes. But he was. You see, when we lived in Kiev, he'd tell people that I was born in Minsk. When we lived in Bialystok, he'd say that I was born in Kiev. And so it went. But he never once mentioned Saint Petersburg. I discovered, quite by accident, that I was born there."

"Really?"

"Uh-huh. During one of our frequent moves, I came across some hidden documents, specifically my birth certificate. And reading it, it also became clear that my father had changed our name after we left Saint Petersburg. I was born Dorrit Tzacheroff. Not Zache."

"Why did he change his name?"

"I don't know. For the sake of convenience perhaps. And it wasn't a complete change. He merely lopped off the first letter and the last four. He really just shortened it."

Suddenly Dorrit wondered if she ought to be divulging these details. Her father had always warned her about confiding in strangers. Except this morning of course, when he specifically told her to speak freely, implying that it was all right because they now lived in Berlin.

"Have you ever confronted him about any of this?" Silently Johann questioned the professor's motives and duplicity.

Dorrit shook her head.

"It didn't seem all that important. I was very young when I found the documents. Later, when I was older, and for the sake of satisfying my own curiosity, I couldn't possibly distress him with questions. Any mention of the past, any talk of my mother, made him awfully gloomy. He's carried a torch for her all these years. She was the light of his life. There's never been anyone since."

"Except you."

Dorrit smiled; the green of her eyes took on a lighter shade.

"I'd like to think that he is proud of me at least."

"That's a safe bet in view of his campaign yesterday on your behalf."

Despite herself, Dorrit laughed.

"Yes, he was rather pompous. You must forgive him. Believe me, he normally doesn't run on like that. I don't know what set him off, and I assure you that little of what he said was true."

"I believed him." Johann switched deftly into French; Dr. Zache had claimed his daughter was fluent. "I believed every single word."

"Then you are extremely gullible," Dorrit said, having responded in French without missing a beat.

Johann was impressed; the professor had not exaggerated. "I'm afraid you've exposed a weakness," he laughed.

"One of many, I'm sure," she retorted glibly, instantly regretting the slur.

Johann leaned over and refilled her empty wine glass.

Taking a carefully measured sip to hide her shame, Dorrit wondered how she could have let such an impertinent comment slip. Bold as brass, she'd implied that Dr. von Renz was a man of weaknesses, which was the same as suggesting he enjoyed gambling, foolishness with women, and drinking. Plus she'd called him gullible! The magnitude of her indiscretion rushed to her cheeks. The unfortunate thing about having red hair, she agonized silently, was the inclination to blush, which tended to incriminate one. But at least she'd been spared the freckles. If not, they'd now be goose-stepping across the bridge of her nose.

While her embarrassment subsided, and in an attempt to avoid her host's penetrating eyes, Dorrit busied herself with a petit four from the silver tray on the small table in front of her.

It was a delicious brandied sponge cake glazed in rich, dark chocolate with a candy violet on top. She couldn't resist taking another, and after a while she was again able to glance toward Dr. von Renz without reddening.

He was smiling at her! Perhaps he was not offended? Moreover, he topped off her wine glass, something she didn't think an angry host would do.

"Did you know, Fraulein Zache," he said as he put the decanter back into its silver coaster, "that we've actually met once before?"

"Yes, of course. Yesterday."

"No. Before that."

"Really? Where?" Dorrit stared at him; she didn't meet many people and couldn't imagine she'd have forgotten such an imposing individual.

"In Ladeburg."

"Ladeburg?" She looked puzzled.

"It's a small place some twenty-five miles east of Berlin. It was about a year ago. Last December to be precise. Your coach stopped at a local inn. I advised you about the poor road conditions."

"Oh? My goodness, yes!" Dorrit exclaimed, her eyes suddenly glowing with the memory. "Forgive me for not recognizing you. I'm afraid I was a bit tired at that point in our journey. The tram strike made it a long and strenuous trip by coach. But what brought you to Ladeburg?"

"I was just killing time with a friend. We were sampling the inn's famous brew and listening to the fiddler. I was born in nearby Bernau. I still keep a home there. I always spend the holidays in the country."

"But not this year?" Dorrit asked in reference to his invitation for next Thursday.

"No. This year I had other plans." In a silent tribute to those plans, Johann raised his glass.

Figuring he expected her to do the same, Dorrit did so and quite spontaneously smiled over the rim at him.

Johann felt her smile like a pleasant punch.

SEVENTEEN

Arriving home from Wirchow late Thursday afternoon, Johann made a quick tour of the downstairs. As he had instructed, logs were burning in the fireplaces throughout, supplementing a temperamental coal burner in the basement and insuring that the drawing room, in particular, was invitingly warm despite its size. As he now walked through this large room, he frowned from force of habit at the fragile antiques upholstered in striped pastels with skimpy cushions not made for comfort. While guests seemed not to mind that in the least, Johann was partial to the small sitting alcove—reached through an archway at the far end of the room. Here the chairs were big and firm and the glass veranda doors provided a splendid view of the terrace and garden beyond.

Peering outside, he saw it had started to snow. The sky had threatened all day, and inasmuch as it'd soon be dark, Johann opened the doors and went out to light the gas lamps in each corner of the terrace. Brushing wet flakes from his shoulders, he stepped back inside the alcove to admire the scene. The snow looked sensational, glittering like confetti in the yellow circles of the gas lights.

He rearranged a couple of chairs; this was where he would entertain Dorrit and her father before dinner. That decided, he walked briskly back to the center hall and closed the doors to the salon opposite the library; the salon was for dancing and large crowds and tonight would only serve to draw heat away from other rooms. A quick glance into the dining room told him the table was set and ready.

Being in exceptionally good spirits, he broke his own rules and intervened between two maids squabbling over where to hang the last of the ornaments on the tall evergreen standing at the base of the long curving staircase. A Christmas tree was decor he could not dispense with, regardless of his guest's religious affiliation. The maids were not accustomed to attention from their employer, and his affable mood immediately caused their argument to lose steam.

Johann settled down in the library with some reading, until the mantle clock chimed the hour of six, reminding him that Schmidt had better get going. He was picking up Dr. Zache and his daughter and the weather was bound to slow the horses.

After Schmidt left, Johann went upstairs to change. Flicking impatiently through his bedroom closets, he finally selected a gray velvet dinner jacket, paired with black gabardine slacks. He tied a maroon ascot into the open neck of his white silk shirt, fastened it with a plain gold pin, and ran a comb through his hair and the back of his hand over the lower part of his face. Satisfied he didn't need to shave, he went back downstairs to the library to await his guests. He poured himself a shot of smooth English bourbon, sloshing it around in the heavy crystal goblet before tossing it down in one quick motion.

Schmidt returned with his passengers at precisely seven o'clock. He ushered them into the hall, where a maid stood ready to take their coats.

"Good evening!" Johann emerged from the library and reached for Dr. Zache's hand. "I trust the trip was comfortable?"

"Thank you, yes," the professor replied, sniffing appreciatively as he surveyed the grand surroundings. He gave the large crystal chandelier suspended from the high-domed ceiling a second look, while his feet tested the luxurious thick carpets scattered about on the parquet. Dorrit had not embellished the truth, he realized. This home was even more spectacular than she had described. "It was awfully good of you to send the coach. I daresay it would have been difficult to find public transportation this evening."

Johann laughed at the very idea and turned his attention to Dorrit, something that caused a rush of pleasure to sweep over him. Her auburn hair was fastened into a soft chignon glistening with the moisture of melting snowflakes gathered during the short walk from the curb to the house. Small wispy curls had worked free and framed her exquisite face.

The maid was helping her out of her coat, and underneath the coarse outer garment, she was wearing a cream-colored blouse and a green watered-silk skirt. Although unsightly boots peeked out from beneath the hem of the skirt, the entire ensemble was adequate for the occasion.

"It's a pleasure to see you again, Fraulein Zache," Johann said as he took her hand and put it to his lips.

Reciprocating with a similar comment, she smiled, flashing her pretty teeth. And taking full advantage of her accommodating mood, a far cry from her reticent arrival last Saturday, Johann placed her hand on his arm and, with the professor pulling up the rear, escorted his guests from the hall and through the drawing room to the more intimate environment of the alcove.

Schmidt appeared with aperitif wines, bowls of exotic candied nuts, assorted relishes, and the promise that dinner would be served precisely at eight o'clock.

"Welcome!" Johann lifted his glass.

"Thank you. It's awfully nice to be here," Dr. Zache said, then added with a shrewd twinkle in his eye: "And a very merry Christmas!"

"*Shalom aleichem!*" Johann pronounced the carefully rehearsed salute with facility.

Chuckling, both men concluded the evening was off to an excellent start.

The paintings in the library had impressed Dorrit on her visit last week, and minutes ago when she walked through the drawing room, her eyes hadn't missed a single art work on the pale-blue walls. Having worn the soles off her shoes, perusing Berlin's famous museums during the past year and attending endless lectures, she almost considered herself something of an expert, enough of one anyway to be astonished that so many exhibition-quality treasures existed in a private home. So as long as her father and their host were discussing things of a professional nature, she was blissfully content to study the pictures here in the alcove until there was a lull in the men's conversation, when bursting with curiosity, she finally asked Dr. von Renz if the painting on the wall behind her father's chair was by the Dutch painter...Jungkind.

"It is indeed." Johann smiled and, being partial to the courtyard scene, was pleased that she had identified it, because it was unsigned and eluded many a trained eye. "Lacking a signature," he explained, "it's not considered particularly valuable. But Jungkind did initial the back of the canvas. I've been told it's a proof. I suppose that's why it was relegated to this far corner of the house. Still, it happens to be a favorite of mine."

"It's wonderful," Dorrit agreed. "An early morning scene."

"Early morning?"

"Well, yes. The weak yellows would indicate that. And the sky is very light. Later in the day, everything would be more vibrant in tone and there'd be longer shadows."

"Hm, yes, I suppose so." Johann put his glass down on the table next to his chair and placed the thin cheroot he'd been smoking in a Limoges ashtray. He looked at the professor. "I see you made sure your daughter studied art as well as languages," he said.

"Actually, much as I'd like to take credit, Dorrit developed that all on her own," the professor admitted.

"With a great deal of help from museum curators," she grinned self-consciously. "Especially those at Berlin's National Gallery of Art."

"Then you've been taught by the very best. Would you like to see one of Jungkind's works that's signed?"

"I'd love to!"

Johann got up. "Professor Zache, will you join us?"

"No, thanks. I'll stay put and keep the wine and nutmeats company. Paintings are not my forte. My ignorance on the subject would quickly become embarrassing."

As she toured the drawing room, Dorrit took inventory of a host of celebrated signatures. She found a Renoir, a Signac, and a Cezanne sharing the same wall.

"This house belonged to my maternal grandparents before it passed to my mother," Johann was telling her. "But my parents are solely responsible for the art collection. When they inherited the place, it was full of ghastly old family portraits, of the flat and somber variety. Brown and gray being the predominant colors. Pictures that looked as though they'd been painted posthumously. They were grouped on the walls like a grim reunion of the dead. The one over the fireplace in the library is the only one that did not offend. And so it hangs there still."

Dorrit remembered that she'd been curious about it last week.

"The girl is so pretty and so cheerful. Who is it?" she now asked.

"My mother at a tender age."

"She had a plucky and sweet smile."

106

"And you're wondering how she could have brought forth a scoundrel like me?"

"Oh, no! Not at all." Flustered at how close he'd come to reading her mind, Dorrit forgot to ask about the artist. "What happened to the other portraits?" she said instead. "The somber ones?"

"They were banished to the basement long ago."

"Oh, dear, such rude treatment! The damp can't be very good for them. Aren't you afraid of ghostly visits?" Dorrit laughed.

"No, because I can't help but think that my ancestors approve wholeheartedly of the change. Surely colorful landscapes are preferable to dour faces. Even their own."

Johann drew Dorrit's attention to the opposite wall. They crossed the floor and stopped in front of a large, exquisitely detailed pastoral, a country scene so realistic, she was tempted to test the air for the sweet fragrance of the fields and flowers.

"That's by an American artist," Johann explained when Dorrit couldn't tear her eyes away. "Ridgeway Knight. He lives and works in Paris."

"It's beautiful," Dorrit murmured. "Your parents had wonderful taste."

"And a good amount of dumb luck. Many of these artists are now coming into their own and gaining recognition."

"Have you done any collecting?"

"No."

"Just as well, I suppose. It'd be difficult to find space on the walls." Dorrit glanced around. "I'd hate to see any of these sent into exile."

Johann agreed.

"If I were to collect anything, it'd have to be something very small, so it'd fit in a drawer."

"Insects?" Dorrit cocked her head and smiled up at him, recalling that she had once collected butterflies.

"God forbid! My housekeeper has an abhorrence of bugs. Dead or alive, none would be tolerated."

"Stamps then?"

"Stamps would be practical," Johann acknowledged.

Dorrit was examining the signed Jungkind, when she suddenly felt a hand on her elbow. It was warm, yet it made her shiver. Was Dr. von Renz signaling they ought to move on?

107

She turned toward him and surprised herself by colliding with his shoulder. He didn't step back and kept his hand on her arm. His touch caused a strange warmth to flow through her, but as pleasant as that was, her inexperienced soul began to suspect that he was acting improperly. He was certainly standing much too close for any meaningful conversation.

A heady silence fell between them.

Bewildered, Dorrit lifted her eyes and looked at him; one corner of his mouth was pulled into a half-smile. The breath caught in her throat, and try as she might, she couldn't draw her eyes away. His amused and speculative gaze held her strangely captive. She felt his hand slide up her arm and cup her chin. For a moment he seemed to be studying her face as if something about it pleased him. Suddenly he bent his head down.

Something pounded in Dorrit's ears; heat was rising into her cheeks, and realizing that she was holding her breath and becoming dizzy from the effort, she quickly stepped back in order to requisition some equilibrium. It would be the height of bad manners to sink to her knees from lack of air.

As she backed away, she saw a shadow of disappointment cross Dr. von Renz's fine features. His jaunty half-smile vanished. His hand let go of her and fell to his side. As she widened the distance between them with another step backwards, she herself felt an odd sense of regret.

Discreetly brushing the back of her hands against her burning cheeks in a futile effort to cool them, she turned toward the wall and forced herself to concentrate on another painting. But it was with great reluctance that she came back to reality. She had never before been stirred to feel carnal passion and could hardly credit its existence. But if this strange tempest in the pit of her stomach was the harbinger of the exquisite emotions she'd read about in *pfennig* novels, maybe she ought to welcome it, because in the books everything always turned out so wonderfully.

"Shall we rejoin your father?" Dr. von Renz asked in the next instant, as if the awkward moment had not passed between them. He offered his arm, which she gladly accepted because her legs felt like jelly and might not support her.

Had he been on the verge of kissing her, she wondered all the way across the carpeted expanse of the drawing room. No, he wouldn't have dared, not with her father sitting in the adjoining alcove. Then again, maybe he would? Instinct stronger than reason told her that neither her father nor anyone else could have stopped Johann von Renz from doing exactly as he pleased. And with that thought came the painful knowledge that apparently he had changed his mind and decided not to kiss her.

Disappointment settled in hard and fast, because Dorrit suddenly owned up to the fact that she would have liked being kissed. Of course, a moment later she was ashamed of herself for such hedonistic thoughts. It wasn't like her at all.

"Papa," she cried on the way home, "how could you possibly tell that man that I'd be delighted to go to a dance?"

"'That man...'"? Professor Zache frowned. "Surely a poor way to refer to a host who has just entertained us lavishly. And furthermore, insisted we be on first name basis. I'd expect you to remember that his name is Johann."

It was midnight, it had snowed steadily for hours, and the snorts of the horses laboring through the deep drifts, could be heard inside the coach. And likewise, afraid that Schmidt, riding outside in the driver's box, might hear her, Dorrit now lowered her voice to a whisper.

"I will remember, papa. Just tell me why you gave your consent when you know I can't dance! I can't distinguish a simple box step from a sarabande!"

"Don't fret so, child. You can learn."

"Learn? By New Year's Eve? It's only a week away!"

"I've raised you to be clever. Your mind is sharp. Surely a few fancy steps won't overwhelm your feet."

"Dear God, I am destined to die of shame! I just know it."

"Nonsense, my dear. Dancing will come naturally for you. It's in your blood. You'll see."

"In my blood? Please, papa, make sense. You yourself have admitted to having two left feet. Was my mother perhaps a Bolshoi ballerina?"

"No, dearest, that she was not." Professor Zache sighed and closed his eyes as if he was experiencing pain. He leaned his head back against the thick squabs in the comfortable coach. It was clear to Dorrit that he did not wish to say any more. And, of course, she didn't push him. She was all too familiar with his stony silence whenever her mother was mentioned.

EIGHTEEN

Dorrit accepted Johann's arm and made her way along a labyrinth of gilded corridors inside the Beckstein *schloss*, her expensive taffeta hems and her confidence both scraping the floor.

Johann stopped briefly at the top of a wide staircase, where he handed a card to a steward clad in white satin breeches, red coat, and powdered wig. In the next instant, the man's sonorous voice buffeted Dorrit's ears as he loudly announced:

"The Baron von Renz . . . and . . . Fraulein Zache!"

At the sound of an unfamiliar female name, three hundred of Berlin's most illustrious citizens fell silent in the salon below and raised their eyes, some fumbling with their monocles to get a better look at the girl on the arm of a very popular member of their set.

Caught completely off guard by Johann's title, Dorrit snatched a sideways glance, then wished she hadn't. Dressed in black formal attire, white silk cravat, and ruffled shirt with diamond studs in place of buttons, this . . . ah, *baron!* was much too handsome for his own good—*her* own good. God forbid she falter this early in the evening! And as she now found tenuous footing on the softly carpeted stairs and began a slow descent, she silently thanked her father for his largess.

As soon as the stores opened after the Christmas holidays, he'd fished into the well of the old pendulum clock that held their life savings and handed her a fistful of crumpled marks, with the instructions to buy cloth for a gown and a pair of pretty dancing shoes. When she questioned the prudence of squandering money on fancy clothes, since the outfit she'd worn last Thursday night could be put into service again, he snorted: "The time has come to invest, not save! Mind you, buy the very best!"

She had and was now glad of it, because this was clearly no ordinary dance, neither were these people your garden-variety mortals and suddenly swallowing convulsively, Dorrit realized that besides proper evening apparel, there were other things she should have concerned herself with. Namely, what was expected of her once she reached the salon? Was she supposed to curtsy when presented to the host and hostess? Was happy New Year a proper greeting? She knew about poets and politicians, but her father had not thought to include deportment at balls in her education, and sooner or later this deficiency was bound to become apparent. Moreover, she had come to this magnificent ball without knowing how to dance.

Miserable and tense, Dorrit turned cold with the scope of her predicament. She could fake a number of things, but her clumsy feet would fool no one. She and Hannah had practiced various dance steps on the kitchen floor until the green linoleum began to show bare spots; still, she knew her limitations. And suddenly panicking in the face of her shortcomings, she inadvertently dug her clammy fingers into the fine fabric of Johann's sleeve.

"No one here kicks, scratches, or bites," he whispered, leaning so close, she felt his warm breath on her face. And placing his hand across the one that was digging into his arm, he grinned: "Their tongues occasionally sting, but they've not been known to draw blood. I'll personally vouch for their behavior."

The promise wrung a tight laugh from Dorrit's throat. Later she was to wonder if this was the moment she fell in love with him.

"If only you could also vouch for mine," she now said. "I'm not very good at . . . at formal balls." Anything formal, she would have liked to add, but she didn't want to confess too much all at once. Why ruin his good humor this early? He'd soon enough discover that he was saddled with a social illiterate. Besides, there was no time to explain. They had reached the salon, where Johann engaged expertly in the formalities necessary to move along the glittering reception line.

Dorrit was presented to the Count and Countess von Beckstein, tonight's hosts; their son, Wolfgang Reinhard; and their daughter, Monika Marie, standing with her affianced, Herr Anton Jurgen Widermann. The aging Duke Henry Francis von Strelitz and his much younger duchess were also part of the reception committee, and with so many names to concentrate on, Dorrit neglected to curtsy. But since no one swooned, perhaps it wasn't expected. And after clearing this first hurdle without a scratch, she hoped to lose herself in the crowded salon and catch a second wind.

But that was not to be, because Johann's friends, and there were many of them, tripped over each other in order to make her acquaintance. However, after the initial introductions, these same people quickly lost interest when it became clear that this newcomer didn't have anything to add to their light and frivolous banter. Of course, Dorrit knew that Ciro's was a supremely elegant nightclub in Berlin and that San Sebastian was an exclusive seaside resort in Spain. But inasmuch as she had never been to either place, she could hardly sing their praises or lament their flaws. Thus forced to remain silent among the revelry, she concentrated on the scenery, which did absolutely nothing for her self-confidence either.

Never before had she seen such magnificent gowns and such dazzling jewelry. It was as if she were standing in the middle of a stage production where everything was too fabulous to be real. And though she had never actually thought of herself as poor, Dorrit suddenly felt impoverished.

One thing was clear. Her gown didn't measure up, this despite the fact that she had slaved for three days sewing it and the material had been very expensive. While working on it, she'd been convinced the silvery blue taffeta was stunning, but here, in this sparkling salon, it lost its shine and looked as pale as water. Moreover, she was wearing no jewelry except for small pearl earrings her father had given her last year on her seventeenth birthday.

Her spirits hit the skids. Immersed in conversation and laughing uproariously with his friends, even Johann seemed to have written her off. And who could blame him? Among these fine feathers, she was as nondescript as a patch of dry grass.

Still, while wallowing in self-belittlement, Dorrit did her best to look unconcerned, carefully molding an expression of bored amusement such as she'd seen on the young Duchess von Strelitz in the receiving line. However, when a stunning raven-haired girl in a yellow gown of exquisite style approached, Dorrit's composure slipped. Wildly envious, she stared at the girl throwing greetings and kisses all around before blithely leaving her escort on the perimeter of the cluster of people and elbowing herself through. Without acknowledging Dorrit with as much as a look, she put a hand on Johann's arm, and, judging from the warm smile he bestowed upon her, he was obviously pleased to see her. Dorrit bit her lip as she watched the girl chatter and laugh and toss her head just so to assure the huge diamonds in her ears caught the light and everyone's attention.

It seemed a lifetime before Johann remembered that Dorrit needed to be introduced to this shimmering butttercup of satin and tulle. And when he finally did, Louisa von Tirpitz—bless her—didn't waste a minute before pulling Dorrit aside for a private *tête-à-tête*, which pleased her so immensely, she failed to see the malicious gleam in the girl's eye.

"So, do tell me." Louisa, though hardly able to contain her burning curiosity, lowered her voice lest someone discover her obsessive interest. "How did you and Johann meet? I mean...who exactly introduced you?"

"Oh, no one did," Dorrit was happy to report. "We met quite by chance."

"Really? When?"

"Last December."

"Last December?" Louisa looked surprised, her eyes narrowing with her next comment. "That's an awfully long time ago. Strange that we haven't seen you before this."

"Well, we only had a brief encounter at an inn and immediately lost track—" Dorrit clapped her mouth shut. Too late she realized her mistake.

"How quaint." The words carried a horrible accusation.

Dorrit's cheeks flushed a deep pink further damning her.

Enjoying Dorrit's mortification, Louisa prolonged the moment as she opened her reticule and popped a mint into her mouth.

"Want one?" she asked as an afterthought, and held out the small tin container.

Dorrit shook her head.

"So..." Louisa put the mints back and closed her purse, "you obviously managed to...ah, track Johann down."

Having recovered, Dorrit now seethed. Of all the impudence!

"No," she said hotly, "he became acquainted with my father."

"Well, now that's convenient. What does your father do?"

"He's a professor at the university. At the medical school."

"I see." A bit of respect slipped into Louisa's voice. "It figures then," she said and shrugged. "Johann spends all his free time at that musty old place experimenting on cadavers. I suppose your father does that as well?"

"No. His hands are not steady enough. He only lectures now."

"Which is much more sanitary of course. One can catch dreadful diseases tinkering with the dead." Louisa shuddered and changed the subject. "Where do you live?"

"On Niederlag Gasse."

Dorrit realized Louisa was nosy to the point of being rude, but decided it was better than being ignored. And just in case someone was looking their way, she fashioned an expression of intense fascination, as if she and Louisa were discussing world-shattering events.

"Niederlag?" Louisa von Tirpitz raised a finely penciled eyebrow. "That's in Charlottenburg? Isn't it?" It was obvious from her tone that she knew perfectly well it wasn't.

"No. It's near the university."

"Oh, just off Unter den Linden then?"

"Not exactly. A handful of blocks east of there."

Louisa's nose wrinkled imperceptibly, that general location was not a chic residential area by any stretch of the imagination. She eyed Dorrit with a queer twist on her lips before she seemed to remember that she had abandoned her escort. Without ceremony she turned on her heel and weaved through the crowd. A moment later, Dorrit saw her smile at the plain-faced, but exquisitely dressed gentleman. He turned red to the roots of his blond hair with pleasure.

After Louisa's departure, when no one picked up the slack, Dorrit felt more deserted than before and toyed with the idea of seeking refuge in the ladies' lounge. Johann had his back to her, she probably wouldn't even need to excuse herself. And once she'd visited the lounge, she could try to strike up a conversation with some of the elderly guests seated in the various comfortable corners of the salon. As a rule, older people had poor eyesight and might not notice her lackluster appearance. And although they usually liked to discuss the weather or their rheumatism, she might be lucky and find someone with an interest in politics.

But before she could melt away, Johann looked around as if

114

he had temporarily misplaced something.

"Ah, there you are!" he said and slipped an arm around her waist, spoiling her vanishing act. "Enjoying yourself?" he asked without a drop of penitence for having neglected her all this time.

"Yes, very much," she lied stoutly.

"Wonderful." Switching into French, he suddenly ignored everyone else and asked if she would care to dance.

"I suppose we could make a gauche effort while waiting for the music," she said, her expression mocking him for his oversight; the musicians in the adjoining ballroom were playing . . . yes, but only scales and chords while warming up their instruments.

"Ouch!" Johann laughed. "You've exposed another weakness! It seems that I'm tone deaf." He tightened his grip on her waist and persisted in French. "Let's keep that between the two of us. All right? I attend the opera regularly, and it'd be very embarrassing if word got out."

"I see what you mean." Dorrit smiled and wondered if Johann would hold her so possessively if he was contemplating the ambrosial attributes of the beautiful Louisa with the flashy earrings?

The doors to the ballroom were eventually thrown wide open as the orchestra burst forth with the first dance. A Strauss waltz.

"Now may I have the pleasure?" Without waiting for an answer, Johann took Dorrit's arm and led her through the doors among a glittering mass of people spilling into the enormous ballroom.

Her heart sank to abysmal depths. Her kneecaps went rigid. The moment of truth had come. A moment she should have dreaded all along, and would have, except there had been too many other things to worry about.

Perhaps she could fake a twisted ankle, she thought miserably. After a few steps, she'd falter anyway, so any injury was bound to look convincing. But could she fool a doctor, who'd presumably insist on examining her? No. It might be safer to claim a blinding headache; stomach cramps she already had—no pretense was needed—but it was too embarrassing to mention.

In desperation, Dorrit finally chose the path of least resistance: candor. Forcing a pretty smile, and with a measure of grit inherited from some unknown ancestor, she came clean.

"I feel obliged to warn you," she said in French, since Johann appeared to prefer it and she needed to stack the deck in her favor, "my footwork could prove to be a painful lesson in self-defense. Even for the most accomplished partner."

He threw back his head and laughed.

"Well, in that case, permit me to prove my courage." He bowed elegantly.

Dorrit allowed herself a moment to enjoy his laughter and gallantry.

However, an instant later, she found herself on the dance floor, begging her feet to make the proper moves. Frantically counting in her head while visualizing the diagram Hannah had sketched on the kitchen floor in chalk, she followed Johann's lead, managing not to scuff his shoes disproportionately to her foul-ups. Thank God, it was a waltz! She and Hannah had practiced it more than any other dance, and Dorrit happily discovered it was much easier to dance with Johann than a giddy maid. Soon she could stop counting and leave her feet to their own devices while she took stock of the glorious ballroom.

A dozen chandeliers, twinkling with thousands of prisms, sent flashes of light darting among the dancers on the polished parquet. Garlands of fresh flowers were draped around sconces and gold-leafed mirrors along the walls of the vast room. Tall potted palms stood bunched together in the four corners like tropical forests, and dressed in eighteenth-century satins and powdered wigs such as the steward at the top of the stairs had worn, the musicians played on a raised platform surrounded by miniature fruit trees forced into bloom, releasing a sweet fragrance. However, whenever she and Johann brushed past other couples, Dorrit suspected the scent in the ballroom actually came from the expensively perfumed ladies. Indeed, she was so mesmerized by the people and the scenery it never occurred to her that as she scrutinized her surroundings she was tit for tat attracting equal billing and was fast becoming the subject of heated speculation.

Who is she? everyone wanted to know, and how could someone never before seen in their midst have snared the most sought-after Berlin bachelor for this prominent occasion? Those who had been introduced could not recall her name from the Register. But, of course, they were spared any mental exertion once

Louisa von Tirpitz passed the word that Dorrit Zache's father was a school teacher and resided somewhere in the industrial part of town. This rumor was not believed by everyone, however. Those of a more charitable nature reminded each other that no one here consorted with individuals of no account. Certainly the Baron von Renz would not insult the Count and Countess von Beckstein by expecting them to entertain a commoner.

Eventually, general consensus subscribed to the opinion that Fraulein Zache was a foreigner. Many declared they had heard her speak French. Others suggested she might be Italian. Obviously her gown was of Italian design because no Berlin or Paris designer would sanction such simple lines and display so much shoulder. Fraulein Zache's dress looked suspiciously akin to a Roman toga.

The music stopped. Johann was leading Dorrit toward one of the champagne tables, when he spotted Kurt Eckart arriving with Lillian Schindel; the two had been an item since meeting at the chancellor's ball this past spring.

"There's someone you must meet," Johann said, forgetting all about the champagne. "A colleague of mine. The girl with him is a cousin of my friend in Bernau."

Dorrit tried to look for all the world as if she wanted to meet these people or die. And in preparation for another frosty confrontation with a glamorous female, she took a steadying breath and kept her head stoically erect as she walked through the crowd, never realizing the posture made her look positively regal.

Kurt had a nose for quality and couldn't take his eyes off the astonishingly beautiful girl at Johann's side, something the latter noticed with a measure of dry amusement as he made the introductions and Dorrit and Lillian shook hands.

"Well . . . well . . . well!" Kurt said when it was his turn to exchange courtesies. "So you're the little lady they're placing bets on in the salon." He took both of Dorrit's hands and put them to his lips with exaggerated ceremony.

"Bets?" Dorrit asked. "Whatever on?"

"On the number of sutures needed to repair Kurt's jaw!" Johann interjected and issued his friend a withering look, one that would have sent a lesser man to his knees. Of course, Johann was well aware of this crowd's penchant for gambling; he was a gambler himself, but only on horses and cards. Were the damn idiots tonight actually betting on the shelf life of Dorrit's charms?

"Gambling is second nature to half the people in this room," Lillian chirped in, attempting to rescue the moment. "I don't give the silly fops a second thought. Some have been known to bet a small fortune on how many flies will land on a sugar cube. Can anything be more droll?" She didn't wait for a reply before quickly changing the subject, efficiently deflecting attention from Kurt's unfortunate mentioning of bets to bubbly details about the Christmas festivities at the Konauers'. "We missed you this year, Johann," she said and slapped his arm playfully with her fan.

"And Johann missed our announcement," Kurt blurted. "Believe it or not, Lillian has agreed to marry me."

"Oh!" Lillian cried. "Now you've spoiled my surprise. I wanted to wait and announce it at midnight." She looked exasperated, although she was actually tickled pink that Kurt had brought it up. After all, that indicated a certain amount of eagerness on his part.

Johann waylaid a passing waiter carrying a tray of champagne flutes.

"Here's to spoiled surprises," he offered as glasses were passed around. "And to long life and much happiness for you both!"

"Thank you. But you won't be hearing wedding bells for a while," Lillian said over the noise of clinking glasses. "We haven't set a date yet. If you wish to hear assorted details, Kurt will clue you in." With that, she turned her back on the men, pulling Dorrit to the side. She wanted to share her tale of woe with another female; men rarely had the patience to listen.

"Although Kurt and I are engaged," she began with pharisaic drama once she'd secured Dorrit's undivided attention, "we haven't agreed on a date yet because we can't be married for at least another year. Maybe longer? Kurt insists on being established first. He's got some absurd notion into his head about making do on his salary. Which is perfectly silly considering what they pay new doctors nowadays. We won't starve, mind you, but we can't live on such a pittance either. And he stubbornly refuses to accept financial assistance from his family. Or from mine."

"I think that's commendable," Dorrit said.

"Well, I don't! I'll be turning twenty-one next month. I'm practically an old maid."

Dorrit laughed; it was impossible to imagine that someone as pretty as Lillian could ever be a spinster.

"Not you!" she said. "If you were ten years older you'd never pass for an old maid."

"Thank you." Lillian smiled ruefully. "But try telling that to my parents. They want grandchildren in the worst way. I had a brother who died from scarlet fever a number of years ago. My parents have never recovered and probably won't until I present them with some grandsons. In fact, they have already expressed their wish to have my first son named Gerhardt. After my brother. Isn't that a bit morbid?"

"No. I don't think so," Dorrit said, and although the subject of a dead boy was not a cheerful one, she was enjoying herself in Lillian's company.

Every bit as glamorous as any female at the ball, Lillian was not commensurately haughty, nor did she seem to notice Dorrit's lack of finery. A row of perfectly matched diamonds glittered around Lillian's neck, and her pink panne velvet gown was so lustrous, it, too, reflected the light and dazzled the senses. She had a soft, round face, a small, pert nose, a mouth like a rosebud, and short, curly blond hair that was a striking contrast to her brown eyes. Next to Louisa von Tirpitz, Lillian was the most attractive girl in the entire ballroom, Dorrit decided in a burst of gratitude for her overture at friendship. In the same vein, she also concluded that although Kurt was not as tall and athletically lean as Johann, he was imposing. His features were well defined, his chin firm. His hair was jet black, his eyes the pale blue of a winter morning. Dorrit guessed he had a good sense of humor and laughed readily, evidenced by the small lines around his eyes.

NINETEEN

Dorrit felt a hand on her elbow and, turning away from Lillian's pleasant chitchat, thought it to be Johann's. But no, it was Kurt's. She experienced an odd pang of disappointment and wondered why that should be.

"I've been granted permission to ask for one dance," Kurt grinned. "Which should attest to the strength of the friendship with yours truly."

"Just one!" Dorrit laughed, exhilarated with her sudden popularity. "We'll have to make it memorable then."

"Not too memorable," Johann raised an eyebrow, then turned to Lillian, inviting her to the floor.

It was a polka. Dorrit had been right about Kurt. He had a great sense of humor, which he displayed every time she tripped him.

When the music stopped, he had barely returned her to Johann and waltzed away with Lillian, when Count von Beckstein appeared and requested a dance with Fraulein Zache. Johann had no choice but to surrender Dorrit and then go in search of the countess to assure she was not idle while her husband danced. She was not. Philip von Brandt had arrived, solo as usual, and was delighting the eminent hostess with his suave footwork.

Johann smiled inwardly as he watched Philip von Brandt. His blond hair meticulously combed, there was not a crease to be found on his black recherché attire. And of course, Philip banked on his early chivalry with the countess to carry him through to the end of the evening, when he might be in dire need of forgiveness. The distinguished Herr Doctor von Brandt, member of one of Berlin's most celebrated families, and religiously sober in the laboratories at Wirchow, was not expected to remain tidy or temperate more than an hour at any social function.

As his eyes continued to roam the floor, Johann decided to cut in on *Graf* Zollern and dance with Louisa; he might as well

120

get it over with, because if he didn't dance with her, tongues would wag, which wouldn't be fair to her. But while dancing with the girl he had once considered marrying, he craned his neck to catch sight of another wearing a neat French braid entwined with blue ribbons matching the color of her simple taffeta dress.

"You seem distracted, Johann," Louisa murmured after a while, when his distinct lack of attention became all too apparent. "You haven't once commented on my gown."

"Forgive me," he said automatically. "It's lovely of course. Yellow becomes you."

"Then I shall wear it again for the kaiser's ball next month. Just to please you," she purred. "My father will be honored that evening. You are planning to attend, aren't you?"

"I'll be there." Johann looked at the beauty in his arms but felt not the slightest stirring. "Is Wilhelm finally putting your father in charge of the fleet?"

"Yes. He's to be made state secretary for the navy. Isn't it exciting? But it's still very hush-hush. So don't breathe a word until it's official."

"My lips are sealed."

"He'll be ever so famous, you know. He might even have a city *platz* named after him one day."

"Well deserved, I'm sure," Johann drawled, and immediately regretting his tone, tried to make amends with a glamorous smile. Its seductive charm was not lost on Louisa, whose nose was out of joint because he was not her escort tonight and, moreover, appeared to be settling his affection on someone of no consequence. Even with the mentioning of the kaiser's ball, he had not taken the hint and secured Louisa for that important affair. She quite forgot herself now as she succumbed to an insane jealousy that had smoldered all evening.

"Everyone is in a stew, wondering about the girl you're with," she said. Surely if Johann realized what people thought of the chit, he'd own up to his mistake, which would do much to ease a cramp in her chest.

"Hmm, is that so?"

"Yes. No one recognizes her of course. And she doesn't have anything to say for herself which is of no help to those of us who'd like to be friends. I don't suppose her family is listed?"

"They're not."

121

"Well, in that case, I should think she'd want to talk a little bit about herself to help us get to know her better. I hate to pass along gossip, but everyone says she is strange. You know, too quiet. And just imagine if the kaiser makes an appearance. It's rumored he might stop in later. One can only guess what she might say if she were presented to him."

"Dorrit Zache will make a good account of herself."

"I sincerely hope so. But I can tell you, I tried very hard to be pleasant earlier. It got me nowhere. And, of course, there's the problem of her gown."

"Her gown? A problem?"

"Well, not a problem exactly. But it is rather plain." Louisa wrinkled her nose for effect. "And another thing, everyone knows that a French braid is much too causal a coiffure for a ball. And—"

"I think I get the picture, Louisa."

"Of course. It's a good thing—"

"It's a good thing," Johann interrupted, "that fashion hasn't entered into any of my conversations tonight. I'd be pronounced a half-wit on the spot."

"Do be serious, Johann! You are no half-wit. Which only deepens the mystery."

"Mystery?"

"Yes. As to what you can possibly talk to Dorte, er, Doris about?" Louisa was experiencing some difficulty with Dorrit's name; perhaps because it wasn't listed in the Register.

"I see." Johann adopted a grave expression rather than risk laughing out loud. "Actually, Louisa, you can put your pretty head at ease. On the drive here tonight Fraulein Zache and I had a lively exchange about Fontane and Dehmel."

"For heaven's sake, who are they?"

"German poets."

"Oh." Louisa's lips fashioned a sour little moue; this conversation wasn't going exactly as she'd hoped, but that didn't keep her from continuing. "Well, you're obviously temporarily..." She shrugged wearily. "Uh, what's it called?" When Johann didn't come to her rescue, she lunged ahead. "Anyway, whatever it's called, some have placed bets. *Graf* Zollern wagered his finest race horse that your interest in the girl would be very temporary. He gave it a month. At the most."

"Pity."

"Pity?" Louisa looked confused.

"I hate to see the man lose a good steed. He can hardly afford it."

There was a pause in the music. Johann returned the suddenly speechless Louisa to *Graf* Zollern before he stopped at a champagne table. From there he saw Count von Beckstein keep Dorrit on the floor between dances.

"Now, as I was saying," Count von Beckstein was loath to relinquish Fraulein Zache, because it was rare to find a young woman with an appreciation for the workings of government, "we must pray the kaiser can frustrate von Bulow into resigning. A full term under his chancellorship could spell trouble with our foreign neighbors. The man's too militant. Too aggressive."

"Maybe he's trying to get all the unpleasant confrontations out of the way early in his term," Dorrit suggested.

"Yes, I suppose he could be putting Europe on notice. Warning everyone that he's a chancellor to be reckoned with."

"Unlike his predecessor," Dorrit smiled.

"Schillingfurst was an old fool." Count von Beckstein realized the orchestra was again playing. "And so am I, it seems, not to have noticed the music. Let's have another dance!" He took hold of Dorrit and fell into a box step she was happily familiar with.

They had circled the floor only once, when she saw a steward frantically wind his way through the dancers. He was quite out of breath when he reached the count, and after first begging Dorrit a million pardons, he whispered something in his ear. Count von Beckstein flushed a deep red.

"Good God!" he exclaimed. "Here? Now?" He looked around as if the sky was about to fall but that such a calamity would please him. "Forgive me," he said to Dorrit, suddenly as breathless as the steward. "It seems the kaiser is about to grace our festivities with his presence. His coach has just pulled up. The kaiserin has been ill with influenza, and so I didn't really expect His Majesty tonight." The portly count pulled a handkerchief from his breast pocket and wiped it across a sudden sheen on his forehead. "I must leave you and go find my wife." His balding head pivoted around in all directions. "Ah, there she is! Over there . . . dancing with that rascal, Philip von Brandt!" Stuffing the handkerchief back in his pocket, he took Dorrit's arm, plowed unceremoniously through the crowd to tap Philip on the shoulder. "Philip, my good man, please see to Fraulein Zache!" To Dorrit he said: "We'll finish our dance later, my dear." He kissed her hand, then quickly headed for the salon with his wife on his arm.

Philip grinned at Dorrit; he knew exactly who she was because Johann had told him about the gorgeous redhead he planned to take to this ball. And although the room was full of beautiful women—some with red hair—none were this lovely. He bowed elegantly.

"Philip von Brandt at your service," he said, still grinning. "Now, let me guess . . . you are with Johann tonight?"

"Yes." Dorrit smiled, surprised. "How did you know?"

"I will tell you while we dance." *And maybe,* Philip thought, *maybe she'll tell me why I have the feeling we have met before.*

Amazingly, Dorrit was thinking the very same thing until she suddenly realized that this was the doctor she'd seen months ago in the emergency ward at Wirchow the time her father's bronchitis needed medical attention. But she vowed not to bring that particular occasion up, because if she remembered correctly, she'd been so wild-eyed and unkempt that the nurse who was sent home with her avoided any close contact. Something Dorrit had blamed on the smelly scarf from Herr Ziegler's shop.

Kaiser Wilhelm and his entourage of distinguished aides had entered the salon.

"Eduard!" The kaiser's eyes twinkled merrily; it was clear he enjoyed pulling surprises.

"You do us a wonderful honor, Your Majesty." Count Eduard Hugo von Beckstein bowed.

"I trust the kaiserin is convalescing comfortably?" the countess added, recovering from her deep curtsy.

"I can report that she has made a remarkable recovery and would have liked to come tonight," the kaiser assured the countless, "but alas, Dr. Renvers wouldn't allow it. So here I am. Quite alone!"

This declaration was a flagrant insult to the esteemed acolytes hovering at his side, none of whom thought to correct the kaiser, who without further ado strolled into the ballroom where the orchestra abruptly fell silent. The guests, too, fell silent when they realized Germany's exalted monarch was in their midst. Bowing, they parted like the biblical waters to allow him to walk among them. Bejeweled fans fluttered as the emperor strolled about, stopping now and again to exchange cordialities with a chosen few.

When he came so near that Dorrit could see the blue of his eyes, she drew in her breath with awe at his persona and the splendor of his regalia. Dressed in white and gold with a colorful red sash across his chest, heavy with medals and honors, he looked every inch a king.

"Would you like to meet him?" a voice on her right wanted to know.

"More than anything," she answered dreamily, without thinking, and never guessing that Philip was serious.

"All right, come on then!" Philip took her arm and pulled her forward.

"Oh, no! I didn't mean it! Not literally, anyway." But Dorrit's protest came too late, because the kaiser had recognized Philip von Brandt.

"Philip! How nice to see you."

Philip executed a dandy bow from the waist. Dorrit curtsied deeply, keeping her eyes on the floor.

"So tell me, . . . how is the general?" Kaiser Wilhelm was evidently still addressing Philip. Dorrit didn't dare look up to confirm it.

"My father suffers the weight of his years, but he is otherwise quite fit."

"I'm glad to hear it. He is a great man, one Germany can be proud of. We wish him a long and comfortable retirement."

"Thank you, Your Majesty. And may I present Fraulein Zache!"

In a state of panic, Dorrit sank further to the floor in what she hoped was an adequate and graceful show of reverence. She didn't know what else to do. Offering her hand seemed too plebeian.

"Fraulein Zache, I'm delighted!" The kaiser reached out and lifted her chin, when she seemed intent on studying the floor.

Dorrit snapped her head back.

"Your Majesty, the pleasure is all mine," she said, a small nervous smile forming on her lips. Dear God, was she expected to say anything more? She cherished the hope he would quickly move on.

He didn't. He continued to study her face before suddenly announcing:

"I should like to dance!" He turned to Count von Beckstein who'd followed close on his elbow. "Eduard! Why is the orchestra silent?"

Count von Beckstein motioned for the musicians to earn their keep.

"A waltz? Your Majesty?" he asked.

"Yes. A waltz to the New Year. Will you give me the pleasure, Fraulein Zache?"

"It would be a great honor," Dorrit heard herself say. But she didn't recognize her own voice.

The crowd fell back, leaving an expanse of parquet that to Dorrit loomed as immense as Alexander Platz, and then some. The kaiser put his good arm on her waist; she placed her left hand on his shoulder and with the other, held out her skirts. She had read about his lame arm and instinctively guessed that this was the way to manage the situation.

From across the ballroom, Johann watched her with quiet pride.

A few feet away, Louisa's face took on a strange color, which didn't compliment her gown.

After the kaiser's waltz, Dorrit was immensely popular. As if ordained to a higher plateau by the kaiser's dance, the grandest of endorsements, every gentleman in the ballroom wanted a turn with her, and none minded her faulty steps when anything other than a waltz was played. While she reveled in her new-found prominence, Johann seemed content to stand at the champagne tables, glass in hand, watching the dance floor as he talked with other men similarly occupied.

When a sumptuous buffet, every dish known to the discriminating palate, was served in the salon, Johann pried her away from a Hungarian duke to eat supper with her. And once the last piece of succulent lobster had been dipped in butter and disposed of and the countdown toward midnight drew near, he jostled the crowd to secure her a wonderful spot by the large windows facing the sloping lawns, where a fireworks display was being readied.

As the clock struck the hour of midnight, the ballroom erupted with shouts of Happy New Year, while one rocket after an-

126

other exploded in the black heavens outside, sending brilliant showers of stars cascading toward earth. Groups of people in the ballroom broke into song and amid this noisy hoopla, Johann turned to Dorrit and lifted her hand to his lips.

"Happy New Year, darling," he whispered.

Darling . . . ? Her heart leapt into her throat, cutting off her voice, and before she could regain it, the magic of the moment was gone. It was too late to respond with anything she'd not later regret as inadequate. Besides, a number of ladies were coming by to throw their arms around Johann, including Louisa who had regarded Dorrit with nothing less than cold hatred ever since the kaiser's waltz, and who now pretended she simply didn't exist. But determined not to be separated from Johann in the melee—after all he had just called her darling—Dorrit stood her ground. She kept her hand on his arm, only to wish she hadn't, because she now heard him call everyone darling.

That he used the endearment so cavalierly hurt. But after the initial wave of disappointment passed over her, leaving only a small knot in the pit of her stomach, she took a deep breath, pushed out her chin, and clenched her fists in a silent vow that no one, least of all her aristocratic escort, guess her foolishness in taking any affectionate word at face value. Used so freely, it obviously meant nothing. And since she had always entertained an active contempt for vapid emotions, she quickly tossed off any and all romantic illusions.

She jettisoned another illusion as well when she realized that she was peculiarly unpopular with the same gentlemen who had happily walked through fire for a dance earlier. Popularity was evidently a fleeting thing in this crowd; not a single man made a pass at her. So far, only Count von Beckstein and Kurt had come around to give her a peck on the cheek. Lillian had embraced her, which was nice, and Philip had meant to kiss her, except he was now so drunk, he kissed Johann instead. All the other gentlemen who approached, abruptly backed off after they discerned something in Johann's face. Was he silently telling them that she wasn't worth the trouble?

Yes, obviously, and with that sorry conclusion the last of the stardust settled heavily into the bottom of Dorrit's novice heart like pebbles thrown into a pond, spreading ripples in ever-widening circles of diminishing pride. Pride? She abruptly took herself by the scruff of the neck. *Pride . . .* her father had once said . . . *will see you through the worst of times. Never let go of it!* Now heeding his advice, she greedily gathered it about her because it was all she had left.

When the last dance of the evening was announced, Johann turned to her and claimed it. And as his smooth steps guided her effortlessly across the floor, Dorrit wondered how she could possibly have enjoyed any of her earlier partners. But she didn't dwell on her present luxury. And in order to keep her susceptible heart from intimidating her good sense, she began a conversation such as Count von Beckstein had enjoyed.

But Johann couldn't be baited, and after a while she gave up, figuring the champagne had dulled his taste for talk; something he confirmed a moment later when he pulled her so close that her breasts were pressed against the black satiny lapels of his jacket, which alone guaranteed to stifle any dialogue. She was silently questioning the propriety of such intimacy, when she heard soft whispering near her ear. She missed much of it to the din of the music, until she suddenly felt his lips graze her temple at the same time she distinctly heard:

"Darling, . . . I'm madly in love with you—"

"What . . . !"

Her back became a picket fence, and her heart stopped with such a jolt, she felt spasms of real pain. She stumbled and tripped them both to within inches of the floor. His shoulders shaking with muffled laughter, Johann regained their dignity, and once their feet were again in sync with the music, he repeated himself.

"I love you," he said. "I'm afraid you'll have to marry me or risk having a madman on your conscience."

Dorrit died and went to heaven.

Of course, an instant later, she realized that like Philip, Johann was intoxicated. While she had danced with others, he had spent a great deal of time at the champagne tables. It was quite clear that he was simply toying with her. But for some unfathomable reason, she didn't mind. And although she knew that when he sobered, he wouldn't remember his proposal, she'd treasure the extravagant memory for as long as she lived.

TWENTY

As soon as Herr Baron and Fraulein Zache were comfortably settled inside the coach, Schmidt clucked to the horses, pushed his hat down over his ears, pulled a woolen muffler up over his lower face, and drove away from the Beckstein *schloss* among a succession of sleek carriages, moving along the dark road like a miniature train. Johann spread a fur blanket around Dorrit's waist, for although the chill inside the coach was tempered by the hot bricks under the floorboards, the winter morning was bitterly cold and the ride from Dallgow to Berlin was a long one.

After a few moments of gazing out of the window at the bleak wintry landscape of frozen fields and darkened farmhouses, Dorrit sank back against the soft cordovan cushions. Exhausted from hours of dancing and unaccustomed rich food and champagne, she abruptly fell asleep.

As the carriage springs creaked and the wheels rattled across the uneven cobblestone streets on the outskirts of Berlin, she awoke with a start to discover that she was lying with her head in Johann's lap, his arms cradling her.

"Good morning," he said, grinning down at her and brushing a silky lock of hair off her forehead with the back of his hand.

"Good mor—? Ohh!" Mortified and instantly awake, Dorrit sat up, smoothed her hair, and checked the buttons on her coat. "I . . . I'm sorry. I c . . . can't imagine how I could have fallen asleep," she mumbled, quickly throwing off the last traces of drowsiness while carefully avoiding Johann's eyes. It was much too awkward to look at the person whose lap she'd brazenly occupied, and so she turned toward the window and pretended to study the dark streets passing by outside. Soon they were taking a shortcut through Tiergarten toward Pariser Platz and would shortly be rolling along Unter den Linden.

Johann pushed back the carriage curtain on his side, noted the route as well and wished he had told Schmidt to stay on the city streets to buy more time. He hadn't expected Dorrit to sleep the entire trip. With the hour growing short, he now pulled her chin around so that she faced him.

"There's precious little to see in the park at night," he said in reference to her continued interest in the scenery. "Dare I hope that your studied silence means you're giving undivided attention to my proposal?" He groped under the fur blanket and found her hand. "Or did you think me drunk and disorderly on the dance floor and not to be taken seriously?"

Dorrit's lips twitched in a small grin at his correct assessment. But her amusement was arrested an instant later by wonderful shivers playing on her spine as his fingers laced themselves tightly with hers. She nodded.

"I thought so," Johann grimaced. "Well, for the record, with the exception of an adventure with strong spirits at the age of fifteen, I generally don't disgrace myself in public. Of course, I admit that an offer of marriage on a crowded ballroom floor was somewhat out of character. But it was extended under conditions of complete sobriety and with a great deal of forethought." When Dorrit slanted him a dubious look, he challenged her. "I can prove it!"

He let go of her hand, leaned over to fumble with the latch on a compartment under the seats facing theirs, and had soon extracted a small box stashed among maps, gloves, and other paraphernalia.

"Here," he said handing her the box. "Here's something that caught my attention at Friedlander's a few days ago. It was in the display window, and the minute I saw it, I decided it would suit you perfectly because it matches the color of your eyes. Indisputable proof of forethought." He grinned, devilishly sure of himself.

Friedlander's? Dorrit didn't trust herself to speak. Her mind was in turmoil; first by the knowledge that Johann's proposal had been real and now was accompanied by a gift from the most expensive jeweler in Berlin. Her father had cautioned her never to accept anything other than candy or flowers from a gentleman since expensive gifts could compromise one. And with that warning ringing loud and clear in her ears, how could she possibly accept a gift from Friedlander's. Of all places! At a loss of what to do, she simply stared at the box not daring to open it. Except for Ivar Kozlowski many years ago, and a young man in Warsaw who'd sent her flowers anonymously until her father discovered his identity and cooled his ardor by means she never learned of, she'd had no experience with amorous members of the opposite sex. And positively never with a sophisticated individual such as the one sitting next to her.

"Go ahead open it!" he now urged her. "It won't bite." He smiled ruefully. In his memory, women never needed pressure to accept his gifts. Curiosity finally got the upper hand and discarding her father's time-honored advice, Dorrit unfastened the gold filigree clasp. The lid fell back, revealing an enormous stone, cut in the shape of a heart, attached to a gold chain.

She gasped. She knew the gem was real, because only a genuine emerald could sparkle so brilliantly in the dim light of a coach lamp.

"It is exquisite," she breathed, unable to tear her eyes away. *Thank you* was on the tip of her tongue, except words seemed too inadequate.

Figuring Dorrit might never get around to trying it on before they reached Niederlagstrasse, rapidly bearing down on them, Johann lifted the jewel off its velvet cushion and nimbly fastened it around her neck.

"There we are!" he said and looked pleased with himself. "I was right. It suits you. Now we'll just have to get a dress to go with it. Green, maybe? Frankly," he pretended to consider something of enormous importance, "it will probably look best on white. White as in . . . ," he reached out and cupped her chin in his hand and looked at her with a penetrating and serious mien, "white as in . . . wedding gown. What do you say? Yes?"

Dorrit tipped her face up; the shiny heart around her neck and the one beating wildly inside her rib cage were both reflected in her eyes. No other response was needed.

A smile flashed across Johann's face. He shifted in his seat and slipped an arm around her shoulders, while his left hand caressed her delicate satin-smooth cheek, on its way down to tenderly cradle her neck. His eyes traveled to her lips and lingered there as his smile disappeared, relaxing the corners of his mouth.

Dorrit felt a strange craving; she knew she was about to be kissed, and unlike last Thursday, she was not going to discourage him. She wanted to be kissed and in the worst way. Her

131

hands slid stealthily up the smooth wool of his overcoat and came to rest against his lapels a moment before her fingertips touched his chin. The invitation was as unmistakable as her innocent touch was powerful, and, keeping a firm check on his passion so as not to overwhelm her, Johann found her mouth in a soft hesitant kiss testing the contours of her lips, as if he were merely exploring any number of possibilities before proceeding.

A sweet madness rushed over Dorrit with this exquisite intimacy. And as his mouth grew more insistent, heat and fire fought for space inside her pounding heart. She clutched savagely at his lapels, soon winding her arms around his neck in an attempt to garner support from the very person who was undermining her balance.

Johann kissed her with an unhurried thoroughness, and when he finally pulled away to allow them both to draw breath, his fingers fanned into her hair. Tousling the silky curls that had come undone from the French braid, he held her head between his palms and looked at her with something equivalent to reverence.

Dorrit felt she had reached the summit of happiness, and although her lips were bruised from the raw force of his, she ached for more of the same. She looked at him, a silent request written on her flushed face.

"I think you've had enough kissing for one night," he teased in an odd, choked voice as he ran his fingertips across her moist lower lip to calm its trembling. "Besides, I can no longer trust myself to behave." He fastened a button on her coat he'd tackled with before coming to his senses. "We'd better tidy up. I can't bring you home like this. Your father will take one look at you and throw me out the door before I can convince him of my honorable intentions."

Dorrit squelched a giggle at the vision of her less than robust father hauling this giant of a man out of the apartment.

"Papa is a staunch believer in a good night's sleep," she said and looked cagily at Johann. "You have nothing to fear. He was planning to go to bed early tonight and welcome the New Year from beneath the warmth of his eiderdown. He explicitly said that since he was entrusting me to the company of a true gentleman, he saw no reason to wait up."

Johann laughed.

"Your father is a clever man, but he's obviously a poor judge of people. His faith in me is flattering. Pray he never learns of his misplaced trust. Let's suffice to say that I'm not worthy of his daughter, an auburn-haired princess who tonight danced with the emperor."

"Please! Don't remind me!" Dorrit wailed. "Dear God, to think how easily I could have tripped His Majesty!"

"He didn't look the least bit worried," Johann smiled. "On the contrary. He appeared to enjoy himself immensely. And not just the waltz."

"What else was there?"

"Your attention to his small talk. It's well known that in addition to raking a keen eye over the ladies, the kaiser enjoys smothering them with gallant conversation."

"Gallant conversation? Hah! Absurd is more like it. Can you imagine . . . he claimed I had Romanov eyes!"

TWENTY-ONE

Hannah had taken Friday off to go visit a sister who was ill, and so Dorrit was in the kitchen when her father returned home from the university.

"Hi!" she called out to him. "Tea will be ready in a minute. How was your day?"

"Wonderful!" Dr. Zache chuckled as he hung his coat in the hall closet and retrieved the books and papers he'd balanced on the umbrella stand. "For once I was allowed to conduct my lecture in peace. Your fiancé wasn't there to baffle me with polemic abstractions."

"I know. Johann told me he'd be in surgery all afternoon and would miss your seminar."

Herman Zache came into the kitchen to give his daughter a kiss.

"That young doctor works awfully hard for someone who doesn't have to make a living."

"That's because he enjoys it, papa."

"A man with inherited wealth who does not succumb to a life of leisure," the professor mumbled to himself, "is refreshing, indeed. Oh, and ... ah, Dorrit, I think I'll take a spot of brandy with my tea."

"Brandy?" her eyebrows shot up.

"Yes. And without any moralizing my dear." Herman Zache turned and walked out of the kitchen.

Dorrit found the rarely used bottle in the cupboard and put it on the tray she carried into the living room a moment later. Her father was seated in the sofa, rubbing circulation into his hands. The newspapers were strewn on the old plaid-covered ottoman by his feet, but his lecture notes and books were carefully placed on the corner of the small table next to the sofa, leaving enough space for the tea tray. The one window in the room, though small, allowed enough late afternoon sunlight to filter through; it was not yet necessary to switch on any lamps. The scene was tranquil and ordinary, except for Herman Zache's odd reluctance to meet Dorrit's eyes as she set out cups and saucers and poured the steaming brew. He looked at a wooden peg in the floor with great fascination, as if he were contemplating dissecting it, and finally around the room as if seeing it for the first time.

Having asked for brandy, a drink he used strictly for medicinal purposes and only in the dead of winter, Dorrit wondered if he was now conscience-smitten. After all, it was mid-April, the weather was warm and pleasant, and his lungs weren't troubling him. But she stirred a spoonful into his cup without comment and sweetened her own tea with a bit of honey. She pushed a plate of *linzertorte* within her father's reach and, settling herself down in the wing chair, picked up one of the newspapers he had brought home and waited for him to relate details of his day. He always did; it was a pleasant afternoon ritual.

But he remained silent. He sipped his drink and reached for a thin wedge of *linzertorte* without a word. Dorrit checked one of the more reliable clocks in the room. Not yet five. Good. It was still early. She had plenty of time before Johann arrived. She had already fixed her father's supper, his favorite chicken soup with dumplings was simmering on the gas burner in the kitchen; all that remained for her to do was to change into her blue suit. She and Johann were going to dinner and the theater tonight, and since Hannah wasn't here to help braid her hair or fashion a chignon, she'd simply wear it loose.

Reflecting on the wonderful evening ahead, Dorrit put the newspapers down and studied her father, disturbed by his continued silence. His brow was deeply furrowed and he was clawing at his beard as if bothered by troubling thoughts. Moreover, he looked pale, something she hadn't noticed when he came home. Was he not feeling well? Always alert to any change in his appearance, Dorrit grew worried. Something was wrong. Maybe she ought to stay home with him tonight.

"Papa, are you feeling all right?" she asked at length.

"Yes, of course, *bubeleh*."

Bubeleh? Dorrit's heart felt a pleasant little lurch with the endearment; he hadn't called her that since she was a little girl.

"You might be a bit less frugal with the brandy though." Herman Zache held out his cup between his palms like a mendicant monk and nodded toward the bottle. When she reached for the teapot first, he shook his head and smiled queerily. "Just some brandy."

"What? Without tea?"

"Yes."

Dorrit hesitated.

"Come, . . . come, now. The stuff can't possibly harm an old fellow like me."

Against her better judgment, Dorrit poured, then watched him closely as he put the cup to his lips, and in order to take his mind off the brandy—God forbid he wanted more—she began to describe her day, most of which was spent at the dressmaker for the final fitting of several gowns, including her wedding dress. It was hard to believe that professionals were making her entire trousseau, when sewing was something she could do perfectly well herself. But overriding her objections, Johann had hired the famous Madame Mimieux and given Dorrit carte blanche. She was just now telling her father about the splendid progress on a green chiffon gown sprinkled with flecks of gold thread, when he stunned her by reaching for the brandy himself, splashing it clumsily into his cup.

"That's it, papa!" she cried. "Keep that, but you'll get no more." Dorrit took the bottle away from him, plugged in the stopper, and got up to put it in the kitchen before he could drink himself to death. She returned to see him shudder as the burning liquid cut a path down his unseasoned throat. He had apparently tossed some of it down too fast; tears sprang to his eyes. In the next instant his chest heaved with a sudden and frantic struggle for air as a convulsive cough wrenched his body.

"Dear God!" Dorrit flew to the sofa and beat her palms on his back. "Papa! Papa!" she cried.

"I . . . I'll thank you not to p . . . puncture m . . . my lungs," he sputtered when he had recovered enough to speak. "I'm fine. Really, I am. I just haven't learned to drink this infernal stuff like a gentleman." He realigned his shoulders inside his baggy tweed jacket, took off his glasses, and ran his sleeve across his watery eyes before reaching into his pocket for a handkerchief.

Dorrit looked at him; his face was contorted and twisted with an expression she didn't recognize. She watched as he blew his nose and folded the handkerchief and put his glasses back on. Like he had done earlier, he again avoided her eyes, now staring into the distance with the detached mien of a daydreamer. But his reverie appeared to be anything but pleasant.

A strange fear crept over Dorrit. There was something on his mind, something terrible, the room was heavy with it. Of course, she was used to his lachrymose moods; he had suffered them in the past. But this was different somehow, if only because he had never before tried to drown his misery in brandy. She moved closer, took his hand, and put an arm around him. Now that her wedding day was fast approaching, perhaps he was already feeling lonely, already tasting the emptiness of the apartment once she was no longer living here.

"Won't you reconsider Johann's offer," she said in an attempt to dispel his desolation, "and move with me to Lindenstrasse? The house is so very large. Your bedroom alone would be as spacious as this entire apartment. There's room for all your books and clocks and—"

"No, my dear." Herman Zache shook his head to stop a sales pitch he'd heard a hundred times since January. "That place is entirely too big. I'd wander around lost half the time and never get any work done. Besides, how could I ever put my feet up without damaging all that fancy furniture?"

"Those are poor excuses, and you know it."

"Maybe...." Dr. Zache sighed. "The truth is I have moved too often. When you and I finally made it this far west, I promised myself that I'd never again budge. Berlin is my home now."

"Grunewald is Berlin."

"I know." The professor nodded. "Which means you'll be nearby. And that makes me very happy, *bubeleh*. So why spoil anything by asking an old man to adjust to new surroundings?" Herman Zache reached for his cup. As Dorrit watched him drink, she held her breath expecting another attack. It didn't materialize.

"But there is something else," he said and put the cup down, his hand suddenly shaking so violently, he almost dropped it, "something else that might spoil...ah.... What I mean to say...there's something I must tell you." He cleared his throat noisily, pulled another handkerchief from an inside pocket, only to fold and refold it as if he needed to occupy his hands.

"What, papa? What is it?" Dorrit prompted when he hesitated. "Have you . . . have you had some bad news?" she asked gently a moment later when he continued to waver and she was reminded of former times when "bad news" meant depression followed by upheaval in terms of a quick move to another town.

"No. I've had no bad news. Except for the fact that I'm a coward."

"You're no such thing!"

"Unfortunately, I am. And it's not news. It's something I've known for a long time. Longer than I care to admit. I have spent a lifetime, . . . your lifetime, my dear, cowardly deluding myself—"

"Deluding yourself?" Dorrit interrupted. "I don't understand. What do you mean?"

"I mean . . . I've been . . . lying. An ugly word, indeed, and so I prefer to use delude. Still, it's all the same. The truth is . . . I've lived a lie while fabricating one cowardly excuse after another . . . convincing myself that each . . . each deception was justified because you were too young."

"Too young? For what?"

"The truth. I found a thousand reasons to keep it from you, all the while promising myself that I would tell you later when you were grown and old enough to understand. And now, lo and behold, I discover that you are grown and about to be married, yet I still lack the courage and find that I need a wretched crutch." The professor eyed his cup with disgust. "Plus, I'm cowardly pinning my hopes . . . on . . ." he faltered and began kneading his hands.

"Pinning your hopes on what?"

"Your . . . happiness. As well as your financial security, now that you're about to step into the very niche you were born to occupy."

"Born to? What niche, papa? What are you talking about?"

"Johann. I'm talking about Johann—"

"Johann?" Goose bumps were creeping up Dorrit's neck; her father never spoke in broken sentences or riddles. Was the brandy causing it? "What does this absurd talk have to do with Johann?" she asked.

"Everything, I'm afraid. Because I'm hoping that if you find hatred in your heart for me or think ill of your mother, he'll help you bear it. You'll have a husband. You no longer need a father. A devious one, at that."

138

Devious? Dorrit sat perfectly still; an unreal atmosphere descended over the small room. Hatred for her father? Preposterous! And how could she ever think ill of a mother she'd never known?

"Does any of this have something to do with Saint Petersburg?" she asked softly.

"Y . . . yes."

"Well, don't torture yourself, papa. I know I was born there. I also know that you changed our name when we left."

"Huh?" the professor looked at her, shocked.

"I've known it for years."

"Years? But . . . but how?"

"I came across some papers once."

"Papers?"

"Yes. My birth certificate."

"Oh. . . . Why didn't you tell me?"

"Because I didn't care where I was born. And it certainly didn't matter to me that you'd shortened our name. I figured you had a good reason. Also, I didn't want to upset you by asking questions. You always had so much on your mind. You were often . . . well, you know, sad."

"I see." The professor looked around for the brandy bottle before he remembered that Dorrit had put it away. He steadied himself with a deep breath instead. He had far worse to tell her. Finding the birth certificate was just the tip of the iceberg.

"I kept you in the dark, *bubeleh*," he began slowly and reached for her hand, "to shield you from the drama surrounding your birth. You were completely innocent in a tragedy that touched us all . . . touched your mother in particular. I guess I simply hoped to spare you for as long as possible. But more than that, I kept silent because I wanted to keep you to myself. It was selfish of me."

Drama? Tragedy? Selfish? Dorrit flinched at the strong words and, again, when her father's grip on her hand tightened, plunging the huge diamonds in her engagement ring into her fingers.

"I loved your mother very much—"

"I've always known that, papa. Tell me about her."

"I will. I should have done so long ago. I regret my silence. I kept quiet because to say anything meant to say too much.

139

There was no halfway. It was all or nothing. And like I just said, I was afraid to lose you." Herman Zache's shoulders sank into the sofa cushions, as if pushed there by an iron block, invisible but of considerable weight. "Being selfish . . . being a coward is a terrible thing—"

"And you're not!" Dorrit almost shrieked, recalling the many times her father had picked up and moved, facing an unknown destination fearlessly. "You are the bravest person in the world. And the most unselfish!"

The professor sighed; he could take no comfort in her heated declaration, for she had not yet heard his story.

"When you came into the world," he began in a raw whisper, uttering the words slowly as if each letter and syllable caused him a great deal of pain, "healthy and strong less than six months after my marriage to your mother, I knew of course that you weren't mine."

What! Dorrit's heart catapulted into her throat.

Not his! Her mind screamed in protest at such utter nonsense, but she couldn't move her lips to phrase a single word. Not his? Her wonderful father was not her father! It couldn't be! It was simply not possible! She wanted to rail at him for saying such a ridiculous thing. But all she could do was stare in bewilderment, shock silencing her because she realized he would never ever say anything of the kind if it weren't absolutely true.

"Your sturdy condition," he continued, "despite your very 'premature' birth, confirmed what I had already suspected when your mother showed signs of pregnancy immediately after our marriage. But it didn't matter to me in the least. I loved her desperately. And—the father be damned—I loved the child she was carrying. I cried with profound happiness the first time I held you, and I thanked God for the miracle of your birth. I vowed to raise you with all the love I had to give and all the worldly possessions I could provide. With regard to the latter, I fell sadly short."

"No . . . no you didn't! Don't say that!" Dorrit's protests were barely audible, strangled as they were by a rubber band somewhere in her throat. Hot tears blurred her vision. She blinked to keep them from spilling over; her father had more to tell her, and she must not distract him with the flow of tears.

"It was not until many months after your birth that your

mother told me who he was." Dorrit held her breath. "I never asked. I didn't care. I was your father. Legally at any rate, and no man could love his child more than I did. But the day came when she insisted on telling me. I suppose she wanted to clear her conscience and not play me for a fool any longer. I was a doctor and knew a full-term baby when I saw one. Something she realized. And as her story poured forth, it became quite evident that she still loved the rascal who had violated her. Which didn't surprise me."

"Why? Wh...who w...was he? Is he...still alive?"

"No, he is dead, *bubeleh*. He preceded your mother to the grave."

"Oh..." Dorrit felt an odd stab in her heart.

"His name was Alexeyev Romanov. He was the only son of a Russian grand duke who enjoyed direct blood ties to the czar. And like most of his class, he was spoiled rotten. But I can tell you that he was a handsome devil. I'd seen him riding through the streets of Saint Petersburg with his entourage of highborn friends. He sat well on horseback. Girls swooned while older women twittered about his dashing looks. He was blond, and his eyes were a vivid green, peculiar to that branch of the Romanovs. You inherited those eyes, my dear, and his proud chin. But you have your mother's auburn hair and pretty nose. And, thankfully, you have your good old-fashioned practical common sense from me." The professor allowed himself a half-chuckle.

"Your mother, rest her soul, was neither practical nor sensible. She was a hopeless romantic. She believed the prince loved her because for a time he gave up his other liaisons and only had eyes for her. Which was not surprising. She was an enchanting creature. But she was also young and naive. Alexeyev, an experienced rogue, filled her ears with pretty words, her heart with hope, and her hands with expensive trinkets. She mistook it for commitment. And had someone told her that a Russian aristocrat would never take a Jewish wife, she probably wouldn't have believed it. Of course, when she told him that she was expecting his child, he vanished on a grand tour of Europe. A long absence that included a visit with his relatives in the Danish Royal House, where his betrothal to a Danish princess was soon announced. Since the bride-to-be was only twelve, the wedding could not take place for another three years. But news of this eventual royal union was celebrated with much fanfare at home in Saint Petersburg.

"In her desperation, knowing the prince was lost to her, your mother turned to her parents, who, in turn, immediately approached me. I was well known to the family. They had a number of children, and I was frequently summoned when one of them was ill. However, suddenly, I was being invited to the house as a regular guest. I found myself at their supper table with the lovely Arina sitting next to me, smiling and listening to my didactic conversation with rapt attention.

"I was forty-one, she was only sixteen, and when her parents pulled me aside one evening and suggested that I marry her, I was quite frankly stunned. Of course, once I established that they were perfectly serious, I happily agreed. In my elation, in my incredible joy, I never stopped to question why this beautiful girl would consent to have me for a husband. I was neither handsome nor clever with sweet words. But I was dependable. I made a good living as a surgeon, and under the delicate circumstances, which I was not aware of then, a dependable husband was more than Arina's parents could hope for. Also, I had no living relatives who might raise bothersome questions and burden them with requests for a dowry. They had three additional daughters to marry off and no money for a matchmaker.

"As for myself, I felt that I was the luckiest man on earth. I had never been one with the ladies, and now, this dainty female was being thrust into my arms. I was completely infatuated. I never thought such happiness could be mine.

"Weeks into our marriage, when it became apparent that Arina was expecting and already pretty well along, I realized of course that I was not the one responsible. But I said nothing. I played the proud and happy father-to-be. I loved her unconditionally. A love that was not reciprocated. Her smile, her flirtations faded the day we took our vows. Still, I lived with the false hope that after the baby was born, she might look at me differently. It was not to be. After you arrived, she grew even more distant, and no matter what I did to cheer her, a strange quiet sadness overwhelmed her. I realized it had nothing to do with me. If I'd been twenty years younger, a sight more handsome and witty, she could no more love me than she could forget Alexeyev.

"When word spread that the prince had returned from his

142

travels, a strange anticipation began to glow in her face. I saw signs of her former brightness. She took an interest in eating and shopping and dressed herself and the baby each morning as if she expected an important visitor. She must have thought that he would come to see her. And he did. But she never knew. I alone saw him.

"As fate would have it, I was home with a bad case of bronchitis and your mother had taken you to her parents' house for a few days to avoid any contagion. And sure enough, on one of those days, one early afternoon, he came visiting. He came alone. No entourage. His horse neighed, and since I was expecting no visitors, certainly none on horseback, I immediately went to the window, peered out, and was not really surprised to see who the caller was. I was only surprised that he had troubled himself to learn that Arina was married and where she now lived. And, of course, I was angry. And jealous. Had I been in good health, I would have shown myself. I would have stormed out of the house and given him a piece of my mind, damned be the consequences!

"But ill as I was, I could only hover behind the curtains and pretend that no one was at home. I watched him get off his horse. He walked up to the door, raised his hand and prepared to knock at the precise moment I suffered a terrible coughing spell. The sound of it shocked him. He had not expected to find a husband at home in the middle of the day. He turned on his elegant heel and rode off without a backward glance. I never told your mother that he had come. I still believed she would forget him, that time would work its miracle. I was a fool.

"Some months later, all of Saint Petersburg was buzzing with terrible news. The prince had been killed in a duel. Rumors abounded the duel had been with the irate husband of one of his new conquests.

"Arina became demented in her grief. She shut herself off from everyone. Even from you. She grew listless, thin, and in her weakened state, she contracted pneumonia. There was a dreadful epidemic that winter and it quickly claimed her tragic young life. But she died oddly happy. There was a smile on her feverish lips when she took her last breath. I think she went to her eternal rest believing Alexeyev was waiting for her in a better world and that death would grant them what life had denied."

Burning tears were streaming down Dorrit's face. She

couldn't move a muscle to wipe them away. But it didn't matter. Her father was past the point of being distracted by tears, and the flood from her eyes loosened the painful pressure in her throat.

Herman Zache went on with his story.

"Shortly after your mother's funeral, and quite by chance while tending patients in the city hospital, I heard gossip that sent chills through me. Word circulated that as soon as the official mourning period for Prince Alexeyev ended, his family expected to find and raise a child they had reason to believe was his. I could only guess that as he lay mortally wounded, he must have unburdened his conscience.

"I became deathly afraid. I didn't know what he'd told or how much. But I knew one thing, that armed with even the flimsiest of leads, they'd soon enough find you and take you away from me. The power of the palace was at their disposal. And I was a Jew. It'd be child's play for a Russian aristocrat to arrest me. My life and property was expendable. Any trumped-up charge would send me to Siberia, if not the gallows. Jews had taken part in the assassination of Alexander II, and it was well known that his son and present czar, Alexander III, believed an underground plot was being hatched to end the Russian monarchy. It was generally accepted that Jews were at the core of any conspiracy.

"I made desperate plans to flee. I told no one. Not even your mother's family. They were sure to be questioned. It was better for them if they knew nothing. I left everything behind except for important documents and whatever money I had. Carrying you in my arms, I walked out of the house in the middle of the night and made my way to the railway station on foot, leaving no hackney driver to bear witness. Likewise, I didn't buy tickets from the stationmaster. Hiding in the shadows behind a closed kiosk, I jumped aboard a westbound midnight train just before it pulled away from the station.

"Several stops later, a tired conductor came around, and from him I bought tickets to Minsk. But even as the train lumbered toward daylight, putting comforting miles between us and Saint Petersburg and I no longer needed to fear immediate arrest, I was not to experience any peace of mind. From that time forward, any curious look or suspicious comment from total strangers drove me into a panic. I dared not make friends be-

144

cause they might ask questions. Even after I changed our name—made it very German—I lived in constant fear of the long arm of the czar's police. I became paranoid. I stopped practicing medicine and became a teacher. I lied about our origins. I lied about your birthplace. I taught you foreign languages. German and French. And, of course, we continually moved west. There were bloody *pogroms* throughout Eastern Europe. We had barely left Kiev, when two thousand of our people were rounded up and murdered for no godly reason except their Jewishness. But it was well known that Berlin was a haven for Jews and other expatriates. And so . . . I slowly worked my way here."

Dr. Zache fell silent. His story finished, he loosened his grip on Dorrit's hand and looked at her with trepidation, afraid at what he might find. Knowing he had lived a lie, would she denounce him? Would she be angry that he had robbed her of a royal upbringing?

As he searched her tear-stained face, he found no bitterness on her brow, no condemnation fell from her lips, her eyes remained soft and bright; soft with love, bright with tears. The love he recognized, the tears he understood, and when her arms suddenly fell around his neck, a profound happiness swelled in his chest.

"Popi," she cried. "I . . . I love you so."

His heart squeezed with joy. *Popi?* She hadn't used that engaging term since she'd been a little slip of a girl. Smiling, he stroked her hair just as he'd done that night when he fled Saint Petersburg, carrying her onto the train, fear of discovery all but buckling his knees. Her sweet little face had been wide-eyed with wonder, the snow had swirled about them, and she had clung to his neck, afraid of the huge belching locomotive already moving as he jumped onboard, afraid to lose her popi in the darkness.

"Had I confessed earlier," he now said, his voice thick with the memory, "you could have returned to Saint Petersburg and—"

"And what? Don't say such a thing! I would not have wanted to go back. You're my father, . . . my family! I could never love anyone but you."

"Except that good-looking doctor, eh?"

"Y . . . yes." Dorrit whispered, smiling through her tears.

"Well, then, you'd better go change your dress, my dear. Just leave me with the tea tray." Dr. Zache turned to consult a clock on a shelf above the sofa. "*Ach*, time is running!" he said and patted her hand. "And you'd better wash your face," he added and ran a clean corner of his handkerchief across her wet cheeks. "It certainly won't do to let Johann know you've been crying. He might never forgive me for being the cause of it. I'd like to remain on good terms with my son-in-law."

"Should I tell him?"

"By all means! When the moment is right, tell him everything." Dr. Zache suddenly grinned. "I dare say he'll be pleased to learn that half your blood is blue. Besides, I'm sure he has often wondered how a homely creature like myself came to have such a beautiful daughter."

Dorrit pinched his nose playfully and got up. On her way out of the living room, she switched on some lights and stopped to draw the curtain across the window.

Without either one of them noticing, dusk had settled in.

TWENTY-TWO

The fifth of May dawned to a cloudless blue sky. By afternoon, it was as warm as a day in August, and riding through the streets of Berlin on the way to her wedding, Dorrit's heightened senses tingled with the rare beauty of the city.

Colorful petunias spilled from window boxes along Niederlagstrasse, giving the drab apartment buildings a whole new look. The goddess of peace, riding her golden chariot atop the Brandenburg Gate at the foot of Unter den Linden, glinted in the sun. Pariser Platz just beyond these impressive portals was alive with beds of red tulips bending showy heads on fragile stems in deference to the benign breeze. The sound of the dancing waters in the sparkling fountains in front of the Adlon Hotel was as sweet as the sound of song birds. Sunday strollers sauntered leisurely along the forested paths of Tiergarten, where majestic groves strutted their new foliage and children chased each other across lawns dotted with glossy buttercups. Somewhere in the distance, sonorous church bells chimed the hour of four, one carillon right after another, in turn, so as not to compete for God's ear all at once.

Searching for reality, Dorrit looked wistfully at her father. Was she dreaming, and would she momentarily hear his dear voice calling: "Wake up, Dorrit! Wake up! It's time for school."

But she heard no such command. Her father sat silent next to her, an unmistakable impish twinkle in his eyes softening his stern deportment, while the constant smoothing of his gray beard bespoke of a touch of nerves. The carriage was presently rumbling west along the elegant Kurfurstendamm and under the dabbled shade of the ancient oaks dominating its center divide.

"Oh, no!" Dorrit cried when Schmidt, at length, pulled into Lindenstrasse, where as far as the eye could see, elegant rigs were haphazardly parked on both sides of the street. "We're late, papa! Everybody is already here."

"Well, I should hope so," the professor said and climbed out of the carriage first so he could help Dorrit down. "Guests are supposed to arrive ahead of the bride."

"Oh . . . ? Of course, . . . yes. How silly of me." Dorrit alighted and adjusted the voluminous folds in her gown, a sheer dotted Swiss that fell like a white cloud to her ankles. She gazed at the magnificent house, recalling that frigid December day a few months ago when she'd stood by these same gates, wondering if she dared pass through them.

The grand villa looked infinitely more approachable at this time of the year, she decided. The large windows reflected the warm golden tint of the afternoon sun, and the gnarled vines clinging to the wrought-iron fence drooped with grapelike clusters of light purple. Blooming white lilacs along the south wall of the house scented the air, and urns lining the walkway were filled with yellow primrose and pink sweet William.

Suddenly Dorrit bit her lip, reached for her father's arm and rushed him inside the gates and up the footpath, in blind determination as though she feared the curtain would fall on this exquisite scene if she delayed another minute.

The hall was milling with the last of the guests making their way toward the salon and the neat rows of folding chairs set up for the ceremony, a civil ceremony with respect to the different religions of the bride and groom. Actually, Herman Zache would have agreed to a church service, had Johann insisted, so anxious was he for this marriage to take place. Security for his precious daughter in a world where he himself had experienced none, was first on Dr. Zache's list of priorities, and he would personally and devoutly plead his case before his creator before long. Herman Zache did not expect to make it through another winter.

Gerlinde and Lillian had been watching for Dorrit, and as soon as she and her father stepped through the front door, they whisked them into the library, quickly closing the doors behind them before any of the guests were the wiser to the bride's presence.

Hans was flower bearer and was huddled in a corner of the library with his grandmother, who was giving him last-minute instructions and fretting over several creases in his handsome navy sailor's suit, complete with white piping and a shiny brass whistle attached to a gold braid and placed in a breast pocket, where Ursula dearly prayed it'd remain.

The minute she saw the bride, she straightened and greeted Dr. Zache and Dorrit effusively. The Konauers had met both Dorrit and her father this past January, when Johann brought his fiancé to Bernau. Now, with a look toward Gerlinde that said *I've done my best with the boy,* Ursula left for the salon where her husband was saving her a seat in a front row.

Smug and excited at being included in the ceremony, when his sisters were banished to an upstairs room with Fraulein Kruse, Hans was careful not to forget his instructions. No sooner was his *oma* gone, when he dashed over to Uncle Johann's desk for a boutonniere of lilies of the valley, which he handed to the bride's father. Running back to the desk a second time, he grabbed a bouquet of red roses tied with white silk streamers and proudly presented them—upside down—to Dorrit.

"Thank you, Hans," she exclaimed and carefully righted the delicate spray before she bent down to give the boy a kiss. "They're beautiful!"

Grinning from ear to ear, Hans shuffled back to the desk. This time to pick up the basket of rose petals he was to distribute along the aisle when he marched into the salon at the head of the procession.

Glancing at the clock on the mantle, Gerlinde gave him a gentle shove in the direction of the closed French doors.

"Time is drawing near," she said. "Be a good boy and go stand guard. Alert us the minute the music starts."

Feeling enormously important with this assignment, Hans skipped across the floor, kicking up the corner of a Persian Tabritz.

"He's so excited, one would think that he was getting married," Gerlinde said, shaking her head indulgently as she bent over to straighten the rug before quickly turning her attention back to Dorrit. "I hope to live to see the day. But now, let's have a proper look at you." She tilted her head, her eyes misting with emotion as she made Dorrit pivot full circle. "You look like a dream. I often wondered why Johann didn't marry. When he telephoned us on New Year's Day to spring the surprise, I thought he was rushing to the altar because—" she suddenly giggled self-consciously, "well, because he was . . . pushing thirty, getting dreadfully old, and beginning to worry about the lack of an heir.

But now, you know what?"

Dorrit shook her head.

"Now I see that he was just being very picky and waiting for perfection." Gerlinde dabbed a lace handkerchief at the corner of her eye and all of a sudden threw her small thin arms around the bride. "Years ago, Johann became family to me," she cried with happy emotion. "It was the day I married Karl-Heinz. He and Karl-Heinz were like brothers, so I guess I just kind of took it for granted that he'd be mine as well. And in the same manner I hope you'll think of me as a sister from this day forward. You, Lillian, and me . . . the three of us! Sisters! How about it?"

"There's nothing I'd like more," Dorrit stammered, on the verge of tears with Gerlinde's offer.

Lillian stood apart and looked askance at the scene, which was not to say that she was displeased with Gerlinde's pact. Still, the latter tended to get all mushy at the slightest provocation, which, as Dorrit proved, was catching and not particularly kind to one's complexion. Therefore, Lillian staunchly avoided any maudlin emotion for the time being. After all, she would shortly be on display walking down the aisle. Kurt was in the front row, and she certainly didn't want him to see red-rimmed eyes or blotched cheeks.

"Are you nervous?" she now asked Dorrit and, instead of hugs and kisses, stroked the frothy bridal gown gathered at the waist with a pearl encrusted sash. The scooped neckline was softly scalloped as were the elbow-length sleeves. Dorrit's abundant hair was pulled back from her face and held in place by a band of tiny silk rosebuds sparkling with dewdrops. Real diamonds, Lillian guessed, figuring Johann would insist on that.

"Very," Dorrit admitted. "I collected butterflies once. To properly display them, I had to stick pins through their thoraxes. I am afraid it's payback time. They're needling me now and swarming in my stomach."

All three girls giggled. Gerlinde reached up to adjust Dorrit's off-the-face veil; not that it needed it, but she needed to keep her hands busy.

The hum of subdued conversation in the salon ceased abruptly and was replaced by a lively Mozart minuet. Flailing his arms, Hans jumped up and down by the doors to get his mother's attention.

"All right, all right!" Gerlinde patted the air with her palms to calm him and turned to Dr. Zache, who was happily perusing the abundant bookshelves. "We've just had our two-minute warning," she said to him. "The next piece will be the Mendelssohn. I promised Johann we'd be alert. If I miss my cue, he might be tempted to dunk my head in the punch bowl later." She laughed, abrogating any such fear, and pulled a compact from her beaded purse. Making a face at her own reflection, she pushed some thin strands of pale blond hair under the netting of her hat and adjusted the layers of chiffon in her blue gown. Lillian was similarly dressed—in yellow—and so confident in her appearance that she didn't need to check the mirror. Gerlinde stopped preening.

"All right. Is everyone ready?" She snapped the compact shut and banded the small group together.

A moment later, they walked across the hall behind Hans, who sprinted ahead. When the appropriate moment came, Gerlinde gave him the signal to proceed into the salon. In his excitement, he emptied the entire basket of petals on the floor just inside the doors. Tossing an exasperated look of sincere apology toward the bride, Gerlinde motioned Lillian to ignore the spilled flowers and follow Hans. Then she, too, stepped around the pile of petals and disappeared into the salon.

Dorrit clamped her lips together to keep her mouth from quivering. She tightened her hold on her father's arm. He straightened his new silk vest under his new silk suit and molded an expression she had never before seen.

"Well, my dearest treasure," he said and squeezed her hand, "we've traveled a rocky road, you and I. But I promise you that the next few steps will be smooth. Then I'll leave the rest to Johann." He puffed out his chest with unabashed pride even as his voice cracked and his arm trembled. But good as his word, his steps were firm as he walked his daughter down the aisle.

A hundred of Berlin's elite turned in their seats and cranked their heads to look at the bride, their faces melting into a gray blur before her. She saw only Johann. Dressed in black attire, as splendid as that he'd worn on New Year's Eve, he was standing at the far end of the large room, flanked by the solemn-faced officiating judge and a grinning Karl-Heinz.

As she drew near, Johann's eyes dipped to below her throat

where an emerald heart hung suspended on a gold chain. He smiled.

They were married.

Following the ceremony, the bride and groom mingled with the guest in the drawing room, where toasts and speeches continued to delay a lavish six-course dinner until Frau Schmidt finally threw up her hands, ordered her husband to ring the silver bell one last time, after which, she told the staff to commence serving whether or not a single person had found the dining room. Food in the mouth was better than pretty speeches any day—wedding days included—she decided. Besides, her light-as-air salmon mousse could not wait another minute and still expect to draw raves.

The evening remained delightfully warm, and as dinner drew to a close, the strolling violins in the house joined a band of musicians on the terrace. The music soon pulled the guests outside as well. The terrace was large enough to accommodate the dancing and the trees throughout the garden were strung with colorful lanterns, lending a festive glow as shadows lengthened and darkness fell.

As he suspected would be the case, Johann managed only one dance with Dorrit. The first. From that moment on, friends sabotaged his best-laid plans. However, just before midnight and before these same friends could invent more duplicitous means of keeping him from his bride and delay his honeymoon, he saw her in the arms of easy game, the aging Duke von Hertlinge.

With a lopsided grin and a blunt "excuse me," Johann cut in, held Dorrit's hand as if it was attached to his own, and though somewhat hampered by her full skirts, managed a quick beeline around the side of the house. Not swiftly enough, however, to avoid the blizzard of confetti that some fleet-footed guests and a very sloshed Philip von Brandt staged by taking a shortcut through the salon.

Schmidt was waiting at the curb. Tonight he would drive the baron and baroness to the Grand Hof Hotel in Potsdam. Tomorrow they would proceed by train to Paris. After crisscrossing France, they would spend the latter part of their honeymoon in Spain.

TWENTY-THREE

It was the beginning of June, the honeymooners were heading for the Bay of Biscay and San Sebastian, seaside retreat of wealthy Europeans and official summer residence of the Spanish court.

"The Villa Solana is the choicest hotel here, but somewhat isolated," Johann explained when Dorrit registered surprise as their driver left the main road from the train station and, instead of continuing into San Sebastian, cracked the whip over the horses and guided them onto a steep, narrow lane sliced into the foothills of the Urgull Mountains. "It doesn't attract your typical tourist."

"I can see why," Dorrit gulped, eyeing the sheer drop-off on the right side of the road. The sun was at its highest point, the bay shimmered, and she could hear waves crashing onto the rocks below, but she dared not lean over to look and judge the distance down, it might tilt the precarious balance their carriage held on the small strip of dirt. Instead, she inhaled the tangy and pleasant smell of seawater and kelp trapped and drying in shallow pools between the rocks.

"In fact, this place is so inaccessible it appeals to an odd clientele."

"Such as?" Dorrit said, absorbing the spectacular scenery all the while wondering how the driver might manage any on-coming traffic.

"Disgraced royals living in exile and an occasional ambassador with his paramour," Johann grinned. "International jewel thieves on the lam have also been known to hide out here. And of course today a couple of ordinary citizens from Berlin intend to take advantage of the delightful seclusion as well. To avoid being badgered with invitations from those of social rank who might wish to investigate ours, I reserved our accommodations simply as 'Doctor and Frau von Renz.'"

"Oh . . . ?" Dorrit contrived to look piqued. "But Herr Doctor!

153

How could you? I had so hoped to meet a Spanish duke and—"

"The hotel has an excellent library, darling. And marvelous gardens. The weather is guaranteed, and the surf is refreshing."

"Is that supposed to take the edge off my disappointment?" Dorrit laughed, incredibly happy. But in the next instant, she felt a cold and strange shudder run up her spine. Her fingertips tingled. Someone was walking on her grave. She sobered. Was it bad luck to wallow in contentment?

On their first evening at the Villa Solana, and as if God was in collusion with the Spanish ministry of tourism, Dorrit and Johann were greeted by a sunset of such profundity that it was a while before they could turn their backs on it and go downstairs for dinner. Lingering on the balcony outside their suite, they stood mesmerized, gazing at the broad strokes of orange and pink brushed across the endless sky above a tranquil sea.

But just as the last rounded trace of the sun sank into the bay, taking with it the brilliant colors from the sky, enormous waves began crashing against the rocky shore. It was as if the water was suddenly determined to devour the strip of sand between the surf and the hotel. Sea gulls that had been roosting peacefully on the breakwater only moments before, now shrieked and swooped into the air, gliding and diving over the churning sea.

"How odd," Dorrit reflected, leaning on her elbows over the vine-covered balustrade and fully expecting to feel salty spray on her face and to see the surf lap right up against the road and flower beds just below. "The water changed so suddenly. How can that be?"

"Crosswinds spring up without warning," Johann said. "They cause sudden and high swells. This bay is known for unpredictable and treacherous currents. Which reminds me," he put his arm around Dorrit's shoulder, "no swimming on your own! That's an order. In years past, when I came here with my parents, I was never allowed on the beach without a male escort, a proven and expert swimmer." Johann grinned sheepishly. "I suffered in embarrassed silence till I was seventeen."

"I am eighteen!" Dorrit laughed. "By your own yardstick, too old for an escort on the beach."

"The order still stands," Johann said, dead serious. "Each year there are several drownings along this coast. As picturesque as this place is, it can be dangerous. In fact, I forbid you to set foot on the beach without me."

"Well, I suppose it'll be easy to remember," Dorrit grinned up at him. "On the Champs Elysees where ornamental fountains posed the only danger of drowning, you didn't once allow me to walk alone. You even tagged along the morning I went out to look for a clock for my father. This after you'd made it quite clear that you found souvenir-hunting a pastime for tourists and to be avoided at all costs."

"There were other hazards in Paris."

"Such as?"

"Frenchmen."

"Oh, come now!" Dorrit sputtered.

Turning her toward him, Johann's hands moved up to cradle her face.

"Haven't you noticed I'm incurably possessive?" he said and kissed the tip of her nose. "And jealous."

"Be serious, please!"

"I am being serious."

"Well, if I have attracted unwanted attention, you have only yourself to blame. I tried to tell you that Madam Mimieux's seamstresses were too expensive. Are you now telling me that the styles are too risqué as well?"

"Perhaps," Johann mumbled and drew her up against him. The breeze sent her fragrant hair tumbling into his face. He was instantly ready to ignore his stomach and cater to that other more powerful need. He kept his arms tightly around her while the last traces of daylight faded from the horizon, melting together a purple sea and sky.

Somewhere in the distant interior of the hotel, the final dinner bell rang. The gulls began settling down on the pilings, some still alert with their heads pointed into the wind, while others rested their orange beaks across the black feathery pillow atop their wings.

Days later, after strolling along the beach and finding a restful place among some rock formations well away from the water,

Dorrit decided the moment was right to tell Johann the story of her mother's tragic love affair, which resulted in her unconventional parentage.

"Just goes to show that I was right," Johann said when she had finished her account.

"Right? Right about what?"

"About you. I always suspected you were a princess. From the very first time I saw you."

Dorrit laughed.

"Well, it's easy to see how you got that idea."

"Oh?"

"Yes. It was obviously the way I dressed. Off the bargain racks for everyday wear and homespun for balls."

"Exactly!" Johann said. "Only one of noble birth could carry herself so regally in simple garments."

"Then why," Dorrit demanded to know, "why all this fuss, to say nothing of the expense, to outfit me in haute couture?" She brushed some sand off her white pleated skirt trimmed with half a dozen rows of navy piping at the hem. By contrast, her blouse was blue with white piping on the sleeves and collar, while shiny brass buttons ran down the front and across the epaulets. "I'll have you know that to justify the cost, Madam Mimieux felt compelled to inform me that every stitch was 'zee rage! Zee pinnacle of zee high fashion!' At such heights, I began to question if her *mode et parure* would fall from favor long before I had a chance to wear everything."

"You asked her that?"

"No. I didn't dare. She intimidated me."

"She did what?" Johann glowered and stood ready to fire the woman.

"Well, you see, she always had me at a disadvantage. Atop an awkward stool with a hundred pins stuck in my side."

Johann burst out laughing.

Watching him, Dorrit's heart skipped a beat. His brown hair was windblown, it looked irresistible that way, and his teeth were so incredibly white against his deeply tanned face; the Spanish sun had quickly done its work on him. The neck of his light blue shirt was open, showing a patch of bronze chest as dark as his face. A crumbled white linen jacket hung negligently on his broad shoulders. Without any conscious thought, she snuggled up against him. His arms immediately closed about her.

She tilted her face up to his, reached out her hand, and, knowing full well what she was doing, traced the outline of his firm wide mouth with her forefinger.

"Stop that, you little tease!" he hissed between his teeth and snatched her fingers away while his gray eyes began to smolder. "Stop tempting me in broad daylight, unless you want your shapely little bottom in the sand and a public display of our intimacy."

Dorrit peered over their rock fortress.

"Public? Herr Doctor?" she murmured, devising a capricious expression. "There's no one here but us."

"Hm, that pleasant observation," he lowered his mouth toward hers, speaking against her lips with feather-light kisses, "could get you into a heap of trouble." His hand slid under her blouse the same time his mouth began exploring hers with sweet and scorching madness. Of course, he would stop before it went too far, he told himself. After all, he was not about to make love to his wife on the beach, even if they were alone. Still, it was an enticing thought.

A hair-raising scream pulled Johann back to earth. But believing he'd been startled by the battle cry of an offended sea gull, he ignored it. However, when another high-pitched shriek was again carried on the wind, it sounded remarkably human.

Instantly alert, Johann let go of Dorrit and stood up and scanned the beach in both directions. This spot was a couple of miles from the hotel. They hadn't met a soul during their walk earlier.

"What was that noise?" Fastening her blouse, Dorrit picked up her wide-brimmed straw hat and hit it against her knees to shake off the sand.

"I'm not sure." Johann took her arm and helped her climb over the rocks. Once out on the beach, he held up his hand to shield his eyes from the glare of the sun. That's when he spotted a couple of women silhouetted at the water's edge, some distance away. Their presence, in and of itself, was no surprise, because the beach directly in front of the resort was rocky; most bathers chose to walk the distance to this area, where a smooth sandy bottom was much kinder to the feet. However, when one of the women suddenly plunged into the surf fully dressed and the other began running back and forth raising her arms toward heaven, the scene took on another suggestion entirely.

"Good God!" In the belief that he was about to witness a suicide attempt, Johann shook off his jacket, tossed it negligently onto the sand, and leaving Dorrit to follow at her own pace, raced toward the women. It was a one-way ticket to hell to go swimming now. The bay had been rough earlier; at the moment, it was positively dangerous, with white foam topping each crashing wave.

He reached the frantic woman running circles on the sand; her uniform immediately identified her as a maid. He took hold of her arm. She began gasping incoherently: *"Mon...madame ...noyer! Mon madame....noyer!"*

Of course, Johann didn't need to be told in French or any other language that the woman in the surf might drown. Waves were breaking all around her, the swirling water reaching to her shoulders; even so, she continued heading further out to sea.

Turning his back on the hysterical maid, Johann kicked off his sandals, dove in, and with a few determined strokes, reached the spot where the woman was floundering, hopelessly trapped in the heavy wet folds of her skirts. As he lunged for her, she threw herself forward. A swell knocked the feet out from under him, but not before he'd gotten hold of her arm. However, the minute they both found footing, the woman began a desperate struggle to free herself. She beat her fists against Johann's chest, her face distorted in harsh contours of wild-eyed panic. Her mouth moved, but no sounds came forth. Dodging her assaults as best he could, Johann dragged his uncooperative catch back toward shore. *Why in God's name was she trying to drown herself?*

Once they reached shallow water, she stopped resisting and looked at her savior as if seeing him for the first time. Sanity softened her features for an instant before she slumped to her knees in the foam of a retreating wave.

"Please...let me go." she cried with heart-wrenching sobs and pounded the wet sand. "My son is out there. Oh, God, my little boy! Please, let me go! Marcel!" she moaned and, struggling to her feet, faced the churning surf, screaming: "Marcel!"

Marcel...? Stunned, Johann turned and strained his eyes

out across the hostile sea. But he saw no little boy. There was no one in the breakers.

"It's true, monsieur. It's true!" The maid, hitching up her skirts and braving the ankle-deep water, now rushed to her mistress's side. "We let Marcel go swimming with his cork float. We were watching him. But a large wave caught him. It came out of nowhere. It swept him out. It happened so quickly. And then we saw him lose his hold on the float!" The maid wrung her hands, tears sprung to her eyes. *"S'il vous plait,* can you help us? It's such a long way to the hotel. I would have run for help, except I was afraid to leave. I was afraid Madame de Loncourt would drown herself."

Johann was about to chastise the maid and Madame de Loncourt for letting a boy go swimming in this surf, with or without a cork float, but this was no time for conversation. He turned back toward the seething green water, narrowed his eyes, and searched the top of the swells. Sure enough, a small head and one thin flailing arm suddenly popped up well beyond the breakers. Good God! How had the boy gotten himself out that far? Well, never mind. There was only one thing to do. Less than idea conditions notwithstanding, it was time to go for a swim.

"Keep your mistress out of the water. No matter what!" Johann ordered the maid clinging to the distraught woman. "If need be, my wife will help you." He waved to Dorrit, who was standing on dry sand clutching his jacket that she'd picked up where he had dropped it. Her frightened eyes were pleading with him not to go in. But, of course, she knew that he would.

Popping the buttons, Johann ripped off his wet shirt, discarded it at his feet, and dove into the pounding surf for the second time in as many minutes. His body sliced through the water with unbelievable speed, but when he reached the spot where he'd seen the boy, there was no sign of him; only the slab of cork was visible, bobbing far beyond reach.

Diving again and again, Johann searched frantically. Time was critical. The water was surprisingly deep, he noted, and there was a bottomless drop-off on the sandy floor a short distance away. He felt uneasy because it was unusual to have a trench so close to shore.

Close to shore?

Good night! After surfacing for a gulp of air, a quick glance told him that he was no longer close to shore. But how could that be? He'd been diving and crisscrossing the water just beyond the breakers.

Suddenly a sick feeling made his skin crawl.

Riptide!

In the event he was trapped in one of the cruel currents the bay was notorious for, that would of course explain the boy's distance from the beach when first spotted. After being caught by a wave, the lad had not ventured further out on his own. He had been . . . pulled!

Cold fear such as Johann had never before experienced and was loath to credit, rushed over him as he realized that, yes, he too was being pulled out to sea by an invisible force of a terrifying strength. And though he was an accomplished swimmer, he was as helpless as Marcel to fight the savage tow.

But not to panic. One thing at a time, he told himself severely. Keep your head. Find Marcel. Then swim like the devil and pray like a saint.

Diving repeatedly, Johann caught sight of the boy, submerged some thirty feet away. The child hung suspended under the water, not struggling, not attempting to swim. *The first stage of drowning!*

Johann raced forward.

A heartbeat later, his own lungs bursting, he surfaced with the limp form. And holding Marcel's head above water, he applied upward thrusts of pressure on his diaphragm until the boy began vomiting and spewing seawater. Once his stomach and lungs cleared, and as soon as he was breathing more or less normally, Johann gave a victory sign toward shore. Then cradling Marcel against his chest, he began an arduous journey, using the backstroke.

Marcel, who appeared to be eight or nine years old, was in shock and did not fight the rescue, as victims of the sea frequently do. A small blessing, because Johann knew he would need total concentration if he was to reach shore, a goal that was far from assured. As fast as he swam in one direction, the current had other plans and pulled him in the opposite.

Alternating every stroke he knew, he soon realized he was gaining no ground and only exhausting himself. He was at odds with a powerful element. With every passing minute, staying afloat became a major victory, hard won and not guaranteed to last. But he persevered, keeping his strokes even to conserve energy.

Occasionally glancing over the top of the choppy waves breaking against his face, Johann caught sight of the three women on the beach. The distance had grown so great that they looked like small black dots. He couldn't make out which one was Dorrit. Dorrit . . .! A sudden surge of renewed energy launched him forward. But the precious feet won were immediately lost to the deadly tow.

"Dammit!" he swore out loud. He was no marathoner. The trips to the Baltic as a boy, his former visits to these shores, and the times he and Karl-Heinz had pitted themselves against the rain-swollen river in Bernau was not enough preparation for this inequitable test against an ill-tempered sea. Hands down, the sea held the advantage over any mortal.

Johann continued swimming.

His legs soon felt like lead weights, and his shoulders ached with a remorseless pain; breathing was a labor in itself, and chilled to the bones, his teeth began to rattle in his mouth like ill-fitting dentures.

Again and again he stopped to rest and to shift the weight of the semiconscious boy. He couldn't tell which arm hurt the most; the one holding Marcel or the one he used for swimming.

His rest stops grew more frequent. A numbing weariness was creeping over him. His mind became as battered as his body. He was growing tired of a battle he wasn't winning. His energy was spent, his reserves drained; what little remained was imprisoned in rigid muscles rendered useless by the cold. Crazy thoughts of yielding to the pull and welcoming the soft underwater environment began to seduce him.

It seemed an eternity since he'd gone into the surf. The shoreline was still slipping further and further away. His situation was desperate. He could not hope to resist the tow indefinitely, and even if its icy tentacles were to let go of him, he was too spent now to swim with one arm while dragging the weight of the boy.

His eyes searched the beach for the women. They were no longer directly in his line of vision. Was the current pulling him down the beach or had they moved? Minutes ago they had staunchly waved to him. Or was that hours ago? It felt like days.

A swell lifted Johann up long enough to allow him to look over another cresting wave. He spotted the women again. There were only two now; a third was running along the beach in the direction of the hotel. Was the maid going for help? Had they finally decided he was in trouble and couldn't make it on his own?

Too exhausted to worry about his pride, he hoped so! Of course the hotel was some distance away, and sand was a slow track to run on. Even if she had left the minute he dove into the surf, it was doubtful that any meaningful help could be mobilized. Certainly, no local familiar with this ornery sea was fool enough to dive in. And could the small dinghy the hotel kept on quaint display be launched in these high seas? Probably not. It would be swamped at once, and then there'd be more bodies needing rescue.

Johann could no longer swim, it was no use kidding himself. He was barely staying afloat. He was swallowing large amounts of water. He didn't care. It didn't matter somehow. The numbness in his muscles spread to every part of his body and brought blessed relief from the burning pain. He was no longer cold, and this new anesthetized state was rather pleasant.

Again a large wave hoisted him above the surface of the water. He scanned the coastline and the mountains rising in the distance. It was ruggedly beautiful. Dorrit loved being here. He suspected that she loved it much more than Paris. Too bad he had to spoil it for her by getting himself drowned. She was awfully young to be widowed. From bride to widow in five easy weeks.

Good God! What am I thinking? What is happening to me? Am I losing my mind? Johann didn't take lightly to dying. Not quite thirty, it'd be premature to join his ancestors. Surely he wasn't finished yet?

Again he strained to see the beach and the two women. Which one was Dorrit? He couldn't tell from here. But as long as he could see two women walking along the water's edge, at least he was still afloat, still in the game.

Walking? Actually, they appeared to be running. What did that mean?

All at once the women waved. They pointed. But at what?

The shoreline had changed, Johann noted—less large rock formations and longer stretches of sand. He must have been dragged some distance down the beach, because he didn't recognize the backdrop.

A measure of new hope suddenly surged through him. Perhaps all was not lost? If the current had changed direction and was no longer pulling him out to sea but instead pulling him parallel to the shore, he might eventually be deposited on a spit of dry land like a piece of driftwood. If he could just stay afloat long enough, then maybe, just maybe—?

An instant later, he caught sight of an old sea wall jutting out into the water half a mile away. Was that what the women were pointing at? Were they signaling that he ought to try for that wall?

Yes! The women, bless them, were on to something. Because if he was no longer being pulled out to sea, then all he had to do was tread water, hang onto the boy, and point himself toward that divine and beautiful pile of ancient barnacle-encrusted rock.

Again he looked toward the beach. He could now distinguish Dorrit from Madame de Loncourt. In fact, he could see Dorrit quite clearly. She was still clutching his jacket.

Dorrit and that sea wall! He forced his mind to think of nothing else.

Dorrit and that sea wall!

TWENTY-FOUR

Exhausted from the afternoon's misadventure, Johann fell into a comalike sleep early in the evening. The following morning, however, after stuffing down four eggs, half a dozen buttered buns and gallons of coffee in the hotel's excellent dining room, he was himself again, as if yesterday's ordeal had never taken place.

"How about a swim?" he teased, put down his napkin, and stood up to help Dorrit from her chair.

"Sure! But only if there's a nice challenging undertow. Of course with all you just ate, we'd have to wait three hours."

Laughing, they left the sunny dining room to a sedate dilatory crowd sipping coffee and lingering over the morning papers.

"All kidding aside," Johann took Dorrit's arm and, once outside in the courtyard, walked through a bougainvillea-covered arch and headed for the hotel's fabulous gardens behind the main buildings, "solid ground feels mighty comforting. Let's keep it under our feet for the rest of today."

Dorrit smiled and nodded toward a dignified elderly couple sitting in the shade of a latticewood pavilion, sketching the rosebushes growing in a semicircle around a triple dolphin fountain near the entrance to the gazebo. The gentle splash of water into the pool mingled pleasantly with the sound of bees buzzing around the fragrant flower beds.

"Might that activity appeal to you? Would you like to try to paint?"

"Definitely. Better yet, how about going into town? We can play tourist and look for souvenirs."

"You're that anxious to avoid the beach?"

"Actually, I was thinking of your father." Johann stopped to nip two showy white gardenias from a prolific shrub.

"My father?" Dorrit stood still while he fastened the flowers into the barrettes keeping her hair in place.

"Yes, you see, you got him a clock in Paris. So I thought I'd

164

bring him one from here. He collects them, doesn't he?"

"He's passionate about old timepieces."

"Then it's decided." Johann stepped back to admire his handiwork. "You look wonderful," he smiled. "Only one of us will now be mistaken for a tourist. You, darling, will pass for a local senorita at the market."

"Or at a wake," Dorrit said, inhaling the gardenias' heady perfume. "I smell like a funeral parlor."

"Watch your tongue! I don't like the reference." Johann grinned, remembering how close he'd come and again gave thanks to the sea wall. He took Dorrit's hand and continued through the magnificent gardens toward the guest bungalows behind the main buildings.

There had been a great to-do in this part of the hotel compound yesterday when a semiconscious boy was carried home; Dorrit guessed Johann's destination long before he spoke.

"Would you mind stopping in for a brief visit with Madame de Loncourt before we head off to town?" he asked. "I'd like to check on Marcel to make sure he's experiencing no ill effects from his exposure and shock."

Although she could whip up zero enthusiasm for a visit with a boy who had almost cost Johann his life, Dorrit agreed to it. And, of course, she mustn't blame Marcel for the near tragedy. It was the foolish Madame de Loncourt whom Dorrit should be angry with. And had she not been paralyzed yesterday with terror for Johann's safety, she might have strangled the woman for being so incredibly naive to think that a piece of cork would keep the boy safe in a high surf. The hotel posted warnings whenever the water was too rough for swimming, in four languages yet! The sign had been prominently displayed yesterday by noon. Only a nitwit would have ignored it.

The door to Madame de Loncourt's bungalow was opened by a fully restored maid. Smiling broadly, she ushered the visitors in, one of whom she equated with the Second Coming of Christ.

Marcel was lying prostrate and penitent on the sofa in the large airy living room. A breakfast tray on the table next to him had been picked clean. A good sign, Johann noted, and his subsequent examination of the little fellow established that Marcel was suffering from nothing more than a case of remorse for having caused such a drama.

"Promise me," Johann sat down on the edge of the sofa and spoke gently in French, "that you'll never again venture out in rough seas." The boy nodded solemnly. "And don't ever rely on a piece of cork to keep you safe. Even when the water is calm."

"Oh, I won't. Never again. Cross my heart."

"Good." Johann smiled and tousled the boy's hair. "Actually, I was very pleased with the way you cooperated while we were swimming toward shore."

"Really?" Curious, Marcel pushed himself up on his elbows. He remembered little from that swim.

"Indeed. Had you kicked and thrashed about, we might have had a much worse time of it."

Grinning like the Cheshire cat, Marcel glanced toward his mother to see if she had heard him being praised.

She had. She looked pleased.

When Dorrit and Johann made ready to leave, Madame de Loncourt walked her visitors to the door. Once out in the garden, out of sight of her son, tears welled up in her eyes.

"We will forever be in your debt," she cried softly. "Words can not express our *remerciement*. If you had not happened along and been willing to risk your life, my little Marcel would be dead. And I would have drowned as well. I know that I would have wanted to die."

"Everything turned out fine. Don't dwell on it," Johann smiled. "If anything, be grateful to the old sea wall. It should rightly have crumbled ages ago." On a lighter note, he added: "My wife will attest to the fact that I was badly in need of some exercise. The hotel's *cuisinier extraordinaire* has wrought havoc with my waistline."

His flippancy brought a sweet smile to Madame de Loncourt's lips. She dried her tears, all the while thinking that her saviour was exceptionally lean and enormously attractive.

"We've been here just a few days," she said. "My husband is attending to some business in Madrid. He's due back tonight. We're supposed to stay another week, but I'm suddenly very anxious to get back home."

"I understand," Johann said.

"We'll probably return to Paris tomorrow morning. Still, I do hope my husband will have a chance to meet you both before then."

"It'd be our pleasure."

After Madame de Loncourt and Dorrit exchanged a few words about the charms of San Sebastian and where to find the best coral and amber trinkets, the visitors left.

In addition to the main dining room, the Villa Solana served meals in the enclosed courtyard, where discriminating guests, those who wished for complete solitude, could dine alfresco under a black velvet sky. Tables were discreetly separated from one another by decorative wooden trellises and canopies of lush red bougainvillea. A lone guitarist strumming unobtrusively in the shadows added to the ambiance with soulful Spanish ballads.

Dorrit and Johann, regulars in the courtyard, had just been served their main course and were discussing plans to go back into town after dinner to see a Barcelona flamenco troupe making a celebrated appearance at the Casa Verde nightclub, when an impeccably dressed gentleman entered their sanctuary, disregarding their obvious wish for privacy.

After bowing to Dorrit and begging her forgiveness for the intrusion, he turned to Johann and inquired if he was addressing the physician from Berlin?

Believing that a hotel guest had taken ill and that the inevitable call, is there a doctor in the house, summoned him, Johann rose and acknowledged with a slight nod.

But instead of the expected appeal for help, he found himself imprisoned in a masculine hug, complete with a thorough back-pounding, while his cheeks suffered the ardor of a madman.

Astonished, he stared at the individual assaulting his person. Of course, he quickly realized who it was, even before Monsieur de Loncourt began his emotional speech.

Johann immediately down-played the rescue.

"A small matter—"

"Non!" Monsieur de Loncourt held up his hand to silence him. "Small matter? Indeed! It is everything in the world to me. Everything I live for. Without my wife and son, I would have no reason to exist." His eyes bright with emotion, Monsieur de Loncourt expounded a moment longer before he turned back to Dorrit, placed a gallant kiss on her hand, then

167

left as abruptly as he had arrived.

Johann remained standing and watched him go.

"The French are a demonstrative lot," he grinned and sat back down again to attend to the delicious stone crabs.

A week later, in preparation for their return to Berlin, a maid and a valet were summoned to the von Renz suite to assist with the packing. While Dorrit supervised, Johann went downstairs to settle the bill.

"God damn!" he uttered, and expletives of a much stronger caliber followed in rapid succession.

The hotel manager spread his hands in a helpless gesture, drew his shoulders clear up to his earlobes—forcing three double chins—while remaining disdainfully silent against the tirade and the two smoking barrels of this German's gun-powder-gray eyes. This resort catered to a twenty-four-carat clientele, he reminded himself; how had this doctor and his wife managed to secure reservations in the first place? Furthermore, he was baffled that any guest saw fit to complain about an account being settled by some philanthropic soul who wished to remain anonymous.

Johann left the man and stormed up to his suite. He took the stairs rather than the elevator in order to vent some of his fury.

Loncourt...? De Loncourt!

The manager's lips had been sealed, but Johann knew it was that emotional Frenchman who had paid the bill. Damn! And what was de Loncourt's first name? Of course there were probably a thousand de Loncourts in Paris. It'd be a hell of a job to locate the right one.

By the time Johann reached the second landing, he realized that even if he found Monsieur de Loncourt, he could not try to reimburse him. The man's pride would be severely damaged, such as his own was now. To shred another man's vanity for the sake of his own was not Johann's style. Dammit! He would have to let it go.

Still scowling with impotent indignation, he reached the suite and tersely dismissed the maid and the valet, handing each a week's wages. Shock and delight mingled on their faces. First at being so roughly discharged, secondly at being so handsomely paid.

"That bloody Frenchman covered my account!" Johann muttered under his breath to Dorrit as he snapped the suitcases closed and opened the door for the porter who had come to take the luggage downstairs. "It's an outrage! I can't imagine how the hotel can allow such a thing!"

The old porter took the valises and placed them carefully on a cart in the hall. Turning back on the still-fuming guest, he touched his cap and smiled, displaying the unfortunate spaces of several missing teeth. He didn't understand German, but the timbre of this tall gentleman's voice was decipherable in any language.

"I'll have the suitcases by the curb in a jiffy," he promised and left with celerity, fully believing that he had intruded on a terrible marital tiff.

While Johann made a quick visual check of the rooms and gathered the morning papers together for reading on the train, Dorrit wandered out on the balcony for one last look at the magnificent view.

Iridescent hummingbirds were buzzing around the colorful blooms on the herbaceous vines clinging to the stucco railing. The scent of the flowers mixed pleasantly with the smell of kelp and salt water. She would treasure the memory of the Villa Solana for the rest of her life, every minute spent here except that dreadful day when this beautiful bay almost took Johann from her. She shivered, and for the thousandth time, thanked God no harm had come to anyone. No harm until today, when Johann's pride had suffered a severe blow. Smiling inwardly, she suspected that he would probably rather have drowned than find himself the recipient of charity.

She leaned over the balustrade. The old porter had reached the sidewalk in front of the hotel and was loading the suitcases into the carriage that stood ready for the drive to the train station.

Dorrit took a deep breath, filling her lungs with the wonderful balmy air, and, heedless of her complexion, aimed her face toward the sun, letting its tingling heat turn her cheeks pink. Johann would be furious that she was ruining her skin. But he was already furious, a bit of a sunburn could hardly add to his

169

anger, and she would have kept her face toward the blistering sphere in the sky if she hadn't been distracted by a sharp voice from below. She opened her eyes, glanced over the railing, and recognized the hotel manager, who regularly rode herd on his employees. At the moment, his tongue was lashing the old porter, and while Dorrit didn't understand his rapid-fire Spanish, the tone was patently cruel.

She felt bad for the porter; surely the old man had done nothing to deserve such a dressing down. Why, no one around the place worked harder or more cheerfully. He was always on hand opening doors, carrying packages, and wielding luggage heavier than himself. On the day of the near-drowning, he'd been first on the scene. With the agility of a cat and with no concern for the distinct possibility that he could break his neck, he had scampered out on the dangerous sea wall with warm blankets for the two human forms the sea had spared.

"Ah, there you are!" Johann joined Dorrit on the balcony. "Sorry to be leaving?"

"Yes and no," she smiled and ran her hand through her loose hair, causing it to gleam like red fire in the sun.

"Well, make up your mind, *liebchen*."

"I can't. The view is so completely intoxicating. It inhibits all rational thought."

"In that case, I guess I'll be stuck with a tipsy wife from now on," Johann grinned.

"What do you mean?"

"You'll have this view when we get home."

"That's silly, Johann. How can that possibly be?"

"Remember the painting we saw in San Sebastian last week? The same day we shopped for a clock for your father. The painting you didn't want because your sense of thrift got in the way of your excellent eye for art?"

"Oh, no! Not the Georges Seurat! The picture of this bay? The beach . . . the breakwater . . . the gulls?"

"That's the one."

"You . . . you didn't . . . ?"

"It's on its way to Berlin."

"Oh, Johann!" Dorrit flew into his arms. "How could you? It was so expensive! And . . . and where will we put it? There's no room on the walls!"

170

"We'll find space in Bernau."

A malicious bark from the curb below intruded on Dorrit's happiness. She slipped out of Johann's embrace and leaned over the balustrade.

"Not again!" she said, exasperated. "The hotel manager keeps picking on that poor porter. He scolded him terribly just a minute ago. I can't imagine what he has done to warrant public humiliation? And I'll just bet that trite manager cracks the whip even worse in private. He knows full well that a menial worker with a large family to support won't dare become mutinous."

Moments later, while riding down in the elevator, it occurred to Johann that Dorrit had been mighty quick to stir up compassion for an old hotel lackey, as well as remind him of the tiresome manager. Was she suggesting that there existed a God-given opportunity to rid himself of Monsieur de Loncourt's unwelcomed beneficence?

Before the carriage pulled away from the curb, Johann did precisely that when he pressed the amount of a month's stay at the most expensive hotel in San Sebastian into the porter's bony hands.

Dorrit noticed the exchange out of the corner of her eye and smiled brightly. But even so, her smile did not match the one spreading on the old man's furrowed face when he looked at the fortune he was holding.

"Sir, . . . there must be s . . . some mistake here. . . ." he mumbled, completely bewildered.

"Maybe, but it's not yours," Johann assured him just before the carriage drove off.

"May God be good to you," the old man whispered from the curb and took off his cap in reverence to such generosity. He was not sure whether to laugh, cry, or kick up his heels and whistle.

He went back to work.

TWENTY-FIVE

The house in Bernau was so large, it took a couple of days before Dorrit was able to find her way around.

From the center hall, an archway opened to a salon the size of a ballroom, next to which was an exquisitely appointed drawing room of near equal dimensions. The dining room lay directly opposite with two sets of French doors that opened out onto a beautiful flagstone terrace and exquisite rose gardens. The terrace rounded the corner of the house and so was also accessible through doors at the far end of the center hall. A library, an intimate ladies' tea room, kitchen and servants' wing completed the downstairs.

The second floor was reached by a wide staircase that rose gently from the middle of the center hall to a landing before it split and continued in opposite directions toward the master bedroom suites plus a maze of dressing rooms and guest rooms. The third floor had a schoolroom and sleeping quarters for staff not housed in the servants' wing. Dorrit immediately made it her business to learn the names of everyone employed on the estate, from the adipose housekeeper, Frau Erdmann, right on down to the most menial maid. It was the least she could do, since each of them curtsied her and addressed her as *mein baroness*. She often wondered if she'd ever get used to her new life.

Another thing and a far less pleasant one that she also had to get used to, was Johann's absence. She'd been spoiled during their honeymoon, when he was around every minute of the day and night. Now she saw him mainly at night, just before dinner, and as wonderful as that was, she missed his company during the day. But he spent his entire day with the horses, and how could she possibly compete with forty magnificent animals? Perhaps if she learned to like them? As it were, with the exception of the old bays that pulled coaches, she was afraid of horses. Even the well-tempered gelding Johann bought at auction as a surprise gift for her only days after arriving in Bernau made her uneasy.

"For you, darling!" he had announced proudly the morning it was delivered and was brought right up to the front steps of the house so she could admire it as it was led out of its transport cart, saddle and all. "Of course it comes with strings attached."

"Strings?" Dorrit croaked.

"Yes. Riding lessons," Johann qualified and grinned. "Which is something I'll personally attend to."

"R . . . riding lessons?" Dorrit smiled to cover her horror; there was nothing she wanted less than to ride this horse. But being careful not to let Johann see the scope of her fear and the dismal impact of his gift, she managed a cheerful: "He's beautiful. Thank you."

"Do you want to try him now?" Johann checked the straps on the saddle and bent down to tighten the girth.

"Uh, no!" Dorrit said quickly. "That's to say . . . I'm . . . I'm not dressed for riding." She wondered that Johann hadn't noticed she was wearing a delicate yellow morning dress with a splash of appliqued white roses at the hem. Hardly riding garb.

"Yeah, I guess you're right," Johann gave her pretty dress an appreciative look. "Anyway, now that you've met him, decide on a good name and tell Otto. He'll make a sign for the stall." Johann winked, turned the animal around, and led him down toward the stables, leaving Dorrit to ponder how terrific her husband looked in jodhpurs and long, sleek boots. And, afraid of the creatures or not, she concluded she must go visit the stables. She could no longer put it off. She ought to at least pretend to be interested in this new gelding. She watched him cross the courtyard, swishing his tail with self-important affectation. His coat was a mottled gray like the sky in advance of a terrible cloudburst. Actually, she could think of a number of fitting names for him, Foul Weather being the most benign.

Once Johann and the gelding had left the courtyard and disappeared down the graveled path behind some poplars, Dorrit went back inside the house and ran upstairs to change into a sensible cotton frock, but not so sensible it could be construed as riding attire. Minutes later, on her way out the front door, she grabbed a hat for protection against the sun as well as a handful of sugar cubes from the bowl on the sideboard in the dining room. She put the sugar carefully into her pocket. It was a bribe for Foul Weather.

As she rounded the corner of the corrals, she spotted Johann down at the timing track. He was sitting astride the fence, stopwatch in hand, and, along with the trainer, cheered a horse running the oval, apparently to everyone's satisfaction. *Thank Goodness he's busy*, Dorrit thought, *I can tour at my own pace.* And of course, on this, her first real trip inside the stables, she planned not to get any too close to the animals. If the new gelding was securely restrained, she'd offer him the sugar cubes. Ride him? No! That would only scare her unconscious.

"Good mornin'!" Otto smiled, removed his cap, and quickly sized up the baroness. "I hear the new gelding be yours. Did you come to visit with 'im?" he asked slyly; he could smell fear a mile away.

"Good morning, Otto. Yes." Dorrit stepped gingerly through the stable doors, careful not to make any sudden movements that might incite the horses. "Do you think it'd be all right if I fed him some sugar cubes?"

"Sure! Go on in. He's in stall number twelve. A mighty fine horse he is. Mighty fine. Needs a very special name, that one."

"Winter's Sky!" Dorrit said, suddenly inspired; besides, she didn't think Otto would approve of Foul Weather. "His coloring reminds me of gathering clouds before a storm," she explained with a feeble shrug.

"Well, now that's a fittin' and proper name for 'im!" A smile spread on Otto's wrinkled face, one Dorrit took to heart as personal praise. "I'll get busy and make a sign for his stall. Hm, Winter's Sky? A fittin' name all right. But, . . . here, you come along with me now. You came here wantin' to give 'im a treat."

As Otto walked Dorrit along the enclosures, he was still nodding approvingly at the name she'd chosen. She felt flattered and was, moreover, very appreciative of his company. If any of the animals became riotous, Otto would surely know how to handle it. Furthermore, he walked on the inside, next to the stalls, thus shielding her from several beasts who poked their heads over the portals as she walked by. And when they came to the new gelding, Otto kindly held on to his halter as she put out her hand

174

and offered the sugar. But although she delighted in the feel of the soft muzzle exploring her palm, she held her breath in abject terror until Winter's Sky had eaten the sugar and left her fingers surprisingly intact.

When she left the stables a short time later, it was with the sensation that Otto was watching her departure with an odd expression.

Once clear of the compound, a quick glance over her shoulder confirmed that Johann was still at the timing track. But having had her fill of horses for one day, Dorrit quickly continued up the path and back toward the house before he could spot her and ask her to join him.

The midmorning sun was warm, another scorcher was on tap. She pulled down the brim of her straw chapeau to shield her face. Berlin would be particularly stifling today, she ruminated and decided that she must pressure her father to come out for a visit. He was as obstinate as a mule when it came to leaving the apartment for any overnight excursion.

Halfway up the hill, thinking she'd go cut some roses before the heat opened them, Dorrit took a detour toward the greenhouse near the orchards, where sheers and baskets were kept. Of course, Jens would probably spy her and then follow on her heels like an alert watchdog. Yesterday, he'd all but gnashed his teeth when she pruned the hollyhocks and cut some gladiolus. It was clear the gardener didn't like any meddling in his domain. But she refused to be cowed; she had little with which to occupy her time, and she particularly enjoyed working in the flower beds. Besides, the large vases throughout the house needed fresh splashes of color regularly, a responsibility she was determined to take on. And as she now picked up her steps, she decided on pink roses for the hall and a mixture of white and red peonies for the table and sideboards in the dining room.

She had scarcely started for the greenhouse when the ground behind her shook. Without turning, she knew Johann was approaching, because only he dared ride so recklessly on this narrow garden path. She experienced an overpowering impulse to run, and would have, except her knees went soft and would not support flight. She stepped off the path and stood rock-still, discreetly wiping her suddenly moist palms in the folds of her dress as she faced the huge black beast her husband brought to a stop only inches away.

The horse turned his head toward her, laid his ears back, and snorted.

Dorrit jumped.

"Don't be afraid," Johann laughed, then leaned down to whisper to Dorrit as if he was worried about insulting the animal with what he was about to say. "Asmodeus is the gentlest of creatures. He's practically a house cat. A declawed house cat."

"Well, you could have fooled me," Dorrit managed a short nervous laugh. Asmodeus, she thought. In Jewish demonology, that meant evil spirit. The name fit like a glove, she decided.

"And he's very partial to sugar cubes."

"Oh!" Dorrit's hand dove into her pocket, glad to find she had some pieces left while wondering how Johann knew about the sugar. But never mind that, she quickly dropped the treat on the path in front of Asmodeus, because she was not about to tempt fate a second time today by letting this horse within an inch of her hand. Momentarily preoccupied watching him nuzzle the dirt, she failed to see Johann bend down. Before she realized what was happening, he grabbed her around the waist and deposited her into the saddle in front of him.

"Let's go beg some lunch from Gerlinde," he mumbled against her ear. Then without waiting for as much as a nod of assent, turned the stallion, who didn't balk at the additional weight, up the hill toward the poplar-lined avenue that led from the house to the village road.

Light-headed with terror, convinced the horse would toss her off at any moment, Dorrit dearly wished she'd had more sugar cubes; those measly few clumps she'd thrown into the dirt couldn't have bought much consideration from this brute. But clenching her teeth, and gulping down her fear, she kept her head pointed straight forward, glad Johann couldn't see her face. It would give her away. It had drained of all color. Ironically, she had wanted to spend more time with him, but this was not what she'd had in mind.

"You'll be riding the gray gelding within a week," Johann declared after they were out on the road. He kissed the back of her neck, brushing her hair aside to do so. "By the way, I like the name you gave him. Otto told me about it."

"Oh...thank you." As pleasant as his kisses were, Dorrit wished he'd stop and concentrate on Asmodeus, who might well be waiting for precisely this kind of inattentiveness to bolt.

"Otto thinks you will make a fine equestrienne. I tend to agree with him. You show tremendous endurance."

"Really? We haven't gone very far yet."

"I mean endurance," Johann chuckled, "as in holding your breath."

"Oh..." Considering the state of her nerves, her repartee came quickly. "Your arm's so tight it makes breathing impossible." Her voice shook, something she hoped Johann would assume was due to the movement of the horse.

"What's this?" cried Karl-Heinz in sham outrage when he saw a horse approach with two riders. He was in the courtyard, coaxing a stud stallion into a horse cart for a trip to a neighboring farm. Now with arriving visitors, he threw the reins to a groom, letting him deal with the skittish animal. Hands on hips, Karl-Heinz cocked his head and mocked Johann. "Does this mean your overrated stables have succumbed to neglect and disease, stranding you with a lone survivor?"

"Can't say that I'd ride all the way over here to bring you the satisfaction of such news," Johann said. "But perhaps we can temper your disappointment over lunch?"

"Lunch? I can't afford your appetite," Karl-Heinz snorted and caught Dorrit around the waist as Johann swung her down.

Gerlinde came to the front door the minute she heard the familiar insults. She rushed down the steps, pushing her hair in place under a hair net.

"Of course you're staying for lunch," she said and hugged Dorrit fiercely, noting the poor thing was pale as a ghost, which was why when Gerlinde turned to greet Johann, her kiss was accompanied by a stern look, blaming him squarely for Dorrit's pallor. Gerlinde harbored no fondness for horses and understood the fear they gave rise to in some. "But first I want to give Dorrit the grand tour," she said. "I want to show off my new house before we eat and get lazy." With that, the two women linked arms and went inside, leaving the men with the obstinate stallion.

"Come on ol' boy." Karl-Heinz reclaimed the reins from the groom and tried to sweet-talk the horse up the ramp. "If only you knew the fun you're gonna have, you'd be a helluva lot more cooperative. I hear that mare over at Borst's place is mighty pretty." He tugged on the bit. "A glossy coat soft as silk. You're a lucky fella—" The animal reared up and nickered.

"Whoa!" Johann slapped its flanks and, pushing at its hind quarters, while Karl-Heinz and the groom pulled, the men finally got the animal into the cart.

After a full year and an army of construction workers, Gerlinde's house was nearly completed. Of yellow masonry with ornamental wooden slats decorating the upper story, the steep roof was laid with glazed red tiles. Only a few inside touches, such as ceiling moldings being carved in Italy, remained to be added. But ignoring those small details, the family had taken occupancy. Several rooms were already completely furnished in light modern Biedermeier. However, the library was being finished in the mahogany of old, hunter-green leather furniture, and dark antique side tables. Throughout, a feeling of space was enhanced by larger than normal windows, and of course, every room was equipped with sleek new radiators; the latest in winter heating.

Lunch at the Konauers' was a relaxed affair on the terrace, under a large striped canvas umbrella where the four friends sat around a wrought iron patio table with a mesh surface and put away a delicious meal of weisswurst steamed in home-brewed beer. Side dishes of apple fritters and cucumber salad accompanied the fare, along with baskets of crusty Bavarian bread.

"Summers are short; it's imperative to spend as much of it as possible in the out-of-doors," Gerlinde said, apologizing for entertaining on the unfinished terrace, strewn with building supplies. But countless pots of red geraniums were strategically placed to conceal the worst mess.

Dorrit commented on the treillage being erected against the back of the house and said she could visualize bougainvillea climbing onto the roof with a mass of color such as she'd seen in San Sebastian.

"Of course I doubt it'd survive our winters," she added.

"Yes, that kind of shrubbery might be a bit optimistic," Gerlinde agreed. "Anyway it's too late to start anything that'll bloom this year. But by next June, in time for a garden party I'm already planning, I promise you that this treillage will be covered from end to end with climbing roses."

"That'll require a miracle," Karl-Heinz sniped under his

breath, thinking that women were often unrealistic.

Plates were being pushed aside just as Ursula and Karl Konauer were spotted trudging arm in arm down the long hill from the old mansion, Karl's predictable cigar smoke arriving well ahead of them.

"You've missed lunch!" Gerlinde called out as her in-laws rounded the corner to the terrace, where they stepped cautiously across boards of lumber serving as makeshift walkways. "But how about some dessert?" Without waiting for an answer, she instructed the maid who was clearing the dishes to set two more places.

"We didn't come to eat, my dear girl," declared Karl Konauer, winded from the hike. "We came to see you and the grandchildren. And our timing," he said as he and Ursula greeted Dorrit and Johann, "couldn't be better. It's always a special treat to see our favorite neighbors, absent as they've been most the summer."

Hans, who had been eating in the kitchen with Fraulein Kruse and the twins, heard his grandfather's voice through the open windows and immediately came running. For although he knew he was not to intrude on the grown-ups' lunch, his grandparents' arrival changed all the rules.

"Opa, you wanna come watch me ride?" he said, tripping over a flower pot in his excitement.

"I'll tell you what," Karl Konauer plunked down on a chair. "I'm going to have some coffee and visit with your *Onkel* Johann and your brand new *Tante* Dorrit for a while. Maybe you can bring your pony around here? Then we can all watch you."

Hans looked toward his father for permission and, getting it, ran off like a bullet toward the stables.

"At least we don't have any lawns yet that the pony might ruin," Gerlinde smiled indulgently as she watched her son disappear around the side of the house.

Minutes later, Hans came back riding on a show-quality miniature Russian pony, a birthday gift from his grandfather. Hollering "watch me! watch me!" he rode in proud circles in the large open field behind the terrace. Johann was glad to see that Hans kept the pace slow and didn't try to race the poor animal's heart out on this hot summer day.

During the latter part of August, at Dorrit's urging, Herman Zache finally conceded that a short trip to Bernau would not set him back immeasurably if he took some work along.

Dorrit was gripped by anxiety the day he arrived. He looked awful, much thinner and more stooped and gray than she remembered. She had of course seen him in Berlin immediately after she returned from her honeymoon, but she had not noticed any change then. Maybe there had been a change, she now realized, except she'd been too absorbed in her wonderful new life to see it. A pang of guilt for her neglect put a damper on her initial elation with his arrival, and while helping him unpack and settle into the loveliest of guest rooms, a room she had filled with dahlias cut this morning, she decided she would speak to Hannah as soon as she got back to Berlin. Herman Zache was a man who never complained. It would be easy for a maid to become neglectful if no demands were made of her. But for now, Dorrit would indulge him iniquitously and instruct Frau Erdmann to keep a pot of fresh fruit soup on the stove at all times regardless of the heat of the day. Elderberry soup with a dab of sour cream was her father's favorite summer meal, something Hannah had probably forgotten.

Dr. Zache's appearance improved with Dorrit's pampering, the languid country life, and stimulating nights when assorted neighbors came for dinner. He strutted around proud as a peacock for an entire day after his dinner partner the evening before had turned out to be a countess. But more beneficial than anything else were the quiet evenings spent in the library alone with his son-in-law, tackling contemplative medical topics and watching Dorrit, content in her reading, curled up on the sofa. Dr. Zache noted that Johann couldn't take his eyes off her, something that was far more salutary for a father's well-being than any amount of fruit soup.

TWENTY-SIX

Once back in Berlin, Johann resumed his duties at Wirchow where he had firmly established himself and with seniority, enjoyed regular hours. Dorrit entertained callers, met Lillian in town, or visited with her father. But she was always back by five o'clock, long before she heard the front door groan on its heavy brass hinges, signaling Johann was home, at which point she ran out into the hall and threw her arms around him.

"Missed me, *liebchen?*" he asked and squeezed her.

"Uh-huh," she mumbled, and though she wrinkled her nose at the strong smell of hospital antiseptics that clung to his pin-striped suit, she tipped her face up for a kiss, not caring a hoot if the servants were watching. Johann was never embarrassed when she came flying into his arms. The staff existed and, with the exception of the Schmidts, he rarely noticed any of them.

One day in October, Johann came home carrying a large box under his arm which he proceeded to carry upstairs, motioning Dorrit to follow him.

"This," he said as he put it down on her dressing table, "has been in a bank vault since my mother died. I'm afraid there's a lot of stuff to sort through. Some of it may not suit you. But you can have reset any of the stones that appeal to you."

Dorrit could scarcely contain her curiosity as she eyed the tortoise-and-ebony-inlaid miniature chiffonier. She opened a drawer and lifted a protective layer of velvet, revealing a number of exquisite diamond necklaces, paired with bracelets and earrings. She drew back in surprise and her eyes were fairly bulging as she tested other drawers where she found matching emerald sets and sapphires in all sizes and shapes. There were amethyst and topaz chokers, lavalieres, elaborate pins, and an enormous brooch with a ruby the size of a door knocker. An entire drawer held strings of pearls in various lengths. On the periphery of this *Arabian Nights'* fantasy, she heard Johann explain that his ancestry had not been a very prolific one.

"Rarely have more than one child survived to a marriageable age," he was saying. "My father had two brothers that died in infancy, and my mother was an only child. So these trinkets have accumulated instead of being split up. But if you and I have better luck," he grabbed her suggestively around the waist and kissed her neck, scraping his teeth on a row of sparkling diamonds she was fastening around her throat, "then maybe this stuff will be distributed democratically among our daughters and daughters-in-law, and no longer be a burden for any one woman to care for."

"Hah! Some burden!" Dorrit giggled and pushed Johann away in order to try on yet another glittering piece. She stood in front of the mirror and was almost blinded by her own reflection. "These rubies will do wonders for my white velvet gown," she said dreamily. "And, of course, these fabulous opals will enhance the strapless blue satin. Now, as for the emeralds," she rummaged through a drawer full of green stones, "they'll go well with—"

"Your greedy green eyes!" Johann laughed. "Alas! My sweet and unassuming wife is turning gluttonous. But let's make one thing clear right now. With or without the opals, you're not to wear the blue strapless in public. That gown is . . . well . . . it's indecent. Only to be worn when entertaining at home."

"Madame Mimieux called it 'zee rage.'"

"Outrage is more like it," Johann grinned and cupped Dorrit's chin in his hand. "You can wear it when it's just the two of us. Which I much prefer anyway. In fact, I plan to spend a good many evenings at home this winter in the pleasant pursuit of enriching our family tree. A game that requires only two players and definitely no company."

Dorrit looked up into her husband's jaunty gray eyes, dropped a strand of luminous olive-sized pearls into the chest, and threw her arms around his neck, while she silently and, not without considerable pain, questioned why after six months of marriage, she was still not expecting a baby. Only a week ago, at a dinner party, the Count and Countess von Beckstein had announced that they were going to be grandparents. This in spite of the fact that their daughter, Monika Marie's wedding had taken place a whole month after Dorrit's.

There were days when Dorrit worried that there was some-

182

thing wrong with her; yet she couldn't bring herself to consult her father. They had never discussed discreet female subjects, and if she suddenly started now, he might wonder why she didn't just speak with Johann, her husband, a practicing physician. But to bring her fears to Johann was even more unthinkable, because she couldn't bear to see his disappointment if it was discovered that she was, God forbid, barren!

By the end of January, Berliners would have welcomed a blinding blizzard. Anything was preferable to the steady gray drizzle that sent shooting pains through their bones and put many a fine wine cellar under water.

Increasingly bothered by labored breathing, Professor Zache found little stamina for even simple tasks. The three flights of stairs to his apartment might as well have been the sheer face of the Zugspitze. He cut back on his teaching schedule.

The weather dried out in February, but Herman Zache's lungs did not. Dorrit was immensely relieved when Johann finally threatened him with a hospital stay unless he agreed to move in with them and submit to their care.

Too weak to argue, Herman Zache swallowed his stubborn pride and let himself be settled into the guest suite on the ground floor on Lindenstrasse, where no stairs taxed his strength and where the fireplace would be stoked around the clock. Frau Schmidt made gallons of hot soup, Johann attended to his medication, and Dorrit provided her father with the cheer of her ever-present company. All assumed their duties with faithfulness and prayed for his convalescence.

However, by the end of March, Johann knew his father-in-law's condition was terminal. Nurses were hired in eight-hour shifts while everyone waited for a miracle.

The miracle never came. In the middle of April, Herman Zache died in his sleep after days of convulsive coughing, which had spent his ravaged lungs.

Dorrit was slow to recover from her father's death. And in June, just when she was beginning to take an interest in her surroundings again and was looking forward to spending the summer in the country, she suffered a terrible setback.

Arriving in Bernau, her mood plummeted to new depths, because suddenly everything reminded her of her father's visit last year. He had loved it here. He had been so happy, and realizing that he would never again enjoy this beautiful countryside, it lost its allure for Dorrit. She felt ill, she felt dispirited, and Johann's attempts to restore her humor only irritated her. She found herself snapping at him and, though immediately remorseful, she was unable to control herself. Prudently, she began to stay out of his way. And unlike last summer, she was glad that he was busy with the horses, so busy, in fact, that he forgot to mention riding lessons. She cloistered herself in her rooms, reading and sleeping, mostly sleeping, insofar as it was a wonderful escape from her sorrow.

Occasionally she sought refuge in the rose gardens, where she puttered around, fully determined to vent her black mood on Jens if he dared appear with a scowl on his face. She had enjoyed working in the gardens last summer, but now the perfume of the exquisite flowers made her feel wretched. After only minutes of pruning, she felt faint and was forced to retreat to a shady bench. A retreat she suspected pleased the groundskeeper no end, but depressed her to a point where she often started to cry. She'd sit on the bench and sob without caring a speck who saw her. Just as long as it wasn't Johann.

Dorrit blamed herself for her father's death. She had not been diligent in attending to his welfare. She should have known better than to marry and leave him. It had killed him, same as if she'd put a knife in his heart. And although Johann had carefully explained the ravages of pulmonary consumption, which had led to Herman Zache's death, Dorrit felt responsible and allowed a terrible guilt to gnaw at her innards, dulling her. Listless and despondent, she stayed in bed till noon without reaping any benefit, because by supper, and no matter who graced their table, she had to fight a constant need to yawn.

Friends sent her pitying glances. The glances hurt, but not nearly as much as Johann's grim looks from the other end of the vast dining-room table. There were times when she was grateful for the distance, for she feared he'd like to kick her. It was all he could do to look civil in the face of her colorless conversation, which did nothing to help him entertain their guests.

To make matters worse, Dorrit suspected that she looked awful. For weeks after her father's funeral, she had been too distraught to take an interest in her appearance, and now she was too tired to bother. Tonight she had made the mistake of wearing a mauve, empire-waisted gown, a gown that didn't suit her at all, something she had discovered at a reception in Berlin, during the early spring when Louisa von Tirpitz had gone to great lengths to gush about its style and color. Like so much about Louisa, her flattery had not been genuine. Still, Dorrit wore the gown tonight because it was the first thing to fall from her closets when she was getting dressed.

It was a wonder Johann didn't say anything; he was usually very opinionated.

Didn't he care?

Was his marriage not wearing well? Now that Dorrit exhibited such lackluster traits, was he tolerating his wife because he was stuck with her, while finding pleasant diversion elsewhere? Johann was the kind of man women couldn't keep their eyes or hands off. She'd seen that often enough. Tonight, no less than three ladies at the table were squirming for his attention. He seemed particularly charmed by Countess von Richthofen, whose husband was drinking a great deal and so didn't notice what was going on between his wife and Johann. But Dorrit noticed. She saw Johann laugh at every snippet of conversation that fell from the countess's pretty lips. Perhaps the two of them were even now making plans for a bit of dalliance, which Dorrit had heard was accepted among the *haute monde*. In fact, Johann himself had once told her that Karl-Heinz was unfaithful on occasions, but only because it would kill Gerlinde if he wasn't, since another pregnancy would put her in the grave. But Johann certainly didn't need to take precautions with his wife. Dorrit would welcome a baby—if it killed her.

Dear God! Johann? Unfaithful! Dorrit could stand a lot of things, but not that! She'd rather he beat her than ignore her and look elsewhere.

When had he stopped loving her and why? Actually she knew why. Her hair was limp, her complexion sallow, and tonight her personality was so unilluminating it earned weird looks from everyone around the table. Even Gerlinde eyed her with a strange frown. And dinner was not halfway over before Dorrit realized that those who didn't ignore her outright simply humored her like a senile aunt. Her guests appeased her with a bland comment now and again, half-hearted comments that eventually tapered off until conversation simply ground to a halt and a pall settled over her end of the table. A pall that didn't reach the opposite end, nor did it affect the effervescent Countess von Richthofen. She remained in a decidedly festive mood while engaging Johann's attention.

Dorrit grew increasingly miserable. Things came to a head when at one point, during dessert, she saw the gorgeous countess reach over and put her hand across Johann's. *A lover's caress!* How dare that woman? And right here for all to see!

Anger boiled over in Dorrit's chest, sending bile into her throat, strangling her. She couldn't breathe. The room swayed. Her stomach lurched. Covering her mouth, she rose in defiant desperation and committed a hostess' most unforgivable act. Without a word she left the table.

Behind her, she heard a chair scrape violently against the floor. In the next instant, Johann was at her side, his arm around her waist. He was obviously furious. She turned to look at him, fully expecting a public reprimand. But although his brows had snapped together, he was displaying no visible anger. Of course, she immediately realized that he would not compound her rude behavior and give their guests further indigestion by parading his own ill temper. On the contrary. He clearly meant to mitigate everyone by playing the role of attentive husband. Which he confirmed when he addressed those present.

"Dorrit appears to be ill," he said with his flair for correctness. "She needs to lie down. Carry on. I'll be right back."

Dorrit's knees buckled in shame.

Gerlinde rushed from her seat and came to hug her.

"Feel better," she whispered.

Gerlinde's gesture brought Dorrit to tears, but thankfully, no one saw, because Johann was already marching her into the hall and up the stairs, summoning a maid as he went.

"Help my wife undress!" he commanded when the three of them had reached Dorrit's rooms. "And have someone bring up tea. Under no circumstance leave my wife alone until she's in bed. Is that clear?" His tone was so blunt, he could have used Latin, and the girl, nodding so fervently that it was setting her cap askew, would have understood him.

Dorrit wondered why he was taking out his anger on a poor

maid who had done nothing wrong. And had she dared, she would have intervened. However, she was hardly in a position now to question her husband's tone when it was her own conduct that had pushed him to be short-tempered.

Satisfied that his orders would be carried out, Johann returned to the guests.

Dorrit had barely undressed, finished a cup of chamomile tea, and sunk into her soft feather bed before Johann reappeared, claiming everyone had shown the good sense to leave early. And although she knew that he enjoyed nothing better than late hours of high-staked card games after dinner, she discerned no irritation in his voice when he commented on the party's premature adjournment.

Though puzzled, she was much too weary to try to figure it out. She could not keep her eyes open. Her head felt as heavy as a boulder. She was asleep before Johann left her rooms, closing the connecting door to his bedroom behind him.

But in her semiconscious state, before oblivion claimed her, Dorrit sensed that he had stood by her bed, brooding dangerously.

Had he contemplated strangling her?

TWENTY-SEVEN

The morning following the aborted dinner party, Gerlinde walked uninvited into Dorrit's bedroom. The timing couldn't have been worse. Dorrit felt horrible and wished to see no one, least of all a perky neighbor who might inform the entire county of her wretchedness, describe to the curious how her hair was tangled in stringy clumps, and worse, the way her room smelled. She had just vomited in a chamber pot that had not yet been removed because she was too weak to tug at the bellpull. Her pink satin sheets were stained and crumbled. Yards of Valenciennes lace, normally gracefully draped from the canopy of her bed, hung lopsided and torn; Dorrit could only think that she must have yanked on these panels during the night in her sleep. Withal, she wished she were dead and hated Gerlinde for seeing her like this, hated her smug smile and greeting. Dorrit returned both with a glare, as harsh a one as she could manage, given her illness.

But the cold reception did not deter Gerlinde, whose mission was precisely to clarify why Dorrit had been so miserable last night and why she felt even worse this morning.

"Your sickness," Gerlinde began and walked briskly across the soft gray carpet to pull back the pink and pearl striped curtains on the twin dormers; instantly the fresh July morning spread cheer in the room. She turned toward the bed. "Mind if I open a window?"

"No. Please do."

Gerlinde opened two and leaned out to fill her lungs with the fragrant air, momentarily silencing the chirping birds flitting about in the ancient ivy clinging to the red brick. She came back to sit down on the edge of Dorrit's bed.

"Now, as I was saying," her small frame fairly bristled with self-importance at the wealth of information she carried in her sparse bosom, "your sickness... the reason you feel lousy and only want to sleep—"

"Oh, I know!" Dorrit interrupted.

"You do?"

"Of course. I . . . I have a stomach ailment of sorts. A nasty strain. It won't go away. Please," Dorrit pointed to the bellrope, "I need to get rid of the chamber pot. It's so disgusting! The open windows help but . . ." having to admit to the mess under the bed was mortifying; Dorrit turned into the pillow so she wouldn't have to face Gerlinde. "The smell alone is making me ill," she finished lamely.

Forgoing the bell, Gerlinde stuck her head out into the hall and called a maid; at her own house that usually got quicker results, and as soon as the offending pot was removed and replaced with a clean one, she sat back down and looked as if she was about to burst if she didn't speak soon.

"Dorrit," she said, "look at me!" Dorrit obeyed reluctantly. "I know you're suffering from nausea, but you don't have a stomach complaint."

"I don't?" Dorrit wondered how Gerlinde could so cavalierly dismiss the foul proof in the chamber pot.

"That's right. Sure, certain foods turn your stomach. Particularly that custard cobbler Frau Erdmann served last night. Still, you're mostly ill in the mornings. Right?" Dorrit nodded. "And you've had none of that monthly . . . well, you know . . . that stuff lately. Right?"

A spot of scarlet crept into each of Dorrit's cheeks; acute embarrassment at such frank talk prevented her from answering. She averted her eyes, pulled the sheet clear up to her neck, and realized that she had completely forgotten about the absence of a period all these weeks. Again she nodded.

"I thought so," Gerlinde said and folded her arms across her chest like a school mistress about to lecture the class. For although she'd once been as uninformed as Dorrit, plus a hundred times more shy, at the age of twenty-three and with three children to her credit, she was now a woman of experience.

Remaining mute as a stone, Dorrit sank even further into the bedding as Gerlinde blithely began to share this abundant experience, ending with a dramatic statement:

"All your symptoms point to the simple fact that you are pregnant!"

"Huh . . . ?"

"You heard me, silly! You are going to have a baby!"

The corner of the sheet was in Dorrit's mouth; she didn't know how it had gotten there, but she was suddenly chewing on it, while her heart made squishy sounds in her chest. And overwhelmed by a great need to laugh or cry—she didn't know which—except all at once she was so happy that laughter seemed most appropriate.

"Are you sure . . . " her voice bubbled with giggles, "are you sure that's all that's wr . . . wrong with me?"

"Positive. But," Gerlinde looked devilishly sly, "if you want a second opinion, Johann can examine you."

"Good gracious, no!" Dorrit looked horrified. "I mean . . . what I mean to say is that . . . that he probably wouldn't want to. I don't think he wants to come near me unless it's to wring my neck." She didn't go so far as to elaborate on his absence in her bed during the past weeks.

"Wring your neck? Why on earth?"

"Because . . . " it felt so good to confide in someone that Dorrit couldn't stop herself, she had never before had any close friends, and it was a heavenly picnic to talk her heart out, "because I deserve it," she admitted.

"You what?"

"I deserve it. I've been a monster lately. I haven't been myself since my father died. I've gone from bad to worse since coming to Bernau. Last night, I hit bottom, as you saw. Johann was very angry. I can't say that I blame him. I behaved miserably in front of his friends."

"Wait a minute! What do you mean 'his friends'? We're just as much your friends. Most of us anyway." Gerlinde's small heart-shaped face was an open book; it was obvious that she had seen Countess von Richthofen trifle with Johann at the dinner table. "And I can tell you that Johann is not angry with you. Far from it! He is worried. Worried to death about you. Particularly about your condition."

"My condition? Do you think he has guessed?" Dorrit's spine tingled with the idea that Johann might know.

"Guessed?" Gerlinde snorted as if someone's intelligence had come into question. "Of course, he has guessed! He's a doctor, for heaven's sake. And the best! My daughters and I are living testimony to that. He's only dumbfounded that you haven't wanted to share your good news with him. Being an impatient man, he has shown remarkable patience waiting for you to mention the fact that he's going to be a father. Men are quite silly about that sort of thing."

"But how could I tell him? I didn't know."

"That's precisely what he began to suspect, and why he felt obliged to enlist my services. He looked pretty sheepish last night after you went to bed, and he threw us all out. But before Karl-Heinz and I got the boot, Johann ordered me to come back here first thing in the morning. He figured a heart-to-heart talk with another female might do you a world of good. He was quite exasperated and stammered something about the fact that you had grown up without a mother and might therefore not know about certain things."

Dorrit smiled. Johann never stammered.

"Besides," Gerlinde continued, "haven't you wondered why he hasn't pestered you to ride? He's been ribbing Karl-Heinz for years for failing to get me up on a horse. Believe me, my husband was getting ready to dish out some crow; you're saving yours the trouble of eating it."

"Please don't mention eating."

"Sorry." Gerlinde laughed and got off the bed. She bent down and kissed Dorrit's forehead. "I'll be leaving now. Johann is waiting downstairs. He hasn't gone out to the stables yet. That's how anxious he is about our little chat. So do get dressed and go on down and put him out of his misery." At the door, Gerlinde turned. "He's stretching it, you know, putting you ahead of the horses this morning." She laughed, waved gaily, and was gone.

Dorrit had barely put her feet on the floor before Johann burst into her room. For a moment, he just stood there, grinning broadly, looking at his disheveled wife as if she was the eighth wonder of the world. Then he crossed the floor, ignored the traces of vomit on her nightgown, and gathered her into his arms.

*   *   *

Lillian Schindel and Kurt Eckart came to Bernau for a week in August. But inasmuch as they were engaged and not yet married, propriety required that they maintain separate roofs. Lillian stayed with the Konauers, relatives were the most exemplary chaperones, and Kurt stayed at the barony, where

Dorrit and Johann hosted a party the first night of their visit.

Desperately wanting to look her best, Dorrit perused her closets very carefully for this occasion, finally settling on a green organdy, although she would have to wear it minus its pretty sash or risk fainting from being cinched too tightly. Her figure was thickening, she would soon have to let out all the seams to accommodate her expanding midriff. But she had never been particularly vain, losing her waistline was of no account, and as she admired her swelling figure in the full length mirror hung on the inside of the wardrobe doors, a deep sense of contentment put color into her cheeks. She smiled back at her own reflection, went over to her dressing table, picked up a brush, and gave her hair a hundred strokes before twisting it into a chic knot at the nape, the latest in Berlin hair fashion. To soften the severity of the style, she pulled a few springy curls loose around her forehead and chose dainty clusters of seed pearls for her ears. Around her neck she hung the emerald heart. It went well with the dress, and Johann was always pleased when she wore it.

Satisfied with the way she looked, she took a deep breath and realized that she was actually looking forward to the evening ahead. At least she felt pretty sure her stomach would not riot at the mere sight of spinach souffle or cream cakes. Twenty people were expected for dinner, but as Johann had commented earlier when he walked through her rooms, fastening his tie and buttoning his evening jacket before going downstairs, they could never be quite sure about Philip von Brandt. It was common knowledge that the fair-haired Philip would arrive punctually only if he did not stop at a tavern on the way and fall in with a full tankard and an overripe female, in which case, he would roll in the next day, after her charms and his headache had both worn off. Parties in the country could easily go on for a week; it was generally no disaster to miss the first night.

Making her way downstairs and crossing the enormous foyer, Dorrit blew a whimsical kiss to the George Seurat seascape from San Sebastian hanging in a prominent spot near the library. The doors to the terrace at the far end of the hall were open, and gales of merriment wafted in from the group gathered outside. Dorrit was late because she had been slow to awaken from a nap earlier, but Johann had promised to make her excuses. Now she quickened her steps, ready to carry out her role as hostess.

Johann extricated himself from a conversation and came to her side the minute she stepped out on the terrace. Taking her arm, he led her across the flagstones.

"Twenty minutes on your feet, and I'll begin scowling like a black devil if you are not sitting in a chair," he whispered as they went.

"But I feel terrific, Johann."

"That's wonderful, sweetheart. Still, I expect you to be obedient. If not, I'll put a bug in Anna's ear about how you are dying to hear about her and Enno's Mediterranean cruise. That ought to keep you nicely pinned in a seat till dinner."

"You are assuming that I wouldn't be delighted to hear about her trip."

"That's right. They encountered rough seas, and her details are quite graphic. And as always, far too lengthy."

Dorrit laughed at his reference to Anna von Steigert's gift for gab, and she was about to protest that her stomach had called a truce, when the very person being discussed, Enno's new wife, spotted her and immediately rushed over.

Enno von Steigert had been a friend of Johann's since childhood when the two small boys had first studied each other through a hole in the hedge which separated their parents' respective properties on Lindenstrasse. The opening was eventually expanded to allow easy access, and the boys had become inseparable whenever Johann visited Berlin. Years later, when Enno's parents left the villa to his older sister and left him the money to build a home of similar grandeur, he did so in neighboring Wannsee. However, he had little time to enjoy his new residence, since his work as a foreign diplomat necessitated living abroad. There had only been one exception, a tragic one, when some three years ago, a vacation in Kenya ended in horror when his first wife suffered a snake bite and died.

Nearly losing his mind over the incident, Enno was sedated and housebound in Wannsee for months. No one expected him to remarry, certainly not anytime soon. However, while on a visit in Hamburg last year, he met the vivacious Anna Schellenberg, who convinced him in a remarkably short period of time that her dearest wish was to move in diplomatic circles. Not one to let a lady's wish go begging, Enno married her, and Anna immediately proved her veracity and her ability to adjust to all manner of hardships associated with living abroad. She packed and unpacked her suitcases with scientific precision and made lifelong friends in all four corners of the continent.

As the party on this balmy evening in August drew to a close and the wise went home or retired to the guest rooms, stalwarts like Kurt and Johann were abandoned to polish off a bottle of 1880 English bourbon along with a highly wagered game of tarok.

It was long past midnight when Johann staggered into Dorrit's bedroom and noticed that her lights were still on. Thinking she had fallen asleep, he intended to turn the lamps off. He was surprised to find her awake and reading. Realizing he looked like hell's picnic, he raked a hand self-consciously through his hair. His collar was open, a crumpled tie was slung negligently over his shoulder, and the red fissures in his eyes could only be repaired with a good night's sleep.

"I wore Kurt down and sent him to his room broke," he grinned and bent down to kiss Dorrit good night.

"In that case you had better lay low tomorrow or prepare yourself to face Lillian's wrath. She has finally convinced Kurt that he's financially solvent and able to set a wedding date. They have settled on November the first."

"I'll forgive Kurt's debt first thing in the morning," Johann laughed.

Dorrit reached for his hand. It only required a slight tug to make him sit down on the edge of her bed. She put her book away, pushed an extra pillow behind her back, and began to play with the lapels of his evening jacket, all the while thinking how extraordinarily handsome he was despite his rumpled appearance.

Johann took her hands, kissed the inside of her wrists, while silently reminding himself of her *enceinte* condition. However, the bourbon was impinging upon his good judgment; it was proving a struggle to get off her bed. Especially in the wake of her next words.

"Aren't you going to keep me company?" she slipped her hands inside his open jacket.

"No, darling," he mumbled and soothed the piqued frown off

her forehead with his lips. "We have to be careful a little while longer. Until you feel better. The first few months are the most critical."

"But I do feel better," she whispered against his face. "It's only the mornings that are so dreadful. And tomorrow is a long way off."

"It's later than you think. You need sleep and definitely no exertion." Grinning, he added, "Doctor's orders."

"Perhaps we ought to get a second opinion." Dorrit managed a face as sly as Gerlinde's the day she had suggested something similar. "Not that I question your professional competence, of course, but since Dr. Eckart is conveniently on the premises."

"Why, you little . . ." Johann's words died away as her arms locked around his neck and he felt her breasts, enlarged by pregnancy, press against his thin silk shirt. But after all, a man's starved body can stand only so much stimulation, every fiber of his being went AWOL with her pleasant invitation. A heartbeat later, his resolve and his good intentions disintegrated completely when she moved over to make room for him in the bed, displaying her very shapely legs in the process.

TWENTY-EIGHT

In February, on a night when Berlin was buffeted by an ice storm that snapped trees and brought down power lines, Dorrit gave birth to a fine healthy boy. Johann had finished his shift at Wirchow, arrived home to find her in labor, and taking no chances, immediately put her in the coach and made a U-turn back to Wirchow, all along the way cursing Schmidt for attacking the icy roads with sound caution.

Nature was rarely kind to first-time mothers. Dorrit's labor was long, and toward morning, when Johann's own exhaustion made him ineffectual, he turned her over to a trusted colleague, Dr. Benjamin Tarnoff, who was just coming on duty. Secure in the knowledge that Dorrit was in the best of hands, Johann plunked down on a cot in the physician's lounge, intending to catch a short nap. But even as he clamped down his eyelids, numb to the lumpy mattress and deaf to the scraping noise of sleet blowing against the windows, he was not able to sleep. His mind, refusing to rest, was needled by age-old gossip concerning the birth of Kaiser Wilhelm; a botched affair known in professional circles as the great insult to German medicine because Britain's Queen Victoria sent her personal physician to Berlin with instructions that if it came to a decision, he was to save the life of her daughter, the kaiserin, over that of the child.

In his eagerness to obey this royal command, the English doctor pulled on the baby with unnecessary force, causing one arm to become separated from its shoulder socket. And immediately turning all his attention back to the mother, the baby was wrapped by a distracted nurse, the damage ignored for critical hours when it might have been corrected. This bungling condemned Wilhelm II to carry a useless arm.

Johann had frequently wondered at the mind-set of those involved. Until today. Today, when all his own concern was for Dorrit, he finally understood the queen's orders. Nothing on earth mattered to him except Dorrit. *And if it came to a decision—*

Instantly alert, he jumped off the cot, left the physicians' lounge, and, his white surgeon's coat flying behind him, ran down the narrow corridor, sending hospital personnel diving into doorways.

He had neglected to instruct Dr. Tarnoff that if it came to a decision...

Johann barged into the delivery room just in time to have a nurse place his son, squealing lustily, into his arms.

They named him Maximilian Johannes.

They called him Max.

*　　*　　*

Kaiser Wilhelm's personal physician, Theodor Renvers, had on numerous occasions been present as an observer in Wirchow's operating rooms, where the ability of a certain surgeon had come to his attention. Therefore, it was not surprising that this particular individual was on Dr. Renvers' mind one morning in early June of 1905, when he accompanied the kaiser on his regular constitutional through the palace gardens on Unter den Linden. Wilhelm II was an early riser, fond of fresh air and exercise, which included beating his chest with his good arm while he inhaled and exhaled ten times, treatment Dr. Renvers had not prescribed and which invariably caused a smirk to form on his lips; something he was careful not to let the kaiser see.

Wilhelm took great pride in perfect health, ignored his deformity, and people who wished to serve him learned never to cast a glance toward his withered arm. Lately, however, he'd been bothered by painful growths in his throat, something he could not ignore. His father, Emperor Frederick III, had died only months after being diagnosed with throat cancer, and the possibility of suffering the same fate disturbed the forty-five year old kaiser. He and Dr. Renvers had discussed various medical options, all pointing to surgery. But Theodor Renvers, a physician entrusted with the health of the entire imperial household, was a man of some sixty-plus years and past his prime as a surgeon; especially for something as delicate as the sovereign trachea, which was why he today sang the praises of a younger man.

197

"There's not a steadier pair of hands in all of Germany," he avowed once the kaiser had finished his chest-pounding ritual. "The man has nerves of steel."

"I see." Wilhelm started to walk again, the gravel crunching beneath his mirror-polished boots as he strolled along a path through a sea of pink and white azaleas. He stopped to pull a dandelion out of the ground; *how on earth had thirty gardeners missed such a large weed?* Holding the offending plant pinched between two fingers, he resumed walking. "Nerves of steel, you say. And good hands. But can he be trusted to be discreet?"

"Absolutely." Renvers was forced to pick up his steps to keep abreast of the monarch, exertion that left him short of breath. "He's a very private individual. He shuns any professional acclaim. He's not out to make a name for himself. He is a baron with a large estate in Bernau."

"A baron toils at Wirchow!" The kaiser looked surprised.

"Not to make a living, I can assure Your Majesty. Something else drives him. The challenge of the profession, I believe. Some call him an eccentric. Others say he's a dreamer. He talks of spare parts for humans and the possibility of reattaching severed limbs." Renvers allowed himself a hearty chuckle. "His outlandish theories provide those of us in the profession with provocative entertainment now and again. As for his own amusement, I'm told he regularly experiments on cadavers."

Pursing his lips, Wilhelm gazed skyward. Dr. Renvers waited patiently for him to speak. If this surgeon was not acceptable to the kaiser, who could he possibly recommend? There were so many butchers, and gifted doctors were ambitious and might threaten his own position with the royal family. Renvers did not want to be sent out to pasture quite yet, which was why Dr. von Renz was so perfect. He was far too talented to aspire to playing nursemaid to the kaiser and far too keen on spending long summers on his estate to risk being at the beck and call whenever someone sneezed at the palace. But it was safe to assume that he'd consider it his patriotic duty to help out in a pinch. And this was a pinch, because a slight—hopefully, a very temporary—trembling bedeviled Dr. Renvers' right hand and prevented him from attempting the precarious incisions of the kaiser's throat.

"Hmm . . . a baron who derives pleasure from evisceration of the dead." Wilhelm found an appropriate receptacle for the dandelion and wiped the sharp smell of the weed from his fingers with a handkerchief. "Sounds like an intriguing individual. What did you say his name was? Or did you?"

"Forgive me. No, I don't believe I mentioned it. His name is Baron Johann Maximilian von Renz."

"Oh!" Wilhelm's eyes widened with surprise. "I know the man. He is received at Court. This is indeed a coincidence. Emperor Frederick enjoyed a long association with a Baron Edmund Bernhard von Renz. Obviously, this remarkable surgeon's father. Send for him at once!"

That very afternoon, summoned by a cryptic but urgent message, Johann was shown into a private chamber in the Imperial Palace on Unter den Linden. Clasping his hands behind his back, he wondered what this was all about as he strolled the floor and studied a number of royal portraits in heavy gold frames. The entire room was gilded, walls, ceiling, every piece of furniture was clad with an aurous finish, and the coverings on chairs and settees were of a gold-colored fabric as well. The blue porcelain *Kamin* in the corner looked completely out of place.

A door opened at the far end of the room. Johann immediately recognized Dr. Renvers as the man crossed the expanse of shiny golden parquet, his shoes clicking noisily as he approached.

"Herr Baron! I am delighted to see you!" Dr. Renvers pumped Johann's hand enthusiastically and motioned for him to sit down on a gilded chair. And after first glancing around to assure himself that they were quite alone, he pulled up a similar national treasure and sat down opposite the visitor. Servants were known to have extraordinary hearing, and taking no chances, Dr. Renvers barely spoke above a whisper as he came right to the point and explained how Johann could be of immeasurable service to the Crown.

"If you accept this assignment," he said as he finished detailing the kaiser's complaint, "you must perform the surgery forthwith. Our kaiser has suffered many a sleepless night and wishes to have it over with. And I must stress that word of it cannot leave these walls. It is crucial that the population at large not suspect any illness at the palace. We're living in a volatile time. There is unrest in the streets, unemployment being what it is. Too many young people are leaving the land for the glamour of the cities. I don't need to tell you that it's straining the job market. We're increasingly having to put down street riots. Each a crisis. I don't know where it'll end. But I know that in times of turmoil, there must be no hint of vulnerability at the top. Panic could ensue." Renvers looked grim. "Not even our dear kaiserin has been told of her husband's ailment. Of course, if . . . *Gott bewahre*, a malignancy is found, we shall naturally be forced to make an official statement."

Johann nodded. He was aware of the tension and strife among workers and jobless alike; casualties from riots and street fights were regularly admitted to Wirchow.

"I've taken the liberty of assuring His Majesty that I can have your complete discretion in this matter," Dr. Renvers said.

"Of course." Johann rose, indicating the interview was over.

Dr. Renvers ignored the snub to his position and led the haughty aristocrat through the interior maze of the royal residence, finally arriving at his private offices, next to which was a state-of-the-art hospital.

Impressed with the facility, Johann took quick mental notes. He had recently toyed with the idea of establishing a clinic of his own, and, to the last detail, this was precisely what he'd envisioned. Remembering that a house on the corner of Lindenstrasse, and the well-traveled Halensee had come on the market, he decided—here on the spot—to buy it and immediately put his architects to work designing its conversion, a project that was sure to please Dorrit. She was not always reconciled to his long hours at Wirchow, especially when an emergency caused him to arrive home too late to see Max before the boy's bedtime.

While both doctors scrubbed, Dr. Renvers elaborated on the kaiser's health history, underscoring his tolerance for pain.

"He's hard as nails," he promised, smiling with apology at his choice of words; the same time, he eyed Johann's hands, hands that would momentarily be entrusted with the life of the most powerful man in all of Europe. One slip of the scalpel and the kaiser might drown in his own blood. Watching the younger surgeon scrub, it actually began to bother Dr. Renvers that he was so utterly calm in the face of this paramount assignment.

The patient, who had gone to great lengths to arrive without being spotted by servants who might wonder why he was heading for the infirmary, strolled in moments later. He had enjoyed outwitting one and all, and giving no clue to his fear of cancer, his piercing blue eyes flickered with recognition as he greeted Johann warmly and engaged him in conversation.

When it appeared that the kaiser was enjoying himself far too much and might have forgotten the urgency that existed, Dr. Renvers stepped in.

"Ahem . . ." He cleared his throat discreetly, then bluntly reminded everyone about the consequential situation that had brought them together. "Shall we get started?"

Wilhelm proved to be an excellent patient. He required a minimum amount of sedation and Johann removed the growths and cauterized the incisions with routine perfection.

While the kaiser remained recumbent, Dr. Renvers hovered at his side, checking the royal throat for any unusual bleeding, all the while congratulating himself for choosing Dr. von Renz for this delicate assignment. In all his years in the profession, he had never before seen such quick and neat work. Dr. von Renz was a damned miracle worker. Wilhelm might well be on his feet in an hour. Tonight he could simply claim a touch of laryngitis and insist on broth for dinner.

After carefully examining the removed throat tissue under several microscopes, Johann announced that although the specimens were large, they were, in fact, harmless polyps. No cancer was found.

That verdict revived the monarch considerably. He clasped Johann's hand in his. "I'm in your debt," he whispered in a raw postoperative voice.

"Not at all," Johann protested.

The kaiser wanted to say more, but both doctors cautioned him not to speak, there was a danger of hemorrhaging.

"A bland liquid diet for one week and no public speaking for two," Johann instructed, and after assuring himself that the kaiser was resting comfortably, he left him in Dr. Renvers' care.

Johann was not to dwell on this surgery, and as he made his way back to Wirchow, it never occurred to him that this service to the Crown would someday impact a tragedy of proportions he could not possibly begin to imagine on this benign June day.

TWENTY-NINE

From the day it opened its door, Johann's clinic on Halensee Strasse met with tremendous success. Specializing in plastic surgery, a new field few physicians ventured into, the clinic attracted a discriminating clientele, those who wished for the complete privacy large city hospitals could not offer. Patients were also occasionally transferred from Wirchow or from Charite when an industrial accident taxed their resources. Dr. von Renz never turned away a charity case; he engaged two full-time assistants but personally handled all trauma and burn victims, which meant that, following a civic disaster, those who endured the additional ride in the ambulance to the Halensee Strasse Clinic were the lucky ones.

In the years following Max's birth, Dorrit suffered two miscarriages. But in 1908, she gave birth to another son. They named him Frederick Alexander, soon shortening it to Fritz.

With the arrival of this much-wanted second child, Johann decided to lessen his responsibilities. Max was going on five and he did not want to miss out on either one of his sons' tender years altogether. He approached Dr. Benjamin Tarnoff, a trusted colleague from Wirchow who had assisted in both of Dorrit's difficult deliveries, with an offer of a professional partnership.

Ben accepted and, with his wife, Gertrude, moved into the spacious quarters on the top floor of the clinic. In addition to the convenience of residing on the premises, the move was a pleasant one, because not only was this apartment larger than the flat they'd occupied near Wirchow, it came with a garden. And having reached middle-age childless and resigned, Gertrude was soon directing all her untapped maternal instincts to the rebirth of this wonderful green spot behind the clinic.

Once she'd unpacked the last cup and saucer, she immediately set about breathing new life into the garden, where, in defiance of years of neglect, several fruit trees thrived. A good pruning encouraged them further. The soil in the old flower beds was weeded, fed and turned over and showed its gratitude by producing blooms in rare size and color. Gertrude trimmed overgrown bushes choking the boxwood hedges bordering the property, she raked mulch into the lawn and stopped its invasion of a graveled foot path. The only greenery that didn't suffer the clippers, a shovel, or a pinch, were the gnarled grapevines clinging to an ancient trellis along the sunny side of the red-brick terrace. The vines were spared because, after a thorough inspection, Gertrude could not decide if the trellis was supporting the grapes or if it was the other way around. But she figured that if neither one was disturbed, their collaboration might outlast her expectations.

Despite an age difference of some twenty years, Dorrit found a new friend in Ben Tarnoff's wife. Their origins were similar. Both Ben and Gertrude were Russian-Jewish expatriates. He a doctor, she a nurse, they had met and married in Moscow in 1887, months before a sudden round-up of Jews. Tipped off by one of Ben's Christian colleagues only hours before the hospital was under siege by the czar's police, they managed to escape and, from that day forward, fled steadily toward the west, eventually settling in Berlin.

"Berlin's been good to us," Gertrude was glad to report and tucked a loose strand of hair behind her ears. Her conservative coiffure, a tight bun wrapped in a hair net at the nape, was still more black than gray, and her brown eyes were full of youthful curiosity; only her square build and slightly swollen ankles gave her age away. It was a lovely afternoon in May and she and Dorrit were sitting on the brick terrace, enjoying the view of the rejuvenated garden waking up to a new season. Dorrit often stopped in to admire Gertrude's handiwork, and the two women never tired of comparing a past with so many similarities it had forged a bond between them. "Both Ben and I lost relatives to the *pogroms*," Gertrude went on to say. "Neither one of us felt truly safe until we reached Germany."

Dorrit nodded and explained the reason her father had felt precisely the same way.

*　　*　　*

At the age of twenty-seven, Dorrit had remained lithe of

body and her hair was still a vibrant auburn, while the sparkle in her luminous green eyes regularly outshone the fabulous jewels she wore. Without question, the Baroness von Renz was one of the most glamorous of Berlin's elite. And the evening in 1909, when she and Johann attended a palace ball in honor of Germany's new chancellor, Theobald von Bethmann-Hollweg, was to be no exception. She wore a king's ransom in diamonds and a low-cut shimmering green satin gown, flaring with gold-spun lace at the wrists and at the flounced hem.

The former chancellor, *Furts* von Bulow, had resigned earlier in the year when he lost the support of both the Reichstag and the kaiser. His tenure had been difficult and his departure bitter, but he and his wife, Princess Maria, showed no battle scars during this night of celebration for the successor. On the contrary.

"He has fallen from power, yet I've never seen *Furst* von Bulow look more pleased with himself," Dorrit whispered to Johann while they strolled the salon, stopping now and again to chat with friends and acquaintances.

"I suppose he's relieved not to be involved in the daily turmoil."

"Most of which he created," Dorrit pointed out. "His aggressive foreign policy turned out to be disastrous."

"Yes. We haven't got a single association in Europe that's worth a damn. The French are still angry with our interference in Morocco, and it doesn't look like the Russians are going to let the Bosnian crisis pass." Johann made a wry face. "And now the British are mad."

"Why?"

"They don't like rivalry in the Middle East. Our plan for a Baghdad railway irritates the hell out of them."

Dorrit was swift to come to Germany's defense; she loved her adopted country.

"Well, let's see the British build a railroad. They are free to compete," she said.

"They don't want to. They'd rather stop us. And Wilhelm's constant talk of German superiority hardens their resolve."

"You sound like Count von Beckstein."

"He and I occasionally see eye to eye," Johann grinned and

stopped at a champagne table, where he and Dorrit exchanged pleasantries with those gathered there. Handing Dorrit a glass and taking one for himself, they soon took their leave.

"Count von Beckstein likes our new chancellor." Dorrit returned to their conversation as they walked away.

"If he can soothe our troubles abroad and ease economic tension at home plus retain the kaiser's support, he'll be on my A list as well."

"That's a tall order, Johann."

"I'm simply quoting his campaign promises."

"What about his pledge to expand the army? He claims to be a dove, yet he's mighty eager to build up the military. I don't particularly like that."

"He's hoping to absorb the unemployed. Joblessness has got to be brought under control, or we could be facing turmoil unlike any in recent memory. And not just strikes and street riots."

"Revolution?"

"Maybe worse. There are times I fear we're sitting on a powder keg. Tension around Europe being what it is, it'll take very little to set it off. In which case there'll be war."

"Please, you're depressing me!"

"That's the last thing I want to do, darling." Johann deposited his empty glass on the tray of a passing waiter. "So let's change the subject and dance." He nodded toward her champagne. "Do you want to get rid of that?"

"Yes."

The waiter was gone, so Johann placed Dorrit's glass on a mezzanine ledge where it'd be safe until another waiter could collect it. Then he led her down into the ballroom and out among other dancers.

"In fact, and on a different subject," he said once their feet were in step with the music, "ever since we left the house this evening, I've been wondering what on earth possessed my virtuous wife to display herself so immodestly?" Johann bent down and kissed her neck and bare shoulders, attracting a number of disapproving looks from Berlin's *prominente* matrons silently questioning why this particular baron always insisted on molesting his wife in public.

"What do you mean?"

"Don't play innocent with me. You know very well that you are encouraging half the men in the ballroom to commit mental adultery."

"Only half? How disappointing," Dorrit laughed.

"The other half, my dear, are foreigners, seething with envy because not only are our railroads superior, our women are as well."

Their dance was all too soon interrupted by the predictable tap on Johann's shoulder, obliging him to relinquish Dorrit to none other than the devil or savior, depending on how one perceived Chancellor Theobald von Bethmann-Hollweg this early in his administration.

When Dorrit's next partner turned out to be none other than the exalted Kaiser Wilhelm himself, who astonished one and all by keeping the Baroness von Renz in his company for the entire length of two complete waltzes—generating a buzz of furious whispering—Johann danced with the kaiserin and then with Louisa. She had some years ago married *Graf* Zollern; given birth three times and grown so plump that ball gowns were no longer flattering.

"Did you enjoy yourself, darling?" Johann asked in the car on the way home. During the latter part of the evening, Dorrit had been monopolized by others.

"Um, except for the snitty remarks that floated around the ballroom about a certain individual who needed to behave with more dignity at Court, or risk being banished. Apparently the kaiserin finds anything other than a chaste waltz highly inappropriate."

Johann threw back his head and laughed.

"Good God! The kaiserin's had seven children. I suppose she'd like us to think that we are in the presence of a blushing virgin." Johann slipped an arm around Dorrit and drew her close. "Imagine, seven children with a one-armed husband. I'll bet she's promiscuous as hell."

"What a thing to say!" Dorrit giggled. "Have you no respect?"

"None for hypocrisy. And by the way, I'm still trying to decide whether to credit you or the celebrated Madama Mimieux for this gown you're wearing."

"What?"

"You heard me. Now tell me, what compelled a matronly

mother of two strapping boys to display her bosom so immodestly?"

"Promiscuity, of course."

Grinning, Johann kissed her but was rewarded with a not entirely painless bite, for his one ill-chosen word, "matronly."

Schmidt kept his eyes discreetly peering into the dark road ahead. He knew better than to direct as much as a glance toward the rear view mirror. Besides, he had enough to concentrate on now that he was driving a motor car. The carriages had recently been retired when the baron purchased two Daimler-Benz automobiles. A seven-liter Mercedes touring car for summer driving, and a heavier, longer sedan for the winter months.

THIRTY

Five years later...

Spring of 1914 saw the tense and long-simmering atmosphere in Europe reach levels of near hysteria. Crowned heads eyed each other with cold suspicion, increased their military preparedness, and rushed to line up with their allies. The stages of war were being set.

Germany joined ranks with Austria-Hungary and Turkey, and Kaiser Wilhelm put out feelers to assure himself of a friendly alliance with Russia. After all, he and his cousin, Czar Nicholas, had generally enjoyed a pleasant relationship. Indeed, years back when the indecisive Nicholas had been too shy to request the hand of Princess Alix of Hesse in marriage, Wilhelm, who suffered no reticence around the ladies, came to his aid. During a family holiday, he thrust some roses into Nicholas's hand, took him by the arm, and said: "Alix is crazy about you. Let's go propose to her!" Alix, also a cousin to the kaiser, became Empress Alexandra of Russia, and since she and Nicholas were completely devoted to each other, Wilhelm took some credit for their happiness.

However, when the German ambassador to the Court of Saint Petersburg rushed back to Berlin in May of 1914 with stories of mounting unrest inside Russia that weakened the czar daily, Wilhelm decided that the giant country to the east could not be counted on, and might not even be trusted. In fact, this could be the perfect opportunity to strike. A turbulent Russia, with an irresolute and vulnerable ruler, might fall quickly, and be a juicy plum in German hands.

Wilhelm summoned his generals to discuss an invasion of Russia along with the planned assault on France, and would hear none of it when they warned him about fighting on two fronts; a strategy that was bound to tax their, albeit superior, military machinery.

While talk of war reached fever-pitch proportions, the fuse

was lit when a Serbian nationalist, with hope of Slavic freedom mixed with hatred for Austria-Hungary, assassinated Austria's Archduke Ferdinand at Sarajevo, Yugoslavia, on June 18, 1914.

At the time of this shattering event, Dorrit and Johann were spending a pleasant summer in Bernau with their two sons.

Max, at eleven years of age, was a handsome boy with a head of blond hair, compliments of his princely Russian grandfather, and green eyes as startling as Dorrit's. Long in the legs like his father, the boy sat well in the saddle, and this summer, Johann finally let him choose a full-sized thoroughbred for his own. Without hesitation, Max picked the most spirited two-year-old in the stables and set about training the excitable animal with a firm voice and grip, triumphing in record time—no surprise to anyone—because once his mind was made up, Max usually prevailed, no matter the obstacle.

In direct contrast, his younger brother, Fritz, preferred to spend long hours by himself in the quiet pursuit of some solitary activity. He would soon celebrate his sixth birthday and was perfectly content to ride his small, fat Welsh pony around in the confines of the paddocks, only occasionally venturing beyond these safe enclosures when he rode up to the terrace at the back of the house where his mother regularly entertained friends for afternoon tea. There he would show off his limited riding skills and bask in the limelight, because Max could be depended upon to be nowhere in sight.

Physically, Fritz bore an uncanny resemblance to his father. He had his deep-set gray eyes, the strong square jaw and the dark brown hair, and although he was inclined to be reserved and quiet, his face shone with curiosity. Timid or not, both Dorrit and Johann agreed the boy was intelligent beyond his years.

It was nearly noon when Johann and Max returned from their morning ride on a warm day in late June. Max remained in the stables to scrub down his horse. Johann left his to the grooms and walked up to the house, where he expected to find Dorrit on the terrace. He was not disappointed.

The minute she spotted him cutting across the lawns, she put down the book she was reading and quickly unfolded a parasol so he wouldn't scold her for sitting unprotected in the sun.

"Hm, is that bumbershoot for my benefit or yours?" Johann

hadn't missed the umbrella's sudden release and cocked a censorious eyebrow as he bent down to kiss her.

Dorrit managed to look as if she didn't know what on earth he was talking about.

"Really Johann!" she laughed and pushed him away. "You smell like a stable rat!" She wrinkled her nose and pretended to be offended when, in fact, she didn't at all mind the redolence of old leather and horse sweat that clung to his clothes whenever he'd been riding. "In a minute we'll be bothered by flies," she teased for good measure.

"Sorry." He grinned and raked a hand through his hair as he pulled out a chair and fell into it. Johann was forty-two but there was not a strand of gray on his head. His damp shirt was partially unbuttoned, the sleeves were negligently rolled up, and he hadn't shaved before setting out this morning. "Do you want me to clean up before lunch?" he asked, in all seriousness, realizing his present condition might offend.

"No. Not as long as we're eating outside and the wind doesn't shift." Dorrit laughed and decided he'd never looked more splendid.

"Where's our Fritz?" Johann stretched his booted feet out in front of him, crossing them at the ankles.

"He was here until a few minutes ago, when he suddenly got hungry and went inside to have Frau Erdmann fix him something to eat." Dorrit pointed to a pile of coloring books strewn on the flagstones. "As you can see, he worked up an appetite."

"I've never known a boy to eat so much and yet remain so skinny." Johann smiled indulgently but was in the next instant distracted by the loud revving of a well-tuned engine in the courtyard at the front of the house, a familiar announcement that Hans Konauer, who had given up horses in favor of the automobile, had pulled up in the Dusenberg.

"At least he didn't lean on the horn." Johann frowned good-naturedly and turned to look toward the young man now coming into view, strolling around the side of the house. Hans jumped a boxwood hedge and, with the impatience of youth, cut through the rose gardens to the terrace, raising his hands to shoulder level to avoid snagging his shirt sleeves on any thorns.

"Hi, there!" Hans swung one arm in a sweeping greeting. "Rolf told me I'd find you out here. But he wasn't about to let me walk through the house. I think he's afraid I'll drag engine oil across the floors. Isn't it time he retired? The old boy must be a hundred." Stepping carefully around the coloring books, Hans sauntered over to the glass-topped patio table and kissed Dorrit. "You look ravishing as always, *Tante* Dorrit. How are you?"

"Fine, Hans. And yourself?"

"Never felt better." He boxed Johann's shoulders, then plunked down on a chair, propping a foot up on an empty one.

Although there'd be deep wheel ruts in the driveway to tend to after Hans's visit, Johann was enormously pleased to see him and signaled the butler hovering behind the terrace doors. Rolf disappeared, moments later materializing with three tankards of beer.

Without waiting for formalities, Hans reached for his glass, blew away the foam, slouched back in his chair and took a thirst-quenching gulp. He was as comfortable here as he was at home on a kitchen stool and, ignoring the linen napkin, wiped his mouth on the back of his hand.

Hans Konauer had grown into a good-looking eighteen-year-old. He was of medium build, his hair was light blond like Gerlinde's, and his eyes were blue, but of a deeper shade, more like his father's. He had a ruddy, healthy complexion regardless of the season, and Johann did not doubt that local frauleins were charmed when he came calling.

After an initial round of pleasant chitchat about nothing more consequential than the perfect weather Bernau was enjoying, Hans suddenly set his glass down hard and sat up straight as if he was bursting with news that couldn't wait. He pushed the center bowl of lavender star dahlias to the side and flicked at the small insects that dropped from the showy blooms. Having established a clear line of vision across the tabletop, he came right to the point of his visit.

"If this nasty business," he began, "you know, the assassination of the archduke, turns out to be the catalyst that blows the lid off Europe . . . what I mean to say . . . if it starts a war, I have decided to enlist in the kaiser's army."

Stunned by this unexpected declaration, Dorrit's mouth dropped open. Her eyes flew across the table to Johann. His glass was halted halfway to his lips, and she saw his eyes narrow over

211

the rim before he set it down abruptly as if it was poison. Frowning, he straightened in his chair, lending rapt attention as Hans continued.

"I haven't told the folks yet. I expect they'll be dead set against it. But that's where you . . . Uncle Johann, come in." Idly rotating the cold tankard between his palms while he spoke, Hans failed to notice the terrible effect his words were having on the very people he was trying to impress. "The way I see it, if I sign up early, I stand an excellent chance of getting a commission. I'd like to go to the front as an officer. If I wait to be inducted, I'll have to go as an infantryman." He glanced up and finally realized there was a distinct lack of enthusiasm on the part of his listeners; it didn't deter him, however. "Grandfather agrees with me," he went on. "I've discussed it with him at length. As you know, he's a veteran of the Franco-Prussian War. Of course family military tradition won't sway my parents. Nothing grandfather says has any impact. Papa humors him whenever he talks about his glory days. And mother? Well, . . . you know, she makes sour faces at any mention of war."

Hans leaned his elbows on the table and pressed his point. "But I know they'll listen to you, Uncle Johann." Suddenly he grinned. "Mother thinks the sun rises and sets on your shoulders, sentiment I intend to take advantage of. That's why I'm here. I've come to ask you to speak to my parents. To mother in particular. Perhaps as early as tomorrow during her garden party. It's an all day affair, so you'll have plenty of time to break into the topic casually. All I ask is that you help prepare her to accept my decision. I'm of age. I don't need parental consent. Still, I'd like to have it. And I want to get in on the action before it's over. The papers say if war breaks out, it'll be a short one. A few months at the most."

"Yes, that's what they say," Johann signed; he had read the reports, too. "But be that as it may, Hans, let's hope it can still be avoided." He looked at the young man seated across from him, a boy he loved as his own, a sturdy lad with a soft heart; to this day Hans still manned an elaborate feeding station for the birds that wintered in Bernau. Of course, at the moment, he was restless and, like most his age, had a romanticized view of war. Having grown up in the quiet countryside, he craved adventure.

Johann remembered only too well the boredom that had propelled him to move to Berlin years ago. And in that vein, he now again suggested a stint at the university, something he had done last summer when Hans became fascinated with U-boats and had threatened to run off and join the navy.

"Actually, Uncle Johann, the university is not a bad idea," Hans agreed. "And I promise you that I'll consider it. I'll give it very serious thought. But after the war. Hell, . . . uh, I beg your pardon, *Tante* Dorrit, but by next summer, Germany might rule over twice as much geography as what we've got now. Then there'll be all the more to learn." Hans grinned, his eyes were swimming; it was obvious he had already measured himself for a snappy uniform.

Johann finished his beer and did not mince words.

"I'm sorry, Hans," he finally said, "but I can't possibly try to influence your parents. My heart wouldn't be in it. In truth, I'd like to try to dissuade you from enlisting. War is a serious and dangerous business. The kaiser has a large professional army. Tough, well-trained men. Let them prove themselves. You are the only male heir. Consider your responsibilities to your family." Suddenly Johann looked downright grim. "Indeed, if you volunteer, I believe it would kill your mother."

"Uncle Johann, with all due respect, you're missing the point." Hans, not daunted by sobering statements, forged ahead. "Once the war starts, there will be battles on several fronts. The kaiser's army won't be enough. If I don't sign up, I'll be drafted. The papers are full of talk of inductions. Mother reads the papers. She knows that anyone between eighteen and thirty can expect to be called up. And like I just said, I want to get a jump on the rest of them and get some proper training as an officer. Mother will have to agree it'd be wise. I can't believe she'd want me to go as a foot soldier."

"Officers are the first the enemy try to pick off," Johann mumbled morosely. "Because once a lieutenant goes down, the men lose their focus." He argued a while longer, putting war in its worst possible light; in other words, sticking to the facts as best he knew them.

Hans enjoyed the debate because Uncle Johann didn't lose his temper or pound his fists on the table. How differently this scene would be played out at home. Karl-Heinz hated to be contradicted and would immediately take personal offense and begin to roar like a lion.

Fritz came out on the terrace, chewing on a hunk of black bread liberally spread with butter. Johann patted his knee, and the boy immediately came running over. Johann's arms closed around him, and as he hugged him, he thanked God that Max and Fritz were too young for the army.

Hans Konauer stayed for lunch. Frau Erdmann brought baked Brie, chilled buttermilk soup, and poached cod in parsley sauce and small round potatoes in their skins out to the table. She was miffed when the butler insisted on carrying one of the heavier trays. She bristled at him for not sticking to his own duties. The food was best left to the maids and herself, thank you very much.

Dorrit had long ago lightened the elderly housekeeper's duties. However, the woman clung to her habits with sanguine pride. Heaven forbid she be found lacking and pensioned off. Frau Erdmann had no intentions of leaving the baron's employ until the good Lord saw fit to take her like He had taken Otto last year, when the old groom was found in the tack room, asleep, a peaceful, natural death; his weather-beaten face strangely free of lines.

THIRTY-ONE

On August third, two days after declaring war on Russia, the kaiser's army marched across Belgium toward France. When England did not remain neutral, as he had hoped, Wilhelm sent his navy into combat against the British fleet rushing to the aid of France. At about the same time, and much to his surprise, Russia went on the offensive with unanticipated strength, immediately forcing Germany into blistering battles on two fronts. Privately, the kaiser's generals shook their heads. They had warned Wilhelm about inciting Russia, but they kept their backs straight and threw their full weight into the maneuvers of a two-fronted war, not yet aware that they had disastrously underestimated the power of their enemies.

September saw Hans leaving for the eastern front. Only his grandfather watched him depart with pride. Gerlinde and Ursula sobbed uncontrollably, and since Karl-Heinz's own emotions were too raw to attempt to console the women, he ordered the twins to comfort their mother and grandmother while he went to the stables and mucked out the horse stalls with such determination that embarrassed grooms began attacking every piece of equipment with spit and polish, giving the entire compound the appearance of being spanking new within hours.

Karl-Heinz was at a loss as to why this war was being waged and sincerely hoped the kaiser was being completely candid when he promised it'd be short and that victory would come swiftly. Conceivably, the whole bacchanalian farce might be over with before Hans saw combat. Karl-Heinz hoped so. In fact, he did more than hope. He prayed. He prayed for his son's safety and he prayed for Germany, no minor undertaking because he had never been a praying man.

The war spread. *Where was God?* Karl-Heinz stepped up his prayers. *Was no one listening?* New countries entered the conflict, and it rapidly became a world venture of death and destruction never before witnessed on the face of the earth.

Eventually Karl-Heinz stopped his appeal when it seemed to fall on deaf ears.

The Konauers came to Grunewald in mid-December to let the fourteen-year-old twins, Klara and Leni, indulge in some Christmas shopping at the fabulous stores in Berlin. However, while her daughters were giddy with excitement and insisted on going into town the minute they arrived, it was impossible for Gerlinde to feel any enthusiasm for the coming holidays, knowing they would be spent without Hans. Mechanically, she walked along the festively decorated Tauentzienstrasse with Dorrit and the twins. She had no interest in shopping, neither was she in the mood to satisfy her sweet tooth at Kranzler's Konditorei as the day wore on. Only when she spotted a handsome one-of-a-kind cashmere sweater in the windows at Kaufhaus des Westens did she brighten.

"It'll be perfect for Hans!" she cried and rushed inside to buy it, never glancing at the price rag. "I'll mail it to him." But though the purchase cheered her, the gaiety didn't last till evening.

"We've had no word from him in three weeks," she reported with a look more pitiful than tears when, during dinner, Johann immediately inquired about Hans.

"Where was his last letter mailed from?" Johann asked while signaling a maid to pass the brown-braised potatoes.

"Grodno. His unit was pushing into Russia the following morning. It scares me to think that he's now inside enemy territory." Gerlinde waved the potatoes away and also declined an additional helping of sliced duck in orange sauce; she had no appetite for the portion she'd already taken. "I wish he'd write again. And soon. Just a word to let us know that he is safe." Her small shoulders suddenly collapsed under the weight of her fear, making the padded sleeves of her red velvet gown look like bat wings.

"I'm sure he has," Johann said. "Mail delivery from the front is often unreliable. But even if he is fifty miles east of Grodno now, he's still behind the furthest German advance. As it is, conditions are not all that bad on the eastern front. We hold the advantage. The Russians are ill-equipped. Their armies are undisciplined and regularly depleted by an inordinate number of deserters. Since their initial strikes into Poland, which caught us by surprise, they've enjoyed no victories. Be glad Hans is not in France where I hear we're using *yellow cross.*"

"What's that?" Gerlinde looked puzzled.

"Mustard gas. A God-awful compound. A ground-seeking mist with the tendency to drift back over our own troops at the slightest change in the wind. And once it seeps into the trenches, there's no escaping it. Apparently it dissolves exposed skin on contact. Our men are issued masks. But some are careless about using them. As you can imagine the gas is terribly disfiguring."

The fourteen-year-old Klara stiffened. She had a beau at the front. Their neighbors in Bernau, the Borsts, had four sons. The oldest was seventeen and exceedingly handsome. During the past year, he had always sought her out at dances; he was a divine dancer, and at the last one, he had asked if he might write to her once he enlisted. He was now in France. So far, she'd received three wonderful letters that she kept in a heart-shaped box on the table next to her bed.

"Philip has been involved in some lab work of a military nature," Klara heard Uncle Johann elaborate, and though adult conversation usually bored her, she sat up and paid rapt attention. "He's familiar with the chemicals used in this poisonous gas. It's highly classified, so he can't talk about it except to say that a small dose of the stuff is so excruciatingly painful, afflicted soldiers shoot themselves to end the torment."

Klara paled and shot a meaningful look toward her sister, the only one at the table who knew about her beau. But Leni shrugged negligently; she'd not yet developed a fondness for boys, preferred horses and thought Klara's newfound love interest was sappy. Though twins, the two girls were as different as night and day.

"Those who survive the gas are hideously deformed and—"

"Please, Johann! That's enough! Spare us the details." Dorrit sent a quelling look the length of the table. "Hans is not in France. Even so, I don't think your little lecture on chemical warfare is cheering Gerlinde." Dorrit glanced toward the boys. Max was all ears, but, thankfully, Fritz appeared more concerned with cleaning his plate; he had a vivid imagination and this kind of talk might give him nightmares.

"Quite right, darling. I'm sorry." Johann turned to Gerlinde.

217

"How about a game of bridge?" he said. "Will you be my partner?" The servants were clearing the table; coffee and dessert would be served in the library.

"Losing at cards won't cheer my wife either!" Karl-Heinz muttered as he pushed himself away from the table, his stab at humor conspicuously bland. The jovial bite was gone from his jaw. He missed Hans and, mustard gas or not, he was plenty worried. However, he kept a stiff upper lip for the sake of the females in his family. They outnumbered him, and if they went on a crying jag all at the same time, he wondered how he'd handle it.

Over the course of the next few days, the normal atmosphere in Berlin served as a wonderful tonic for all concerned. Holiday lights and decorations were strung throughout the city; an early snowfall added to the ambiance; and it was at times possible to forget that war was raging across Europe. Germany was not fighting on her own soil. Except for some food rationing, those at home suffered few hardships. The Berlin papers reported wonderful victories, particularly on the eastern front. Moreover, Dorrit made sure that there was no time to brood. She had secured tickets to several plays, and planned to fill the box at the opera with her friends. Plus, everyone was attending Eckart's annual holiday party.

The Eckarts' marriage had only produced one child, a girl, two years younger than Fritz. Since it was unlikely there'd be any more children, Lillian and Kurt were left to squander all their love and material wealth on little Elsie, spoiling her with every excess known to mankind.

Philip von Brandt had remained a bachelor, which surprised no one, because the coarse and painted women who attracted him were not the sort he could possibly marry. However, on the occasion of the Eckarts' Christmas party, he surprised one and all when he arrived with a lovely, refined lady by the name of Isabel Thimm. She was a widow in her late thirties, an attractive brunette socialite from Dusseldorf with two teenaged daughters. Delightful girls, as poised as their mother, but not above giggling with the Konauer twins when the four girls quickly found each other at the party and just as quickly disappeared upstairs, where they could talk their hearts out and squeal without bothering any of the adults. And, of course, Klara immediately told her new friends about her beau who faced mustard gas daily without flinching, because she was sure that he was as brave as he was handsome.

Enno von Steigert had been temporarily recalled from his diplomatic post in London. He and Anna were enjoying their Wannsee villa for the duration of the war. And when the effusive Anna von Steigert cornered Gerlinde during the course of the evening at the Eckarts' with tales from the trenches, Gerlinde was an eager listener. Everyone else at the party hesitated to discuss the war within her earshot because of Hans's participation. But since Anna's marriage to Enno had yielded no children, she could not imagine the pain carried in a mother's heart at a time like this. She rambled on without whitewashing the horror stories that her brother, Georg Schellenberg, a prolific correspondent sent home from his post along the River Marne.

"Georg is thirty-three. Past the optimum age for the military," she explained. "Still, he enlisted the minute war broke out. He's a graduate of Krampnitz Academy."

"Really!" Gerlinde had heard of the exclusive officer training school on the outskirts of Berlin and was duly impressed.

"Indeed. He placed right at the top of his class. And, of course, he didn't hesitate when it came time to serve the kaiser. He left a wife and four children behind in Hamburg. He's now a full commissioned front-line *Korvetten-kapitan!*"

"Ah. . . ." Although she didn't quite know what that was, Gerlinde was again impressed.

"Of course, high rank doesn't preclude him being up to his waist in mud and up to his neck in danger. Living in vermin-infested trenches with bullets flying overhead can't be much of a picnic."

"No, I can't imagine." Gerlinde was all at once glad that Hans was on the march in Russia, and not in any trenches.

"But I suppose, it's even worse for the enemy," Anna went on without drawing breath. "Just last week, Georg wrote that he had helped pick several French soldiers out of some barbed-wire coils. Leaving their trenches, whooping and hollering, they'd run so fast during a raid on our lines that they hadn't seen the traps in time. Their skin torn to shreds, they were put in a medical tent where they died of blood poisoning before they could be traded for some of our own. Imagine, getting stuck in wire! Rather clumsy of the elegant French, don't you think? But obviously our traps are clever. We are superbly equipped. Far better than the French and the British combined!"

Anna patted her blond coiffure; she might as well have patted herself on the back, the message was the same. "Of course, we do lose a few of our own men now and again. Georg says that some of the soldiers in the trenches are such greenhorns, they freeze the first time they come face to face with the enemy. They make the mistake of looking him in the eye, and finding a boy no older than themselves, they hesitate to kill him. That split second gives the other scoundrel a chance to ram a bayonet right into... ah, into their ribs."

Anna faltered with the vision of such a gruesome fate, but recovered quickly; the pleasure of Gerlinde's intense attention taking precedence over indelicate details. "It bothers Georg terribly. He's responsible for these young men. Some were so anxious to go to war, they lied about their age and signed-up at sixteen, only to now suddenly look around shocked and bewildered, clutching at the hole in their chests, wondering what happened. They invariably cry out for their mothers before they die."

Gerlinde had turned ashen. "Do... do you think the Russians are using b... bayonets?"

"I doubt it. They have little in the way of fancy weaponry. Their ranks are full of peasants with pitchforks, who'd rather farm than fight. Most have no allegiance to Czar Nicholas. I hear the Russian army is hopelessly divided."

"Still, I'm worried."

"Well, certainly. But at least Hans is not in those dreadful trenches in the west, facing two enemies!"

"Yes. I suppose I should be grateful for that."

"Sure. Besides, the war will end first thing in the New Year. And it'll end sooner in the east, because the Russians are going to collapse from starvation. Everyone was put in uniform in August. No one was left to bring in the harvest. Come January, there'll be nothing to eat."

Anna took Gerlinde's arm and moved through the Eckarts's glittering rooms to engage others in conversation; she was not one to stand still for too long in such a delightful crowd.

"You'll see," she said. "Hans will be home within weeks. So will my brother. I'll host a party to celebrate the end of the war.

A big bash before we go back to London. Actually, Enno is hoping for a post in Madrid. The weather is dreadful in London. Ah, look! There's Philip! Come, let's go meet his new lady friend. If she can keep him sober past ten o'clock, she'll have Lillian's undying gratitude."

THIRTY-TWO

Spring came, but there was nothing to celebrate. In fact, the mood in and around Berlin grew increasingly caustic. Everyone agreed that the swift victories Kaiser Wilhelm promised were long overdue. The war was dragging on. Germany had not yet taken France. Naval battles with the British were at a stalemate, and the Russians were regrouping. They had yet to be starved into submission and were showing sporadic signs of strength.

Dorrit was both surprised and delighted on the first day of April when Johann came home from the clinic much earlier than usual. However, her pleasure was short-lived when in the next instant, she sensed that something was wrong. He kissed her with his usual "hello darling" and handed his coat to Schmidt, but then he walked into the library all too briskly and without his typical questions as to Max's and Fritz's whereabouts.

Dorrit followed him. Had a surgical procedure gone wrong? Had a patient died? Or...? Dear God! Had Karl-Heinz telephoned? Hans...?

"What's wrong, Johann?" she asked.

"Wrong? Nothing is wrong."

"But you're home so early," she said and plucked at his sleeve when he turned away from her to pour himself some sherry from the cart near his desk.

"And I can't come home early without something being wrong?" He cocked an eyebrow and held out the decanter questioningly.

Dorrit shook her head.

"Of course you can. It's just that you look like you're carrying a ton of bad news. Have you heard from Karl-Heinz? Any word of Hans?"

"No."

"Well, thank God for that," Dorrit felt better. "No news is good news nowadays."

"Yes." Johann put his glass down on the green blotter on his desk and walked over to close the doors into the hall. Dorrit braced herself anew. He never closed those doors.

"Come here," he said, leaning against them.

She ran into his arms. She felt the smooth expensive gabardine of his jacket against her cheek and heard his heart beating rhythmically. Her fear evaporated somewhat, because if something was truly wrong, how could his heart beat so calmly?

"So what have the boys been up to today?" he asked against her hair.

"The usual," she smiled. "School. And since the weather is so nice, Fraulein Werner took them over to the playground in the park this afternoon."

"She is still in our employ?"

"Of course."

"Then the boys must have done something unusual."

Dorrit laughed.

"Actually, Fraulein Werner has merely abdicated her position as governess and, befitting the times, become a sergeant."

"I see," Johann grinned. "Remind me to raise her salary proportionately."

He released Dorrit, picked up his drink, and went to stand by the window next to the fireplace, where a small heap of gray ashes reminded one that winter was now only a memory. It was a beautiful, sunny day outside. Spring was fooling around in Grunewald Park across the street, waking everything up. On a day like this, it was hard to believe that so much was wrong in the world.

"I don't know why Max and Fritz insist on waging war with each other," Dorrit said, coming to stand next to Johann. "There's enough of the real thing. Of course they come home from school with such glorious reports of battles and victories that I suppose it's only natural they act out a few skirmishes of their own. I'm only afraid someone will get hurt. Fraulein Werner, dear soul, gets in the middle trying to restore order when she ought to stay clear of it, because as the third intervening party, the boys occasionally forget their own fight, join forces, and gang up on her."

"I'll speak to Max."

"And to Fritz. He gives as much as he takes. The boys are equally guilty."

"All right," Johann grinned. "I'll take them both by the scruff of the neck...and...." his voice faded. He was stalling. *Dammit! Any longer would be cowardly.* He put an arm around Dorrit's shoulder. "But first there's something I have to talk to you about." Still gazing out the window and without turning to meet her eyes, he said: "As you've already suspected, I'm home early today for a reason. I do have some news." Dorrit's head snapped around to look at him. "I don't expect you will applaud it," he went on. "But with our sons' newfound lust for war, I suppose they'll find it rather interesting." Johann put his glass down on the mantelpiece and turned to face Dorrit. He took her chin and said quietly: "I have volunteered—"

She flung off his hand.

"What?" She had seen the posters in town asking for volunteers. Men from all walks of life were presenting themselves. Young men! "You're joking!" she said, reminding herself that today was April the first. "Is this some sort of an April Fools' joke?" She demanded hotly. "If it is, it's not very funny."

"It's not, darling," he said somberly. "I have—"

"But...but you can't be serious!" she cried again interrupting him. She wanted to scold him good for scaring her, except her throat tightened with the realization that although Johann occasionally played a practical joke, this was not such a time. He would never make sport with such a serious announcement. "You're too old," she said lamely. "You know nothing about being a soldier."

"A soldier? Good lord, Dorrit! I didn't sign up to be a soldier." Johann took her lovely face between his hands and smiled, because she had jumped to the wrong conclusion. "Of course I'm too old...difficult as that is to admit. I'm not going to be a soldier, darling. The kaiser is not that desperate yet."

"What then?"

"I've volunteered as an army surgeon."

"Oh...." Dorrit exhaled, immensely relieved.

"A few weeks ago when the call went out, I put my name in the hopper. This morning my number came up. I've been assigned to a field hospital near Kapsukas, in Lithuania."

"Is that anywhere near the front?"

"Yes. And an area that's disastrously short of medical personnel. Battle lines are spread pretty thin in the east. So are dressing stations. Since the severely wounded can't be moved, experienced surgeons are needed near the trenches. Medics in the field are doing a heroic job. But they are not surgeons."

As she listened, Dorrit was twisting a long, double strand of perfectly matched pearls around her neck. *Battle lines! Trenches!* When Johann initially said army surgeon, she was appeased. Now, she didn't know what to think, because she couldn't imagine that a physician at the front was any better off than a soldier. Enemy artillery shells could not possibly distinguish between a man in uniform versus one in a white coat. Her heart cringed. The strings that held the pearls snapped in her hands.

"The situation is getting more desperate by the day," Johann said and calmly bent down to retrieve the luminous spheres rolling on the carpet. "Interns fresh out of medical school are being sent out on a rotation system. Dedicated men, but men with no real experience. Few attempt amputations. The wounded are dying needlessly from gangrene left to spread. I can't sit by and listen to the stories, shake my head in commiseration, then do nothing. You do understand that, don't you?" He placed a fistful of priceless olive-sized pearls in a crystal dish on the Queen Anne desk by the window.

Dorrit nodded reluctantly.

"How . . . how long will you be gone?" she asked, her eyes on the floor, pretending to look for any pearls he might have missed. She did not want Johann to see the disappointment and anger in her face. Anger with the war and disappointment that he had not sought her opinion before committing himself—that he had committed himself at all!

"I honestly don't know. Probably a year. Of course, the war may be over long before that. If not, I'll be replaced by another volunteer."

"A year!" Dorrit almost sank to the floor; shock slowed her mind like a clock running down, allowing her emotions to get the upper hand. "H . . . how could you?" Her tone was suddenly stern and accusing. "How could you volunteer when you knew it'd be for so long? And couldn't you just have signed up for a couple of months? Did it have to be a whole year? My God! What about Max and Fritz? Did you consider them? They need you. They need their father. I . . . I need you." More bitter words raced to her lips but died before they could be spoken; quelled by sobs breaking in her chest.

"Please, darling, don't cry." Johann had not expected such an outburst. Dorrit was usually so levelheaded. He dug a handkerchief out of his pocket and offered it to her. She snatched it from him roughly. "Please, . . . please get a hold of yourself," he pleaded. "Try to understand that I have no choice. This war is a catastrophe in terms of maimed bodies and lives lost. And if I can do something, however little, I'm personally willing to make some sacrifices."

"Such as your . . . life?" Dorrit hollered louder than she intended.

"I don't believe it'll come to that. Besides, if I don't go, I couldn't live with myself." He pulled her around so that she faced him and, searching her tear-swollen face, said: "I had hoped that you would feel the same way. That you would understand that I can't sit idly by while boys are dying. For God's sake, think of Hans. He's out there somewhere. Suppose he's been wounded."

"I . . . I do think of Hans. And I do understand . . . ," Dorrit blew her nose and ran her sleeve across her wet eyes. "It's just that you . . . you surprised me. This is so sudden. All these many months I've been thankful that you were too old and Max and Fritz too young to serve in the war. Every time I talk to poor Gerlinde, I feel awful . . . and . . . glad at the same time. Glad I don't have a loved one at the front. Gerlinde is dying a slow death worrying about Hans. And . . . now . . ." Dorrit's voice broke. "I don't know if I can stand it. I'll be so afraid for you. And I don't know if I can stand to be alone. I . . . I have never been alone."

"But darling, you have the children. A house full of servants. And friends. You'll not be alone for a single minute."

Friends? Dorrit hit upon an idea.

"How about Philip?" she said, her eyes suddenly dry and shining. "Can't he go instead of you! He has no wife. If he hasn't decided that Isabel is perfect for him, he never will. Why, all he does is sit and tinker in that old laboratory. He's not seeing patients. If he left for twelve months, no one would miss him."

"His lab work is precisely why he is not suited for the front. He's had little surgery experience. He would be of no more help out there than a young intern."

226

"Oh . . . yes, I forgot. It's really ironic."

"What is?"

"That I have always been so proud of your work, practically bursting at the seams whenever people talk about the wonders you perform at the clinic." Her lips twitched with a smile. "Did you know that you've been called a miracle worker?"

"Good God, no!" Johann grimaced.

"It's true. But right now I wish you were a . . . a . . . chimney sweep." Johann pulled her close.

"When do you leave?" she asked as she clung to him.

"In a week."

"So soon?" She had hoped for more time but made no mention of it. "What about your patients?"

"Ben Tarnoff will have to manage. I've already talked with him. In fact, he might have to run the clinic alone for a while. Both of our associates have volunteered and can be called up at any time."

"Has Ben volunteered?" Dorrit asked, inspired by another idea. "I mean if he has, maybe he could go first? He and Gert have no children. It would only be fair."

"Ben has not volunteered. Most doctors are now being sent east and he does not wish to set foot on Russian soil. No one can ask that of him. Have you forgotten his and Gertrude's stories?"

"No. I guess I spoke without thinking," Dorrit said evenly while her heart cried. A week! A measly week left to them, then a whole year apart. The first too short, the latter too long. Her eyes burned, but they were dry. Her heart was full of anguish, but she remained silent, if only for a moment.

"Has Kurt volunteered?" she heard herself ask.

"No. And I don't expect that he will. Actually, I think he's slowly distancing himself from the medical profession. He's keen on politics. It wouldn't surprise me if he changed careers altogether."

THIRTY-THREE

A week to the day of this emotion-charged conversation, Johann joined an eastbound regiment and boarded a troop train moments before it slipped out of Potsdam Platz station in the rainy predawn darkness.

Hours into the journey, as daylight slowly crept across the horizon, the transport was chugging through East Prussia, where as far as the eye could see the black earth was dotted with tufts of green seedlings stretching their fragile stems toward a pale but determined sun that by noon had pushed the clouds aside and dried the landscape. Farmers in the fields stopped their labors, wiped brows as furrowed as the soil they tilled, and saluted the passing train. Children waving paper flags gathered at village railroad crossings, where boys, a couple of years short of enlistment age, raced along the tracks and shouted encouragement to their heroes leaning out of the windows. When the train stopped at major stations to take on coal and water, it was welcomed by smiling brigades of local matrons and their nubile daughters. The women handed slices of brown sugar pastries through the windows, the girls blew shy kisses loaded with promise, and the soldiers, to the man, made solemn vows to return.

By nightfall when the transport lumbered into Tannen-berg, Red Cross sisters were on hand to dispense food packets to the disembarking troops. The space vacated on the train was promptly filled with furloughed soldiers. Come morning, they'd be home in Germany, with all the comforts that went with military leave, while the newcomers continued east toward the battlefields. Yet this latter group was a sight more cheerful, joking with the veterans, calling them slackers and promising them that they needn't come back because real men had come to finish the job. But the joking stopped abruptly when the last to board the homebound train did so on stretchers. Even carefully tucked sheets couldn't hide the fact that these "slackers" had left an arm or a leg at the front.

Aroused before daybreak, the following morning, the men on the floor in the Tannenberg station were given five minutes to collect their gear, scoff a bowl of oat porridge and a cup of coffee. No cream, but no one grumbled. It was common knowledge that luxuries were scarce near the front, and all stood ready to make concessions for the Fatherland.

On account of his peerage, Johann had been given the rank of major, issued the appropriate uniform, plus a pistol he was required to wear at all times. Only a large white armband appliqued with the red medical cross distinguished him from a front line commanding officer. And although he'd been obliged to sleep on a threadbare rug in a drafty station cubicle last night, this morning he would enjoy the dignity of rank and travel up front in the cab with the driver. A distinct privilege, inasmuch as the rest of the journey was by truck convoy over bumpy dirt roads, where the men riding in the open vehicles had to contend with blinding clouds of dust and exhaust fumes that turned the strongest stomach and put a green tinge on the healthiest complexion.

By midafternoon, choking and bruised, the convoy sputtered into Kapsukas. Five hundred elite combat trained troops alighted from the vehicles and fell into formation—every pair of knees uniformly slow to snap to attention—and after an hour's rest they were on the march to the front. The men didn't know it then, but the trip just endured would be their last pleasure for some time to come.

Kapsukas was Johann's final destination. After signing in at army headquarters, he was given a tour of the amenities available to officers—canteen, bath, and barber shop—before catching a ride to the medical facility, which he learned lay some five miles outside of town. His driver, a young sergeant, who reminded him achingly of Hans, saluted smartly before throwing Johann's personal effects into the rear seats of a battered vehicle that suffered internal injuries as well when he stripped the gears, backing out of a tight spot.

The center of town was teeming with German militia. Local citizens venturing about had to jump for their lives as army trucks barreled through the streets with no concern for pedestrians, a situation the Lithuanians accepted good-naturedly, because the Germans had liberated them from the Russians, who had occupied their city with no concern at all.

"We secured our position here less than a month ago," the driver explained when his passenger commented on the scorched buildings they passed. "Of course the czar's troops weren't keen on leaving. We had to persuade a lot of them with flame-throwers. In fact, we had to burn some buildings clear to the ground to get the rats out. We'd been bogged down outside town for quite a while. Taking it was an important victory. It allows us to supply a critical stretch of trenches."

"The Memel Line?"

"Yeah. The part that runs parallel with the Niemen River. Some two hundred miles of it. Of course the Russians are now regrouping on the other side. Still, we've got the bridges covered and tons of coal boxes ready to launch. Plenty of daisy-cutters too. Hell, just the whistle of a flying d-cutter," the sergeant grinned and looked sideways at his passenger, "scares the living Jesus out of the bastards long before the hardware hits."

Johann shuddered. *A daisy-cutter.* An insanely pleasant name for an explosive shell that scatters shrapnel in wide circles close to the ground, mowing down men and shrubs alike.

"And lemme tell you—oh, shit!" The driver stood on the brakes to avoid two old women carrying bundles of firewood across the road. Screeching to a halt in a cloud of dust against the curb, he doffed his hat to the ladies, smiled, gunned the car, and drove on, cursing them soundly.

THIRTY-FOUR

Nothing he'd heard in Berlin could have prepared Johann for what he encountered after the driver dropped him off and made a quick U-turn, speeding back toward Kapsukas as if he feared that his passenger, having seen the place, might burden him with requests for a round-trip.

Bags under his arms, Johann stood alone and incredulous, looking at a squat building with a crude hand-painted medical cross splashed on its crumbling edifice. His eyes traveled beyond the structure to an undisciplined pine forest encroaching from the west, stopping just short of the back of the property and denying it any afternoon sun. Enveloped in a general and depressing neglect, this hospital facility appeared to have been established in a former roadside tavern; a weather-beaten sign over the door promised voluptuous barmaids and bottomless kegs. But no running water. An ancient cast-iron pump stood in the middle of the front yard in a puddle, indicating it was still very much in use. A stable to the right of the building was not, its rotten beams having been abandoned to woodworm a hundred years ago. The tavern's tiled roof was of adequate repair. Still, Johann figured that any scorched building in town would have served the purpose better. Of course, being closer to the front lines was crucial; it could mean the difference between life and death for a wounded man.

Perusing this desolate spot, Johann's ears pricked. The boom of howitzers could suddenly be heard in the distance where a battle was commencing, giving proof that location alone was why this cheerless and godless building had been resurrected as a field hospital. Shivering involuntarily, Johann lifted his eyes skyward. White clouds barreled furiously overhead, chased by black smoke from the big guns, smudging the clouds and dulling the patches of blue in a yellow haze. Reminding himself why he'd come, Johann put both bags under one arm and pushed resolutely at the door with the other.

It creaked open on a rusty hinge.

He stepped inside and found himself in a dingy hall, where from the general looks of things, he guessed there'd be no reception committee. The doors on either side of a warped center staircase were closed, and while the hum of voices could be heard behind one, behind the other, there was nothing but an eerie silence broken by an occasional moan. Johann was wondering how best to make his presence known, when this door opened and an orderly, balancing a stack of bedpans and dragging a lame foot, shuffled into the hall.

"Excuse me," he said, waylaying the man. "I'm Dr. von Renz. Can you tell me where I might find Dr. Bergen?"

"You're our new man from Berlin?"

"Yes."

"Welcome. Herr Director will be glad to know you've arrived. He's right down this corridor. Second door." The orderly pointed with his chin as his eyes settled on the luggage under Johann's arm. "Doctors' quarters are upstairs," he said. "But just leave your gear here in the hall. I'll bring everything up the minute I dump this." Without further comment, he ambled off, awkwardly supporting himself and the cargo he was carrying, on one good foot.

The air quality improved dramatically with the fellow's retreat, and depositing his bags against the wall, Johann quickly found the designated door, knocked, and entered when bid to do so by what sounded like an angry grunt. Once inside the small room, the climate didn't improve. Herr Director, a graying, balding man in his sixties, had his back to the door and was far too preoccupied tending a sedated soldier to look up and acknowledge the newcomer.

Johann circled around the gurney, inadvertently blocking the light from the window.

"I'm Dr. Von Renz," he said.

"I know." Dr. Bergen raised his head with a scowl that looked as if he'd like to eat him. "Glad to see you finally made it." He waved him away from the window, and again bent over the patient to tug at a stubborn bomb fragment embedded in the man's shoulder. "One of our wards have been without a doctor for two weeks," he appeared to hold Johann personally responsible, "and we're short of chloroform as well. This patient will get no more. I'm sure you can appreciate that I have to be done with him before he comes around. So, if you'll excuse me."

"Certainly. I'll go unpack." Johann turned toward the door, glad to leave this testy individual.

"Unpack? That can wait. Time is at a premium around here. We have to take advantage of every minute of daylight. There's no guarantee we'll have electricity at night."

"All right. I'll start with some rounds then."

"Good. Take charge of ward B. On the left where you entered this building. Most of the men there are terminal. At best, they'll go home with only half the limbs they came with. I trust you have no qualms about amputations? Our esteemed Dr. Reymann hasn't got the stomach for it."

"Dr. Reymann . . . ?"

"Our colleague. Humph!" Dr. Bergen snorted with asperse mockery. "Six months out of medical school . . . graduated summa cum laude, but I'm afraid he's not cut out for the profession. I've had to put him in charge of ward A, where most of the patients are expected to survive unless Dr. Reymann slips up." Herr Director consulted a clipboard on the instrument tray. "All right. Let's see. Where are we now? Oh, yes. Ward B. Cot number ten. Leg amputation. Advanced gangrene. You'll have to operate immediately. Use the room next to this one. It's got running water. And, mind you, ether is to be administered only during amputations. Under no circumstances are you to waste it on any other procedure no matter how loudly anyone hollers. The way I figure it, if a soldier can yell, he's strong enough to stand the pain."

"I'll examine the patient immediately," Johann said.

"I've already done that. Take the leg off mid femur."

"I'll determine the extent of the surgery after I've seen the patient," Johann said in a deceptively smooth tone; he was not accustomed to taking orders.

Dr. Bergen ignored any message given and bent over the comatose man.

"Rule of thumb around here," he said as he went back to work, "start with the worst cases first and pray the others don't deteriorate before you can get to them. Occasionally, along with our own, some wounded Russians are dragged in. Treat everyone equally. POWs are worth more in trade if they're alive."

The large piece of shrapnel finally loosened and slipped out of the soldier's arm. Dr. Bergen reached for sutures with one hand while he groped the wound for any small fragments with the other. Finding it clean, he wiped his hands on his surgeon's coat, grabbed a piece of gauze and swabbed at the blood oozing from the gaping hole before plunging the bow-shaped needle into the flesh, quickly sewing flaps of skin together.

"A word of caution," he continued. "Never turn your back on a POW. Crippled or unconscious, they can make weapons out of a mess tin. You're replacing the doctor we lost two weeks ago to a Russian patient believed to be comatose. The scoundrel had fashioned a sharp instrument from a bedspring. When Dr. Buhler bent down to examine him, he sunk it right into his heart."

"Christ Almighty!" Johann exclaimed.

"Don't waste your time calling on Him. He can't hear you for the mortar shells. And I'm telling you about the late Dr. Buhler simply to illustrate that one can't be too careful." Dr. Bergen looked up, peered over horn-rimmed spectacles splattered with dried blood, at the new physician and wondered how such a clean-shaven individual would fare in this hell hole. Not well, he suspected. He was much too elegant for this duty. Of course, he'd soon enough get dirty, if he lasted a week. "Be on guard at all times," Herr Director finished.

"Thanks for the warning. I'll keep it in mind." Johann turned toward the door. "Is a surgery nurse available?" he asked, remembering the impending amputation. "And can someone perhaps give me a quick cook's tour?"

Dr. Bergen jerked his head around, scarcely able to contain his scorn. If this individual was expecting to be escorted around the premises like a visiting dignitary, forget a week! He wouldn't last the day, and it was already three o'clock. Surgery nurse, indeed! Why did Berlin persist in sending prima donnas and neophytes out here? Didn't those idiots at the war ministry realize that professionals were needed? Surgeons who'd clamp an artery with their teeth, if necessary.

Dr. Bergen was moving his lips to vent his spleen, when some scuffling in the hall outside distracted him. Someone was leaning against the door, trying to push it open. Johann, about to exit, pulled the knob.

"Ah, Nurse Hofmeyer!" Dr. Bergen's face softened imperceptibly as his eyes flicked over the woman carrying in a large basin of clean instruments.

Johann stepped forward and took the heavy tray from her, placing it on an empty table in the corner.

"Thanks!" she smiled. Her smile was a nice contrast to the caustic demeanor of Herr Director.

"Hofmeyer, this is our new surgeon from Berlin. Dr. von Renz." Herr Director was accomplishing the necessary introductions with a distinct frugality of words. "He will take charge of ward B."

Olivia Hofmeyer offered her hand.

"Welcome to the front," she said, her smile still in place.

"Thank you."

Herr Director cleared his throat and waved his hand in a pointed dismissal.

"I suppose you can take a few minutes and show Dr. von Renz around," he said to the nurse. "But step lively. There's work to be done."

Once out in the hall, Olivia Hofmeyer looked at the newcomer and guessed his thoughts.

"No time for pleasantries around here," she said in reference to the contumelious Dr. Bergen.

"It doesn't matter. None of us are here on a social call."

"Far from it," she laughed, her lively blue eyes playing on his face. "In these godforsaken parts, a good time means getting two hours' sleep. Have you seen your quarters?"

"Not yet."

"Just as well. It can wait. By tonight you'll be too tired to care. It'll be less of a shock that way. Doctors' accommodations are upstairs. Small...drafty, spartan, pretty much describes them. But at least they are private. Nurses sleep dormitory style in a room at the back of the building, and the nuns go back to the cloister in Kapsukas each evening before dinner so the army won't have to feed them."

Smiling at her candor, Johann studied Olivia Hofmeyer as she spoke. He guessed she was in her early forties. Her blond hair, cut as short as a man's, was streaked with silver and various shades of dye, indicating a valiant attempt to stave off middle age. It worked, helped by the fact that her figure was trim and her face had a pixie quality about it, round and soft, the kind that's slow to age. She'd probably been cute as a button in her youth and had now matured into a very handsome woman.

She walked next door and stepped into a room that appeared to have been a laundry facility at one time.

"This is where you'll be doing amputations," she said and went over to a cast-iron sink standing under a cracked window. She turned the tap, bleeding rust from the line. "Running water," she grimaced, raised and dropped her shoulders in resignation. "But at least this room is somewhat removed from the wards. Screams won't carry the distance."

Frowning at such unprofessional talk, Johann's frown deepened when he realized that a tavern table, mottled with years of accumulated food stains, served as an operating platform. Moreover, a pile of sheets, dirtied by blood and other body fluids, lay folded in one corner, the heap attracting scores of enthusiastic flies.

"Linens have to be washed and changed with each patient," he said sharply, attesting to his level of outrage.

"Sure," Nurse Hofmeyer agreed, "And they would be if we had enough of them. This two-fronted war is overwhelming the medical community. There are not enough doctors, supplies, or linens to go around. So while we wait for headquarters to fill our requisitions, we conclude that clean sheets won't save the men who need this facility and dirty sheets won't kill them. The nuns wash every day, bless them, but they can't keep up with the demand." Olivia Hofmeyer leveled her bright blue eyes on Johann, challenging him. "Have you done many amputations?" she asked bluntly.

"Only on cadavers."

It was her turn to frown. According to Berlin, this new surgeon was supposed to be experienced. And if not, why had Dr. Bergen put him in charge of ward B? Concealing her dismay, she walked from the room.

"I meant no offense about the state of the sheets," Johann said, somewhat chastened, as he followed her out.

"And I didn't take any," she said, turned, cocked her head, and looked up at him, deciding that he was incredibly good-looking. She forgave him his sharp words.

Walking back up the corridor toward the wards, she glanced at his left hand, not surprised to see that he was married. It was the story of her life; she invariably fell like a rock for men she couldn't have. In fact, a disastrous affair with a married man

236

back home in Paderborn was the reason she had volunteered for duty in this remote outpost, and had, like Herr Director Bergen, committed herself for the duration of the war.

Olivia Hofmeyer took the new doctor through ward A, where he was introduced to the nurses and to Dr. Reymann, the intern Herr Director had all but crucified. And, sure enough, the young man looked pathetically relieved, when Johann assured him that he'd take charge of ward B.

"I was saving the worst for last," Nurse Hofmeyer whispered as she now crossed the hall and led Dr. von Renz into the ward occupied by the desperately ill, men long past making conversation with one another. And although he had smelled death before, without cringing, Johann found that his breath caught in his throat like a sticky obstruction with the fetid stench hanging over the entire room. He immediately made a beeline for the windows, intending to open them. They wouldn't budge. They'd been painted shut decades ago. He turned on the two nuns in the ward and ordered that the door into the hall remain open at all times to insure ventilation.

"Ah, but Herr Doctor," one of the nuns spoke up, "the noise these men make disturbs the patients across the hall."

"I see." Johann glowered at the woman. "I suppose you haven't considered that the lack of air might well kill these men?" He looked around at the broken and bandaged bodies. "Are we making a conscious choice here?"

"No . . . no of course not." The nun shook her wimpled head and turned to take flight.

As Johann watched her go, he realized that it had taken him exactly five minutes to become as petulant as Dr. Bergen. He smiled at the remaining nun.

"I'm sorry if I was rude," he mumbled. Then without wasting another moment, he began to walk among the casualties, aware that Nurse Hofmeyer stayed at his side. It pleased him.

There were some twenty beds in this infirmary, and reading individual charts as he went, Johann spoke to every man who was not comatose. Olivia Hofmeyer added personal particulars and warned him well ahead of time that the two men in the corner were Russians.

"They're not expected to last till morning," she whispered as Johann approached their cots.

Remembering Dr. Bergen's story about the sharpened bed-spring, Johann studied their pale yellow skin and tested their rigid limbs without bending down too far. Both men suffered advanced tetanus; nothing could be done for them at this stage. While he jotted a note on their charts, he felt their eyes on him. He tried a few Russian words. One of the men smiled, the other turned angry eyes away; apparently he was still fighting the war. But he didn't have long to wage any personal battles. Death was on the march in his body and would defeat him within hours.

Crossing the center aisle, Johann made his way to the cot of the soldier whose chart carried the dreaded code for amputation. He approached the young man's bed slowly as if no emergency existed; no sense alarming him any sooner than necessary.

A wisp of a girl, a local Lithuanian volunteer, was bent over him, holding a cup and helping him drink some water. Seeing the new doctor, she immediately put the cup down, straightened, and introduced herself. Her name was Marja. She had a fresh-scrubbed face, a smile that lit up the room, and whatever she lacked in age and nursing experience was compensated for by her eye-appealing presence; as beneficial in this pitiful ward as a shot of morphine, Johann ruminated.

"So, how are we doing today?" he asked the fellow in a cheerful voice as he peeled back the sheet covering his legs, one of which was mangled beyond repair below the knee. Red tell-tale lines of gangrene were spreading upward into healthy tissue. Dr. Bergen's diagnosis had been on the mark. Amputation could not wait.

The lieutenant—his military jacket and appropriate insignia hung on a hook behind his bed—muttered something unintelligible. Johann glanced at his chart. He'd been given a dose of medication an hour ago, and groggy from the effects, he was obviously not up to conversing. Just as well, Johann thought, in view of what was in store for him.

"Don't give this patient any more to drink." Johann addressed himself to Marja, and carefully replaced the sheet over the man's legs, if only to keep the flies off the festering flesh. "And please stay with him till I get back." She nodded.

"What for?"

"Pardon?" Johann turned and saw the patient rise up on one elbow, apparently not as dazed as first believed.

238

"What for?" the lieutenant repeated. "Why . . . why are you coming back?" He fell heavily down on the pillow, drained with the effort of speech.

Johann was about to level with him, but when the man's eyes closed, he realized that he probably wouldn't hear him. Again he instructed Marja to stay put. And as he walked away, checking other patients on his way out, he saw that there were two other possible amputations. *Welcome to the front,* he reflected bitterly.

"Show me the supply room," he asked of Olivia Hofmeyer once they were out in the hall; he hoped to God there was plenty of ether. "And tell me what you know about the circumstances surrounding the lieutenant. Has he been told anything?"

"No. He came in only about an hour ago, shouting at the top of his lungs that we'd better not take off his leg. We gathered from the medics who brought him that he'd stepped on a land mine, after which he spent two days in the field ducking bullets from both sides before they could get to him. The pain must have been horrible, as horrible as wondering who would find him first. The enemy or his own men. While pinned down in the muddy field, he apparently had enough wherewithal to apply a tourniquet from a piece of his shirt. That saved his life. But God knows, he arrived here knowing his leg was in bad shape and needed immediate attention. Yet he flung his arms at anyone who tried to touch it."

"I suppose that lying wounded for days in no-man's-land with rotting corpses of friend and foe alike as company, can do terrible things to the mind," Johann said.

"Yes. Dr. Bergen couldn't work on him while he was in such a wild state. We gave him a sedative. He's much calmer now. Still, you'll need two orderlies to hold him down. Ether is not always a hundred percent effective. I sometimes think our supplies are diluted. I'll assist you as well. Some of our nurses don't like the gore in the back rooms." While she spoke, Nurse Hofmeyer sincerely hoped Dr. von Renz was up to the task at hand. How much had he learned from cadavers who don't bleed or fight back when a leg is sawed off?

THIRTY-FIVE

April slipped by. May came and went. It was June . . . then July. Daylight lingered past ten in the evening and returned a couple of hours after midnight, melting the days together. Weeks became months, Johann lost track of time. Dates were important only when a soldier died and the particulars had to be reported to headquarters so a telegram could be sent to the man's family. A short and standard one, there were too many deaths and no time to be original.

Death happened so frequently, Johann felt numbed by it, a numbness he fought because it'd breed indifference, dull his judgment, and slow his hands. There could be no lax surgeons at the front, where men came in trailing their intestines behind them. Some arrived with mud-impacted faces, then no face at all once the mud was cleaned away. A seventeen-year-old had hobbled in on a bloody and clumsily wrapped stump, all that remained of his right foot. He had supported himself on a homemade crutch on the long trek from the hinterlands because those with worse injuries than his needed the space on the lorries. His desperate effort was for nought. He died of blood poisoning.

Feverish men staggered in with burns and lacerations treated in the field, but which now refused to heal and smelled abominably of ham gone bad. Some came with wounds full of maggots, others with once-mended scabs ripped open by yet another volley of enemy fire. They came with typhoid and lockjaw, came to have antitetanus needles plunged into their chests in the desperate hope that it wasn't too late. Some, blinded by shrapnel, arrived tied to the walking wounded; those with enough strength to leave the trenches on their own in search of the hospital. Sometimes the men simply came to die in a bed, friends dragging in their mortally wounded comrades for this last bit of dignity. To die in the field meant to rot in the open or be ground into the mud under the spoors of Russian tanks.

After his initial harsh assessment of the Berlin surgeon, who upon arrival had looked much too elegant to be of any practical use at the front, Dr. Bergen soon realized his error. Men pulled through against all odds because Dr. von Renz refused to give up on them. Operating through the night by the light of a kerosene lamp, he performed impossible feats, which included repairing facial wounds so that a soldier could look into a mirror without begging for a *coup de grâce*.

Intrigued by the man's ability, Dr. Bergen began to seek out this indefatigable colleague during meals, the only lull in their hectic routine for any kind of socializing. Conversation helped flavor the bland rations sent down from headquarters for staff and patients alike, and of course, the food was even more palatable when the nurses joined the men at supper. Female company was always pleasant. Johann found Olivia Hofmeyer's particularly so and suspected Herr Director did as well. The strenuous work and long hours had not hardened her face, she laughed readily, and without the brittle and discordant sound of the other nurses.

During the worst of times, when a patient screamed in agony and she all but tripped over amputated limbs rolling on the floor in the "blue room"—as the place in back became known among the soldiers because of the color of those who returned from there—Olivia Hofmeyer remained calm, her expression beatific like the nuns at prayer. She let soldiers clutch at her arms till they were bruised; she stroked feverish brows, listened to and painstakingly wrote down last messages for mothers, wives, and sweethearts back home.

Each morning before starting his rounds, Johann glanced around the infirmary, hoping to catch her eye and perhaps a smile, which invariably chased some of the gloom that pervaded ward B like a dank fog. He enjoyed the very sight of Olivia Hofmeyer, enjoyed the way her uniform hugged her slender hips and the way her full breasts strained against the bib of her apron. She looked incredibly good. Of course, with the passing of time, even the old nuns in their black, roomy habits looked good and Johann occasionally wondered if he was becoming some sort of a pervert. While he scrupulously kept all contact with any female staff member on a professional level, he soon discovered that it was becoming increasingly difficult to remain impartial to Olivia Hofmeyer.

She didn't talk much about herself, but he gleaned that she'd been widowed while still in her twenties, when she lost both her husband and a small child to pneumonia in the span of one month. She had never remarried, was now forty-two, had volunteered the day the war started, and for reasons she kept to herself, never requested the home furloughs that nurses were entitled to.

On an evening in September when, in lieu of a dinner break, the nurses went to headquarters to soak in a real bathtub and Dr. Reymann remained on duty in the wards with Marja; Johann and Dr. Bergen were left to have supper alone.

The weather on this late summer evening was balmy, and taking full advantage of it, the two doctors took their food trays out to the back steps of the hospital and sat down in separate corners, leaning into the same rotting banister and listening to the all-too-familiar rumbles of a terrible skirmish somewhere in the woods. Both doctors expected to hear a stray shell whistling overhead at any moment. Last week, one had made a deep crater only fifty feet from where they now sat.

By and by, the noise of the big guns silenced as the battle lost steam along with daylight. Long shadows of dusk crept through the tall pines that stopped short a stone's throw from the hospital, and as the sun sank further behind the trees, the encroaching darkness obscured the rows of graves rippling the ground along the perimeter of the woods, a foreboding view, and the only thing that interfered with the pleasure of eating in the out-of-doors at the back of the building, where a favorable breeze kept the carbolic odors of the wards at bay.

"One has got to wonder if headquarters retain a local cook with secret allegiance toward the enemy," Dr. Bergen said and eyed his tray suspiciously; the fare was particularly unappetizing tonight. "How in God's name can we hope to win the war on these putrid provisions?"

Johann dunked a rock-hard biscuit he'd been unable to halve into the watery soup in front of him.

"I like to think we're getting the scraps so there will be more for our men out there," he said, pointing toward the woods with his knife.

"I suppose so. If not, starvation will claim them sooner than Russian bullets." Dr. Bergen submerged his spoon into the vegetable soup, exploring the depths of the bowl like a submarine hunting unfriendly objects.

Leaving his biscuit in the bowl to soak, Johann ate a piece of cheese while absently watching his older colleague stirring his soup until it was too cloudy to see the bottom. Finally tasting it, Dr. Bergen made a face that brokered no explanation. Disgusted, he threw down his spoon.

"These damn weeds were furnished by a stagnant swamp," he sputtered and plowed a hand through his thinning hair, uprooting several gray remnants. "And to think what I have refused to eat in the past!"

Johann chuckled.

"Fine! Go ahead and laugh! But when you're through, I'd suggest you check the cheese on your tray. Just look here..." Dr. Bergen jabbed at his piece with his fork, "mine's so inhabited by vile organisms, it's literally trying to walk off the plate!"

Johann felt himself go pale. He had just swallowed a large chunk without examining it for worms.

In November, after a year of service, Dr. Reymann was replaced by another intern, a Dr. Stocker from Bonn.

Before embarking on the trip home, Dr. Reymann made the surprise announcement that he and Marja, the pretty hospital volunteer from town, were getting married. However, since her parents were not particularly pleased about losing her to Germany, they were also not the least bit motivated to step forward and host a wedding. Hence, it was held at the officers' club at headquarters, courtesy of the army.

Leaving the new man, Dr. Stocker, in charge with a skeleton crew, the rest of the hospital's staff crammed into the one vehicle at their disposal and went to the wedding. Olivia Hofmeyer slipped in next to Johann, who'd been elected to drive the overloaded motor lorry to town; it was a trip made pleasant by the feel of her body pressed against his as everyone squeezed together to make room. When he put the car in gear, his hand brushed against her thigh, sending a school boy's rush of pleasure through him. Chagrined, he tried to concentrate on the dusty road ahead, but instead, found himself wondering how Olivia always managed to smell so nice. The staff was allowed one bath a week at headquarters. The rest of the time, the small trickle of water in the common shower used by all at the hospital was supposed to suffice. Johann occasionally questioned if his own lack of hygiene offended anyone.

After the wedding festivities, Dr. Reymann and his bride stayed in a Kapsukas hotel for an early morning departure to Germany. Everyone else returned to the hospital and tended patients until long past midnight.

Johann was last to stagger upstairs.

Once in his room, he shrugged out of his blood-smeared surgeon's coat and hung it on a hook behind the door. It slipped off. He let it be. Already dirty, it would be none the worse for spending the night on the floor. It was expected to last a week between washings, and he could only imagine what they'd say at Wirchow about that, but he didn't dwell on it. Wirchow's fastidious wards and his own pristine clinic were a million miles away, both a fast-fading memory. Peace time . . . civilian life . . . were all but forgotten out here, existing only at night in short, sweet dreams dispersed in the harsh reality of each morning, when new casualties were brought in.

His body throbbing with fatigue, Johann unbuttoned his military jacket and threw it over a chair. Impatiently loosening his collar, he glanced longingly in the direction of his bed, only to momentarily stiffen. He blinked and looked again, this time staring long and hard. There was no light in the room except what the moon let through one small slanted attic window. But narrowing his eyes, he could see well enough to make out a curve under the rumpled sheets. He inched closer and bent over the bed. His gaze fell on a head of short blond hair on the pillow.

"Nurse Hofmeyer!" he exclaimed, his gray eyes impaling the streamlined female form under the covers. For an instant, he believed he'd walked into the wrong room, until he remembered that the nurses slept downstairs, dormitory style, in only slightly more comfortable digs than the orderlies enjoyed.

"Um . . ." she stirred, turned over, and looked at him, her eyes heavy with sleep. Even so, Johann thought she'd never been more appealing.

"Nurse Hofmeyer?" he repeated, his heart suddenly beating irregularly. For if she really meant to be in his bed, it was indeed a pleasant surprise.

Fully awake, she rose up on her elbows, the blanket fell away revealing a great deal of her. Johann sucked in his breath. The sight drugged his senses. He swallowed clumsily like a man wandering in the desert and finally coming upon a cool spring of fresh water.

"Nurse Hofmeyer," he uttered again and reached out to touch her shoulder, if only to convince himself that she was no mirage.

"Hush, Herr Doctor," she whispered, her soft mouth curved in a trembling smile; his fingertips on her skin made something leap inside her. "There's no need to alert the entire hospital as to my whereabouts. Someone downstairs might decide to have me report for night duty."

"I wouldn't allow it." Johann grinned down at her, still grabbling with this unexpected windfall. "I'll pull rank on them. I have yet to put those stripes to the test." He nodded toward his jacket on the chair with its fancy gold insignia and continued undressing. All at once, he was not the least bit tired.

"Speaking of rank," Olivia murmured, watching his every move, her pulse quickening at the sight of his hard and lean male body, "don't you think 'Nurse Hofmeyer' is a bit . . . uh, formal under the circumstances?"

"Yes . . ." Johann lifted the covers and slipped into the bed. "But 'Olivia' is much too melodic in this God-awful noisy place."

"Nights are quiet. Use it at night when we're alone." Her arms wrapped around him.

Nights? *When we're alone.* The promise reverberated pleasantly in Johann's ears and acted like an exquisite massage on his weary soul. His pledge to a year of celibacy took a battering as his body immediately responded to her delightful invitation. He had no interest in resisting this alluring woman. His heart rate accelerated dangerously. He cursed middle age, the long dry spell he'd endured, and although he was about to break his marriage vows, it caused him no qualm of conscience. His past life, Berlin and his family were so far away, it seemed another world and his future was not at all assured in this one. Battle lines changed daily. A mortar shell could hit the hospital at any time, while any number of contagious diseases, for which there were no cures, could strike with similar results.

Johann concentrated on the present.

245

Olivia Hofmeyer was the present.

She was a lifeline to *mens sana* on this bleak and godless front where nothing mattered but the moment at hand, nectarean and all absorbing, because there might never be another. He reached greedily for her sweet offerings, finding her lips in a kiss of profound passion. But although he'd grown as large as a stallion and was half-demented with need, he proceeded slowly; male pride forcing him to try to make her enjoyment match his.

"So . . . Herr Doctor," she murmured against his lips, "tit for tat, can I call you . . . Johann?" Although they were about to become intimate, he hadn't yet suggested that little bit of familiarity; something she hoped was just an oversight on his part.

"Of course . . . darling . . . anything you wish." The moonlight that fell across the bed made her silver-streaked blond hair appear iridescent. Johann felt as if he were holding an angel in his arms. "Call me whatever you want—"

Whispering his name, she moved her mouth against his as if sampling a luscious morsel.

A groan escaped his chest; and pressing his hand against the small of her back, he pulled her tightly against him, shifting and forging their bodies together as one, before spiraling toward nirvana.

In December, in one of her weekly letters, Dorrit wrote that she had seen Hans while he was home on furlough. He was thin but otherwise well, had distinguished himself in battle and had been promoted to first lieutenant. The remainder of her letter was full of glowing reports about Max and Fritz's exemplary behavior; reports Johann didn't quite believe. He suspected Dorrit embellished her accounts so as not to worry him. Especially since Max's letters were invariably full of complaints about his younger brother, while Fritz sent drawings of a violent nature.

In their Christmas letters to Johann, both Gerlinde and Karl-Heinz essentially repeated what Dorrit had already written about Hans. In fact, they were so chock full of their son's wonderful home leave, they quite neglected to mention the twins. Gerlinde added a poignant postscript.

"Hans's battalion has been assigned to the Niemen," she wrote in her neat cramped hand. "I'm so very comforted knowing that you are nearby. Dearest Johann, please look out for him!"

Johann smiled wryly at Gerlinde's naive words. The front was enormous and the Niemen River was a thousand miles long. How could he possibly look out for Hans? In fact, he sincerely hoped that he would never come across him out here. If he did, it could only means Hans had been wounded.

But Gerlinde's plea haunted Johann all that winter. And whenever new casualties were carried in and he spotted a tuft of blond hair from beneath the spiked helmet, he felt an icy draft race through his heart until he removed the *Pickelhaube*, cleaned the grime from the face, and confirmed that the wounded man was, *Gott sei Dank,* not Hans.

THIRTY-SIX

The war had passed the point of being a short war. Victory was not at hand. While battles were at a stalemate in the west, the eastern front expanded. Tanks and mortar shells became more numerous on both sides, and with practice Russian tactics improved.

In April, a year after arriving and the month during which Johann expected to be sent home, his replacement failed to materialize. So he stayed on, eventually spending his second summer at Kapsukas.

During the long, hot days of August, the air around the hospital became unbreathable and the sun was frequently all but obscured by thick black smoke from artillery fire. Battles seemed to be deadlocked around Kapsukas, and when the sound of combat was particularly persistent in nearby woods and fields, extra beds were quickly made ready for the newly wounded bound to arrive once the howitzers silenced at nightfall.

It was on one such day, a day of great rumbling activity along the front lines, creating vibrations that cracked windows in the wards, that Johann went to headquarters for additional supplies. The chief provisions officer, Captain Fellner, was a difficult man to deal with on a good day, and on this—an exceptionally bad day—it was Johann's poor luck to find the obnoxious man on duty.

Captain Fellner briefly scanned the list Johann gave him.

"I wish I could help you," he said before handing it back. "But our trucks are still in transit. None of these items are available."

"I beg your pardon?" This office and its agents had been a constant source of frustration for the hospital; Johann hadn't come here expecting a smooth ride or he would have sent an orderly.

"Thursday's shipment hasn't come in yet." Captain Fellner shrugged and spread his hands in a helpless gesture.

"But today is Saturday! Where are the trucks?"

"At the moment, I don't know. A convoy left Tannenberg on schedule. Unfortunately, it's now overdue."

"You mean to say that the Russians have again ambushed our supply trucks?"

"No. I'm saying that the trucks are late."

"And probably in the hands of the enemy."

"Herr Doctor, I didn't say that!"

"No, I guess you didn't," Johann sighed wearily. "All right, I'll just sign for some morphine then."

"*Ach,* the last of it was dispatched only this morning to the medics in the trenches."

"What?" Johann gnashed his teeth to keep his temper in check. "There is no morphine at all at headquarters?"

"None."

Johann stared dumbfounded at the man; this was a new low.

"All right," he finally said and slapped the list down on the desk. "Fill this when the shipment comes in. I'll send someone to pick it up." He turned to go.

Captain Fellner appeared to suddenly remember something.

"Herr Doctor! Wait a minute! You can't just leave this list here. You'll have to complete and sign itemized requisition forms. We have new orders from Berlin." He selected some papers from a pile on his desk and passed them across to Johann. "If you wish, you can do the paperwork now. It'll save you a trip."

That last suggestion had much to recommend it. Johann took the forms and sat down at a table in the corner to attend to this bizarre new regulation. His hand flew across the paper as he scratched out the hospital's requirements, copying from his list.

"Men are dying," he fumed under his breath but loud enough for the supply officer to hear, "and I'm having to waste time with this!"

Captain Fellner busied himself at his desk and wondered why a few forms should cause such a fuss.

"Let me assure you," he said and forced a pleasant enough tone, "the hospital is not being singled out—"

"Just stymied with unnecessary paperwork. Is that it?" Johann got up, walked over, and handed him the finished forms.

"Unnecessary? Quite the contrary. These forms are vital for fair and efficient distribution. We must account for everything now. Certain materials are becoming scarce, and we're deluged with orders from the front lines." Captain Fellner pointed toward an impressive accumulation of requisitions on his desk. "We are under immense pressure to get supplies to our men in the trenches, where it is a matter of victory! Of life and death."

"Supplying the hospital is also a matter of life and death," Johann said, knowing any sentiment was wasted on this man. He had been here often enough to know that this agent didn't consider the hospital a top priority. The wounded could no longer help determine the outcome of the war, therefore it was counterproductive to give them any consideration. It was more important to get supplies to the front, to those who could still make a difference.

As Johann left the building, he made a snap decision and walked next door to the officers' club. If he had to wait for morphine until tomorrow, or until God knows when, he could at least attempt to get his hands on some brandy to ease his patients' pain. Otherwise this trip to town would have been a complete waste. He raked his brain for a ruse as he went. Liquor was strictly rationed, even for the high brass. Nonetheless, and just before entering the club, he decided it might be an advantage to strut the stripes on his uniform. He quickly removed his surgeon's coat and left it outside the door on a wood pile bleached gray from sitting around all summer.

It was early in the afternoon, the lounge was empty except for a burly corporal planted behind the counter guarding the goods. Evenings, this canteen came to life with a bevy of local girls, some who served as barmaids, and others who picked up extra change from lonely officers who didn't mind a tryst out back among beer crates and other debris.

Faking an extravagant limp, Johann strolled toward the watchdog at the bar, still formulating a pretext and not quite sure how he'd pull it off. But it was key to act casual.

"I've come to pick up a bottle of brandy," he announced cavalierly as he approached the counter, clad in sticky green oilcloth battened down with a thousand thumb tacks. He hadn't seen this fellow before and, what luck, he appeared to be easy game. A slackness around his wet mouth that looked as if it'd drool with little provocation, indicated border-line idiot. The army had a prevalence of the witless and mostly they were kept far from the trenches where they wouldn't last twenty minutes.

"Brandy . . . ,Herr Major?" The corporal clicked his heels together noisily. He'd been trained to recognize rank, if little else.

"Yes. At ease, corporal."

"Thank you, sir." The flesh bulging around the man's tight collar undulated as he relaxed his spine. "Did you say a full bottle, sir?"

"Yes."

"Uh . . . well, in that case, may I have your voucher, please?"

"Of course." Johann's mind raced to come up with something plausible. He had no voucher, and this corporal might not be as cracked as he appeared. "Let's see . . ." Johann pretended to search his pockets. "Hm, it's amazing how small slips of paper can get lost." He continued searching with feigned urgency. "I know I had one."

"Never mind. I can check the ledger," the corporal said, happy to oblige a superior officer. "Excuse me for one moment." He turned and reached behind the counter for a thick book lying on a shelf, one Johann was all too familiar with, one that would expose him. He could buy a single drink to be consumed on the premises anytime, but he couldn't get his hands on a whole bottle. Liquor was more precious to the army than ammunition; this corporal staked his pension on its safekeeping, and while Johann didn't begrudge front line officers on leave a bit of libation, he felt the numbing benefits of a good schnapps was better spent on dying soldiers. A point he'd argued to a brick wall at headquarters months ago . . . and lost, which left him with no options but to resort to deceit. Both he and Dr. Bergen had managed to get vouchers from various provision officers for an occasional bottle by claiming disabling insomnia, but they'd never peeled a voucher off Captain Fellner. The man was a fusspot not impressed by rank. A five-star general couldn't twist his arm.

Hm . . . general?

"Actually, corporal, forget the ledger," Johann said to the man's back. "The bottle in question is not assigned to me from the regular inventory."

The young man turned around.

"Oh . . . ?"

251

"No. You see, it's a gift for the hospital. A gift from ...ah...from General Kinzl. We patched up his nephew last week. Saved the lad's life. The general is grateful and wants to show his appreciation. He sent word that a bottle is set aside in the basement. From his private reserve. It is clearly labeled for the hospital staff."

The corporal looked confused and scratched the back of his considerable neck. The sergeant he'd relieved half an hour ago had not told him about this. However, he had told him not to abandon his station. Leaving this counter, even for a few minutes, would be viewed as dereliction of duty. He shifted his weight from one foot to the other, neither one was anxious to disobey the sergeant's order and head for the basement.

"I'd get it myself, corporal but I've suffered a recent sprain," Johann persevered, counting on his initial appraisal that this fellow was a born fool. "Steps are out of the question." And still attempting to appear casual, he removed his hat and limped over to a small table where a chess game had been abandoned, pulled out a chair, sat down, and massaged his knee with great ceremony while he studied the black king's position. "To the basement, corporal! We haven't got all day." The man hesitated. "That's an order!" Johann bellowed.

The corporal snapped to attention.

"Of course, sir!" A major outranked a sergeant. Still, the sergeant's order had been issued first. Which took priority? Which was he supposed to heed? It was sure confusing being in the military. No one explained things properly. But he finally figured that the sergeant was busy elsewhere and would be none the wiser if he left his station. "Er, if you'll pardon me, sir," he now said to Johann, "I first have to secure the front door. Regulations, sir. If I leave, even for a moment, I have to guard the entrance against...well, you know, against unauthorized personnel."

"You're a good man. Dedicated to your duty. See to it then. Secure the premises."

"Thank you, sir."

No sooner had the corporal locked up, disappeared along a narrow hallway and started down the ladder into the basement, when Johann got out of the chair, swung lightly over the bar counter, jimmied the lock on the liquor cabinet, and helped himself to the largest flask of brandy he could find. And, what the hell, he was on a roll and might as well grab some rum while he was at it; rum would help sterilize some surgical instruments. Stuffing the bottles carefully into the inside pockets of his jacket, he rearranged the remaining stock so the theft would not be spotted immediately. Then he bolted across the counter and settled into the chair, again bending over the chess pieces in great concentration.

"Sir . . . ?" the corporal was puffing hard from his climb back up the steep ladder. "I . . . I can't seem to find the brandy," he said as he again took up his position behind the bar counter. "There's nothing down there but spiders." He brushed at some cobwebs clinging to his uniform. "Are you absolutely sure that's where the general meant to leave it?"

"Certainly. He specifically said it'd be stored at headquarters. In the basement. Out of the heat of the day." Though now anxious to leave, Johann got up slowly, grimacing convincingly as he put weight on his left foot.

"That's wise, of course," the corporal nodded. Suddenly lightning struck his small brain. "Say, . . . you know what, sir? I'll bet that when the general said headquarters, he meant 'the' headquarters! Next door. This officers' canteen is part of headquarters of course, but then again, not really. If you know what I mean?"

"Hm, you make a good a point, corporal. I'll check next door." Johann crossed the floor awkwardly holding his hat in front of his chest. "Sorry to have bothered you," he said as he finally put on his hat, carefully flashing the gold band and other trappings of rank to distract the man from the bulges under his jacket.

The corporal had rushed to the door, unlocked it, and sliced a perfect salute as he held it open. After all, one didn't get many brass hats in this establishment, and never at this hour.

As Johann limped away, snatching his surgeon's coat from the wood pile, a couple of lieutenants on their way to the canteen saluted him smartly, glancing at his "war injury" with a flicker of sympathy.

Once he was safely out of view, Johann walked briskly, and somewhat ashamed, to the spot where he had parked the hospital's motor lorry. Imagine, being reduced to faking and thievery! Of course, one did odd things in times of war; surely this ranked among the lesser sins. Besides, the loot was not for personal use, but a substitute for basic supplies, such as ether and isopropyl. Basic? Actually, in all fairness to "crab grass" Fellner, Ben Tarnoff had recently written that those very items were in disastrously short supply in Berlin as well.

"Damn!" Johann swore out loud. "Damn this useless war!" He gripped the steering wheel in a choke hold, his white knuckles straining against the skin, and revving the motor angrily, he pulled out onto the road. As soon as he was free of traffic, he shifted into neutral and cut the engine. The rest of the way was downhill. He could coast. One was under strict orders to conserve benzin.

THIRTY-SEVEN

It was autumn. There was talk the war would end before another winter set in; the last one had sent as many of the kaiser's troops to their deaths as did Russian artillery. It was impossible to keep warm in the dugouts; water for the big guns froze, the weapons misfired, and when enemy shells hit, clods of hard mud and clunks of ice became as dangerous as flying shrapnel for anyone crouched within a hundred feet of the point of impact.

Casualties along the eastern front reached catastrophic levels, and as numbers dwindled, a bulletin reached all field hospitals mandating that convalescing soldiers whole enough to walk and carry a rifle be reassigned to full duty upon discharge. With that edict, the staff at Kapsukas found little to cheer about when a man recovered. It was earnestly hoped that the fighting would stop before any of their patients became repeats.

The last day of October dawned auspiciously to a blue sky without the blemish of a single cloud. And as the sun rose, the bleached and crumbling brick facade of the hospital gleamed pink in its splendid blush. At daybreak, the air was cold and crisp, but by midmorning, it had turned soothingly warm with the embrace of a golden season of its own, *sui generis* and reluctant to depart. However, before the sun would set on this benign and uncommon day, Johann was to be vanquished and feel pain same as if he'd been bludgeoned. And if he thought that he had already experienced the worst at this wretched outpost, he was mistaken.

As it happened, he overslept. Due to an inordinate number of casualties deposited at the doorstep of the hospital the evening before, he had been in the wards until three in the morning, and no staff member was sufficiently heartless to rouse him at five o'clock for his regular rounds. At seven, he woke on his own when a streak of sunlight from the slanted attic window focused itself on his pillow. From habit he swatted the air—before realizing the prickling was not the dozen or so flies that regularly kept everyone company, but rather the tickling of an unfamiliar beam of sun—unfamiliar because he always rose well ahead of it. Turning over, Johann checked his watch, and immediately jumped out of bed in a rush of guilt.

He quickly made his way to the one bath shared by all, entertaining little hope there'd be enough warm water at this hour for an adequate shower. There wasn't, and in his frustration and hurry, he dropped the only towel available. It fell onto the stone and mildewy floor where it promptly absorbed a puddle. Shivering and wet, Johann sought relief in a string of hot curses as he struggled into his uniform. He left the lavatory in a distinctly foul mood, grabbed a clean white surgeons coat from a closet in the hall outside ward B and threw the old one into the bin, although it was supposed to have lasted another three days. Thrusting his arms into the sleeves, he put the stethoscope around his neck and entered the infirmary, ready for another twenty-hour day.

The nuns were in the process of removing the breakfast trays, some of which were hardly touched.

"What's this?" Johann frowned at the plates of black bread dolloped with bacon grease, a boiled egg, and something which resembled applesauce. "Is the breakfast not to our patients' liking this morning?"

"Oh, it's not that, Herr Doctor," one of the nuns spoke up. "It's the same story again, I'm afraid. Several amputees carried on so terribly when they awoke and found parts of their bodies missing that the others lost their appetite."

"Well, that'll never do. Without nourishment, how do they expect to recover?"

"I have long since come to the conclusion that most of them would prefer to die here rather than go home disfigured."

"Something we can't allow, of course." Johann ordered the women to take the food back into the ward. "Force feed the men if necessary," he said. "And account for each and every utensil when you're done." He eyed the senior nun, reminding her to be on the lookout for potential suicides. Ever since the night when a distraught soldier had rammed a fork down his throat and strangled on the metal and his own blood, all flatware was carefully collected after each meal.

Nurse Hofmeyer appeared at Johann's side with a cup of coffee, black and steaming hot. She knew his routine. Coffee first and breakfast after he'd made the rounds.

"Good morning," she smiled and, before handing him the mug, touched her lips surreptitiously to the rim.

Accepting the veiled kiss with a broad grin, Johann wondered if anyone guessed his deep affection for Nurse Hofmeyer or suspected their affair. But quickly dismissing any pleasant musings of Olivia's visits to his room, he took a sip of coffee and began his examinations, starting with a new patient in the bed nearest the door, a soldier who had apparently been admitted just this morning. His face, streaked with tears, was turned toward the cot on his right where a young man lay dead with a gaping hole in his chest. He had not lived long enough to have his chart filled in. Two orderlies, unfolding a waterproof sheet, were preparing to remove him. Space was at a premium. The dead were not allowed to linger.

"I'm sorry we couldn't do anything for your friend," Johann said as he bent over the sobbing boy; a gash in his shoulder was ugly but not life-threatening.

"He...he's...n...not my friend."

"No?"

"He's m...my...kid brother."

"Oh." Johann felt a punch in his chest. "In that case, I am doubly sorry," he said. "Now we'd better get you well quickly so you can go home and be a comfort to your parents." As he examined the shoulder wound, he decided that he would discharge this patient with an incapacitating "internal" injury to make absolutely sure that he was sent home and not back to the trenches.

As Johann made his way to another cot, a strange crawling sensation on the back of his neck caused an icy shiver to run up his spine. He took another swig of the coffee, hoping it would chase the chill. But even as he drank the wonderful black liquid, the only commodity on the front that for some reason hadn't become scarce yet, he was overcome with an odd foreboding and was almost ready to believe he was hearing voices, but not those of the nuns prodding the soldiers to eat. Of course, after a year and a half of this grueling duty, no sleep, and little food, his mind could easily be playing tricks on him. He shrugged, put his cup down on a surgical tray and bent over yet another new patient, one he instantly diagnosed with the dreaded and extremely infectious cholera.

"Why in God's name was this man brought in here?" Johann uttered aghast, turning on Nurse Hofmeyer who was changing the dressing on a head wound of a comatose soldier in an adjacent bed. "This patient must be quarantined! Have him removed at once!"

"The isolation rooms are full, Herr Doctor," she said.

"Well, make space somewhere else then! Move the supplies to the cellar. Use the storage room. Perhaps the . . ."

"Uncle Johann . . . ?"

"Huh?" Johann spun around in the direction of the voice, his heart slamming so violently against his rib cage that his lungs emptied of air; he couldn't breathe.

"It's me . . . over here—"

"Hans?" Johann's lips moved, but no sound came. *Dear God, no! Not Hans!* Walking drunkenly, thrown off balance by the horrible thought that Hans had landed in this ward, Johann waded around pallets and basins, all the while praying that his mind was failing him rather than discover the summons was real.

An agonizing moment later, he stopped and looked down at a cot occupied by someone he immediately recognized. Of course it could still be a mistake, a cruel optical trick brought on by a myriad of personal deprivations. But, as much as he tried to disclaim what he saw, it was Hans. Hans Konauer. None other.

Johann stared in disbelief at the gaunt and dirty face, stared at the achingly familiar features hideously distorted by trauma. The light-blue eyes, now black and hollow, were searching the surroundings with a frantic urgency as if it was growing too dark to see.

"Uncle Johann . . . ?" Again the question formed on the thin pellucid lips stretched across teeth protruding unnaturally, presaging death.

Reaching for a limp hand while fighting to keep his voice steady, Johann bent down.

"I'm here, Hans," he said, "right here."

The young man smiled weakly, his body relaxed, he closed his eyes, his ashen face becoming a mask of contentment, as if he felt safe and was suddenly free of pain. Johann checked for a pulse, but the loud drumming within his own chest interfered with a proper reading.

"Hofmeyer!" he barked in the next instant, dispensing with all professional courtesy. "Hofmeyer! Over here. At once!" It was quite clear he wanted no one else.

She motioned another nurse to finish bandaging the patient she was tending and immediately barreled her way through the maze of beds, picking up instruments, gauze, and a bucket of clean water as she went, figuring it was needed by the harsh sound of the command. She arrived at Johann's side, every pocket on her uniform rattling with instruments, her apron strings bulging and taut with bandages she'd tucked into the belt. Had the situation not been so tragic, he would have smiled at the sight of her.

"Help me cut away his clothes!" he now said, his mind reeling with the seriousness of Hans's injuries. A wound in his hip had been poorly dressed in the field, using a shirt that had probably been ripped from a dead soldier.

"This lieutenant was brought in early this morning," Olivia Hofmeyer explained as she bent down and her nimble hands set about the all-too-familiar task. "Dr. Bergen gave him a bit of morphine." She spoke softly, although the patient had lost consciousness and couldn't hear her. "He said not to bother any further because this one wouldn't last the hour. Another patient with a similarly bad wound has already died."

Johann nodded; he had seen the dead youth.

"Do you want him moved to the operating room?" In view of Dr. Bergen's diagnosis, Olivia Hofmeyer wondered why Johann was fussing over this hopeless case.

"No. He can't be moved," Johann said and began to clean the gash in Hans's side, having first peeled away the crude wadded bandage plug. "I'll have to work on him here. Please, get me some iodine. And more water. Plus whatever painkillers you can get your hands on." His eyes traveled the length of the bed over two limbs outlined under a sheet that lay heavy across them soaked, as it were, in blood. "After I've closed this wound, I'll take a look at his legs. If they're as bad as I suspect, he'll be a burning mass of pain once the morphine wears off." Johann reached into his pockets to see if he had enough sutures for the task ahead. He did.

Nurse Hofmeyer left to fetch the needed items. She returned moments later with everything but the morphine.

"Dr. Bergen is guarding it with his life," she said and while Johann worked on the hip wound, she removed the sheet and began to cut the blood-soaked material away from the patient's legs. "He promised to bring it along personally in a few minutes."

"All right." Johann shrugged, resigned to the scarcity of critical supplies. Besides, as long as Hans was unconscious, he'd feel no pain. Johann finally closed the wounds in Hans's side with quick long sutures, then pulled at the cloth around the legs as Olivia cut. Pieces of the fabric were fused to scorched flesh, and both legs were shattered, white bone slivers protruding through burnt tissue. Johann drew in his breath sharply before exhaling in defeat. Wiping his bloodied hands negligently on his white coat, his broad shoulders sank along with any optimism he might have entertained only moments ago. He sat down on a three-legged stool and stared disbelievingly at the mangled mess. No medical miracle known to man in 1916 could be called upon to mend such damage. And this sorry hospital didn't even have an x-ray machine.

"Do you want to amputate?" Olivia asked quietly.

"No. It wouldn't save his life and only cause him needless suffering. The hip wound alone is fatal. Half the pelvic bone is pulp. He has lost too much blood. It's a wonder he's still alive."

Nodding, Olivia glanced grimly down at a sticky rust colored pool under the bed.

Dr. Bergen came by.

"Do you know this lad?" he asked when he saw his colleague's stricken face.

"Yes." Johann's voice broke, he cleared his throat awkwardly and dismissed Nurse Hofmeyer with a quick nod. "Lieutenant Konauer is as close to me as my own sons."

Dr. Bergen handed over the narcotic.

"Use as much as you want," he said and walked away, knowing he could afford to be generous. That young man wouldn't last long enough to make a dent in the morphine.

Although it was futile, Johann continued to work on Hans, pushing bone back into the flesh of his legs, the same time he fished out bomb fragments and stones. He couldn't give up, he couldn't just sit by and watch him die. He contemplated double amputation, this in spite of the fact that Hans would not survive the short trip to the operating room.

Hans drifted back toward consciousness. Again neglecting to make use of the damp rag that hung at the foot of each bed, Johann wiped his hands on his surgeon's coat, then fingered the precious vial of morphine in his pocket, bracing himself for frantic sounds or gestures indicating pain. But Hans made none. He merely looked around the room in confusion, having apparently forgotten where he was. Suddenly he focused on the person sitting next to his bed. He smiled.

"Uncle Johann? I . . . I can't see clearly. Is it really you?"

"Yes." Johann grasped a cold lifeless hand, squeezing it gently to reassure him. "And I'll stay with you. I've patched you up a bit. You need to rest. Later, when you've gained some strength, I'll go to work on you." Johann hated himself for the cheap promises, and dearly hoped Hans was unaware of the condition of his legs. Johann had discovered that most soldiers eventually accepted the loss of body parts, except the loss of legs which stripped them of the independence of mobility. He motioned a nun to cover Hans's legs with a clean sheet. Thankfully, she was quick about it.

"I'm a mess, huh?"

"Oh, I don't know. I've seen worse." Fighting a storm of emotions, Johann tried to keep his voice light. He touched the back of his hand tenderly to the young face and ran his fingers through the matted blond hair.

"I can't believe my luck."

Johann straightened in the chair.

"Luck?"

"Yeah. Finding you here. I heard you talking to someone earlier. I recognized your voice, I thought I was hallucinating. It seemed too good to be true. An old fellow in a white coat had slipped me some bitter stuff. Opium, I guess. It made me feel like I was floating. So I figured I was dreaming."

"You weren't, and I'm right here."

"I know," Hans smiled before he suddenly grabbed at Johann's arm. "There's only one thing though! Ever since the opium, I haven't been able to feel my legs. They're still there? Aren't they?" He tugged feebly at the sheet covering him, his face a map of panic. "I still have my legs . . . d . . . don't I?"

"Yes." Johann helped him raise his head. "See . . ." He pointed to the outlines under the sheet.

"Well, thank God!" Exhausted from his outburst, Hans sank back down on the pillow. A moment later, and as if there existed a great urgency to talk, he pulled some air into his lungs and continued to speak despite a gurgling in his chest. "The damned Russians . . ." he said, struggling for every word, "came out of the woods like riled boars. They'd shelled our positions for some twelve hours yesterday, and we sure didn't expect them to make noise again before daylight. They roared out of the dark so suddenly, we didn't even have time to shoot off a Verey light. Still, we held them off. The ones who eventually retreated left a lot of dead friends in front of our trenches. One of them, not as dead as his comrades, blew himself up with a hand grenade when we approached to sweep the area for wounded."

"He blew himself up?"

"Yeah. I guess he didn't want to be captured. Or maybe he believed we were coming to finish him off. I thought at first that the explosion got my legs. I'm glad it didn't. But I . . . I guess I took quite a hit anyway. Huh?"

"Yes," Johann said quietly and swallowed past a tight obstruction like a rubber band that threatened to close his throat. He was remembering a boy, a happy lad with straw-colored hair and sturdy legs, riding a pony in the field behind the Konauers' new house, hollering "Watch me! Watch me!" All the while laughing into the wind and urging the animal on but never once using the crop.

"Uncle Johann?"

"Yes?"

"You were right."

"Right about what?"

"The university." Hans's voice rattled; blood was collecting in his throat; Johann recognized the sound, there wasn't much time left. "Did you know that there were days during these past months when I wished I'd followed your advice and signed up for the university instead of the army?"

"You'd be in the war now regardless, Hans. Everyone is being mobilized. The universities have emptied. From *Realschule* on up. I'm here, too. Proof that they're tapping even the very old."

"You're not so old," Hans grinned and closed his eyes, conversation taxed him.

Again Johann heard a raspy struggle for air.

"I'm c . . . cold . . . ," Hans murmured; pink bubbles and trickles of blood were seeping from between his lips.

Johann grabbed the folded blanket at the foot of the bed and spread it over him, knowing it wouldn't help.

"Do you have any pain?" he asked as he gently wiped some swabs across the corners of Hans's mouth.

"No. It's just c . . . cold. And dark. What . . . what time is it? Is it . . . is it late?" Hans's eyes were wide open, groping the surroundings like a blind man. "Is it late?" he persisted, as if the time of day was suddenly very important to him.

Johann couldn't find it in his heart to tell him that it was midmorning and that a pleasant October sun was bathing the entire ward in a cheerful yellow glow. Obviously, Hans could neither see nor feel it.

"It is quite late," he lied and took the cold hands in his.

"Uncle Johann?"

"Yes?"

"Don't tell mother what happened to me. Tell her I took a bullet . . . clean . . . quick. I couldn't bear for her to know about the mess I'm in. Please . . . promise me!"

"All right." Johann pressed the waxy hands; he realized Hans knew he was dying.

"And . . . and tell my grandfather . . . tell him I was in line for another promotion."

"I will. I'll tell everyone. They'll be so proud of you." Johann tightened his grip on the young hands, hands that had shrunk and felt as dry as parchment; it was as if only a thin layer of skin covered the bones.

"I was due for another furlough . . . soon . . . only a few more weeks. I . . . I wish I was going home . . ."

Johann stroked the troubled brow.

"You will, Hans. You'll go home. By God, I swear you will!"

Hans smiled queerly.

"Yes. And it'll be so peaceful at home. So quiet. I'll like that. And . . . and it'll soon be winter. The snow will be so beautiful in Bernau. I wonder if my sisters will remember to . . . to—"

"Feed the birds?" Johann finished for him, knowing that Hans always set up elaborate feeding stations each winter.

Hans nodded and struggled for breath that wouldn't come.

His opaque eyes settled on Johann, while a gush of blood poured from his mouth and ran like a sticky red ribbon down into the small of his neck. He blinked once before his head sank heavily into the pillow.

Johann reached out and touched his face. He ran his hand lovingly through the blond hair and brushed it back off the traumatized forehead before he brought his fingers down and gently closed Hans's eyes.

THIRTY-EIGHT

Johann sat in quiet, paralyzing disbelief for endless moments before he finally, with unaccustomed difficulty, rose. He felt like an old man. He was bone tired. He couldn't straighten his shoulders, and his legs shook as he turned away from Hans and fled the ward, wanting nothing more than to pound his fists into the plaster walls. Once out in the lavatory, he washed the blood from his hands and scrubbed them until they smarted, punishing them for their uselessness.

He returned to the infirmary and went directly to the cot where he had left Hans.

Another man occupied it!

"Where is Lieutenant Konauer?" he barked at the two orderlies who had just brought in the new patient.

"He's dead, sir."

"I know that! But where is he?" Johann's voice rang loud and hoarse.

The orderlies eyed him weirdly. "We . . . uh, we took him outside for burial. Regulations, Herr Doctor. And we needed the bed."

"Damn you!" Johann pushed past the men. "I just promised Lieutenant Konauer that he could go home!"

The orderlies' eyebrows shot up. Go home? This doctor had finally flipped. They watched him run from the premises before they went in search of Herr Director to warn him of trouble.

Johann caught up with the funeral possession a short distance from the hospital and ordered everyone back to the building. Hans was going home. Deathbed promises were sacred, Johann could not go back on his word. Besides, he had to consider the rest of the Konauers, Gerlinde in particular. The thought of her receiving the tragic news was not a pretty picture. But if she could have the small comfort of seeing her son put to rest in Bernau soil, it might ease her grief.

Hans's body was being placed on the floor in the hall at the same time Dr. Bergen was rushing from the operating room, armed with a syringe, ready to restrain someone.

"What's the procedure for having a deceased returned to Germany?" Johann asked and cocked an eyebrow at the weapon poised in his colleague's hand. "You can put that thing away," he added. "I haven't gone berserk. Though only God knows why not."

Relieved to find that the orderlies had exaggerated any bizarre behavior, Dr. Bergen capped the syringe.

"There's no policy," he said. "It can't be done."

"Surely some bodies are returned."

"None that I've ever heard of. We haven't got the manpower or the vehicles for the job."

"Manpower? Vehicles? Christ! We're not discussing a hundred bodies. I'm talking about just one."

"One or a dozen, it can't be done. I don't have to tell you that corpses deteriorate rapidly. Long distance transport would become a health hazard and—"

"Well, Lieutenant Konauer is going home!" Johann snapped. "I'm going to headquarters to make the arrangements. Please make sure no one buries the body before I return."

"All right," Dr. Bergen shrugged. "But I don't know what you expect from headquarters. They're going to repeat exactly what I just said. As you know, they're not especially receptive to our regular demands. I can only imagine how they'll react to an unreasonable one."

"We'll see." Johann turned on his heel and went outside, leaving the older doctor in the hall shaking his head.

Fortunately, no one was using the hospital's motor lorry this morning. Johann took it, gunned it and drove to town in a plume of dust. Speed was imperative, guilt for abandoning the wounded propelled him, he had to be quick about this.

Record-setting minutes later, he screeched to a halt in front of headquarters. In his hurry, he'd forgotten to remove his blood-stained surgeon's coat, the stethoscope still dangled around his neck, and the wind in the open car had given his hair a life of its own. But he was so fixed on his mission that he was completely unaware of the strange and appalling sight he presented when he barged through the doors.

"I'm Dr. von Renz," he wheezed to the sergeant on duty at the front desk. "Where can I find the person in charge of transportation?"

The sergeant eyed the doctor's bloodied coat and immediately decided that calm discretion was called for. Rumors abounded that things were not terrific at the hospital; this sorry-looking individual confirmed it.

"Do you have an appointment, Herr Doctor?" he asked, smiling patronizingly.

"That's ridiculous! Of course not!"

"Then, if you'll please take a seat," the sergeant pointed to a hard-backed chair in a corner and continued in a condescending voice, "I'll see if *Hauptfeldwebel* Mannheim is free at the moment."

"Free...?" Glaring at the man, Johann tossed out a few choice blue words, then pushed his way past him and walked down the hall, reading signs as he went. He'd been along this corridor before. The supply officer, Captain Fellner, held court here. *Christ Almighty! An appointment?*

"Herr Doctor! You cannot pass unannounced." The sergeant was panting on Johann's heels.

"By all means then, return to your station and announce me!"

The man slowed his steps, unsure about how to deal with this. He couldn't very well create a scene by blowing his whistle or pulling his revolver. After all, this was a fellow citizen and no crime had been committed—yet. He turned and ran back to his desk. Better ring Mannheim and alert him.

Johann found the right door and walked in without knocking.

Sergeant Major Mannheim, telephone to his ear, was seated at a large, cluttered desk. The wall behind him was papered with military maps freckled with colored pins, while elaborate radio equipment on a table under the window gave further proof of his importance.

"Ah...Dr. von Renz...?" *Hauptfeldwebel* Mannheim replaced the receiver in its cradle, pushed his chair back, stood up, and extended his hand, hoping that idiot sergeant who'd called from the front desk had gotten this visitor's name right. Mannheim had no contact with the hospital. He didn't know the doctors, and was glad of it. "How can I be of assistance?" he now asked, realizing too late that this intruder was also an officer; the absence of a hat and the white surgeon's coat obscuring the uniform had momentarily escaped him. Likewise, it had obviously escaped that incompetent sergeant out front. Recovering quickly, Mannheim executed a smart salute before taking his seat, after first walking around his desk to pull out a chair for his caller.

Johann ignored the offer to sit and remained standing.

"I have come to arrange transportation for a young officer," he said. "A Lieutenant Konauer. He died this morning in my care. I wish to have his body returned to Germany."

"I see." Leaning forward on his elbows, Mannheim crimped his forehead in an attempt to appear sympathetic. "I'm terribly sorry," he said, "but as you no doubt know, that's quite impossible." He placed his hands together, fingertips to fingertips, forming a steeple against his chin. "Our fallen heroes are buried where they die. For obvious reasons. Of course, we make every effort to send personal belongings home. So if you have any special wishes in regard to the possessions of the deceased, we'll be happy to handle the matter expeditiously."

Johann sat down, incredibly exhausted, and this might take a while.

"I did not leave my patients to discuss a watch or a wallet," he said tersely. "I am here to ask you to make an exception. Naturally, I am prepared to reimburse the army for the expense incurred."

"Herr Doctor, we cannot make exceptions. We don't transport bodies, and the military does not accept payments from private individuals, nor does it cater to personal whims. We are bound to abide by our regulations. If we allowed even one body to go home, every family in Germany would soon demand the same privilege. Our trains would become moving morgues. Imagine the chaos—"

"Sergeant Major!" Johann rose menacingly; this had been a torturous morning, and now this pompous ass was being overbearing as hell. "Please don't lecture me!" he said and leaned his palms on the desk. "Especially not about chaos, because that's something I'm very familiar with. It's alive and well at the hospital. About the only thing that is. And spare me your precious army regulations. Captain Fellner has covered that subject *ad infinitum*. If the hospital had one canister of ether for every useless regulation we've complied with, our infirmary would be airborne. This post is rife with inefficiency and has yet to supply the hospital with adequate rations. Food or medicine. The only thing we get plenty of is paperwork."

Mannheim rose, pulled himself up to his full height of five feet nine inches to gain some ground on this tall intruder.

"May I remind you, Herr Doctor. . . . uh, Herr Major, that we here at headquarters suffer shortages as well. But we manage with what we have. Our orders are to secure the front lines. With our bare hands if necessary. And though rationed severely, we are doing a good job of it."

"I invite you to inspect our facility," Johann said in a soft, blood-chilling voice. "You might arrive at a different conclusion."

The transportation officer chose to ignore that galling remark. He sat down and idly shuffled some papers.

"There's obviously nothing more to be said here," he mumbled. "Now, if you'll excuse me. You ask the impossible, and I really must get back to work. Urgent projects need my attention. I regret that I cannot help you."

"In that case, I must insist on speaking with someone of higher consequence."

The sergeant major winced.

"In this department, I am that person!" he said between clenched teeth. "My word is final. While your appeal for the deceased lieutenant is commendable, I must repeat that it's out of the question. I am in charge of transporting troops. Live troops! I'm sworn to uphold my orders." *Hauptfeldwebel* Mannheim threw his shoulders back so the stubborn doctor would have a clear view of the numerous citations decorating his chest. "It'd take an imperial decree from Berlin to waive my orders."

Imperial decree? Kaiser Wilhelm? Johann sat down, struck by a thought so timely it made him weak in the knees. He might have Hans's ticket home. Yes sir! It was time to cash in a chit. Dammit, why hadn't he thought of that before degrading himself, arguing with this insolent individual preening behind a chest full of cheap hardware?

Kaiser Wilhelm had said at the time of the surgery, "I am deeply in your debt." Moreover, Johann often suspected that he credited him—ridiculous as it were—with a subsequent freedom of throat polyps. His Majesty certainly greeted him with exceptional warmth at palace functions; only Dorrit received a warmer reception. Of course Wilhelm had an eye for beautiful women. But he also had a keen memory. So although it had been a number of years, it was safe to assume that he would remember a favor owed and, as the consummate sovereign, act upon it.

"Sergeant Major."

Mannheim looked across his desk at the doctor and sorely wished a noncommissioned officer could evict a major.

"Yes?"

"I'd like to send a cable."

"A cable . . . ? Why certainly! Right away." Mannheim picked up the telephone and shouted into the mouthpiece. Somebody at the other end must have jumped, because he had barely hung up the receiver before a wire operator presented himself, bid each of the men a "good morning" and then went directly to the radio equipment at the window. Clicking in the origination code, he now looked up and waited for the message, his finger poised on the button.

Johann cleared his throat, got up and braced his hands on the back of his chair.

"Your Imperial Majesty . . ." he began, formulating his words carefully, keeping them to a minimum, "Kaiser Wilhelm . . ."

The room became a tomb. The telegraphist jerked his finger away from the apparatus as if he'd been burned. Mannheim's chair creaked, disturbing the eerie silence, as he tilted forward to stare flabbergasted at the brazen doctor.

"Is this some sort of a joke?" he demanded and rose from his seat with an exaggerated effort. "I have no time for games, Herr Doctor." He was turning puce with anger at being taken for a fool. "You will please not abuse my patience. I am a very busy man."

Johann's expression remained bland, but the acid in his voice could have burned a hole in the floor.

"I might ask you not to abuse *my patience*," he said. "And any interruptions will only serve to keep us both from getting back to work."

The fight went out of *Hauptfeldwebel* Mannheim. He slumped back into his chair.

"Do you actually know the kaiser?" he asked with a sneer that said he wouldn't believe anything other than a plain and honest no.

270

"Well enough."

"I see." Somehow Mannheim had expected that. He motioned for the telegraphist to proceed. What else could he do? His visitor outranked him.

Johann picked up where he'd left off.

"Respectfully request permission to transport the body of Lieutenant Hans Konauer from Kapsukas to Bernau STOP Speed in this matter is crucial STOP Will await reply at this communications station STOP signed Johann von Renz, M.D."

As the machine clicked, Johann wondered if Wilhelm would respond to something he might consider a trifling matter. The kaiser had a raging war on his hands; there was a good chance the telegram would never even come to his attention. It risked being buried under the weight of more important messages.

Hauptfeldwebel Mannheim remained at his desk, fuming and drumming his fingers on the blotter, long after his visitor had left. How had he let this von Renz character get the better of him? How had he been cornered into sending a bogus wire? To the kaiser yet! There were bound to be repercussions. And, of course, he would be held responsible, since the cable had originated from this office. Berlin could not ignore such a violation. Heads would roll. This might be as bad as going AWOL.

That afternoon, when the apparatus by the window began clicking, *Hauptfeldwebel* Mannheim stood by perspiring profusely. He prayed it was a routine war memorandum, not an order to present himself before a military tribune.

It was not the latter; neither was it by any means routine, far from it. The communiqué was from the Imperial Palace on Unter den Linden, and it was for Baron Johann Maximilian von Renz. Baron? Mannheim tore the strip of paper from the machine. The message was very explicit.

Wire received STOP Permission granted for transport of the remains of Lieutenant Konauer STOP Kapsukas Headquarters are ordered to comply immediately STOP At the direct pleasure of Wilhelm II space on convoy to Germany will be available STOP Signed Rudolf Breckt, personal secretary to His Imperial Majesty.

Mannheim pursed his lips and let out a subdued whistle. "Well, I'll be damned!" he muttered out loud. Who would ever have guessed? No wonder that doctor was so cocksure of himself. He did know the kaiser!

Mannheim took the telegram to the sergeant at the front desk.

"Have this delivered to Dr. von Renz at once," he said. "And ask *Oberst* Fuchs to send the standard notification of death to the family of Lieutenant Konauer of Bernau. But add that the body will be returned for burial."

"It will? I . . . I don't understand?"

"You don't have to. It's an order." Mannheim turned and went outside to personally make sure that a coffin and an emergency vehicle could be made ready and be on its way to Tannenberg in time to catch the night train to Germany. The kaiser's orders must be obeyed without delay.

And so Hans went home.

Johann would be eternally grateful to Nurse Hofmeyer, who, with her resourceful ways, managed to procure a uniform—previously worn of course—but one that had belonged to a soldier who'd died from a single gunshot wound. After carefully cleaning the spot, Olivia patched the hole over the heart where the bullet had entered and added Hans's lieutenant stripes. Then she washed his face and combed his tangled hair and dressed him.

As Hans was placed in the coffin, Johann commented on the pains she'd taken.

"You are a marvel," he said watching as the lorry, balancing its grim load, soon lumbered away from the hospital.

"He would want to look good for his parents," Olivia explained quietly.

Suddenly and without caring if the entire hospital witnessed the scene, Johann took Olivia Hofmeyer into his arms. Standing by the old water pump in the yard in broad daylight, he held her tight, held her for endless moments in a lovers' embrace.

"I adore you," he whispered.

That evening, he wrote a long and difficult letter to Gerlinde and Karl-Heinz. And he wrote Dorrit, suggesting she leave the boys in Berlin for a few days. "Go out and spend some time with Gerlinde," he urged her. "She will need you."

THIRTY-NINE

Johann spent another Christmas, such as it were, at Kapsukas. However, since his confrontation with *Hauptfeldwebel* Mannheim, the hospital's food rations improved and medical supplies became almost adequate.

When two cases of wine were delivered to the wards for the patients' and staff's holiday feast, Herr Director Bergen began to seriously ponder on the change. Through a few carefully placed questions around headquarters, he learned that a surgeon at the hospital enjoyed direct access to Kaiser Wilhelm. Inasmuch as Dr. Bergen himself was a widower from Hamburg with little to enjoy except four grandchildren, and since Dr. Stocker was an unillustrious intern from Bonn with positively no ties to royalty, it didn't take much mental juggling to figure out who did.

January was brutal in these parts, and February—a short month—dragged its feet, prolonging the misery till it seemed the longest month of all. The sky was pewter, the ground frozen solid; a bleak landscape, where naked, brittle trees swayed and groaned in the slightest wind; a befitting sound in this mournful, war-ravaged environment.

Grave diggers had worked diligently all during autumn to assure an adequate number of pits were available before the ground became rock hard. Even so it wasn't enough. During the winter, soldiers went to their eternal rest en masse and in old bomb craters covered by handfuls of pine needles and chunks of dirt pried loose from the lip of the hollows. Still, it was with more dignity than that awarded those who fell on the battlefield, where enemy tanks rolled over immobile wounded and dead alike; burying them democratically under caterpillar tracks of ice and snow.

In March of 1917, German battalions advanced to within two hundred miles of Moscow. The Russian plum was within reach, yet there was guarded optimism in Berlin. Reinforcements were needed to keep the lines behind the advancing troops secure, but the worn men fighting on the western front could not be spared. Furthermore, there was heated talk in some quarters that the United States might be entering the war on the side of Great Britain and France; something that would prove catastrophic for the kaiser's tired forces.

A frigid day in March, a day as gray as granite and as unyielding, found Johann walking out from the woods behind the hospital, where yet another casualty had gone to his reward atop the frozen bodies of those who'd departed before him. Ever since last October, since Hans's death, Johann regularly accompanied any man who died in his care to his final resting place. A nun with a hurried prayer on her lips and two orderlies, bored with their repetitive task, seemed too callous a ceremony, too small a cortege. So Johann followed the funeral procession, in full uniform, lending some stature to the occasion. And he frequently remained behind in silent meditation as the others fled back to the warmth of the building.

But on this particular day, he couldn't linger. Icy gusts whistled through the trees, herding and scraping splintered branches over the rimy crust covering the forest floor. The temperature was such that a deep breath could well prove fatal, and blinking against the biting cold to keep his eyes from freezing shut, Johann bent his head, leaned into the wind and followed close on the heels of the others heading back in the direction of shelter.

He was rounding the far corner of the hospital, when he heard the robust roar of a motor lorry along the road from town.

"Crazy fool!" he muttered irritably and stopped to catch his breath; benzin was scarcer than ever. "Cut the damn engine! Coast, dammit!" He had a good mind to chew the fellow out, but lacked the stamina for anger.

The lorry came to a halt by the old water pump glistening in a layer of ice that made it look shiny, giving the false impression that it was new. As Johann picked up his steps and approached, he recognized the driver, a chap from headquarters, when he jumped out to assist a passenger with the luggage.

A passenger...?

Johann stopped dead in his tracks. There was something familiar about that passenger, and in spite of the real danger of losing both feet to frostbite, Johann didn't move. He couldn't. He remained in place studying the black hair, the solid shoulders, the confident stance of the individual, and the expensive cut of his coat.

That man was from Berlin!

Suddenly Johann broke into a full run with reserves he didn't know he had.

"Kurt, you old dog!" he shouted a moment later, painfully aware of the gulps of frozen air he'd inhaled during his sprint. "What in God's name are you doing out here? Don't tell me you have volunteered?"

"I'm afraid so," Kurt laughed as the two old friends embraced, slapping each other soundly on their respective backs.

Johann pulled away first to gawk at Kurt Eckart; the sight of someone from home had taken the sting out of the wind; he felt almost warm.

"I weakened under pressure," Kurt explained as he took his bags from the driver and followed Johann inside. "It was becoming increasingly difficult to go out in public without being mentally flogged for nonparticipation in the war effort. Besides, I was told they needed some competent talent out here."

Johann laughed. It felt incredibly good. It had been so long that he had all but forgotten the wonderful rippling sensation that went with it.

"Sorry it took me so long." Kurt eyed his friend; Johann had aged, he looked gaunt and peculiarly unkempt. "Actually, you can thank Lillian for my being here at all. In her opinion, if I was fool enough to sign on, the least I could do was come out here and replace you. It seems she could no longer enjoy Dorrit's company. All Dorrit wanted to do was read your letters out loud. Lillian was sick of it. No offense, pal. You have a good pen, but Lillian prefers cheerful news. Personally, I'd rather have gone west, of course. More temperate weather. Closer to home. Chance of furloughs, et cetera, et cetera. Frankly, Lillian forced this assignment on me."

"I always knew her to be a peach," Johann said, and he meant it.

"No hard feelings at being abandoned out here for so long?"

"That depends entirely on what you're referring to."

It was Kurt's turn to laugh. He laughed till he choked.

"Say, how long has it been?"

"Just short of two years."

"Good Lord!" Kurt sobered as he looked around the depressing surroundings.

Johann left Kapsukas on the next military convoy bound for Tannenberg, where he would transfer to a train to Berlin. It was not difficult to say his good-byes, except to Olivia Hofmeyer.

Bent over a valise, he turned and looked up, surprised, on the morning of his departure when she slipped into his room for a private moment while he was packing. She closed the door softly behind her and leaned against it, holding on to the knob. She figured she had three minutes before they'd miss her downstairs.

Johann took her into his arms.

"Darling Olivia, I'll never forget you. I will write—"

"No!" she said and pulled away from him.

"But I need to know that you're safe out here. God knows how much longer the war will last."

"Letters are not a good idea, Johann. I don't want your wife to learn about us. No harm's been done. Let's keep it that way. Besides, I'll be too busy."

"Too busy to write a few words?"

"Yes." Suddenly she smiled. "You see, I'll be busy convincing Dr. Bergen to marry me."

"What . . . !"

"I am planning to marry Herr Director."

"You are?"

"Yes. It has recently occurred to me that after all the mayhem out here, I'm entitled to some security once it's over. I'm tired of fending for myself, Johann. The world is geared for couples. I want a husband and the proverbial mountain cottage with a view. And I want some children. Not my own of course. It's a bit late for that. But Dr. Bergen has four grandchildren, and they'll do me fine. I'm sure they'll like to visit us in the Alps. If not, we'll spend some time in his apartment in Hamburg. It's a large one. Dr. Bergen once told me that before the war he was rattling around alone in seven rooms. No one should be alone in seven rooms. Don't you agree?"

Johann nodded. "I had no idea that you even liked him."

"I respect him, which is far more important. And I've worked with him long enough to know that underneath the gruff demeanor, he's as kind a gentleman as one could ever hope to meet. I'm now forty-four. Past the age when men fall madly in love with me. Men under sixty anyway."

"Olivia...darling...that's not true. I—"

"Hush, please don't make this difficult."

Johann took her face in his hands. "Dr. Bergen is a very, very lucky man," he said.

"Let's just hope that he'll be unable to resist me."

"That goes without saying." Johann smiled. "You are definitely irresistible, Olivia."

She grinned. "If all goes according to plan. I will send you a wedding announcement. It will be addressed to both you and your wife. There's no need for any deception with that kind of a letter."

"You're a treasure, Olivia. I wonder if I could have survived out here if not for you. I...I adore you."

She touched her fingertips to his mouth. "Good-bye, Johann. I'll not be downstairs when your lorry leaves..." Her voice struggled with a tightness in her throat. She lifted herself up on her toes and kissed him furtively. "Take care," she whispered hoarsely. "Have a safe journey home. I will always remember you."

He reached out to embrace her. But she had already opened the door.

She slipped through it and was gone.

Dorrit met Johann at Potsdam Platz Bahnhof. She arrived at the station with an hour to spare and spent the time nervously pacing the marble floor of the large concourse, occasionally stopping to peruse magazine covers at a kiosk. The butterflies swarming in her stomach didn't allow her to sit down at the station café. She was as jittery as a new bride and realized she'd been wise not to take Max and Fritz out of school to meet the train. They'd be chasing each other around in the crowded hall, which would make her even more nervous. Far better the boys enjoy their father's homecoming at the house.

When the loudspeaker finally announced an incoming train from Tannenburg, Dorrit ran headlong down the stairs, her heart in her throat. She dashed out onto the blustery open plat-

277

form, bumping travelers and their suitcases alike.

A huge locomotive was pulling in, belching smoke as it screeched to a slow stop. Dorrit elbowed her way along the platform through the throng until she spotted Johann standing in an open door of the train. Afraid he might not see her among the hordes of people, she raised her hand and waved a lace handkerchief to catch his attention.

She needn't have bothered. He had seen her long before the train came to a complete stop. She was wearing his favorite color, green, a sea-green cashmere coat with a black Persian-lamb collar. A matching hat was perched at a jaunty angle on her auburn hair. She was even more beautiful than he remembered. He would have had to come home blind to have missed seeing her, no matter how large the crowd that surrounded her.

He jumped down and plowed a path through the people. A moment later, she was in his arms. Wordlessly he held her tightly, burying his face in her hair, his heart beating against hers.

Snow was falling in large wet flakes. The kind that fall in late March in these parts. The kind that quickly melt.

Soldiers and civilian travelers were stepping off the train, while others rushed to board. Soon a loud whistle sounded. The locomotive jerked forward once or twice before gaining momentum and pulling away toward its next destination.

But Johann was home. Thin, unshaven, gray around the temples, he was home!